THE CHINA GAMBIT

ALSO BY ALLAN TOPOL

FICTION

The Fourth of July War
A Woman of Valor
Spy Dance
Dark Ambition
Conspiracy
Enemy of My Enemy

NON-FICTION

Superfund Law and Procedure (co-author)

THE CHINA GAMBIT

ALLAN TOPOL

Vantage Point Books and the Vantage Point Books colophon are registered trademarks of Vantage Press, Inc.
FIRST EDITION: January 2012

Published by Vantage Point Books
Vantage Press, Inc.
419 Park Avenue South
New York, NY 10016
www.vantagepointbooks.com

Manufactured in the United States of America
ISBN: 978-1-936467-25-9
Library of Congress Cataloging-in-Publication data are on file.

9   8   7   6   5   4   3   2   1

Cover design by Victor Mingovits

For Barbara, as always,
my partner in this literary venture.

PROLOGUE

CALGARY, CANADA

Leaving suite 2100 in the Hyatt Regency and clutching her reporter's steno pad, Francesca Page was excited, more excited than she'd ever been.

Only ten months ago she graduated from Northwestern Journalism School. Now she had the most incredible story. Disclosing what she learned could avoid disaster for the United States.

She practically flew down the corridor to the elevator, her long strides propelling her five eight frame. Impatiently, she pressed the down button, then brushed back a few strands of long brown hair.

Nothing he said in the interview confirmed what she'd learned in Iran. But her father had taught her how to interrogate people. "Watch their facial expressions, particularly the eyes. Voice inflection is critical. What they don't tell you is more important than what they do." All those screamed at her: You're right. That is what they're planning.

The empty elevator arrived. Gripping the brown leather case that held her laptop and cell phone, she charged in. After pressing the lobby button, she was planning her next moves: drive back to the Fairmont; write up the story on the laptop; email it to Elizabeth; then call. Elizabeth will be in her office at the Trib. Still plenty of time to make tomorrow morning's paper. In her mind Francesca was composing the front page headline: "Chinese General Develops Plot Against The United States."

She barreled through the lobby, narrowly missing a heavyset man swaying from too much to drink. Once she exited the revolving door, the biting cold of the mid-March evening smacked her in the face. Snow was beginning to fall. "Cab Miss?" the portly doorman asked.

"No thanks. I have a car in the garage across the street." She zipped up the brown leather jacket and put on her gloves.

She waited for the light to turn green, all the while drafting in her mind. Suddenly, two men were closing in on her, bookends. One short with a pockmarked red face. The other tall and swarthy with a thin mustache.

The short man flashed an ID in a wallet. "Alberta Police. Come with us, Miss Page." At the curb, she saw a black Mercedes sedan, no markings on the side, engine running, rear door open. The car had an Alberta license plate, AP221.

Growing up, she'd heard plenty of stories from her father about the operations of clandestine services.

I'm not being paranoid. Mutt and Jeff aren't real police. I have to seize the initiative and surprise them.

"I can't see your I.D. You'll have to bring it closer."

The short man brought his wallet a foot from her face. As he did, Francesca swung her arm containing the bag with her laptop, fast and hard, hitting him in the face, breaking his nose. Snow had made the sidewalk slick. Caught off guard, bleeding, he slipped and fell. The tall man yanked Francesca's bag away, pulled a gun, and glared at her.

The snow was picking up. Her hair was wet, water dripping down her cheeks. Traffic was moving slowly. She burst into the street threading her way between cars, making a beeline for the garage. Glancing over her shoulder, she expected the tall man to chase her. But he wasn't moving. He had whipped out his cell phone and was making a call.

I have to get to the airport. If I hurry, I'll make the last plane out to Chicago. Then I'll get a plane to New York in the morning. But what if they're not flying? I can't even think that. Besides, Calgary's used to snow.

She roared around curves in the garage. At the exit, she paid the fee. Out on the street, she wanted to floor it, but the surface was slippery, cars skidding. She glanced in the rearview mirror.

The black Mercedes had pulled out and was following, two cars behind.

She turned onto Highway 2, heading north toward the airport. The Mercedes followed her. The snow was coming down harder. The Rocky Mountains on the left were buried in heavy cloud cover.

Through fast moving windshield wipers, she barely discerned a disabled car in the road. At the last possible instant, she swerved around it. She was terrified, clutching the wheel, her palms moist, the defroster and heater running full blast, her legs shaking. Perspiration dripped from her forehead into her eyes and soaked the underarms of her blouse.

The exit for McKnight Boulevard was coming up. She cut sharply on to the ramp, taking it too fast and sliding around, nearly hitting a wall. On the road, she hunched over the wheel, glancing back again. No one was in sight. She breathed a sigh of relief.

Straining to see, she was driving as fast as possible.

Up ahead, she saw a roadblock. She threw on the high beams. A wooden barricade was stretched across the road, blocking traffic in her direction. A man dressed in a police uniform was checking each car, then waving the cars through on the apron. Traffic was light.

She glanced to the side of the road. A car with flashing red and blue lights on the roof was parked on the grass. Next to it, she saw a black Mercedes. License AP221.

One car was between her and the roadblock. The policeman, or whatever the hell he was, let the car pass.

She kept her lights on high and pressed down on the accelerator, driving right at him. He narrowly jumped out of the way. She slammed through the barrier, smashing the wood to shreds.

On the right, she saw a sign: "Airport Five miles." Under it was an arrow pointing left.

She made the turn on to the Barlow Trail, the last leg, two lanes to the airport.

She checked the rearview mirror. A car was right behind her and moving up fast, so close that she saw the Mercedes insignia on the hood. In the snow her Toyota was no match for the Mercedes, which was closing the gap. She felt a jolt as the Mercedes bumped her car. She kept going.

She heard a gunshot. It blew out the rear window. The bullet and glass narrowly missed her. She refused to stop.

While worrying about the Mercedes, she had to watch the road ahead.

Blinding lights were coming at her from the front. A huge truck. She moved to the shoulder of the road. The Mercedes shifted with her, then pulled off.

"Move over you jerk," she shouted at the trucker.

But the truck didn't move. It slammed into her car. And her whole world went black.

PART ONE

FRANCESCA

1

PIAZZA NAVONA, ROME

Craig Page ordered another double espresso in the private room in Tre Scalini and checked his watch. It was ten thirty.

Dammit. Hameed should be here.

He walked over to the window, his eyes scanning the beautiful, baroque, pedestrian-only Piazza Navona. He saw scores of tourists wandering past, stopping at a café or bargaining with vendors, but no sign of the Saudi.

He replayed in his mind the five o'clock call from this morning that woke him in his apartment in Milan, Giuseppe, sounding tense and frantic. "Craig, we need you to come to Rome immediately. A plane's waiting at Linate."

When he arrived at the headquarters of the Italian Intelligence Agency a little before seven, the building was lit up as if it were ten in the morning. "We intercepted a message between two Al Qaeda cells," Giuseppe said. "They're planning something big and soon. 'Operation Water,' they're calling it. We're sending troops to safeguard Rome's water supply. Also the Tiber bridges."

Craig was mulling over Giuseppe's words. "What can I do to help?"

"Use your Al Qaeda contacts. Penetrate their organization. But move fast."

Time to call in a very large IOU, Craig had decided.

Twelve months ago Craig, still with the CIA, followed Achmed, a high ranking Al Qaeda official, from Dubai to New York and thwarted a suicide bombing at Madison Square Garden during a Knicks game. Afterwards, Craig returned to the Middle East to arrest or to kill the other planners of the operation. He located Hameed, a mid-level operative, working at the Arab Euro bank in Dubai. Craig was preparing to arrest Hameed and ship him back to the U.S. for a long jail term. Then he got a better idea. "I'll pretend you weren't involved. In return, I'll want your cooperation in the future." Craig knew the deal was risky. Kirby would never have approved it, but Kirby didn't have to know. Not surprisingly, Hameed jumped at the offer.

Now, if that bastard Hameed doesn't show or cooperate, I've been had.

"Your friend's here," a waiter said.

Craig wheeled around to see the waiter, coming from the kitchen, an espresso on a tray and Hameed behind him, surly-looking with a neatly trimmed black beard sprinkled with gray and a long scar on his left cheek.

"You want something to drink or eat?" Craig asked the Saudi.

"I'm not here to socialize."

Craig reached into his pocket and handed a twenty Euro note to the waiter, who quickly retreated, closing the door behind him.

"How'd you get into the restaurant?" Craig asked.

"A produce truck dropped me at the service entrance. Who told you I was in Rome?"

"After our deal last year, you became a valuable asset of mine. I like to keep track of my assets."

"But I thought you were fired from the CIA because you refused to follow Kirby's orders."

"There was a reorganization. Now I'm a private consultant, working for the Italian government."

Craig pointed to the table. Hameed sat down across from Craig, who sipped the espresso.

"I want to know about Operation Water," Craig said.

"Sorry. Never heard of it."

Craig narrowed his eyes and stared hard at Hameed. "I could still arrest you for Madison Square Garden. If I took you back to the U.S., even under the new rules, you wouldn't enjoy being interrogated. Or I could turn you over to the Saudi government. They don't follow any rules."

Hameed stroked his beard, while weighing his options.

"But just suppose I do know, and I tell you…"

He knows.

"In return for a suitable cash payment, of course," Craig said.

Hameed laughed. "I'd never live to spend it. They'd figure out where you got the information and kill me. But I'll tell you something nobody else knows."

"What's that?"

"I'm sick of this life. I want out. I tried to quit, but the bosses in Al Qaeda told me, with my background in finance, I'm too valuable. If I walk, they'll kill me. So I'm fucked, every which way."

"What a sad story. You're tearing me up."

"You don't believe me?"

"Listen up, Hameed. There's a clinic in Lugano in northern Italy. Just south of the Swiss border. They do great plastic surgery. If you tell me what I need to stop Operation Water, I'll make sure you get a complete makeover at our expense. You'll spend six months recuperating. Then you'll look like an Italian. Even your mother won't recognize you. After that, we'll find you a job in a small town in the lake country."

"Are you authorized by the Italian government to make this offer?"

"Of course not. But I can try and sell it."

"How do I know you'll carry out on your end of the bargain?"

"A year ago I promised you wouldn't be arrested, and you weren't."

Hameed nodded. "Do it."

Craig removed the cell phone from his pocket. "First, let's get the ground rules straight. The Italian police will keep you in protective custody until this is over. And if you're screwing me over, I'll drop the word to one of my other Al Qaeda contacts that you were my informant for Madison Square Garden. It'll be like throwing a bloody body to a bunch of sharks. Is that clear?"

Hameed's whole body shook.

"You still want me to make the call?"

Hameed nodded again.

Craig took his cell into the next room and left the door ajar. He speed-dialed and spoke softly. "Giuseppe, I need your approval. I have an informant who has knowledge about Operation Water. He's willing to talk, but it'll cost you."

"How much?"

"A couple hundred thousand euros. Tops."

"Do it. You can't believe how hard the Prime Minister is leaning on me."

Craig returned to Hameed. "You're on."

"Do I get anything in writing?"

"This isn't the United States. Now tell me about Operation Water."

Hameed took a deep breath. "The target is the Trevi Fountain."

"When?" Craig asked.

"Today at one o'clock. When it's jammed with tourists."

Craig glanced at his watch. Less than three hours.

Hameed continued, "A truck will drop off two boys and one girl a block from the Trevi Fountain. All three will be wearing vests, under their coats, loaded with explosives."

"What's your role in this?"

"Amir's in charge. Hussein's working with him."

"And you?"

"I funneled cash to Amir to buy supplies and to pay the families of the three kids. Ten thousand euros each."

"Where are they now?"

"Their base in Trastevere."

"Address?"

Hameed didn't respond.

"Think about those sharks."

Hameed sucked in his breath. "Number 24 Via Garibaldi. The apartment on the third floor."

"How many people in the apartment?"

"The three kids. Amir. Maybe Hussein. No more than five."

2

TRASTEVERE, ROME

Giuseppe was alone, waiting for Craig in an unmarked blue Fiat on the edge of Piazza Santa Maria, three blocks from the Via Garibaldi address. Craig climbed into the front seat.

"We have the house surrounded," Giuseppe said. "My forces are heavily armed. I told them to remain out of sight. If anyone leaves the building, we grab them. So far, nobody. I think we should wait for them to leave, then snatch them on the street."

Craig shook his head emphatically. "Too risky. At that point, the vests will be armed. All they have to do is pull the triggering device, probably in a pocket. Or someone detonates it from a remote location. The casualties won't be as bad as at the Trevi, but don't forget the market in the square." Craig was pointing. "With powerful bombs, you'll have carnage."

Giuseppe puckered up his lips. "What do *you* think we should do?"

"We may still have a narrow window before the vests are armed. Give me one of your best men."

"Emilio."

"Good. I've met him. Emilio and I will go in and surprise them."

"Suppose the vests are armed when the two of you break in?"

"You lose us, maybe others in the building. Hopefully, that's all."

"You really want to do this?"

"Damn right."

"I could send Emilio and another of my young agents. You're just a consultant."

Craig smiled. "And forty five years old, too. But I can still do the job better than any of them."

"God, you're stubborn."

"None of your guys has my experience."

"Go for it. When you finish, we'll go to Sabatini in the Piazza Santa Maria. We'll celebrate with Prosecco."

"And if I don't make it, have a grappa for me."

Fifteen minutes later, Craig and Emilio, both wearing Kevlar vests, Glocks in their hands, were climbing the inside staircase of number 24 Via Garibaldi. It was old wood and creaked with each step.

Craig was leading the way. He was twenty years older than Emilio. At five ten, he was four inches shorter, and at a hundred and seventy pounds, Craig was thirty pounds lighter.

Craig moved up to the third floor door. He put his ear up to the wood. Not a sound from inside the apartment. He aimed his gun at the door lock, weakened with age and use, nodded to Emilio, then fired. It disintegrated with the single shot. Craig saw a chain on the door. He raised his right foot and slammed it against the door, ripping the wood from the hinges. The door opened into the living room of the apartment.

Gun raised, Craig shouted, "Police. Freeze." His eyes were rapidly scanning the room. He only saw one man: Amir.

The Arab whirled around, stunned. He yanked back his jacket, reaching for a gun at his waist. The instant he had it out of the holster and was raising it in the air, Craig threw himself on the floor, while firing his own gun. Amir's shot flew over Craig's head, but Craig's hit Amir in the chest. The gun fell out of Amir's hand. He slumped to the floor.

Emilio was now in the doorway. Craig dropped to his knee and checked Amir's pulse. The man was dead.

He motioned Emilio to head toward the kitchen, on the right. Craig signaled that he'd cover the rooms on the left.

Moving along the corridor, Craig, gun in hand, passed a bathroom that looked empty. In the bedroom he found two boys and a girl, around sixteen, cowering in a corner behind the bed. Vests and explosives were piled in a corner.

He pointed the gun at them. "Get into the living room. All of you."

The girl led the way. The boys followed. Craig was behind the three of them.

As they went by the bathroom, a man, who'd been hiding behind the door, leapt out with a large knife in his hand. Craig recognized Hussein. Before Craig had a chance to shoot, Hussein hurled himself through the air, knocking Craig off his feet. The gun flew out of his hand. Hussein was powerfully built like a tank, and strong. In seconds, he had Craig on his back, pinned to the floor.

Hussein was trying to plunge the knife into Craig's face. Grasping wildly, Craig seized Hussein's arm and held it in a tight grip. Hussein strained, grimacing, his eyes filled with hatred and determination. Craig felt his grip weakening. The man was too strong. In another couple of seconds, he would force the knife down into Craig's eye.

With a sudden burst of energy, Craig flung Hussein off and rolled over. Now Craig was on top. Hussein still had the knife in his right hand. Craig was clutching Hussein's right arm with both hands. In a swift motion, Craig brought his knee up. With all the force he could muster, Craig viciously plunged his knee into Hussein's groin, smashing his testicles. Hussein screamed in agony. The knife dropped from his hand.

As Craig scrambled to his feet, Emilio ran in, gun in hand. He aimed at Hussein, writhing on the floor, but didn't fire. Craig grabbed his own gun, then kicked the knife away.

"Let's get them out of here," Craig said to Emilio. "You take this bag of shit." He pointed to Hussein. "I'll take the kids."

Ten minutes later, Craig watched the four being loaded into police vans. When they were gone, Giuseppe gave Craig a bear hug. "Thank you so much."

Elated, Craig pulled away. "Now I want that Prosecco."

In Sabatini, they settled into a table in the corner. The waitress popped the cork. They clicked their glasses and sipped the chilled wine.

"You're the best thing that happened to this country since pasta," Giuseppe said.

Craig laughed. "That's one of the things I love about Italy. Nobody exaggerates."

"You've been reluctant to tell me. How did the CIA let you get away?"

"Once Kirby became Director, he insisted on controlling everything. I learned that Al Qaeda planned a huge suicide bombing for Madison Square Garden. Kirby wanted me to stay in Dubai. I had no intention of doing that. I was the only one who knew the M.O. of Achmed, the ringleader. So instead, I followed Achmed to New York and broke it up. That earned me the Medal of Freedom from President Brewster and Kirby's hatred."

"Petty bureaucrats. The same all around the world."

Craig paused to sip some more wine. "Six months later, Kirby eliminated my job as coordinator of Mideast Operations in a so-called reorganization. I came to Milan and opened my private consulting firm."

"Why Milan?"

Before Craig had a chance to answer, his cell phone rang. He didn't recognize the number.

"Craig Page here."

"Mr. Page, this is James Anderson, Deputy Police Chief in Calgary Canada."

Craig's heart was pounding. Two day ago Francesca had sent him an e-mail, telling him she was in Calgary, working on a big story.

"Are you Francesca Page's father?"

"I am."

Craig held his breath.

"Unfortunately, Mr. Page, I have to inform you that your daughter died in an auto accident this evening. Her car collided with a truck on an icy road."

"No," he gave a bloodcurdling cry. "No. It can't be."

Not Francesca. I love her more than anything in the world.

"You're mistaken. It's not Francesca."

"I'm sorry, Mr. Page. She had a passport and other ID in her jacket pocket."

The fool was lying. "You're no Calgary cop."

"I'm very sorry, Mr. Page. She had a Tiffany wristwatch. Engraved on the back 'To Francesca with love…'"

He'd given her that when she graduated from Northwestern.

"And a scar on her left ankle."

He vividly recalled the ski injury she suffered during their trip to Megeve two years ago at Christmas.

The man's accent and inflections were from Calgary. As the reality drove home like a spike through his body, in agony, a rash of grief covered his face, distorting his mouth, turning his grey eyes black. Francesca was dead.

"I'm so sorry," Giuseppe said.

But Craig barely heard his words.

"Leave me alone," Craig said, rising abruptly. "I am alone."

He left Sabatini and wandered the streets of Trastevere. Crossing the Tiber on the Ponte Sisto, he recalled his father, four years old, so alone after the carnage on the farm, his whole family murdered.

Now, I too, am no longer connected to a single living soul.

Aimlessly, in a daze, he crossed streets, disregarding traffic signals, ignoring honking horns and the curses of motorists. He passed churches, but didn't go inside. He wouldn't find solace there.

He walked for two more hours. Then he drifted into a Trattoria. He ordered a bottle of Chianti. The waitress poured a glass, but he didn't touch it. He placed his head into his hands and lowered it to the coarse wooden table. He cried, the tears streaming down his cheeks, dripping into his mouth. "Francesca," he muttered in a barely audible plaintive lament.

He had no idea how long he remained with his head on the table. He heard, "Craig." A powerful set of arms pulled his head up, then raised him to his feet. It was Giuseppe.

"C'mon Craig, we're going to the airport. I'm taking you to Washington."

3

MANASSAS, VIRGINIA

Craig stood in front of Carolyn's grave, and he wept. Through the tears, he mumbled, "Your daughter, Francesca, will be joining you now."

Carolyn was the only woman he'd ever loved. Theirs had been a storybook romance. Childhood sweethearts in Monessen, Pennsylvania, married a week after they both graduated from Carnegie Mellon. Francesca was born a year later, in a difficult birth, leaving Carolyn unable to have other children. But that didn't matter to Craig. The three of them were so close, thriving together during the two years in Houston with the oil company, and then in Washington when he started with the CIA, analyzing developments that affected the flow of oil to the United States.

His grief was overwhelmed by guilt. Fifteen years ago, he recalled, God, it seemed like yesterday, Director Dodson told him they wanted to move him to the Middle East, to Dubai. His cover would be a principle in the Tartan Oil Company, an exploration and development firm. "Your mission will be to ferret out threats to U.S. oil imports, to uncover Al Qaeda operations, and to thwart their plans."

He could have turned down the assignment and remained at headquarters, living the good life in the Washington area with Carolyn and Francesca. But Dodson played on his patriotism. "You will be in the frontline of defending our country." He yearned for action in the field. Carolyn thought he should do it.

Once he took the assignment, he didn't have to uproot Carolyn and Francesca. He could have insisted that the two of them remain in McLean, while he commuted, the way most agent operatives did.

It wouldn't have done much good. Feisty Carolyn, the fiery redhead, the star debater in college, was adamant. She and Francesca were going with him.

He didn't argue. He didn't want to live apart from them. He wanted it all. And he paid for it with Carolyn's life.

Carolyn was marvelous. He loved her so much, but God, was she strong willed at times, even stubborn. After several days of fever and headaches, refusing to see a doctor, insisting, "it's just a cold," he found her vomiting in the bathroom. He picked her up and carried her to the car, then into the hospital. But he was too late. Bacterial Meningitis. Even the words were chilling. He had never heard them before a British doctor in a Dubai hospital announced her diagnosis, making it sound like a death sentence, which it was. The doctors couldn't do anything to save her.

Living in Washington, she'd never have contracted bacterial meningitis. And if she had, the doctors would have known how to treat it.

He pivoted and looked at the open grave, six feet away, Francesca's body suspended above it.

He felt more guilt. Emulating him and seeking his respect had made her into a bold, daring, and sometimes foolish risk-taker. She was always pushing the envelope, a child climbing the jungle gym to the highest level, a teenager skiing the diamond trails. He reveled in it, was so proud of her. And he was convinced those traits had led to her death.

Anderson, the Calgary policeman, had called it an auto accident. That implies someone was careless—negligent, as lawyers say. But murder is no accident. Craig was convinced Francesca was onto a hot story. That's why she was murdered. The rage was boiling in him.

I have to get through the funeral. Then I'll find out who killed Francesca. Their blood will flow.

The chilly wind whipped through the trees as he looked at the people assembling for the graveside ceremony. He spotted Giuseppe. Francesca's high school and college friends were weeping openly.

Lots of former CIA colleagues had come. He saw Betty Richards, the Chief Analyst, sobbing quietly, her black hair, streaked with gray, falling randomly over her head. Ten years his senior, Betty was career CIA, never married, and a workaholic. She wore black framed glasses with thick lenses, resembling old Coca Cola bottles.

Crying, Betty walked up to Craig and hugged him. "So sorry. I loved Francesca. I remember those Saturdays going to the movies with her, when she was a little girl. What a wonderful child. I don't know what to say."

For Craig, the morning was becoming a blur. Images were dancing in his head. But suddenly something came into clear focus. A large black Cadillac sedan was approaching along a winding path. Craig saw the license plate, DCI, Director of Central Intelligence. He did a double take.

Stunned, Craig watched the car stop thirty yards away. The driver scrambled out, ran around, and opened the back door. And there he was.

Kirby left the car and walked toward the grave. Even at five four with platform shoes, with a shaved head too large for his body, Kirby had a sinister look.

Seething with hatred, the taste of bile in his mouth, Craig pulled away from Betty. He charged across the damp grass, cutting Kirby off. "What the hell are you doing here?"

"Paying my respects. I know how close you were with Francesca."

"This is a private ceremony for family and friends. You're neither. Get the hell out."

"I thought it was time to bury the hatchet. Let bygones be bygones. I want to make my peace with you."

"And you figure my daughter's funeral is the time to do that? What kind of asshole are you?"

"I realize now that I was wrong to let you go. You were too valuable. I want to talk to you about coming back."

Kirby looked away from him when he said those words.

What's his real agenda?

"Yeah. Well maybe we'll do lunch sometime. But right now turn around, get your ass into that car, and get the hell out of here."

Kirby didn't retreat. His driver, heavyset with a blond crew cut, moved up to take a position ten feet behind Kirby.

Craig's emotions, raw from grief and anger, boiled over. He picked up a tree branch from the ground and kicked off the thin pieces on top, creating a powerful wooden club. He saw Kirby's driver unbutton his jacket, going for a gun, holstered to his chest.

I'll kill that son of a bitch Kirby with one powerful blow.

Menacingly, Craig raised the club above his head. He moved toward Kirby.

Before he had a chance to swing, he felt a powerful arm around his waist. A hand grabbed his arm with the branch lowering it slowly. He heard Giuseppe's voice, soft and calm. "You don't want to do that."

Giuseppe took the club away, then tossed it on the ground. "I think you should leave," the Italian said to Kirby in the calm voice of authority.

"But..."

"Do it right now," Giuseppe said.

The CIA Director turned and walked back to his car. Craig watched them pull away, the car belching black fumes.

"Thanks," he said to Giuseppe. Then he returned to the graveside.

Moments later, he heard the minister. "We are gathered together, in sight of God, to lay to rest a young woman, incredibly talented, who had so much to offer her country and the world. A woman who was cut down in her vibrant youth by a tragedy none of us can comprehend…"

I will comprehend it. Retribution will be mine.

4

BEIJING

Alone in the cabin of an Air Force jet, General Zhou puffed on a Davidoff he had purchased in Paris. He loved much about the French capital, particularly the high-end restaurants, the women available for a price, and the rich Cuban cigars. Some found them rough, hard, and astringent. For General Zhou, they overwhelmed the senses with their power. He loved that.

He glanced out the window. As the plane approached Beijing, the darkness of northern China at midnight was giving way to a myriad of lights.

The last forty-eight hours had been maddening. Dealing with those Iranian rug merchants, with their endless haggling and histrionics, was equivalent to one of Mao's forms of torture. But in the end he got what he wanted.

Captain Cheng came out of the cockpit and approached General Zhou. "Fifteen minutes to touchdown at the base, Sir."

"And the paperwork?"

"Altered and certified by the base commander. It reads: 'Routine inspection flight over northern China.' The same as our flight out two days ago. Paris never happened."

"What about my brother?" General Zhou asked.

"He's already at the base. He'll meet you at the edge of the airfield, as you requested.

Captain Cheng returned to the cockpit. General Zhou put out his cigar and closed the book resting on his lap. *A History of China... The Long View.* He agreed with the thesis of the author, a brilliant young professor at the University of Shanghai, "Our history has been fashioned by bold, brilliant, and daring individuals, those willing to risk their lives and the lives of millions of others in the quest for national greatness. We have the world's smartest people, extensive resources, and unlimited labor. All that is needed, at any time, is a leader with foresight."

Now, I am that leader. With Operation Dragon Oil, I will leapfrog China over the United States for world domination.

The plane came to a halt in a remote area, at the end of the landing strip, close to a cluster of trees. The instant the door opened, General Zhou, wearing his military uniform and holding a thin black briefcase, bounded down the stairs. Impervious to the subzero temperature, he was charged with energy, despite almost no sleep in the last two days.

He saw his brother, Zhou Yun, dressed in a dark suit, snappy shirt, and tie, standing next to a large, black sedan with tinted windows.

Once General Zhou was in the front passenger seat, Zhou Yun climbed behind the wheel.

"I dismissed my driver," Zhou Yun said, as he shifted into gear and pulled away. "I couldn't take the risk of anyone overhearing our conversation. What happened in Paris?"

"I have good news."

"Did the Iranians agree to our terms?"

"Essentially. After endless quibbling over details. What I yielded on was of no consequence."

"Then it's finished?"

"Yes."

"You have a signed agreement?"

General Zhou reached into his briefcase and pulled out two documents. "An executed copy for you, and one for me. The document is in Chinese, Farsi, and English."

"Why English?"

"The Iranians insisted on it. They aren't literate in Chinese, don't trust me, and said an English version could be useful if disputes arise."

"I have to read it now."

Zhou Yun stopped the car next to the trees, snatched the document from his brother, and turned on the map light. As soon as Zhou Yun finished reading, General Zhou said, "In two weeks, on April first, we will be ushering in a new world order. American domination will be over. The next era, of Chinese supremacy, will begin."

Wolves or wild dogs were barking.

"We have one complication," Zhou Yun said.

"A problem in Canada? With the Canadian Oil companies?"

"No. That went well. I've lined up control of four of the five largest Canadian oil companies. The deals will be announced April 1. The fifth is about to fall into line. A little forceful persuasion will do the job."

"Then what happened?"

Zhou Yun faced his brother. General Zhou was holding his breath, waiting to hear what came next.

"A woman, a nosy American reporter from New York, learned about Operation Dragon Oil and our dealings with Iran."

The General was upset. "How'd… How'd she get the story?"

"I don't know. I called our American friend… The reporter is gone."

The General was still anxious. "Could it be traced to us?"

"Unlikely. However there is one inconvenient fact."

"What's that?"

"After the reporter's death, I had one of my people, with me in Calgary, do some research on the reporter."

"And?"

"Her name was Francesca Page. Her father, Craig Page, had been career CIA, coordinator of Middle East operations, until six months ago, when he was supposedly fired by the CIA in a reorganization."

"You don't believe it?"

Zhou Yun shook his head. "I know the Americans do crazy things, but this makes no sense. Page was one of their stars. He must still be working for one of the U.S. intelligence agencies, but undercover. He and his daughter were probably working together."

"How could our American friend have permitted this to happen?"

"I demanded to know that."

"And?"

"He was apologetic. He insists that Page has nothing to do with the American government."

"I rue the day we ever got involved with him."

"But he's the only one able to deliver what we need. And besides, we can't change horses at this point."

General Zhou shook his head in despair. "I feel success slipping through our hands, like grains of sand."

"You're too pessimistic, my brother. We won't let Page stop us."

5

McLEAN, VIRGINIA

Craig recalled buying the two-floor, red brick colonial when he started working with the CIA twenty years ago, analyzing world oil developments. For the long periods he was out of the country, the house was vacant. But it was still his Washington base. And it had so many memories for him, with Carolyn and Francesca.

When Carolyn died, he was glad he had the house. Francesca, then attending the American school in Dubai, had two more years of high school. Craig decided to move back to Washington for those two years. It was important for her, he decided, to mainstream back into American life. The Agency obliged with an assignment for him at headquarters, evaluating world oil reserves. If they hadn't, he would have quit. Francesca was his top priority. He told them he'd go back to Dubai when she started college.

So for those two years, he and Francesca mourned together in this house, then struggled to pick up their lives without Carolyn, the glue that held the family together. Ironic, he thought, being a single parent forced him to forge a bond with his daughter, he'd never had before.

But now the house was filled with the thirty or so people, who came from the cemetery, wanting to be with him in his grief for a few moments before returning to their own lives.

From his position in the living room, he looked into the dining room. A table was piled with food, but no one was eating. He glanced through the window at the sidewalk in front. Predictably, Betty was outside, smoking a cigarette.

A heavyset man, with a bushy beard and unkempt hair to match, came over. "Mr. Page, I'm Fritz Keller. Francesca was a journalism student of mine at Northwestern. I want you to know she was the best student I've ever had. I'm so sorry. She'd have made a great journalist."

"Thank you, professor. I appreciate your saying that."

"Well I mean it, and I've been teaching for forty-two years. Some of the best reporters for *The New York Times* and *Wall Street Journal* were in my classes. Also, people in television. I've taught them not just to write, but to be resourceful, and to have integrity. Why in my classes…"

Craig tuned the man out.

The cell phone in Craig's pocket rang. He glanced at the caller ID. "Alpha Travel."

Grateful for the interruption, he turned to the Professor, "Excuse me," and moved away, phone up to his ear.

"What do you have for me, Anita?"

"For your flight to Calgary tomorrow, I can get you on a noon flight on United out of Dulles, connecting to their three twenty five in Denver, with a heavily discounted fare in first class."

"Take it. And get me into the Westin."

"What about your return flight?"

"One way only. I have to wait and see what I find in Calgary."

He hung up the phone and returned it to his pocket.

He walked over to a floor-to-ceiling bookcase overflowing with his books about ancient civilizations. But he wasn't looking for a book. Rather, he stared at the picture in front of one of the shelves, taken a year ago in the Oval Office. President Brewster was awarding him the Medal of Freedom for thwarting the Madison Square Garden attack. The President was on his one side, Francesca on the other. He was struck by how much she looked like him. The same thick, dark brown hair, deep gray eyes that locked on a subject like lasers, nose that seemed a little too large in Washington, but just right in Rome, and a winning smile.

He looked at Brewster's note on the bottom, above the President's signature. "On behalf of a grateful nation."

That was the only time he'd met Brewster. And what a wonderful day it had been, he recalled. The President had invited him and Francesca to have breakfast, before the ceremony, with Brewster and his wife, in the residence upstairs. While they were eating, the President asked Craig to describe his pursuit of Achmed, the Madison Square Garden mastermind. He also asked Francesca to talk about the work she expected to do at the *Tribune,* when she started in another two months. Craig vividly recalled an exchange at the end of breakfast. The President asked him, "Why'd you join the CIA, Craig?" And he responded, "I've always loved my country, Mr. President. After two years in the oil business, I realized that imported oil is this country's Achilles heel. If we can't either wean ourselves from it, or keep it flowing, then this country is in deep trouble. Since I can't make policy to change consumption, I want to help keep it flowing. While doing that, I've gotten involved in counter-terrorism work."

The President wasn't merely going through the motions in that conversation, Craig was convinced. He had been warm and gracious, both to him and Francesca. "My door will always be open to you," he said. Craig considered calling Brewster when Kirby fired him, but it seemed inappropriate. Kirby was the Director of Central Intelligence. He could run his agency, however he wanted.

"Mr. Page," a woman said, interrupting his thoughts. She was thirty-something, a brunette in a sleeveless black dress, short hair, good looking, but not beautiful. She had an athletic figure, with muscular arms and legs, accompanied by a serious intense look.

"I'm Elizabeth Crowder, Mr. Page. Foreign Editor at the *New York Tribune*."

"Please, I'm Craig. And I know who you are. Francesca's boss. She spoke about you often."

She pointed to the picture. "Francesca told me all about that day at the White House. I even know what she ate. 'The best day of my life,' she called it. She was very proud of you."

He looked around. People were beginning to leave.

"I imagine you're going back to New York today."

"Yes, but I'm in no hurry."

"Can you stick around? I want to talk to you."

6

McLEAN, VIRGINIA

Giuseppe was among the few remaining people in the house. "My plane to Rome takes off in two hours. I better get going. But before I leave, I want to talk to you for a minute."

"Sure," Craig said. He led the way into the deserted kitchen.

"I don't know when you're coming back to Italy, but I want you to know that the Prime Minister told me, after the Trevi incident, he intends to persuade his counterparts in the EU to start a counter-terrorism unit and put you in charge. You'll be the European Terrorism Czar."

"I'm flattered."

"Money won't be a problem. You'll get generous compensation. For this, the governments will find it. Kept confidential of course. What do you think?"

"I have some things to do here. We can talk about it when I return to Italy."

"Fair enough."

At long last, he and Elizabeth were the only ones in the house. The grandfather clock in the corner chimed four times.

"Get your coat," Craig said to Elizabeth. "The house is stuffy. We'll go out in back. The air will do us good."

She put on a brown leather jacket with a wide belt.

"Hey, Francesca had a coat like that," he said.

"I know. We bought them together at Bloomies last October."

In the back yard, he led the way to an old rusty swing set. "Francesca loved this when she was a kid. I never got around to having it hauled away."

He sat down and slowly swung. Elizabeth sat next to him, not moving, waiting to hear what he had to say.

Toss the words right out. See if she thinks I'm crazy.

"I don't think Francesca died in an accident. I think she was murdered."

Elizabeth's head snapped back in surprise. "You said she was murdered?"

"Exactly."

"I know you're in the espionage business, but…"

He raised his hand. "Hear me out."

"Sure."

"Two days before she died she sent me an e-mail." He removed a print of the message from his pocket and handed it to Elizabeth.

As she unfolded the paper and read, he recited it from memory, "I'm in Calgary, Canada, on a big story. Having lots of memories of the last time I was here with you and Mom. Plan to make it to Milan for your birthday. Your kind of story, Dad. Don't want to say any more now."

She refolded and handed it back. "What's this prove? I don't get it."

"Francesca was a very careful driver." He shook his head. "Big story. Too sensitive to discuss in an e-mail. Then a truck collides with her car, and she dies. That's one helluva coincidence. And I don't believe in unlikely coincidence. You show me a roulette wheel that comes up red twenty straight times, and I'll show you a wheel that's rigged."

She was nodding her head, swinging, while looking at the ground.

Elizabeth said, "James Anderson, from the police department in Calgary, called me."

"He called me, too."

"He said Francesca had been killed in an accident, on the way to the airport, in a head on collision with a truck. 'The roads were icy, treacherous,' he said. So I bought it… But now that I think about it some more… Oh God… You could be right."

"What do you know about the story?"

"A couple weeks ago Francesca spent five days in Tehran, investigating the Iranian oil industry. Her objective was to find out how extensive their reserves are, and more important, who has the inside track to develop and control those reserves. She told me she'd learned a lot about oil from you, and she figured there was a good story. The Russians? The Chinese? The French?"

"What'd she find?"

"I don't know. After leaving Tehran, she flew to Zurich, where she had an overnight layover. She called me from a hotel near the airport. She said she learned something in Iran, which, if true, was so significant and frightening, with such dire consequences for the United States that she didn't want to tell me on the phone. She said she was flying to Calgary to get confirmation of the story."

"What did you do?"

"I knew I had to fly to Calgary, to work with her. Your daughter and I were friends. I had lots of respect for her talent as a journalist, but she was still a rookie, in her first year in the business. She'd stumbled on, or dug up, this huge story. I was afraid she was in over her head. Would she know how to get to the bottom of it?"

"So did you fly to Calgary?"

"I went into the office of Roy McDermott, the publisher of the Trib, and told him about Elizabeth's call. I said I wanted to go to Calgary. McDermott told me, 'positively not.' He said, he needed me too much in New York, that budget considerations were driving him. The Trib's been losing a bundle, and McDermott's trying to squeeze every nickel."

"Did you hear from her in Calgary?"

"One call. On Monday, the day she died, she called me from Calgary about noon, New York time, to say she had scheduled the interview she wanted, at seven that evening. She wouldn't tell me with whom, but she said she'd call immediately after the interview. I told her I'd be waiting by the phone." Elizabeth sighed. "The only call I got that night was from Anderson, twelve hours later."

Elizabeth raised her head. "As I think about it now, something else confirms your conclusion. Iran's involved. In response to threats, they use brute force and terror."

"Precisely."

"So I screwed up." She kicked the ground. "I should have been stronger with McDermott, just told him I was going."

Craig didn't argue with her.

"Then I'd have been in Calgary with Francesca. She might still be alive."

"And if Adam hadn't eaten that apple, none of us would be wearing clothes. You can't give yourself a beating."

"But if you're right, that she was murdered, what can *we* do about it? Enlist the help of the CIA or FBI?"

"Kirby made me persona non grata with those agencies. People have told me I'm not a team player. Not to be trusted. So that's not an option. I have to work on my own. I'm flying to Calgary tomorrow."

Without hesitating, she blurted out, "I want to go with you."

He shook his head. "I'll give you a report when I get back."

"Why not?"

"I prefer operating alone. I've had bad experiences partnering. We'd trip over each other."

"You're wrong. I can help you. With my press credentials, we'll get access."

"And it could be dangerous."

"You don't have to worry. I'm plenty tough. I not only grew up in a rough neighborhood of Brooklyn, but I had three older brothers. Until three years ago, when I got this stupid desk job, which I hate, I was an investigative reporter. I've faced plenty of danger. I was one of the embedded reporters to go with our troops into Iraq."

He was wavering.

"I know how to fire a gun. Growing up, I was one of the boys. Went huntin' and fishin' with my dad and my brothers. Bagged my first deer when I was twelve. I even killed a Taliban thug in Afghanistan, who tried to capture me."

Maybe she can help. Francesca liked her.

"Alright. Tomorrow afternoon, I'm on a three twenty five United flight from Denver to Calgary. I'll meet you at Denver Airport."

"Good. That gives me time to get approval from McDermott."

7

NEW YORK

Elizabeth packed a suitcase in the morning and wheeled it into the Trib's headquarters on Seventh Avenue in midtown Manhattan. After leaving the bag in her office, she headed up to the publisher's suite, rejecting the elevator and climbing three flights, as part of her fitness routine.

"I'm expecting him in about five minutes," Carla, McDermott's secretary said. "Why don't you wait in his office."

Sitting alone in McDermott's office, Elizabeth was struck by how much she disliked the publisher. Until he bought the Trib four years ago, she had her dream job. She was a foreign journalist and investigative reporter with freedom to pick her assignments. The world was her beat. No one ever questioned her travels, and for good reason. Her series, "Poppies and the Taliban," won a Pulitzer. While researching that piece in Afghanistan, she came face to face with death several times, not just the Taliban she killed, but the IED explosions and sniper fire that she barely avoided.

But then, in one of his first moves, McDermott sacked Danny Gross, who made twice her salary, as foreign editor. He gave her the job, with a minimal raise, ignoring her pleas, "I'm a reporter, not an editor." He buttered her up with praise, telling her how good she was. Without asking for a day or two to think about it, she yielded. A week later she decided she was an idiot. She should have quit the Trib, rather than taking that job.

She walked across the office, to the "I love me wall," lined with photos of McDermott with senators, presidents, heads of state, and movie stars. In all of them, he was posing with a phony smile on his round pumpkin-like face, just below his trendy thin wire glasses.

"See something that piques your interest," she heard McDermott say in his booming voice. She turned to face him, staring at her in the doorway.

"Just killing time. Carla told me to wait in here."

He moved to his desk chair, pointing her to one in front. "What's up?"

He looked wary, she thought. "I want to fly to Calgary with Francesca's father. To pick up the story she was working on."

McDermott shook his head. "No way, I need you in New York."

"Russ can cover the editing. And he can e-mail or call me if he has any questions. We won't miss a step."

"Which part of 'no' don't you understand? The 'n' or the 'o'?"

Why is he so adamant?

"The story has to be huge," Elizabeth said. "And Francesca was our reporter. She was murdered. I want to find out who did it."

He laughed as if she were insane. "You've been watching too many movies. You're fantasizing. Francesca died in a road accident. It's done. It's over."

"And the big story she was working on?"

He laughed again. "What story? She was a damn kid, just out of school, chasing a UFO."

"That's ridiculous. She was one of my best reporters."

"What's this? The sisterhood at work?"

"I feel strongly about going."

"I feel even stronger, and I'm the publisher. It's my decision."

"I've busted my ass for this paper for fifteen years." She was raising her voice. "You owe me."

"I don't owe you squat," he shouted back. "I'm not letting you go."

She refused to be intimidated. "I'll go on my own, then. You won't have to pay a cent of expenses. I'll even take the time, as part of my annual leave."

He narrowed his eyes. "You go, and you can forget about your job."

She stormed out of the room, charged down three flights, and into her office.

Without hesitation, she sat down at her computer and typed an e-mail to McDermott: "Effective today, I am resigning from the Tribune."

8

LANGLEY, VIRGINIA

Kirby leaned back in his high, black, leather desk chair and savored his surroundings. He loved the Director's large corner office on the seventh floor of the CIA headquarters in Langley.

He recalled when he was first elected to Congress from Northern California, sixteen years ago, thanks to his father's money as a Silicon Valley venture capitalist and his father's friends. He had joined the House Intelligence committee. He'd always been a compulsive reader of spy novels and intelligence memoirs. Other children wanted to be baseball or football players, but for Kirby, short and uncoordinated, athletics wasn't an option. He wanted to be Director of the CIA. He was still in Congress four years ago, a ranking member of the House Intelligence committee, when President Taylor, Brewster's predecessor, had a chance to pick a new DCI. His father had contributed heavily to Taylor's campaign. The Director's job was part of the payback. When Brewster was swept into the White House,

Kirby leaned on his friends in Congress to persuade the President to retain Kirby. And so far, it had worked. Another couple of weeks was all he needed. Then he'd ride out of Washington on a gold stallion.

The cell phone in his pocket rang. Kirby glanced at caller ID. Roy McDermott.

"Yes, Roy?"

"You asked me to let you know if I heard any more about Francesca Page's accident."

"What happened?"

"Elizabeth Crowder, Francesca's editor, is going to Calgary with Francesca's father to investigate the accident."

Kirby was gripping the phone tightly, perspiring under his arms.

"Why didn't you stop her, the way you did the last time?"

"I tried. Believe me I did. I even threatened to fire her if she went, but she told me to stuff the job. So she no longer works for me. She's one strong willed woman."

"Are you sure Francesca's father's going, too?"

"That's what Elizabeth told me."

Damn. Damn. Damn. Craig Page again. Always Craig Page.

"And there's something else," McDermott said, sounding ominous.

"What's that?"

"Elizabeth thinks Francesca was murdered."

Kirby's blood ran cold. This was his nightmare scenario.

"She told you that?"

"Yeah."

"What'd you say?"

"That she'd seen too many movies. That she was fantasizing. I couldn't change her mind."

"Thanks for the info, Roy."

"Anything else I can do to help?"

"I'll let you know," Kirby said and hung up. He picked up a couple of darts resting on the desk. Cursing under his breath, he fired them at a dartboard on a wall across the room. Both missed the bulls-eye. One landed on the edge of the board.

"Damn," he muttered aloud.

He thought about Madison Square Garden. In Dubai, Craig had uncovered the plot to send suicide bombers into Madison Square Garden and had reported that Achmed was coming to New York to hook up with the other perps. Kirby had asked for Achmed's flight information and told Craig to remain in Dubai. "We'll take it from here."

But Craig had argued, "I have to be there. I know Achmed. Without me, you'll blow it." When Kirby wouldn't relent, Craig refused to turn over Achmed's flight information. Instead, he cut off all communications with Washington and tracked Achmed himself. Then he hooked up with NYPD to foil the attack and catch the plotters, making Kirby seem like a fool. Afterwards, Page sucked up to President Brewster.

He picked up the phone and dialed. "Ali. We have to talk. The usual place in an hour."

9

CULPEPPER, VIRGINIA

Kirby drove himself, over back roads. Only a short distance from posh Washington suburbs and country estates, he was in rural redneck country with places like the Johnnie Reb Saloon. He didn't even know this joint existed until Ali suggested they meet there, for their first project two years ago.

Pulling into the parking lot, all he saw were a couple of motorcycles, two clunkers, and a shiny silver Jaguar XK8 convertible with Ali's vanity plate: DO IT. Too early for the lunch crowd.

He had to hand it to Ali Hariri. The man was more than a survivor. He always managed to come out on top. Once a colonel in the Shah's version of the KGB, known as SAVAK, Ali had made a place for himself in one of the U.S. intelligence agencies. He never seemed to age; no one would have guessed he was in his late sixties. His base was now in Tampa at SOCOM. His specialty was doing jobs off the books, those dicey interrogations or assassinations for which his DOD bosses claimed plausible deniability, and never reported to Congress. Fortunately for Kirby, Ali had a loose leash. He also had time to freelance if the price was right.

Kirby entered the dimly lit Johnnie Reb. He wove his way over sawdust to the booth in the corner, where he and Ali usually met. Ali was already there, sipping a beer, his thin mustache moist with foam. A juke box was playing a Pam Tillis song.

A waitress came over, a skinny kid, looking to be not more than fourteen, in a stained apron that wrapped around her twice.

"Ya want something to drink?"

"Just some coffee."

"And we'll have two barbecue sandwiches," Ali added.

Once the waitress was gone, Kirby looked sternly at Ali. "I pay you plenty of money for special projects. Usually you do good work, but this time you fucked up, big time."

Ali seemed more amused, than upset, which annoyed Kirby.

"I did. How?"

"The woman whose death you arranged in Calgary was Craig Page's daughter. You should have known that."

Ali shrugged. "With what you paid me, I'm willing to take the blame. But it's your fault. All you told me was there's a young woman named Francesca Page in Calgary, a reporter for the *New York Tribune,* conducting an interview in Suite 2100 in the Hyatt, at seven on Monday evening. I was supposed to take care of her. Which I did… very efficiently, I might add."

Kirby didn't argue. It was his fault. Page wasn't an unusual name. Kirby hadn't made the connection to Craig. Acting in haste and near panic, he never even bothered to research her background.

The waitress returned with the sandwiches and coffee.

Ali was eating his sandwich and obviously enjoying it. Kirby took a bite. With everything happening, he didn't have an appetite.

Ali put down the sandwich and wiped his face with a napkin. "I assume you didn't haul me out here to chew me out. No pun intended."

"Right, I'm giving you a chance to redeem yourself."

Ali smiled. "For your mistake. Go ahead."

"Craig Page and Elizabeth Crowder, who used to work for the *Tribune* as Francesca's boss, are going to Calgary to snoop around. They believe Francesca was murdered. And Craig's tough. Resourceful too."

"I know all about Craig Page. Don't worry, I won't underestimate him."

"If it looks like they're getting close to learning what happened to Francesca, I want them both eliminated. The money will be the same as the Francesca job. Another million deposited into your Cayman Island bank account."

"But there are two of them. It should be double. I have expenses. The price of gas is high."

"Then drive a hybrid. One point five and that's final."

"Let's split the difference at one point seven five."

"What is it about you Iranians, that you always have to haggle?"

"So I guess we have a deal at one point seven five."

"Okay," Kirby said reluctantly.

10

CALGARY

"It's been ten years, Mr. Page," the tuxedo-clad maître d' at Caesar's Steakhouse said to Craig, as he and Elizabeth entered the elegant room, decorated in dark woods.

"Gino, you have an amazing recollection of names and faces."

"Only special people. And ones I like."

Gino led them to a table along the wall, with comfortable leather chairs, separated from others, so they could talk. The aroma of grilled steak was in the air. Elizabeth ordered a Cosmopolitan and Craig a Jack Daniels.

"How can you drink something that sweet?"

"I like it."

He made a face. "Yuck."

"Not macho enough for you?"

"Maybe that's it."

"You obviously know your way around. How much time have you spent in Calgary?"

"When I graduated from Carnegie Mellon, I worked for Spartan Oil Exploration Company, based in Houston. They sent me up here for a project. I've been back from time to time, usually seeking information about the oil business. This city's the oil capital of Canada, their Houston and Dallas combined. Calgary's had the most incredible boom time, since the seventies, with some busts along the way when the price of oil plunged. Then ten years ago…"

The waiter returned with their drinks. Craig raised his glass. "To finding answers."

They paused to sip.

"Don't say a word about my drink."

"That trip ten years ago," he said somberly, "was the last family vacation the three of us took. First, we went to Banff and Lake Louise. Afterwards, we spent time here. Francesca was thirteen. Her mother died a year later. Then we moved back to Washington."

"That meant a lot to Francesca. You interrupting your career and moving back until she finished high school. And she said you spent lots of time with her when she was in college, even though you were stationed in Dubai."

"You must have been good friends if she told you all that."

"We were."

A waiter brought menus.

"The Alberta beef is spectacular," Craig said.

"I don't usually eat meat."

"I would have guessed that."

She frowned. "You're stereotyping me. Sounds like an insult."

"Actually, it's a compliment. Healthy, athletic young woman."

"Not so young."

"You probably ran this morning."

"As a matter of fact, I did, five miles in Central Park."

"Good. Then make an exception. You deserve it. Order the beef. It's worth it."

He told the waiter, "Two Caesar salads and sirloin steaks. Medium rare." She didn't object. Craig selected a ninety seven Brunello from Altesino.

Elizabeth said, "As I was telling you, Francesca wasn't merely my ace reporter. We were good friends, as well. We both loved the Mets and hated the Yankees. When she was in town last summer, we spent lots of evenings in the press box at Mets games. She told me she got her love of sports from you."

"Yeah, I played quarterback at Monesson High, in a tough steel town in Western Pennsylvania. My senior year, we went through the season undefeated, winning a state title. I had dreams of playing in the big ten, but the coach at Penn State gave me a sanity check. He said, 'kid, you've got a good arm, but you're not big enough to make it in big time football.' So when the academic scholarship to Carnegie Mellon came through, I took it." He paused, then said wistfully, "I played quarterback at CMU, but we weren't exactly a power."

"Were you an engineer?"

"Chemical engineer."

"You don't seem like a geek to me."

"Now who's stereotyping?"

"I just meant…"

"I know. Pocket computer hooked to the belt and all that. But I also wrote a weekly column on international affairs for our school paper, the *Tartan*. And I took courses in Greek tragedy and ancient civilizations, a real passion of mine."

"I saw the books in the house. Did you ever write on the subject?"

"I hoped to in Milan. So far, starting a business has taken most of my time, but I've begun an article, 'Spies in the Roman Empire.' What about you? Ever want to write a book?"

"When I was at Harvard, I spent a semester in Spain. I became fascinated with medieval history and the Islamic expulsion from Andalusia. I've thought about writing a book one day, but never got beyond that."

She paused to sip her drink. "Francesca admired you so much. She was always striving for your respect."

"And she knew she had it. She wanted to be so much like me that she was hell bent to join the CIA or the military. I convinced her it was too dangerous. Investigative journalism became her next choice."

"That may explain why Francesca always took chances."

Her words stung. Craig grimaced.

"Sorry, Craig. That was tactless of me."

Their salads came. For several minutes they ate in silence. Then Craig put down his fork. "Let's talk about our plan for tomorrow."

"Good. I'm ready."

"We know Francesca's big story involved oil, which is the nexus between Iran and Calgary."

"Correct. And she was focused on another country developing Iran's reserves."

"But we don't know which one."

"I'll put my money on Russia. That's how the Russians operate, using assassination to mow down anyone standing in their way."

"Unfortunately, the Russians aren't alone there."

"But why was she in Canada?" Elizabeth asked, pushing back her hair. "I can't believe the Canadians are cutting a deal with Iran."

"The key, I'll bet, is whom she was interviewing. That's what we have to find out."

Elizabeth nodded. "Agreed. Where should we start?"

"I want to meet with an old oil buddy, Harold Topps, from my Spartan Oil days. We've stayed in touch. He knows everything happening up here in the oil patch. See where it goes from there."

"Makes sense. I'll begin with the police and their investigation of the crash. When I quit my job, I didn't turn in my press credentials.

So I should be able to see Anderson or one of the other top people. I've spent enough time over the years interviewing cops."

Two huge sirloin steaks arrived with fries on the side.

She took a bite of the meat. "I have to admit this tastes good." She said it with enthusiasm.

"Try the wine."

She took a sip and nodded her approval. "Hey I really like this. I'm not a connoisseur. Is it a merlot or a cab?"

"Neither. The Brunello grape is a sangiovese variety. Grown in Tuscany in the hills south of Siena."

"How do you know so much about it?"

"Wine's a hobby of mine. I may corrupt you before this is all over."

"I'm willing to learn. I want to ask you something that's been bugging me."

"Sure. Anything."

"After you left the CIA and decided to open a private security firm, why'd you make Milan your base?"

"I have roots there."

"Page does not sound like an Italian name to me."

"It's a long story."

"It'll take me a while to finish this steak."

She leaned forward in her chair and looked at him with wide chestnut eyes.

"My dad's parents had a farm between Milan and Verona. They grew grapes and some other things. He was the youngest of five children. Four years old at the time the American troops were fighting their way north in Italy and the Germans were retreating.

"The Jews had been able to survive in Italy as long as it was just Mussolini, but once the Germans moved into the country, they rounded up and deported the Jews. Although nobody in my family was Jewish, my grandfather hid in his barn and fed for months a Jewish family he had been friendly with. Two adults and two children. Then one day, the retreating Germans were so close my grandfather could hear them. He hid everybody, including his wife and all five of his children. My grandfather put my father at the bottom of a pile of hay in the field. He faced the German soldiers himself, telling them he lived alone.

"The Germans found everyone except my father. The rest of his family. The four Jews. They killed them all with machine gun fire. My father waited hours before coming out. When he did, the Germans were gone. The dead left behind. Could you imagine what it would be like to deal with that as a four year old?"

She was too stunned to respond. He answered his own question.

"I can't. I heard the story from my father. He told me that he lay down in his bed and cried. All alone. Not knowing where to go or what to do. Four years old.

"The next day the American troops arrived. When a captain by the name of Page was searching the farmhouse, he found my father, who could barely speak. Captain Page pieced the story together from what he saw. He couldn't leave my father on the farm. So he took him with his unit. A couple of weeks later, Captain Page was hit with a bullet in the shoulder. When they shipped him back to the United States, he took my father home with him to Monessen."

Elizabeth asked, "What was your mother like?"

"Blond haired and blue eyed. Her family had been from Sweden. My dad met her when he was in college at Carnegie Tech, where he got an engineering degree. Then they went back to Monessen to live. He began as an engineer and eventually became part of the management team at the local steel mill. My Dad died about six months ago. My mother a year before that. I never had any siblings."

Craig paused for a minute and swallowed hard. "Behaving honorably meant a great deal to my dad. And he loved the United States. He never stopped being grateful to Captain Page and the American Army. All of the freedoms my friends assumed, he wouldn't let me take for granted."

"He must have been proud of what you were doing."

"He was. I wanted him to come to the White House when I received the Medal of Freedom. He was sick so I lined up a car and driver. But he lapsed into a coma two days before. He died a week later."

Craig paused. Remembering was difficult. He still felt a strong bond with his dad.

"When I graduated from college, he gave me a plane ticket and told me to visit the old family farm, so I would never forget where I came from and if it weren't for the U.S. Army, I would never be alive."

"What'd you see?"

"Not much. Developers had built housing on the spot, but that didn't matter. I closed my eyes and imagined my dad lying in bed when Captain Page found him. That story's been pivotal to my whole life. I had to do something to serve the United States. That's why I joined the CIA. I'd still be there if…"

"Francesca told me about Kirby."

"What goes around comes around. Life's long. One day I'll have a chance to get even with that son of a bitch."

11

CALGARY

The morning fog was so thick that Elizabeth could barely see the Rocky Mountains off to the west. She decided to walk the twelve blocks from the Westin to police headquarters.

Last evening before dinner, she stopped in the hotel boutique to buy a guide book. Then at six this morning, once she saw the roads were too icy for running, she took the guidebook with her to read while she peddled on a stationary bike in the fitness center. She wasn't surprised to see Craig already there, running on a treadmill.

On her way to police headquarters, the temperature was in the twenties. The wind had a bite, making it feel well below zero.

She'd read about the interconnecting enclosed sidewalks, elevated fifteen feet above road level, and she sought refuge in one. As she rode up the escalator, she noticed a Middle Eastern-looking man behind her. He was tall and swarthy, with a thin mustache.

At the first chance, she took an escalator down to street level.

She walked fast, while glancing over her shoulder, not seeing him, feeling relief.

But when she hit the bottom he was at the top coming down rapidly.

He's following me.

She made no effort to lose him. Instead, she dawdled on the sidewalk, pretending to window shop.

She walked into the entry way for a women's shoe store. He hung back, a couple doors away. She took out her cell phone and called Craig. "I'm being followed. How did they know we're here?"

"They could have tapped into airline computers and checked manifests for Craig Page. Then hotel registrations. They'd have learned from Westin records that we're sharing a two bedroom suite."

"Another possibility is that bastard McDermott tipped somebody off."

"No sense trying to analyze it. We have to deal with the situation. How many do you think are following you?"

"So far I've only seen one man. Tall, Middle Eastern-looking, an Arab or an Iranian. He made no effort to attack or to grab me."

"He probably wants to see where you're going. Harold can't meet me for another hour. I'm killing time at the hotel. You want me to join you? We can stick together today."

"No, I'm planning to lose him once I get to police headquarters. Meantime, I'll take his picture with my cell phone. Maybe you'll recognize him."

"Good idea."

She ended the call, switched the phone to camera mode, then walked out to the sidewalk with the cell phone plastered to her ear, pretending to look into the front window while moving her lips to give the impression of talking. The tall man was only two shops away.

She waited until he was looking at her, then she aimed and clicked the camera. Gotcha.

She guessed that he noticed her taking the picture. She didn't care.

After moving back into the entry way of the shop, she checked the picture. Perfect. She put the phone back in her bag and resumed walking.

The rest of the way to police headquarters, the tall swarthy man was on her tail, hanging back, never getting too close.

Police headquarters was a spanking-new high-tech, steel and glass, six-floor building. As she climbed the stone steps to the front door, the swarthy man remained on the sidewalk. He bought a newspaper from a box and pretended to read it.

An hour ago she had called and set a meeting with Anderson. He was waiting for her in his office on the top floor, facing the front of the building. Anderson had curly blond hair, blue eyes, and a wide smile, showing white teeth. He was trim and looked fit, the kind of man she expected to meet around a fire at a ski lodge.

"Can I offer you some coffee, Miss Crowder?"

"Call me Elizabeth. And black would be great."

He poured two cups from a carafe on a side table, then pointed her to a chair in front of his desk.

"Thanks for seeing me, Mr. Anderson."

"What was your relationship with Francesca Page?"

"She was a reporter, working for me in the foreign news department at the *New York Tribune*."

He raised his eyebrows. "What story brought her to Calgary?"

"I don't know precisely. Only that it involved oil. We were also friends. I came to get the details of the accident."

"I'm afraid we don't have much. Our emergency line received a cell call from a motorist who came across Francesca's smashed rental on Barlow Trail, which runs to the airport. She was three miles away. The caller said her car, a red Toyota, was crumpled like an accordion, and we should get an ambulance ASAP. It was snowing heavily. A chopper was out of the question. Our ambulance arrived in twelve minutes, but she was dead. Our accident investigation quickly established she was involved in a head on collision with a large truck."

"What happened to the truck driver?"

"We don't know who he was. He left the scene of the accident. We put up roadblocks, but we were too late." Anderson sounded defensive. "Because of the snow, it took us longer to get those road blocks up. The next day, I had my people check all the truck body shops in the area. None of them reported a truck coming in for repairs."

A thin folder was resting on his desk. He slid it forward. "Our accident report. You're welcome to read it."

Elizabeth studied the report while Anderson watched and sipped coffee. Everything was consistent with what he had told her. The police towed Francesca's car to JL Auto and Truck Body Shop on Pine Street.

She closed the folder and pushed it back.

"I'm glad you came in," Anderson said. "Something about this accident has been bothering me. Maybe you can help."

"What's that?"

"In her jacket pocket, Francesca had a plastic room key for the Fairmont Palliser Hotel in town. I went over there myself. I found her suitcase and all her other clothes. Nothing was packed. So I've been asking myself: Why does someone drive to the airport without her suitcase and clothes? All I could figure was she was meeting an arriving passenger. But we checked with all of them on the only flight that arrived. No one even knew her. Do you know whether she was meeting someone?"

Elizabeth shook her head.

"So what's the explanation?"

She took a deep breath and swallowed hard, knowing she was about to toss a live grenade on his desk.

"Francesca was working on a big story, with international implications. It concerned oil and Iran. I believe she was murdered to prevent her from disclosing what she learned."

Anderson didn't flinch. "I wondered if it was something like that. In this town, the trouble's always about oil. Just too damn much money at stake. You can't believe the stuff I've seen, fraud, corruption, extortion, murder. The black gold is usually involved."

"What happened to Francesca's clothes and other personal things?"

"Everything is at the Fairmont, what she was wearing at the time of the accident, the stuff in her hotel room. I spoke with the manager, Donna Humphrey. Asked her to place them in a locked room. I'll call and make sure she'll give you access."

"Thanks. I appreciate that."

Anderson made the call.

"Ask for Donna. She'll be expecting you."

Elizabeth walked over to the window and looked out. The tall, swarthy man with the thin mustache was standing in front of the building, holding a newspaper.

"Could I ask a favor, Mr. Anderson?"

"Sure."

"I don't have a car, and my leg's bothering me."

"You want me to get you a doctor?"

"Naw. I just pulled a muscle running. Any chance someone can drive me to the Fairmont?"

He picked up the phone and arranged it. "Kelly will take you."

Minutes later, a young woman in her twenties, a baby faced blonde, with a name tag, "Kelly Bennett," walked in.

"Call me anytime," Anderson said. "Like you, I want to get to the bottom of this."

Kelly's police cruiser was parked in the basement garage. Elizabeth asked if she could ride in the back and stretch her leg. When the car was on the up ramp, Elizabeth slipped down on the floor.

Kelly stopped the car and turned around. "Hey, are you okay?"

"Yeah. I'm fine. Just getting more comfortable."

"Whatever works for you."

Elizabeth got out in front of the Fairmont and looked around. No sign of the tall swarthy man. Kelly pulled away. She went into the hotel.

12

CALGARY

For several minutes, Elizabeth wandered around the lobby to make sure she wasn't being followed. Then she went back outside and got into the first cab.

Behind the wheel was a young black man, a Nigerian, she saw from the name tag. A tape was playing. She recognized the Nigerian music.

"I want you to take me to JL Auto and Truck Body Shop on Pine. Park about a block away and wait for me. I'll only be a few minutes. Run your meter. I'll give you a big tip."

"Sounds good to me."

He turned off the music.

"It's okay to leave it on. I spent time in your country, a few years ago, doing a story about some brutal murders in the Delta, where the oil and rebels are."

"Very bad people."

As he drove, Elizabeth kept glancing through the back window. Nobody was following.

They arrived in an industrial part of town populated with garages, truck depots, mechanical shops, and small factories.

After the cab parked, Elizabeth walked the block along an oil slick road. JL Auto and Truck Body Shop was exactly what Elizabeth expected: an open garage with mechanics in oil stained overalls, working on cars and trucks, the smell of grease and chemicals in the air. She asked a grease monkey where she could find the manager. He pointed to the rear of the shop. "Mr. Larson's office."

John Larson, in his fifties, was dressed in clean jeans and a red plaid shirt. The boss didn't get down and dirty. Photos of nude women covered one wall.

"Who are you, lady?" he asked, sticking out his jaw and glaring at her.

"I want to talk to you about the red Toyota towed in after an accident last Monday evening."

He looked mystified. "We get lots of cars in here, lady. I can't remember them all."

"It was a snowy night. Friend of mine was killed in that Toyota. A truck hit her, then took off."

He pulled a cigarette from a pack on his desk and lit it.

"What'd you want to know?"

"I want to see the car."

"Not worth repairing. I sent it out to a scrap metal joint."

"Which one?

"Don't waste your time. They already chewed it up."

Now he sounded hostile.

"Did you get any trucks in here that evening, or the next day?"

"Not a one."

"Did you look at the Toyota?"

He took a long drag on the cigarette, then blew perfect smoke rings in the air.

Unimpressed, she looked away glancing at the wall of photos. A blonde dressed only in five inch stilettos, with huge boobs, was staring at her.

"Yeah, why?"

"I wonder if anything on the car would identify the truck."

"Are you out of your fuckin' mind? What could there possibly be?"

She shrugged. "Pieces of metal from the truck. Imprints."

"You don't know shit about trucks. Do you, lady?"

"Well I'm not an expert."

He laughed. "I'll say. Think about an elephant colliding with a fly. What would you find on the fly?"

"Not much. I guess."

"You got it."

"You're in the business, John. Where do you think I should go to find out about the truck?"

"You from New York?"

"Yeah. How'd you know?"

"The accent. My advice, lady, is that you forget about this whole business and go back to New York."

"No fuckin' way."

"Leave it, lady." Now he sounded threatening.

"I won't."

"For your own good, you better."

"Thanks for the advice."

As she walked away, she glanced over her shoulder. She saw Larson picking up the phone.

She was convinced he was calling someone to tell them about her. Whoever had orchestrated Francesca's murder had lots of power in Calgary or plenty of money to get what they wanted. They must have paid Larson to keep his mouth shut. No other explanation for his behavior.

She had reached a dead end on the auto angle. Even worse, she had stirred up a hornet's nest. Now she had one desire: to get the hell out of this part of town before she ended up like Francesca.

At the entrance to the garage, she paused and looked around. The cab was where she had left it. The Nigerian was standing next to the driver's door smoking a cigarette. Nothing unusual on the street.

She walked rapidly, almost running, along the oil slick road toward the cab. Suddenly she heard a powerful engine from behind. She turned and gaped. A silver eighteen wheeler had pulled out of a freight terminal. The truck was barreling down the road, way too fast, coming right at her. Almost on her, the driver blasted his horn, not slowing down. The metal dog on the hood was big as life. Her legs began to freeze up. But her brain sent them a powerful message: Move, or you'll end up like Francesca.

She dove for the side of the road, landing in a pile of oily debris.

"Be careful, bitch," the driver shouted through the open window. Then he sped away.

The Nigerian was out in the street shaking his fist at the truck. "Busturd," he cried out.

She was spread out on the ground. Her arms and legs were bruised and scratched, her suit grimy. Her head ached. In relief, she was gulping deep breaths of air.

The cab driver walked over and helped her to her feet.

"I'm okay," she reassured the Nigerian.

He led her back to the cab.

13

CALGARY

Harold Topps was a gambler. That was the nature of his business: using technology, experience and a gut feel to select a location likely to have oil, then raising money, millions of dollars, his own and investors, and then drilling. If he hit the black gold, he sold off the parcel to an oil company and made a bundle. If he hit a dry hole, the money was lost.

Craig entered the luxurious, wood-paneled reception area of Topps Exploration in the Calgary Tower on Ninth Avenue, one of the city's most famous landmarks, long the city's tallest building. To show for his skill, Harold had a mansion outside of town and a five million dollar "cabin" near Lake Louise, as well as a fleet of boats he loved to race on the lake.

"Mr. Topps will be down shortly," said the busty, mini-skirted blond receptionist with the tight pale green sweater.

Craig realized she was using the word "down" literally, as he looked up at the wide, dark wooden staircase, descending from the floor above. When he was in Calgary on that project for Spartan, Harold told Craig he was planning to start his own business and asked Craig to be his partner. By then, Craig had decided to join the CIA, a decision he never regretted.

He saw Harold, with a thick head of brown hair, a little gray at the temples, making him look debonair, emerge down those stairs looking like God himself. Only the clouds were missing.

"You've upgraded your offices since the last time I was in Calgary," Craig said.

"Damn right. With oil now pushing a hundred dollars a barrel again, I have moola to play with."

Once settled in Harold's cavernous twentieth floor office with a mind-blowing view of the Rockies, Harold said, "We haven't spoken since you called to say you were starting a security firm in Milan. How's that going?"

"Doing well. I'm getting work from the government of Italy. Also private corporations worried about trade secret theft, particularly in the pharma and computer industries."

"Miss the CIA?"

"Yeah, but life moves on."

"What brings you to Calgary, my friend?"

"Very sad news. Francesca died up here last week."

"What? Oh, I had no idea."

"I know that. Or you'd have called."

"I'm so sorry. Great kid. Smart. Good looking. I'd have given anything to set her up with Brian. What happened?"

"She was driving, and a truck crashed into her. Last Monday. A snowy night."

"I didn't see anything in the local paper."

"That's no surprise. Whoever was responsible had plenty of clout."

"You don't think it was an accident?"

"Well, let's put it this way. She was a reporter working for *the New York Tribune*. She was covering a huge story that somehow involved the oil business."

Harold was shaking his head. "With so much money involved, guys play rough in the oil patch. What was the story?"

"I was hoping you could help me there."

"I'd do anything for you.... You know that."

"Tell me what's been happening in the Canadian oil business in the last couple of weeks. Any major developments?"

Harold leaned back in his chair and put his feet up on the glass topped desk. "We've had lots of action. About ten days ago a Chinese delegation, six of them, came to town and made generous offers to take over five Canadian oil companies with the largest reserves. It's all been hush-hush, but I know from people in the companies that the Chinese reached agreements with four of them to close on April 1."

"Did the Chinese talk to you about your company?"

Harold shook his head. "They weren't interested in exploration. They want oil reserves.... Too bad. They were paying a hefty premium above book value."

"What's the situation with the fifth company?"

"Energy Assets. I don't know whether they sold or not. John Saunders, their President and majority stockholder, is in Foothills Hospital."

"What happened to Saunders?"

"I've done work with John over the years. So I went over to see him. Poor bastard has huge casts on both legs and a bandage on his shoulder. His face looks as if he went ten rounds with a heavyweight champion. He claims it was a skiing accident." Harold frowned. "I've seen plenty of those. This sure wasn't any skiing accident."

Harold's face lit up like a slot machine that had a big hit. He dropped his feet and leaned forward. "Jesus. That must be it. You think somebody murdered Francesca?"

"I'm sure."

"And somebody beat the living hell out of John Saunders. These two have to be connected."

"Who headed up the Chinese delegation?"

"Zhou Yun, the CEO of CNOC, the Chinese Oil Company. Guy who negotiated with him said he was one tough SOB. Somebody who made sure he got what he wanted."

"You know where he was staying in town?"

Harold shook his head.

"Did Zhou Yun bring any goons with him?"

"I saw the six of them having dinner one night at Hy's Steakhouse. All looked like businessmen in starched white shirts and ties." He shrugged. "But you can't tell by looks."

"Somebody else could have supplied the goons. Have you seen any Iranians running around town?"

"Nope. Sorry, I can't be more helpful."

"You were incredibly helpful."

"You have time for lunch or dinner?"

"Let's put that on hold."

Craig stood, preparing to leave.

"Let me tell you one more thing," said Harold.

"What's that?"

"Given the business you're in, it's insulting for me to tell you to be careful. But what the hell, you're my friend. When I think about John Saunders, well…"

After leaving the Calgary Tower, Craig, on the sidewalk on Ninth Avenue, took out his cell and called Elizabeth. "Where are you?"

"On my way to the Fairmont Hotel, where Francesca was staying."

"Francesca was probably interviewing Zhou Yun, the head of CNOC, the Chinese Oil Company. I don't know where he was staying."

"I'll find out. This isn't New York. Only a limited number of options. And knowing Francesca, she probably did the interview in his hotel suite."

"Continue to watch your six o'clock. Zhou Yun or some of his cohorts may still be in Calgary. These guys play rough. I just heard what they did to somebody who didn't want to sell his oil company."

"Thanks for the heads up, but I don't need any more warnings. A truck tried to run me down."

"Did you get hurt?"

"Just some scrapes and bruises."

"We'll have to work fast. Get what we can and beat it out of Calgary."

"Agreed. Where are you going?"

"To make a hospital visit."

"My mother taught me: Bring flowers. You can get them in the gift shop on the first floor."

"Thanks. I wouldn't have known that."

14

BEIJING

As midnight approached on still another cold and dreary night, General Zhou looked out of his office in the headquarters of the Peoples Liberation Army. Five floors below, the bright lights of Tiananmen Square illuminated Mao's crypt.

That monster and villain was responsible for the deaths of more Chinese than the total number of people killed by Hitler and Stalin combined. But far more than statistics, Mao's crimes had a personal impact on General Zhou. He and his brother, Zhou Yun, as teenagers in 1967, were separated from their father and mother, who were sent to the countryside for indoctrination. The brothers formed an unbreakable bond. "We can only trust each other," Zhou Yun, older by two years, told him.

In 1973, their father returned to Beijing. He was a shell of the man who had gone away. Tearfully, he explained to his sons that their mother had died of malnutrition.

The irony, General Zhou thought sadly, was that, when Mao had seized power, their father had surrendered his comfortable life in San Francisco to return home for the rebuilding of China. He had a dream of the People's Republic one day becoming the dominant power in the world.

An insomniac, General Zhou loved summoning people to midnight meetings. It let them know how powerful he was, that he was commander in chief of the Chinese armed forces in more than title.

He particularly liked ordering Admiral Xu Shi, the Commander of the Chinese Navy, to these meetings. Admiral Xu always bristled when he felt as if he weren't being treated with respect, which led General Zhou to treat the Admiral like a schoolboy whenever possible. And tonight, perhaps Admiral Xu had even been forced to pull his fat body out of the bed of Lena, his scheming, money hungry mistress, by Captain Cheng's call. But Admiral Xu knew his failure to attend could be classified as insubordination. He might have been removed from his position, or worse.

General Zhou waited until ten minutes after twelve to enter the conference room adjacent to his office, carrying a briefcase. Admiral Xu was seated on one side of the table. Across from the Admiral, sat General Yang Gon, the head of the Chinese Air Force, and Captain Cheng. General Zhou took his usual seat at the head of the table.

He reached into his briefcase, removed two documents, and handed one each to Admiral Xu and General Yang.

"These are copies of the agreement I signed with the Iranians in Paris. We're now moving forward with Operation Dragon Oil on April 1. You both need a copy to prepare for implementation. But I insist that you keep it under lock and key." He hardened his expression and looked directly at Admiral Xu. "Don't take it out of the building and don't make any copies."

He paused for a minute to let the two of them read the document. General Yang said, "You got what you wanted."

"Absolutely."

He turned to the weak livered Admiral Xu. "And what do you think?"

"I'm concerned that, if we go forward…"

"You mean when we go forward."

"It will lead to war with the United Sates."

"You don't have to worry about the United States," he said, his tone dismissive. "I've taken care of the Americans."

"Taken care of them, how?"

"You don't have to know."

"But surely President Brewster will find out before April 1. Their CIA is not totally incompetent. And then…"

How dare he contradict me.

"President Brewster won't find out, and he won't intervene. Subject closed. Now the next topic. I'm prepared to move forward with plans for our invasion and takeover of the island of Taiwan, also scheduled for April 1. I'm giving the order today for ground troops to move up to points across the Strait from Taiwan. Also to add missile batteries at those locations. At the same time, I want both the Navy and Air Force to begin preparation for the Taiwan invasion. Understood?"

"Yes, sir," General Yang said with enthusiasm.

General Zhou looked at Admiral Xu.

"It will be done," he replied reluctantly.

After the meeting, General Zhou returned to his office. He called his brother, waking him. "We have to talk."

"Can't it wait until morning?"

"It is morning. And this can't wait."

15

CALGARY

Elizabeth met Donna Humphrey. The petite manager of the Fairmont, looked even smaller standing in front of a large marble column in the lobby under a sparkling glass chandelier.

"I'll do anything to help you," Humphrey said. "Francesca was staying in room 823. I moved her things into a storage locker. Nobody's been in the room since. This isn't a busy time for us. You're free to examine the room first."

Elizabeth did that, under Humphrey's watchful eye, opening and looking in every drawer. She searched under the bed and in the bathroom. She didn't find a thing.

Then Humphrey took her down to the basement and left her alone with Francesca's personal possessions in a small room with a table. Elizabeth found her task depressing, the physical conditions making it even worse. The hotel was old, the basement damp and musty, the lighting poor.

She put everything on the table: A black roller-board suitcase, a large plastic bag with the bloody clothes Elizabeth was wearing at the time of the accident, other clothes from her hotel room, toiletries, and a couple of hardback books about China. *The Tiananmen Papers* and *A History of China...The Long view,* an English translation of a book by a Shanghai professor.

She stood back for a minute and took a deep breath. Then she began to cry.

With tears running down her cheeks, she leafed through the books, searching for notes. Nothing. She checked the zipper compartments of the suitcase. All empty.

Then she turned to Francesca's clothes—from the hotel room first. She unzipped the toiletry kit and rummaged through it. Nothing remotely helpful.

Finally, she came to the chore she had been dreading: examining Francesca's bloody clothes. On top was the brown leather jacket with a wide belt, identical to her own.

She reached into the pocket and found Francesca's passport, which didn't surprise her. Francesca had once told her, "My dad taught me: Always keep your passport close by. You never know."

She pulled out a thin wallet and looked through it, saw some cash, Canadian and U.S., a driver's license, credit cards, and Francesca's Tribune ID.

She reached back into the pocket and fished around. She found a piece of notepaper from the Fairmont. On it a handwritten note, "7:00 p.m. Hyatt. Suite 2100."

The handwriting was Francesca's. The distinctive number 7 and letter Y.

16

CALGARY

The Hyatt was two blocks from the Fairmont. Elizabeth walked them rapidly, glancing over her shoulder a couple of times to see if the tall swarthy man was following. No sign of him.

Her joy dissipated quickly in the manager's office. As soon as she identified herself as Elizabeth Crowder with the *New York Tribune,* Carl Steele, heavy set, with a red face and bristly gray hair, linked his fingers together, pursed his lips, leaned back in his desk chair, and looked at her with animosity.

"I just have a couple of simple questions," she said.

"I don't talk to the press. It violates company policy."

"Deputy Police Chief James Anderson was so cooperative. He offered to do anything to help." She whipped out her cell phone. "I'll call and tell him you won't talk to me."

He was shooting daggers at her with his eyes. "What do you want to know?"

"Last week, did a Chinese man by the name of Zhou Yun stay in the Hyatt?"

The animosity on his face was replaced by fear. "I can't talk about our guests. Company policy is firm on that. And…" He pointed to her cell phone. "It's against Alberta law. I'm sure your friend James Anderson wouldn't want me to break the law."

She left Steele in his office and returned to the lobby. The concierge was busy. She paused a short distance from his desk, waiting while a woman and her teenage daughter spewed out a string of questions. "If we want to ski, where can we ski.… How can we get there.… Can we rent equipment.… How much does it cost?"

Finally, they exhausted their questions.

Elizabeth approached the blond, handsome young man in a black jacket, with a name tag saying "Chris" on one lapel, and the universal concierge pin on the other. As she did, she removed a hundred dollar bill from her briefcase and held it visibly in her hand.

His eyes were following the money.

"I need some information, Chris."

"That's what I'm here for."

"Earlier this week, and perhaps last week, did you have a Chinese delegation, headed by Zhou Yun, staying here?"

"Absolutely. Six of them for a week. Zhou Yun was in Suite 2100. We had a big snow last Monday evening. They left Tuesday morning in a private plane, as soon as the airport opened."

She slid the hundred dollar bill across the desk. Smoothly, he pocketed it.

"One other question."

Elizabeth removed Francesca's picture from her briefcase and handed it to him. "Did you see this woman in the hotel last Monday evening?"

"Sorry, I can't help you. Monday was my day off."

"Who was on duty then?"

"Bill was on the concierge desk. But a better bet is Vern, the doorman." Chris pointed toward the front door. "He worked Monday evening and he has a memory for faces like you wouldn't believe."

Clutching Francesca's picture, Elizabeth went outside. She watched the portly doorman in his sixties load a heavy suitcase into a cab. Despite the temperature, he was perspiring. She walked over.

"Are you Vern?"

"Yeah?"

"Chris, the concierge, said you might be able to help me. I'm trying to find a friend of mine. She was here last Monday evening. Any chance you saw her?"

She handed him the picture. As he studied it, his chin dropped. "I… I… don't know," he stammered. She studied his crease lined face. He looked around nervously.

"It means a lot to me. I'll pay for the information."

She reached into her briefcase for a couple more hundreds. Before she pulled them out, he whispered, "I don't want your money, Miss, but I will talk to you. Not now, though."

"Tell me where and when."

"I get off in an hour…. Meet me in Sunterra, a little café in Bankers Hall. Three blocks from here. Over on Ninth Avenue."

17

CALGARY

The hospital gift shop had only puny flower arrangements. Craig selected the best of the puny for eighty dollars. "Sorry," the cashier said. "March in Calgary. This is the best we can do."

Flowers in hand, he walked through the doorway into John Saunders's room, stopped dead, and gaped.

In bed, he saw a man with thinning light brown hair and a face battered and bruised, sixteen shades of black and blue. One eye was almost closed. He was missing a couple of teeth. Both legs, raised up on metal contraptions, were in large casts. He had a bandage around one shoulder.

"Well don't stand there and gawk," Saunders called irritably. "I'm not one of the tourist sites in Calgary. Go find whoever you're visiting and leave me alone."

"I'm here to see you."

Craig deposited the flowers on the window sill where they joined half a dozen other puny arrangements.

"I don't know you," Saunders said, his voice trembling. He reached for the call button.

Before Saunders had a chance to press it, Craig said, "I'm not here to harm you. Billy Edwards is my name. A Texas oil man. I came up to talk to you about buying your company, Energy Assets."

Saunders stared at Craig without saying a word.

"Can I sit down?"

"Do I look like I could stop you?"

"I guess not."

Craig pulled up a hard plastic gray chair next to the bed. "What happened to you?"

"Skiing accident. I hit a tree."

"Yeah right," Craig muttered too softly for Saunders to hear.

"I'm sorry. I came because I heard Energy Assets was in play. I'm ready to do an all cash deal. Tell me your asking price."

"You're a day late."

"That's too bad. Who'd you sell to?"

Saunders turned his head to get a better look at Craig and winced. "CNOC. The Chinese National Oil Company. You should have come earlier. I would have preferred selling to you."

"Maybe it's not too late. If all the papers aren't signed, you may have some wiggle room. To show my good faith, I'll get you a deposit by the close of business today."

"Forget it."

"It'll be eight figures."

"Can't do it."

"Listen, I really want Energy Assets. If you tell me who you negotiated with from CNOC, maybe I can reach an arrangement with them that'll make all of us happy."

Saunders reached for the call button again. "I don't know what your game is, Mister. I don't know what anybody's game is anymore. The whole world's gone fuckin' crazy. But if you don't get the hell out of here, I'll call hospital security and have you thrown out."

Craig raised his hand. "Don't worry. I'm leaving."

"Good riddance. All of you."

"I'd give up skiing if I were you."

18

BEIJING

Zhou Yun was wearing a blue silk dressing robe, sipping an Armagnac in the library of his marble-floored mansion with a scattering of Ming vases on the tables and in front of the fire place. Without asking, he poured an Armagnac for General Zhou and handed it to him. "We have reason to celebrate," Zhou Yun said, raising his glass. "I've concluded exclusive supply agreements with Libya, Nigeria, Venezuela, and Sudan. We're cornering much of the world oil supply."

General Zhou put the glass down. "I can't celebrate. This business in Canada with Francesca Page is worrying me."

"I haven't heard anything further. Have you?"

"Not a word, but we're relying heavily on Kirby. I'm not sure we can depend on him."

"You've never liked the idea of involving Kirby."

"That's right. I went along with you reluctantly and now…"

Zhou Yun tapped his fingers on the red leather-topped desk. "What do you want to do?"

"We have to exert additional pressure on Kirby to make certain he carries out his end of the bargain. It's essential that he prevent President Brewster from finding out about Operation Dragon Oil before April 1 and intervening to stop our operation."

"Alright. But how?"

"The hundred million dollar cash payment is due today. Correct?"

"Yes. I was planning to transfer it to his father's Liechtenstein bank account in twelve hours."

"Suppose you don't?"

Zhou Yun gave a long low whistle. "That would get their attention." He paused. "It would be a risky move."

"Why?"

"They could back out."

General Zhou shook his head. "In addition to the hundred million now, if there's no American intervention before April 1, our written agreement gives Mountain Air, their new Silicon Valley startup company, American rights to all computer hardware and software technology developed at fifty leading Chinese universities. Mountain Air will be more powerful than Microsoft, Cisco, and Intel combined. You really think they'd surrender all that? Never."

Zhou Yun's forehead wrinkled. He pursed his lips together. Didn't say a word.

He's not convinced. I have to bring him around.

"Kirby's father doesn't need the cash now," General Zhou said. "Neither does their other stockholder. Tell Kirby's father they'll get the hundred million on April second, if Kirby carries out his end of the bargain, and we succeed."

"The cash might mean a lot to Kirby."

"He can wait a few more weeks. It won't kill him."

Zhou Yun was smiling now.

"I'll call Kirby's father. Tell him that we're doing this because of what happened in Calgary. That we're worried about Craig Page. The old man's a shrewd businessman. He won't like it. But he'll understand."

"And his son?"

"The father dominates the son. He'll lean on him to take care of Craig Page. That's where the leverage will be applied."

19

CALGARY

Vern, the doorman, was waiting for Elizabeth in a deserted area of the café. He was sipping coffee. She picked up a cup at the counter and joined him.

"Thanks for agreeing to meet me," she said.

He glanced around fearfully, "Let's do this fast. Mr. Steele's a monster. If he finds out I'm talking to you, I'll lose my job. I can't afford that. My daughter just moved home with two little kids. Asshole husband was screwing around. At our age, Helen and I can't handle a two and four year old."

"I'm sorry."

"Naw. We'll survive. I want to talk to you. I have to talk to you. Just promise not to involve me in any way."

"You have my word."

He began talking in a soft voice. "Okay, let me tell you what happened."

Elizabeth took a deep breath and blew it out with relief.

"Last Monday evening around eight, your friend, the woman in the picture, walked out of the hotel. Two men came up to her on the sidewalk."

"What'd they look like?"

"One short with a blotchy red face. The other tall. Looked like an Arab."

"Did the tall guy have a mustache?"

"Yeah, a thin one."

Elizabeth pulled out her cell phone and showed Vern the picture she took this morning.

He nodded. "Yeah, he was the tall one."

"What'd they say to her on the sidewalk?"

"They were police, and she should come with them. Your friend was a tough cookie. I'll say that for her. She swung her bag and knocked the little guy down. Broke his nose, I think. He was bleeding a storm. The other guy stole her bag. Pulled a gun on her. But she ran across the street into the parking garage. The guy who was left called somebody on his cell phone. I couldn't make out what he was saying. Alls I heard was airport."

"And then?"

He began coughing. He took a sip to clear his throat, then continued.

"Even though it was snowing hard, your friend raced out of the garage in a red car, a Toyota, I think, and down the street. They got in their car, a black Mercedes parked at the curb, and followed her. I knew they weren't police from how they acted. Cops don't behave like that. And the car they were driving. Those weren't police plates."

"What'd you do then?"

"I went into the hotel, told Mr. Steele what happened, and told him to call the police. He told me to keep my mouth shut if I wanted to keep my job. When I learned the next day about the woman's death on the highway leading to the airport, I felt crummy and guilty as hell. That's why I wanted to tell you. I had to tell somebody. Helen said I should keep quiet. You won't involve me in any way?"

"Absolutely not."

20

CALGARY

Craig entered their suite in the Westin. He shouted, "Elizabeth… Elizabeth." No answer. He called her on her cell. "Where are you?"

"Be back at the Westin in a bit. I just finished a meeting with the doorman at the Hyatt where Zhou Yun was staying. All the pieces are fitting together. Not a pretty picture."

"Not at my end either. Once you get back, we'll decide on our next move."

A few minutes later, Elizabeth walked into the suite. Craig said, "Were you still being followed?"

"I shook the tail this morning. No more threats or attacks since the big rig tried to run me down."

"Jesus, these guys play rough. Let me see the photo of the man following you."

While she pulled it up on her cell, she said, "This guy was

identified by the Hyatt doorman as one of the two men who tried to grab Francesca in front of the hotel."

She handed the cell to Craig, who studied the face. "Definitely an Arab or Iranian. I don't recognize him."

The light was poor where Craig was standing. "Let me take it over to the window. I might get a better view."

He squinted in the sunlight.

"Holy shit."

On the roof of the building across the street, crouching, was a man holding a rifle, light reflecting from the black steel barrel, aiming at him. Acting on instinct, he leaped at Elizabeth, knocking them to the floor and rolling with her away from the window. He threw himself on top of her, covering her face with his body and his own with his hands.

Just as he did, shots rang out shattering the window and spraying flying glass. Shards landed on the backs of his hands.

The firing stopped. He pulled her to her feet, away from the window. "You okay?"

"Thanks to you. You saved my life."

Craig pulled the glass out of his skin. He was bleeding, but not profusely. No need to bother with it. They had only an instant to move.

"They'll be coming for us. Let's get out of the hotel now."

"What about our clothes?"

"That's why they have FedEx."

He raced down seven flights of the inside staircase. Elizabeth was right behind. At the lobby level, they shifted to the adjacent staircase running to the garage. He'd parked their rental, a gray Lexus SUV, on P-3.

Once they were in the car, he roared out of the garage, driving east toward Highway 2. Elizabeth was glancing through the rear window.

"A black Mercedes is following, two cars back," she said. "The doorman told me the men who chased Elizabeth were in a black Mercedes. How'd they find us so easily?"

"They must have planted a homing device on our car when it was in the garage."

"What can we do?"

"Keep your eye on them."

He turned onto Highway 2 and headed north.

"Black Mercedes is still following," she said.

At midday, traffic was light. Craig had the speed up to seventy.

"Where are we going?"

"We have to lose them. Then we'll worry about it."

The highway was three lanes in each direction, Craig in the center lane. He glanced into the rearview mirror and saw the black Mercedes in the left lane, rapidly closing the gap. Two men in the car. The man in Elizabeth's picture was in the front passenger seat leaning out of the window. He had a gun in his hand.

Craig reached down to his ankle holster, pulled out the nine-millimeter Beretta he'd brought from Washington, and handed it to her. "You told me you could shoot. They have a gun, getting ready to aim at us."

"What do you want me to do?"

"Blow out one of their rear tires."

"But they're behind us."

"Roll down your window and wait."

Without any warning, Craig slammed on the brakes, narrowly avoiding being rear-ended by a driver who was honking furiously. But the driver of the Mercedes had no time to react. It sailed by in the left lane. As it did, the gunman fired off a shot, but he had no chance to aim. The bullet flew over their SUV.

Once the Mercedes passed, he yelled to Elizabeth. "Shoot now."

She aimed and scored a direct hit, blowing out the rear tire on the right passenger side. The Mercedes swerved and crashed in to the center guard rail.

Craig resumed driving. As he passed the Mercedes, he saw the gunman and driver flattened against their seats by airbags.

He pushed his speed up to seventy. An exit was approaching for the TransCanada Highway East. He took it, barreling down the exit ramp so fast they almost slipped off the road and over an embankment.

At the bottom, he pulled over, got out, and searched the rear bumper. "Where is that sucker?" he asked himself, feeling around on the bumper.

After thirty seconds, he found the tracking device: a small, black, plastic object, the size of a button, attached to the underside of the rear bumper—the work of an intelligence pro. With a pocket knife, he broke the seal, then smashed the device under the heel of his shoe.

He got back into the car. After checking for cops, he made an illegal U-turn, cutting across the grassy median. They were now driving west on the TransCanada Highway.

"They'll never find us," he said to Elizabeth with confidence. "The last they knew from the tracking device, we were heading east. And by the way, that was a damn good shot."

21

MIDDLEBURG, VIRGINIA

Once he heard that Saturday afternoon would be unseasonably warm, Kirby drove with Sally and Matt to his country estate near Middleburg. Patches of snow were still visible in the mountains, but blossoms were appearing on the trees.

When the mercury hit seventy and the sun was shining brightly, he picked up his putter and a bucket of balls. He walked to the putting green in the back.

Before putting, he stopped to look with pride at Matt, who was taking a beautiful roan over a series of jumps.

Kirby holed a couple of putts. "Not bad for the beginning of the season," he said to himself. He missed the next two which should have been easy. "Damn, that's not good." He put down another ball, then carefully lined up the putt. As he was on the backswing, he heard a woman's screechy voice from behind, in the direction of the house, moving toward him. "Hey, hon, your father called."

He missed the putt, then snapped at her, "You saw I was putting. Couldn't you wait?"

"Don't we always drop everything for your father?"

He hated that voice, and everything else about Sally. The trophy wife had tarnished. Her tits were sagging. The blond hair needed bleaching. On top of all that, following Matt's birth, she lost interest in sex. Once Operation Dragon Oil succeeds, she'll be toast. Women will fight to get into his bed.

She looked at Matt jumping. "Do you really think he should keep doing that?"

"Of course. He won the junior club championship last year."

"But it's so dangerous. I keep thinking about what happened to Christopher Reeve."

Kirby dismissed her concern with a wave of his hand. "You're too risk adverse. In life, you have to take chances to get rewards."

"Anyhow, I came out to tell you that your father called to say he's on his way here to talk to you. He tried your cell, but it wasn't working."

Kirby reached into his pocket. No phone.

"Dammit. I must have left it in the house on the desk." He looked at Sally. "Get my cell."

Obediently, she trooped into the house.

Half an hour later, Kirby's father arrived, looking angry, a scowl on his face. Kirby tightly gripped the putter. His father had a furious temper, and his face was an open book. All his life Kirby had struggled to avoid having that wrath directed at him.

"You've always been a screwup," his father blurted out. "But this time you outdid yourself. And you cost us plenty."

"What are you talking about?"

"Zhou Yun called. He's not making the hundred million dollar payment. He won't make it until after April 1 and then only if Operation Dragon Oil succeeds."

Kirby didn't need an explanation. He felt sick. He thought he might throw up.

His father insisted on pounding it in. "They know Craig Page is Francesca's father, and that Craig's too smart to think his daughter died in an accident. Zhou Yun told me, 'You know what I'd do if somebody killed my daughter? I wouldn't stop at anything until I cut off the pricks of everybody involved and shoved them into their mouths.' Zhou Yun's savvy. He believes, and rightly so, that in the process of finding out who killed Francesca, Craig might stumble across and expose Operation Dragon Oil."

"Maybe you should call his bluff. Tell him, 'unless you make the payment, we won't do a thing. Count us out.'"

His father shook his head in disbelief. "You can't be serious. The payoff in the technology grants is so huge."

"Then I guess we don't have a choice."

"I can't believe you didn't get the background on that reporter before you gave your thug the order to kill her."

"Well, I didn't," Kirby said stubbornly. "And we've been over that a thousand times."

"What the hell were you thinking?"

Kirby looked down at the putting green without responding.

"I asked Zhou Yun whether he'd make the payment if we killed Craig Page. He said that was a definite possibility."

Kirby saw a light at the end of the tunnel. "Hopefully, Ali will do that in Calgary."

Kirby's father walked over to Matt. "Hi Grandpa," Kirby heard. He tried to putt, but couldn't concentrate.

A few minutes later his cell phone rang. He checked caller ID. Ali. Silently, he prayed.

"We missed killing Craig and the girl in Calgary." Ali sounded dejected. "They escaped."

"No," Kirby wailed. His whole body was shaking in despair and anger. "No. Will you people ever do anything right?"

"Don't worry. I have guys covering all the airports. I'll get people to the border crossings. We have the license plate of their car. We'll have a steel wall around the area. We'll catch them."

Kirby grabbed the putter by the handle, hoisted it above his head, and flung it into the pond. "Bunch of fucking incompetents."

22

BANFF, CANADA

"We're going to Tehran," Craig said as he kept the car at a constant seventy, moving west on the TransCanada highway. Nobody was following.

"Tehran?" Elizabeth said in surprise.

"Yeah. We know Francesca was killed for a huge story that she first uncovered in Iran, before she went to Calgary. Until we get that story, we'll never know who killed her or why."

"But we know Zhou Yun was involved."

"He's probably back in China. We'd never get close enough to question him. So we have to peel the onion back, one layer at a time, retracing Francesca's steps in reverse. Iran's next. It'll be dangerous over there. I'd like you to go. We're good together, but if you don't want…"

She was glaring at him. "Stop right there. You can't get rid of me."

"I'm happy to hear that, especially after you shot out that tire. Good job."

He reached over and grabbed her hand. "Ever been in Iran?" he asked.

"Nope. I managed to miss that garden spot. I've heard they have some of the world's best fruits and vegetables."

"Oh, they do, particularly apricots and pomegranates. Also, some of the cruelest, most barbaric police anywhere in the world, supposedly doing God's work."

For several minutes they rode in silence.

Elizabeth said, "My father always accused me of being too hung up on logistics, but I have a question. Are you planning to drive to Iran?"

"That's funny."

"Well if you're not, we have a major problem. We have to assume that whoever tried to kill us has every airport in Western Canada covered."

"A reasonable assumption."

"And no doubt has our license plate. So they'll be checking border crossings. I suppose we could ditch this rental and get another... or buy a car."

"But they know what we look like. And they've probably gotten our pictures on the internet. All they have to do is hit one button, and the whole world gets it. Sometimes, I hate modern technology."

"Okay, Houdini."

"We drive to Vancouver, about six hundred miles. Then take a boat to L.A. The Iranian consul in L.A. will give anybody a visa, in any name, as long as they pay him enough cash. And I have good contacts in Iran. A mid-level official in Iranian intelligence. Also, a CIA covert agent by the name of Jurgenson. A Dutch guy whom I hired for the agency. I saved his life when his cover was blown, and two Iranian intelligence agents had him cornered. I was able to kill both of them. He owes me big time for that."

"That sounds great. I better lose my Trib ID. But I can get press credentials from a friend who works at the *L.A. Times,* a former boyfriend back in New York. With press access, I can go to the Oil Ministry and try to pick up the trail Elizabeth was following."

"Perfect. I know a place in L.A. where I can get you a phony passport on the spot. I've kept several from my CIA days with supporting IDs. One of them's in the name of Jonathan Wilson. You can be Ann Wilson. I'll get the passport. You get the press credentials."

"That's a plan. I assume we're married."

"Yeah. It might avoid a hassle at passport control when we enter the country. The mullahs pretend to be very moral people. What a bunch of fucking hypocrites. They don't like unmarried people traveling together. They'd call you a whore. But in Iran, we have to play by the mullah's rules. In L.A., I'll get you a ring at a novelty store."

"No way. I was thinking about Cartier. They have a shop on Rodeo Drive in Beverly Hills."

He laughed. "I'm afraid that's over budget."

They were driving through a gorge, high in the Rocky Mountains. A fast-moving stream was off to the left. And pure, white snow covered the mountains on both sides of the road. Elizabeth said, "This has to be the most beautiful scenery in the world."

"Too bad we don't have time to enjoy it. Tell me about your former boyfriend in L.A."

"We were teammates on the Trib baseball team, playing in a league against law firms and banks. I pitched. He was my catcher. We dated for a while. No big deal."

"Were you any good?"

She gave a start. "At what?"

"I didn't mean sex. Pitching?"

"Damn good. I'll show you sometime."

"Were you ever married?"

"Once, right after Harvard College. I married a classmate, but that only lasted about a year. Once we got away from the idyllic campus life, I realized I hardly knew him. He wanted to pursue his own activities and didn't care much about me. He was going off to

Africa to work for some NGO. And I was trying to establish a career as a journalist. We had an amicable divorce. We called it our starter marriage. Since then, I've had a number of different relationships, but none I wanted to commit to. And the truth is I love my work. Or at least I did until that asshole McDermott moved me back to New York."

"Something I've been meaning to ask you about him."

"Yeah?"

"How do you explain his refusal to let you go to Calgary?"

"Budget issues. Also, he's a control freak."

"Could it be something else? I read about him socializing with VIPs."

"Maybe he's even scummier than I thought. You think he's in the pocket of the Iranians or the Chinese?"

"Possibly. More likely an American working with them. Does McDermott know Kirby?"

"I never heard him mention Kirby. He doesn't have any pictures in his office with the CIA Director."

"Well, maybe it's not Kirby. But I'm convinced somebody in or out of the administration with lots of clout talked to McDermott."

Elizabeth gave a long low whistle. "So you're telling me this conspiracy is a three-headed monster, one Chinese, one Iranian, and one American."

"Precisely. We have to flush them out, all three of them, and stop them before they can implement whatever it was Francesca uncovered."

"You think we'll be able to figure out all that in Tehran?"

"Maybe not all of it. But we have to get some answers in Tehran. And we're racing against the clock. Harold Topps told me April 1 is the deadline for the Canadian oil deals. I'll bet that's zero hour for the overall conspiracy."

"My God, we only have thirteen days. Drive faster, Craig."

PART TWO

MULLAH'S RULES

23

TEHRAN

Craig and Elizabeth flew on Swiss International from Los Angeles to Tehran, connecting in Zurich. On the second leg of their trip, he noticed that most of the women were in black gowns, with head coverings that permitted only their eyes to show.

"Can you believe this," Elizabeth whispered to Craig, pointing to a group of them across the aisle.

To pass the time, Craig read several newspapers and magazines, he had picked up in Los Angeles Airport. In the *Economist*, he found an article reporting that the hardliners, who now had complete control of the Iranian government, had decided to launch one of their periodic clampdowns on secularism and lack of adherence to strict Islamic principles. One of the opposition leaders had characterized those wielding power as "lunatics."

Craig had seen them in action during the year he spent in Iran on a special assignment for Dodson, Kirby's predecessor. His cover was a Canadian oil man, selling exploration equipment to assist the Iranians in finding new oil fields. His mission was to assess the strength of the opposition to the ruling mullahs.

During that year, he located and spent time with a number of dissidents, all of whom were afraid to go public with their views. He became close with a midlevel Iranian intelligence agent, whom he called Sabi. "If you don't know my real name, it's better for both of us," Sabi had said. "For you alone, I am Sabi. If I hear that name, I'll know it's you."

Craig's relationship with Sabi had been one of the bright spots in a grim year. He also managed to hire and put in place Jurgenson.

The pilot announced, "Fasten your seatbelt. We're beginning our approach into Tehran."

Elizabeth had fallen asleep. He nudged her awake.

The problems began as soon as they reached the airport in Tehran. The line leading up to Passport Control, snaked for almost half a mile and moved at a snail's pace. Each person was subjected to careful scrutiny. Finally, it was their turn to approach the window. The agent on duty, bald, short, and squat, with the straggle of a black beard, spent several minutes examining their passports and staring at the two of them.

Craig could tell Elizabeth was growing more anxious. "Is there a problem," she asked the man. Craig reached down, grabbed her hand out of view of the agent, and squeezed it, signaling her to show restraint. The agent didn't respond to her, but kept his eyes riveted on the computer screen, which Craig couldn't see from their position on the other side of the window.

Finally, the man picked up the phone and said something softly. Straining his ears, Craig, who understood Farsi, couldn't make out what the man was saying because of the glass separating them.

The man pushed down on a button on his desk. Instantly, two soldiers armed with automatic weapons moved up to their position. "You'll have to come with us," one of the soldiers said.

"Why do we have to do that?" Elizabeth said, even though Craig had cautioned her last night at the Peninsula not to argue with any of the military people at the airport. Neither of the soldiers responded. Instead, they led them along a dimly lit corridor, thirty yards long, past a series of closed doors. These were the interrogation rooms Craig knew from the time he had spent in Iran.

Craig and Elizabeth were separated. He watched her disappear with a soldier into the first interrogation room. Another armed soldier led Craig to a room three doors away at the end of the corridor. Inside was an old wooden desk with a soldier sitting behind it. The armed man, who had led Craig into the room, took up a position in the corner, aiming his AKM at Craig. The luggage, which Craig and Elizabeth had checked, was wheeled into the room by a second armed soldier, who moved into another corner and aimed his gun at Craig.

"You speak Farsi?" the man behind the desk asked Craig in English.

"No," Craig lied. "You'll have to speak English to me."

"Why did you come to Iran?"

"My wife is a newspaper reporter with the *Los Angeles Times*. She's doing a story about your oil industry. I plan to tour. See the museums and some of the sites. I've always heard this is a fascinating place."

The man looked at Craig with skepticism. "What's your job?"

"I'm in the administrative department of a Los Angeles steel company."

"Which one?"

"National Steel."

With even more skepticism on his face, the man was staring hard at Craig.

"You're with the CIA. Aren't you?"

Craig got a tight feeling in his stomach.

"That's ridiculous." Craig sounded irate. "I've never had anything to do with the CIA. I work for National Steel."

"I'll bring in one of our steel experts to interrogate you. He'll know you're lying."

Craig shrugged. "Suit yourself. I'm happy to talk to anyone in the steel business. I'll tell him exactly what I do. He'll understand. He'll confirm that you're wasting his time and your time."

The man reached for the phone as if he were about to call a steel expert. The queasy feeling in Craig's stomach hardened, but he didn't show a thing on his face. The man had the phone up to his ear and was pressing buttons, trying to intimidate Craig. When Craig didn't react, he slammed it down.

Relieved, Craig became bolder. "Are you finished with me now?"

"Search him," the man said, pointing toward one of the soldiers. The soldier moved up, ordered Craig to remove the contents from his pockets He then ran his hands roughly over Craig's body. Craig's wallet and all of his papers were carefully examined. Anticipating this, Craig had selected these items with great care. They found nothing remotely interesting.

Next, the man behind the desk pointed to their two black suitcases. While Craig watched helplessly, the soldier opened both of them. He searched the contents and dumped them on the floor. Then he took a knife from his pocket and ripped the suitcases apart, looking for false bottoms.

When he didn't find anything, Craig said, "Can I go now?"

The man at the desk was staring at his computer screen. "I have proof that you're with the CIA. Tell me what your mission is in Iran. Then we'll let you go."

"That's ridiculous. I'm in the steel business."

"You're lying to me."

"No. I'm telling the truth."

"That whore traveling with you. Is she CIA too?"

"I've told you. She's a newspaper reporter."

"Humph," the man said. "We'll interrogate your whore. We'll

find out what story she tells us. Nobody taught her to lie, the way they did you."

The man behind the desk pointed to a chair in the corner. One of the soldiers came over and pushed Craig roughly in that direction. He shoved Craig down in the chair. "You'll wait here until she tells us the truth. Then we'll take you both to jail," the man behind the desk said. He sauntered out, leaving Craig behind with the two soldiers and their AKMs.

Craig checked his watch.

I'll give you thugs two hours to release Elizabeth.

24

TEHRAN

For half an hour no one said anything to Elizabeth. A soldier had led her into a room with dirty beige walls and a battered wooden desk with a computer on top. He pointed her to a hard wooden chair in front of the desk, then stood in the center of the room, staring at her, his gun pointed at her. No one else entered the room.

Periodically, she asked the soldier, "When will somebody come?… When can I go?" He remained mute.

Finally, a tall, thin man with a balding head and unshaven face entered the room. He took a chair behind the desk and booted up the computer. In his hand, he held a passport, which he opened to her picture. He looked at her, and nodded. "Stand up," he ordered Elizabeth.

She did as she was told.

"You're an American citizen," he said with contempt.

"Yes sir," she replied, trying to sound polite.

"When was the last time you came to Iran?"

"This is my first trip."

"And your reason for coming?"

"I'm a newspaper reporter. I want to do an article about Iran's oil industry."

"You've written other articles?"

"Of course. That's my job."

"Show me some of them."

This was becoming dicey. No articles had appeared under the name of Ann Wilson.

"I don't carry them around with me."

"Well, what paper do you work for?"

"The *Los Angeles Times*."

She expected him to use his computer to go online with the *Los Angeles Times*.

Then I'm dead.

He didn't touch the key board. Instead, he said, "What about the man you're traveling with?"

"My husband's a tourist."

"What's his job?"

"He works in the steel industry."

"You're not fooling me. I know he's not your husband. That he's a spy for the CIA."

Her interrogator was staring at her, watching her closely. She stared right back.

"That's ridiculous. I know my husband. He's never worked for the CIA."

Her knees began knocking, her body trembling. She got control and forced herself to stand up straight.

"And you're here to help him when he spies on Iran."

"That's not true. I'm here to research a newspaper article."

"If you tell me the truth, I'll let you go."

"But I am telling you the truth."

"How long do you claim to be married to this man?"

"Twelve years," she said calmly, though she and Craig never covered this question.

"Children?"

"None. Can I go now?"

Without saying a word, he left the room, closing the door behind him.

Minutes later, he returned with a gray-bearded mullah wearing a white turban, and with an obese woman in a dirty, gray army uniform.

The mullah asked, "Why did you come to Iran?"

"I told your colleague, to research a newspaper article about the Iranian oil industry."

"You're lying. The man you're with is a CIA agent."

"That's not true. He's my husband."

The mullah smiled sadistically. "There's no point in your continuing to lie. The man you're traveling with has confessed that he's a CIA agent."

Craig would never do that.

"That can't be. He's not a CIA agent."

"People who tell us the truth have an easier time. Now you're the only one lying. We'll release your friend while we punish you. Would you like that?"

"I'm telling you the truth."

The mullah turned to the woman agent. "Search her."

The woman took off Elizabeth's watch and ring and placed them on the desk. Under the leering gaze of the mullah, the other agent, and the soldier, she ordered Elizabeth to remove all of her clothes, which were carefully checked. She then slipped rubber gloves over her hands and conducted a full body search on Elizabeth. It was horrible, and Elizabeth thought she would die from shame. She kept her eyes closed.

She wanted to throw up. The woman was filthy; the mullah was filthy; the room was filthy. To endure it, she focused on Francesca.

Finally, the woman was finished with her.

"You can get dressed," the woman said.

Elizabeth picked up her clothes and dressed, facing the wall, away from the others. When she was finished, she turned around and walked over to the desk. Gone was her watch… the Piaget she had bought for herself when she won the Pulitzer. She held her anger and put on the ring. "Can I go now?"

The interrogator took over the questioning. "Tell us why you came to Iran," he said.

"To write an article about the Iranian oil industry," Elizabeth replied, now weakly.

"You're lying. You've come with a CIA agent."

"That's not true." She knew she had to keep her wits about her, but they were wearing her down.

Five more times the interrogator asked that same question. Five more times Elizabeth gave the same answer.

"If you won't answer me truthfully here, you'll answer the interrogators in Evin Prison."

The sound of the words "Evin Prison" sent a jolt of fear through her body. The Shah had built that loathsome structure to imprison and to torture political prisoners. The mullahs made it their favorite venue for treating "enemies of the state." In its center courtyard, following summary midnight trials before hooded judges, firing squads executed those who survived endless sessions of torture and solitary confinement.

"But I am answering you truthfully."

The mullah moved toward the door. The interrogator followed. "You wait here. We'll come back and take you to Evin Prison.… Do you have anything else to say?"

"No," Elizabeth replied, trying to sound courageous.

The mullah, the interrogator and the woman agent left the room. Again, it was only Elizabeth and the soldier.

"Think about Mina," she mumbled to herself.

Last year, she'd edited an article for the Sunday Trib magazine by Mina, an Iranian woman in her twenties, a literature student at Tehran University, who was arrested during a dissidents' protest against the rigged election. In the article, Mina described what happened when she was taken to a jail in Tehran, how guards severely beat her with clubs and rubber hoses, then repeatedly raped and sodomized her before tossing her out of a truck along the side of a rural road, expecting her to die. Somehow, the driver of a passing car picked her up and helped her escape across the border into Turkey.

In the worst way, she had to urinate. She asked the soldier if she could go to the bathroom. He remained mute. She couldn't control herself. She felt liquid dripping down her leg. She held back her tears, refusing to give them the satisfaction.

She wanted to be strong, but she was terrified of what they would do to her.

25

TEHRAN

Craig glanced at his wristwatch. Only fifteen minutes until the two hours were up. He wouldn't wait any longer than that. One soldier was in a corner relaxing, holding his automatic weapon casually in his hand. The other soldier was behind the desk, his AKM on the floor and a pistol holstered at his waist. Craig's plan was to stand up, pick up his chair and smash it against the soldier in the corner, then grab his AKM and kill both of them.

Repeatedly, he checked his watch.

Five more minutes.

Suddenly, the door opened. Craig's interrogator entered. He tossed two U.S. passports at Craig's feet. "Take your whore and leave."

Craig could hardly believe his ears. The arbitrariness of despotic regimes constantly amazed him.

"Where is my wife?"

"Two rooms away. Get her fast before we change our minds."

Craig quickly placed their clothes in what was left of their suitcases.

From behind, he heard, "Where are you staying?"

"The Laleh International Hotel."

"For rich foreigners," the man said derisively. "We'll be watching you. Sooner or later you'll slip. We'll find out why you're really here."

One of the soldiers led Craig, wheeling the two battered suitcases, down the corridor. He didn't know in what condition he'd find Elizabeth.

When the door to her room opened, he saw the terrified look on her face, the small puddle at her feet. He walked over, put his arm around her and said, "C'mon, honey, we're leaving now."

Silently, traumatized, she grabbed one of the suitcases and walked alongside him, following a soldier down the corridor and into the arrival hall.

She didn't speak until they were outside in the cold night air, waiting for a cab to pull up to the curb.

"I can't believe we're out," she said. "It was awful." Tears were running down her cheeks.

"It's over now. That's the important thing. We're safe."

"We'll never be safe as long as we're here."

In the cab she was shaking. He put his arm around her and held her tight. "Don't talk," he whispered.

The hotel lobby was deserted except for the fat, sullen-looking man with greasy skin and brown glasses behind the desk. Craig walked up to him and announced, "Mr. and Mrs. Wilson. We have a reservation."

The room clerk shook his head. "You didn't come, Mr. Wilson. And you didn't call. It's past midnight. We couldn't hold your room."

Craig glanced at the wall behind the man. It had a slot for each of the forty rooms in the hotel. The vast majority had keys hanging next to them. Given the hour, they weren't occupied.

He watched Elizabeth collapse into a chair in the corner and put her head into her hands.

"Why don't you look again," Craig said politely. "I'm sure you can find one room."

The man turned to his computer. He began pushing buttons, endlessly Craig thought.

"I'm sorry, Mr. Wilson. We don't have a single room."

"Find one," Craig said, now sharply.

"If you're trying to intimidate me, I'll call the police."

He eyed the phone on the desk. Craig glared at the clerk. His eyes told the fat slob: Touch that phone and I'll break every one of your fingers.

"Check the computer again."

The clerk did. After a couple more minutes, he said, "Perhaps I could find a room for you. Why don't you come with me into the back office, and we'll discuss it."

Craig knew what was coming next: extortion. Welcome to the Middle East. The clerk headed into his office.

"I'll be right back," he told Elizabeth, who was eyeing him anxiously.

Craig took the lead. He and Elizabeth were exhausted. He wanted to wrap this up.

"For a hundred U.S. could you find a room for us?"

"I'm sorry, it's quite impossible. We're sold out."

"Two hundred and that's all."

"I'm sorry, sir…"

Craig rolled his hands into fists.

"For three hundred, I might…"

Craig took the money of out of his pocket and tossed it on the desk.

Once they were in the room, a junior suite with a king-sized bed, and the bellman had gone, Craig raised a finger to his lips, reminding Elizabeth not to talk in the hotel room, as they discussed in Los Angeles.

"Why don't you shower, hon," he said. "I'll unpack."

With Elizabeth in the bathroom, he began a meticulous search of the room. First the walls. He removed the paintings, mountain scenes that looked like they were done by a ten-year-old with no talent. No bugs there. He pulled over the desk chair, stood on it, and checked what seemed to be a smoke detector. It was a sound recorder. If operating, it could transmit to a remote location. He made no effort to disable it. He checked the phone. Someone had installed a recorder into the hand held portion. It was all crude technology, built in Russia.

He walked into the bathroom. The shower curtain was transparent plastic. Elizabeth was letting the water run over her head. As soon as she saw him, she covered herself with her hands.

But he wasn't looking at her. He was searching for more listening devices. By the time he was sure the bathroom was clear, she was out of the shower, drying herself. He turned the water back on. "We can talk in here. The bugs are all in the bedroom."

She was still traumatized, he could tell. "We can leave first thing in the morning if you'd like," he said.

"And let them win. No way."

"But I thought…"

"I just need a little time. I've been through worse with the Taliban. I'll be okay in the morning."

"Good. In the bedroom we'll role-play the Wilsons and their activities in Tehran."

Elizabeth nodded.

As he pulled back the covers on the bed, she slipped a pale blue, silk nightgown over her head. With her back to him, he said, "Are you working on your oil story tomorrow?"

"Absolutely. I'm starting at the Oil Ministry. What are your plans?"

"I want to begin my tour at the National Museum. I'm particularly interested in Darius."

When they were both in bed, she began sobbing, her teeth chattering. He leaned over to comfort her. Her skin was cold. "Hold me," she whispered. "Hold me."

He did. His eyes were focused on the door, expecting it to burst open, until he fell asleep.

26

BEIJING

General Zhou was furious. Sitting in the desk chair in his office, he read with a deep frown, for the fifth time, the message that arrived an hour ago from those rag-head rug merchants in Tehran. Heavy creases etched his forehead below a receding line of still-thick, black hair.

He buzzed for Captain Cheng, sitting in the adjacent room.

"You and I are flying to Paris tomorrow morning. Make all the arrangements. The same as our last trip."

"Yes sir."

"Have the others arrived?"

"General Yang Gan is in the conference room. Admiral Xu is expected momentarily."

"Fine," Zhou snarled. "We'll start without him."

General Zhou went into the conference room with Captain Cheng following. It was hot and stuffy. He crossed over to the window and opened it. As he did, Admiral Xu entered and lowered his six-foot, two-hundred-and-twenty-pound body into a chair across from General Yang.

"I see you decided to honor us with your presence this evening," General Zhou said.

The Admiral didn't respond.

Looking at the Admiral, General Zhou said, "let me explain the situation to you. One of General Yang's pilots brought back a message from Tehran stating that the Iranians wish to renegotiate our agreement. Is that correct?"

"Yes sir."

In a cold fury, General Zhou pounded his fist against the hardwood table. "Those rag-heads in Tehran are impossible. They don't honor agreements like civilized people. They make a decision. Then they change it."

"I agree," Yang replied subserviently.

"There's no order in their country, just chaos. Bunch of incompetent mullahs."

General Zhou paused and closed his eyes for a minute. When he opened them, he turned to Yang. "Are we sure this message is accurate? That it's not disinformation created by the Americans to persuade us to back off?"

Yang answered calmly. "One of my pilots was handed the coded message at the military airport in Tehran by General Peng himself. My own personal assistant decoded it. What do you think the mullahs want from us now?"

"More financial aid… more weapons. Even after we've sent some of our most sophisticated missiles. They have no sense of honor…" His voice, devoid of emotion, was a sharp, cold steel monotone. "An agreement means nothing to them. It's simply a place to begin the next round of negotiation. Claiming they act in the name of their God that lets them do anything they want. Greed is driving them."

"Isn't there another possible explanation?" Yang said.

"What's that?" Zhou asked, sounding skeptical that he could've overlooked anything.

"It's possible," Yang continued in a soft servile voice, "that the ruling mullahs are having second thoughts about the wisdom of acting with us against the Americans. They remember what happened to Saddam Hussein and how anxious Washington has been to attack them since the early days of their revolution. They may fear that, once Washington learns of their involvement in Operation Dragon Oil, the Americans will launch a vicious attack that will break the grip the mullahs have over their people. There will be a new revolution that will sweep the mullahs from power. They know very well that they don't rule for their so-called God. They rule for themselves. Their own power. Their own money. The Revolutionary Guard is now the largest business conglomerate in the country. Doing God's work has never been so profitable."

As Yang was speaking, General Zhou tapped the fingers of his left hand firmly on the table.

Yang continued. "The mullahs still have this awe of the Americans. Even after the disasters Washington incurred in Iraq. They are fearful of confronting the Americans."

General Zhou stopped tapping and locked eyes with Yang. "I can't accept that. Even those rag-heads can't be so stupid. We're providing them with protection from the Americans. No, they're acting like they're in a bazaar. Though I hate to do it, we'll give them one more round. Give one of your most trusted pilots a message to take back to Peng in Tehran, for him to pass on to the Iranians: We'll meet at ten in the morning on Wednesday, in Paris, in my suite at the Bristol. I will meet personally with whoever has authority for the mullahs. Though it pains me, I'll renegotiate one more time. Without them, there can be no Operation Dragon Oil. We will remain on schedule. Implementation begins on April 1. After that, the world will never be the same. Not for us. Not for the United States."

Admiral Xu interjected. "And you think this is wise?"

His words were delivered in a confrontational tone. General Zhou bristled. "Do you doubt that granting the concessions to the rag-heads is necessary for the agreement to be implemented?"

"Not at all. What I question is the wisdom of taking any action—of proceeding with Operation Dragon Oil."

General Zhou sat upright with a start. "You had better explain that."

Xu paused for a minute. The tension in the room was heavy. Yang was squirming in his chair.

General Zhou nodded to Xu. His body language conveyed the message: Speak you fool—if you dare.

"My own personal opinion," Xu began in a hesitant tone, "is that we are locked in a competition with the Americans for economic and military supremacy. Time is on our side. I have no doubt that we will prevail in another ten or twenty years. That we will surpass the United States both economically and militarily as the world's greatest power. We are on the way up; they are on the way down. We have the human resources, the discipline, developing technology that will soon be superior, better education, and greater wisdom. Last year our universities graduated four times more engineers than did the American universities. Even American experts concede that we will surpass the United States in manufacturing by 2020, at the latest. With those ingredients, we will prevail, just as the United States surpassed England in the last century."

He paused to take a breath. "The single most important lesson of history is the inexorability of change. You step into a stream today. You can be certain the water will be different tomorrow."

Xu sounded firm but respectful as he continued, "We should be patient. We don't have to take any action now in order to prevail over the Americans. I will admit that Operation Dragon Oil will hasten our ascension, will permit us to surpass the Americans faster... if we should succeed."

Xu's final words were too much for General Zhou. He pounded

his fist on the table again. "We will succeed."

Xu kept going. "Perhaps you're right. But time alone assures our victory. In another twenty years, our economy will be larger than that of the United States. Why run the risk of provoking the Americans, who may be joined by their allies in Tokyo, with an excuse for war?"

"We can never be certain what will occur in the future. Things happen no one can predict. This way we succeed for sure."

"But twenty years isn't that long to wait."

"I may not have twenty years. Also, you weren't the commander of our forces ten years ago, who was ordered to retreat in humiliation from retaking our province of Taiwan, simply because the Americans moved a couple of ships into the area. Perhaps at the time, when we were so much weaker in sophisticated technological weapons, that decision made sense. We are certainly not weaker now. We may not have the ships that they do, but with our land-based missile capability we could easily destroy every one of their ships in the Pacific."

He stopped for a moment to let his words sink in. Then he continued, "You talk about the inexorability of history. But you miss the point. Great changes don't occur in the world simply by themselves. Individuals shape them. Try to imagine what the world would be like now if Mao, Lenin, and Hitler had never lived."

"Do you," Admiral Xu was raising his voice, "want to be compared with villains like that?"

General Zhou's face reddened. "That's not the point. How dare you say that to me?" Admiral Xu had gone too far. "The discussion is over."

In a rage, General Zhou returned alone to his office. Sitting at his desk, he yanked a Davidoff from the humidor and lit it. Then he reached into the center drawer and removed a photograph album. He began looking at pictures: His grandfather in East Texas standing near a gushing oil well, his father being welcomed to China by Mao after Chiang Kai-shek withdrew to Taiwan, his parents looking frail in the countryside during the cultural revolution—the last picture of his mother.

I won't let that fool destroy everything.

He summoned Captain Cheng. "I don't have to tell you how important confidentiality is for Operation Dragon Oil. We can't tolerate the risk of unauthorized disclosure."

"Yes, sir." Captain Cheng's eyes were blinking.

"After listening to Admiral Xu, I am concerned that he will do anything to block Operation Dragon Oil. He has become an enemy of the state. He must be killed."

Captain Cheng didn't show any emotion. "Yes sir."

"The Admiral has a mistress whom he visits three or four times a week, this evening, if he follows his usual schedule. Lena is her name. They meet at her apartment, which he purchased for her. His driver always waits in the car."

General Zhou wrote the address on a piece of paper and handed it to Captain Cheng.

"She's a cunning little wench in her twenties, about thirty years younger than Admiral Xu. A peasant girl from the country who struck it rich when he met her as a waitress—and she spread her legs for him. Now she wears the latest fashions from France and Italy. She thinks she's an aristocrat; she spends like one. I've had someone investigating her. I learned that, even with what he gives her, she's heavily in debt and growing desperate. If you give her a hundred thousand in cash and the materials, she'll inject potassium chloride into his veins this evening, making it appear as if he had a heart attack. Understood?"

"Yes, sir," Captain Cheng said. "I'll do it exactly that way."

"Good. Afterwards, I want you to arrange her elimination. And make sure he didn't leave any documents in her apartment. When you're finished with the wench, I want you to sanitize his office here in the military compound. Find a copy of the agreement with Iran and anything else relating to Operation Dragon Oil. Destroy it all."

27

TEHRAN

Over the years, Craig had developed the three turn rule. If he was walking and suspected he was being followed, he'd make three turns and if the man—although occasionally it was a woman—was still behind him, he knew he was being followed and acted accordingly.

Two blocks from the hotel, at nine in the morning, Craig was conscious of a man in a black leather jacket, with a gimpy walk, keeping a fixed distance behind him. Stopping to tie his shoe, Craig got a good look. The man was tall and thin, with curly black hair, no mustache or beard.

Craig walked another block and turned left, then right, finally left again. The black leather jacket was still behind him.

Craig knew exactly how to lose the black leather jacket. He walked another half mile to the National Museum. Then climbed the five marble steps to the ticket kiosk. In front of him on the right were about fifty school children. Boys separated from the girls.

He had to wait ten minutes to reach the front of the line. He paid the entrance fee and went inside.

Glancing over his shoulder, he saw black leather jacket flash a government ID at the ticket taker and follow Craig.

Craig knew this museum well from his time in Iran. He had occasionally used it for meetings with Sabi.

For the next half hour, Craig wandered around the three-floor museum, in and out of the rooms, almost at random, stopping to admire the incredible collection of ceramics, pottery, and stone figures. He was walking slowly, casually, as a tourist would do. As he entered a new gallery, he noticed that black leather jacket held back, in the previous gallery, concealing himself in part behind a wall.

Suddenly, Craig, without any warning, rushed up to him in an entranceway. "Pretty amazing stuff, particularly the pottery," Craig said, loudly in English. "Don't you think?"

As he expected, the man pulled away, now increasing his distance from Craig. He didn't want to appear to be seen talking English to an American.

Craig returned to the ground floor and walked into the third room on the left, filled with artifacts from the time of Darius I, who became King of Persia in 521 BC. He paused in front of a relief of the audience hall of the king.

The black leather jacket held his position at the entrance to the room, remaining out of sight for the most part, but occasionally glancing at Craig.

Craig strolled casually toward the men's room on the first floor. When Craig went inside, black leather jacket remained in the corridor.

Craig saw only one other person, an elderly Iranian washing his hands. Craig waited a minute for him to exit, then ran over to the window, opened it and looked out. As he remembered, it was about a twelve foot drop to the ground in back of the museum.

He glanced around. No one in sight. He climbed up on the window sill and jumped, feet first. Fortunately, it had rained last night. The ground was soft and cushioned his landing. He bent at the knees and rolled his body in the thick grass.

Certain no one had spotted him, Craig dashed across a small park. At an open gate, he found a cab stand. He scrambled into the back of the first cab and gave the driver an address three blocks from Jurgenson's Rotterdam Carpet Company.

28

TEHRAN

It was easy for Craig to recall the first time he met Hans Jurgenson. Six months before going undercover in Iran, Dodson, the CIA Director, asked Craig to speak about Middle Eastern terrorism before a gathering of European intelligence agents in Brussels. After his talk, Jurgenson came up to Craig and said, "I'm stationed in Amsterdam and bored stiff. I want to get into the field. If you ever know of anything, let me know."

Once Dodson gave Craig the Tehran assignment, he told the CIA Director about Jurgenson and asked if he could work a deal with the Dutch government to put Jurgenson undercover in a joint U.S.-Dutch operation. "Let's be honest," Craig had told Dodson. "We have so few sources of intelligence in the country." Dodson set it up. At a meeting in Amsterdam, Craig suggested Jurgenson's cover: Director of Rotterdam Carpet Company, which exports to Europe. A month later, the Dutchman set up shop, reporting jointly to Washington and Amsterdam. When he became DCI, Kirby left Jurgenson in place, relying upon him heavily.

Jurgenson had a weakness Craig learned of when he was in Tehran. Missing his wife, Jurgenson was afraid to bed Muslim women, fearing they might be Iranian intelligence agents. So he turned to drinking, which sometimes got him into trouble.

Once when Craig was supposed to meet Jurgenson in a hotel room near Qom, a Muslim religious center, but also site of a nuclear development facility, Craig received a tip from Sabi, telling him that two Iranian intelligence agents, suspecting Jurgenson was a spy because of the things he said in a hotel bar, were preparing to ambush the Dutchman in his hotel room and interrogate him.

Craig burst into the room to find Jurgenson naked on his back in bed, spread eagled, his legs and arms tied to the bed posts. One of the agents was holding a knife, preparing to conduct radical surgery on Jurgenson's genitalia, when Craig showed up, a nine millimeter Beretta with a long silencer in hand. Craig's first shot killed the agent with the knife. He took out the second one before he could pull out his gun. Relieved, Jurgenson had told Craig, "I'll do anything for you. Anytime. Just ask."

Craig got out of the cab in an industrial part of the city, filled with warehouses and small manufacturing plants, and walked three blocks to the Rotterdam Carpet Company, glancing over his shoulder from time to time. No one was following. Rapidly, he climbed the three stairs to the concrete building with a sign in front in Farsi that translated to Rotterdam Carpet Company. He opened the door and stepped into the reception area. In front of him was a sheet of thick glass, behind it, a seated Iranian woman, her face covered in black except for the eyes.

"Can I help you?" she said into a microphone that projected into the reception area.

"I'm here to see Hans Jurgenson."

"Is he expecting you?"

"He'll see me."

"Who are you?"

"Tell him an old friend visiting Tehran."

The woman left her station and returned a few moments later with a short, powerfully built, blond haired, blue eyed man dressed in a western business suit and tie. When Jurgenson took a look at Craig, a stunned expression came over his face. Nervously, his head was twitching.

He opened the door, letting Craig enter the inside of the factory.

"Don't talk until I tell you," Jurgenson whispered to Craig. He led the way along a corridor. To the right, Craig saw carpets being rolled up for shipment and sale in Europe or elsewhere.

At the end of the corridor, Jurgenson opened a door and led the way down a wooden staircase to the basement. There, they entered his private office. A table held a computer, ledger books, and two phones… one black, the other red. A coffee pot rested on top of a small refrigerator.

"We can talk down here," Jurgenson said, sounding hostile as well as nervous. He sat on one side of the table, Craig on the other. "Now you better tell me what the fuck you're doing, showing up like this. You could get us both killed. Do you have any idea what's going on in the country now?"

"There was no other way. I assume you preferred that I come like this rather than taking a chance on calling you and having that call picked up."

"The best would have been leaving me alone."

"That's hardly a way to greet an old friend. We did things for each other not so long ago. You want me to remind you what was about to happen in that hotel room near Qom?"

"That was then. Now is now."

So much for gratitude. "You want to tell me what changed?"

"You may not know this, but you're regarded as a pariah at the agency. Six months ago Kirby called and informed me that you'd been fired for insubordination. He said that if you tried to contact me, I wasn't supposed to have anything to do with you."

"Kirby's an incompetent asshole and a control freak. He fired me because I refused to let him screw up our only chance to thwart a major suicide bombing at Madison Square Garden."

"That may be, but I still work for Kirby. Now why are you here?"

"I'm in Tehran on a private mission for President Brewster. The President has received information that the Iranians are planning a joint operation with China that could have an adverse impact on the United States. The President's unhappy with the information the CIA has given him about Iran's nuclear program, so this time he wants to circumvent the agency by using me to investigate the Iran China matter and report back to him. Kirby knows nothing about my mission."

"That sounds pretty weird. What do you want from me?"

"Any information you have about Iranian-Chinese interaction that I can pass along to President Brewster. You do work for him, you realize?"

"I work for Kirby."

"We all work for the President, Kirby too."

"Are you sure about this?"

"You think I came to Tehran for a vacation? I prefer the south of France or Sardinia."

"No. I guess not."

"So tell me what you know. I'll mention you favorably to Brewster."

Perspiration dotted Jurgenson's forehead. "I don't know if I should talk to you."

"You've got to be kidding."

"Maybe I should call Kirby."

"I've told you Brewster doesn't want Kirby in the loop on this."

"I know the American government's screwed up, but I have a lot of trouble believing…" He reached for the red phone—the direct line to Kirby's office.

Craig couldn't let him pick it up. He leapt over the table and grabbed Jurgenson by the lapels. "Listen you sniveling little blond weasel, you keep fuckin' around with me and I'll finish the job those dudes started on you in that hotel room near Qom."

Craig tightened his grip on Jurgenson's jacket.

"Okay. Okay, let go. I'll tell you what I know."

Craig retreated to his side of the table.

Jurgenson straightened his jacket and sighed deeply. "Something big is going on between Iran and China, but I haven't been able to determine the details or the objectives. My contacts in Iranian intelligence tell me lots of Chinese military people are roaming around Iranian bases. And Chinese weapons are being shipped into the country. That's all I know."

"Is an attack being planned?"

"I haven't heard about it."

"Do you know anything about the Chinese National Oil Company? Has its chairman, Zhou Yun, been here?"

"I don't know. I've told you everything. I swear."

Craig believed him.

"I assume you've told Kirby about the Chinese military activity in the country?"

"Of course. I personally spoke with Kirby."

"What was his reaction?"

"You know what Langley's like. You feed them information, and you feel like it's going into a dark hole." Jurgenson looked at Craig suspiciously. "Why do I think there's more to this than you're telling me? That you're conning me."

"Look, I've been straight with you. I'm on a confidential assignment for President Brewster."

"I've already told you everything I know." Jurgenson was twitching again. "Now will you go?"

"Just one other thing."

"What's that?"

"When I leave, I don't want you calling Kirby to tell him I was here."

"I wouldn't do that."

"Good. If he finds out and asks you about it, I want you to say all we did was small talk. Nothing of substance. Nothing about China. You understand?"

"Absolutely. You can count on me."

From the Rotterdam Carpet Company, Craig took a cab to the Tehran Bazaar.

The bazaar was crowded with housewives shopping. He walked up and down the lanes, darting around shoppers, stopping to check melons and pomegranates until he was certain no one was following him.

Then he whipped the cell phone from his pocket and dialed Sabi's cell, hoping the number was still valid. He was relieved to hear Sabi's usual greeting in his unmistakable voice. "Who's calling please?"

Using a code they'd established when Craig was in the country, he said, "I'm trying to reach my friend Kourosh in Tajrish."

"You must have the wrong number."

"Oh I'm very sorry."

Craig gave a deep sigh of relief. Sabi understood.

29

WASHINGTON

At eleven in the morning, Kirby leaned back in the rear of the car carrying him from CIA headquarters to the White House and closed his eyes, trying to imagine why Ali hadn't been able to find Craig and Elizabeth.

Meantime, he savored the smell of fresh leather in the brand new Cadillac. He loved the many perks of his job, including ordering a new bulletproof car each year. He also loved the immediate access he had to the President. When Kirby had called half an hour ago and told, Kathy, Brewster's secretary, that he wanted to talk to the President about a new issue, she said, "Please hold, Mr. Kirby. He's meeting with a congressional delegation. I'll pass him a note." She was back a minute later. "He'll be able to see you in an hour."

The cell phone in his pocket rang. Kirby checked the caller ID. My God, it was Jurgenson calling from Tehran on the secure line Kirby had installed in the carpet company.

"Kirby here."

"I hate to bother you, Sir, but I thought you should know that I had a surprise visit from Craig Page in my office a little while ago."

Kirby was stunned. "Did you say Craig Page?"

"That's right."

"What did he want?"

"Information about Chinese activity in Iran. He claimed to be on a personal assignment from President Brewster. One so secret that you don't even know about it."

"That's total bullshit. I've been following Craig's movements. He's trying to expand his private consulting firm by utilizing the contacts he had with the agency."

"I figured it was something like that. His cover story made no sense."

"What did you tell him?"

"Not a word. I remembered what you told me six months ago, that if Craig tried to contact me, I wasn't supposed to have anything to do with him. So we had a very brief conversation. Hello and goodbye."

Kirby recognized the hesitation, the trembling in Jurgenson's voice.

"Do you know where Craig is staying in Tehran?" Kirby asked.

"No sir."

"Who else is he talking to?"

"I have no idea. As I said, our conversation was very brief."

"You didn't tell him what you reported to me about Chinese military activity in Tehran?"

"Absolutely not."

"Are you certain?"

"For sure."

The bastard's lying through his teeth.

"This has been very helpful, Hans. As always, your information is valuable. I want you to remain in your office—and close by this secure phone. It may take a few hours for me to get back to you, but I will. Can you do that?"

"Certainly, Mr. Kirby."

Kirby hung up and called Ali. "Meet me in Franklin Square in an hour. The usual bench. If I'm not there, read a newspaper and feed the pigeons."

The car was pulling up to the White House entrance. Kirby got out and was met by a military escort who led him to the oval office.

There were no pleasantries from Brewster. No surprise there. A week after Brewster's inauguration, the President had told Kirby, "You're on borrowed time. I'll keep you in the job for a while to placate your congressional supporters. Don't expect it to last."

As Kirby was sitting down across from the large wooden desk, devoid of any papers, Brewster said gruffly, "You wanted to see me. What's up?"

"We have evidence that the Chinese are preparing for an invasion of Taiwan."

Brewster was visibly shaken.

"What evidence?"

Kirby booted up his computer and began a Power Point presentation.

"The latest satellite photographs show significant Chinese troop and missile movements eastward in China in the direction of Taiwan and specifically toward Nanoping in Fujian Province, a coastal jumping off point for an invasion. They've moved thousands of troops as well as heavy equipment and amphibious landing gear. In short, everything needed to launch a full-scale invasion."

Kirby paused to let those words sink in. Then he continued, "Other photos show the movement of Chinese ships. The newest destroyers and fleet vessels that fire missiles. They, too, are moving in the direction of Taiwan. This data all points to one conclusion: The Chinese are planning to launch a full scale-invasion of Taiwan—and very soon."

"Go back to the photo that shows troop movements," Brewster said.

Kirby pressed some buttons and returned to that photo.

"Isn't it possible," the President said, "that these are only exercises? More saber rattling to alarm us and Japan. Not a prelude to a real attack. Don't the Chinese do that periodically?"

"The movements have never been this extensive. This looks like the real thing. I wanted to get to you as soon as possible, once I satisfied myself that evidence supported a likely attack. I would never come to you with questionable information."

Brewster pursed his lips. "Humph… Keep following their movements closely. Meantime, set up a meeting in the Situation Room today at three. I want the Chairman of the Joint Chiefs here as well as the Secretaries of State and Defense. Tell them to clear their calendars. This is top priority. I'll be there, too. I'll ask my counsel to review our defense agreements with Taiwan." Brewster was frowning. "I do not need a major conflict with China right now."

"We don't need one at any time, Mr. President."

As Kirby left the Oval Office he could barely contain a smile.

30

TEHRAN

Elizabeth was disappointed. She had hoped to meet with a high-ranking official of the Iranian Oil Ministry, someone of authority, but Reza, the Director of Press Relations, about her age, neatly dressed in an Italian suit and tie, who met her in the reception area and led her back to his office, refused to consider it. "I talk to all the foreign press people," he told her in a British-accented English in his office. "No one else does."

Smooth-talking, polished Reza, with his fashionable, thin wire-rimmed glasses and neatly trimmed beard, was such a contrast to those goons who interrogated her at the airport that Elizabeth was astounded. Then it struck her: Reza was the mullahs' window dressing, their public face to deal with the Western media. He was perfect for the part; he could have come from central casting.

But there might be an advantage for her in dealing with Reza. Because he was the only one who talked to foreign press people, he would have spoken to Francesca. He might be able to give Elizabeth some information about what she learned in Tehran.

"Did you go to school in England?" she asked.

"London School of Economics for two years after I completed university here."

"How'd you like London?"

"I loved it. The classes were good. Lots of beautiful women, but not many as beautiful as you."

"You said that so smoothly. You must have had lots of practice with the line."

"And most were very available," he continued. "If you know what I mean."

"So why'd you come back to Iran?"

"It's my home. I have family, though I'm not married. I wanted to spend another year studying in the United States. Harvard accepted me, but your government wasn't giving visas to Iranians. Oh well, I survived. Where'd you go to school?"

"Harvard."

"What a shame. We'd have met in Cambridge. Fate would have brought us together sooner."

I can't believe this jerk.

"Would you like a cup of very good coffee?" he asked.

"That'll be great."

He buzzed for his secretary. Another of those creatures covered in black from head to toe brought two cups on a tray.

She sipped. "It is good."

"Lots of people don't know it, but we grow excellent coffee. We wanted to supply it to Starbucks, but they said that under American law, no American company can do business with Iran."

"That's right."

"I hate the politicians. Is this your first visit to Iran?"

"It is."

"Where are you staying?"

"The Laleh International Hotel."

"The best in the city. You do your research well. You're obviously intelligent. What are you writing about?"

"The Iranian oil industry."

He laughed. "A pretty broad topic."

"You have huge reserves. That's my starting point."

"More than any country except Saudi Arabia."

"Iraq, Canada, and Russia might question that."

"Their information is out of date."

"Perhaps, but you haven't been able to get much of it out of the ground. And you don't even have enough refinery capacity to make gasoline for your own people."

"That's because the United States has prevented foreigners from doing business with us." He sounded defensive. "Is that what you're writing about? More politics. How the U.S. cripples and persecutes Iran?"

She shook her head. "Not at all. As I told you, I write for a Los Angeles paper. We have an enormous number of Iranian émigrés among our readers"

"Traitors," he said sharply.

"They have ties to your country. I want to tell them about the positive steps your country's taking to develop its valuable oil resources."

"Well, we're doing plenty."

"Can you give me any specifics?"

"We have vast numbers of Iranian petroleum engineers with incredible know-how."

She pulled a small steno pad from her purse and made some notes.

"Where were they educated?"

"At Iranian universities. Your readers will be surprised to learn that. The American government makes us appear like uncivilized barbarians. In fact, we're an educated, cultured society."

Elizabeth scribbled some more.

"Also, tell them," Reza added, "that we not only have more oil than those miserable Iraqis, but we have much better oil."

"Let's come back to the development issue. What role are foreigners playing?"

Reza squirmed. "What do you mean?"

"Well for example, do you have development agreements with French companies… or Russians… or Chinese?"

"I'm sorry, but our relationships with other countries are all top secret."

"I've read articles that China is trying to strengthen its relationship with Iran. Is there any truth in that?"

"I can't comment."

"Well, what can you tell me?"

Reza removed a starched white handkerchief from his lapel pocket and cleaned his glasses. He looked around nervously. "Do you know a woman by the name of Francesca Page?"

Elizabeth shook her head. "No. Who is she?"

"A reporter for the *New York Tribune*. She was here a week or so ago, pressing me with all sorts of accusations."

"Accusations about what? China and Iran?"

He whispered, "I don't think we can discuss this in the office. Perhaps tonight we could go to a club. We have some good discotheques that the religious police don't know about. We can dance, drink, like you would in Los Angeles. You're a beautiful woman. We'd enjoy ourselves."

She couldn't believe this sleazebag was coming on to her. "Sorry, but I'm married."

"Your husband will never know."

"He's in Tehran with me."

"Leave him at the hotel. Tell him you have to work."

Elizabeth stood up. "You're not even close."

He seemed flustered. "I only meant we'd talk about foreign oil development at the club."

"Yeah, right. I have to give you credit. That's one of the most original lines I've ever heard."

Reza smiled. "You can't blame a guy for trying. As I said, you're a beautiful woman."

He removed a card from his desk drawer. "It has my cell number. Call me when you change your mind. I look forward to seeing you again."

31

TEHRAN

Craig took the chairlift to the top of the mountain in Tajrash, in northern Tehran. Not surprising, the area was deserted. Midday on a weekday. The café had only two customers: a couple of middle aged women, whom he overheard discussing their marital problems. Tehran stretched out at the bottom. A heavy brown cloud of pollution blanketed the city.

He walked outside in the chilly mountain air to a grassy area. Standing next to a tree was a solitary figure. From the back, Craig recognized Sabi. As Craig approached, the Iranian wheeled around. "I never thought I'd hear from you again, my friend."

"Life's long. One never knows. This is where we had our last meeting."

"Unfortunately, conditions are worse in the country now. When you were here, reform seemed possible. Now…"

"I saw that from the moment I arrived. How are you and your family?"

"I've become a grandfather. A little boy."

"Congratulations."

"My older daughter is a joy. Like her mother."

"And the younger one?"

"She starts the University of Tehran in September. I worry that she'll get into a crowd of dissidents. These are difficult times in the country. And you?"

"Francesca was murdered. That's why I'm here."

"Your only child. Oh, I'm so sorry. What happened?"

"She was a newspaper reporter working on a big story about oil."

"Following in her father's footprints."

"The story concerned China and Iran. I'm hell-bent to find out who was responsible for her death and take revenge."

"You think Iranians were involved in her murder?"

"I don't know. Let me show you something."

This morning, before leaving the hotel, Craig asked Elizabeth to forward to his cell phone the photo of the man who had followed her in Calgary. He wanted to show it to Sabi.

Craig pulled it up on the cell phone. "Recognize him?"

Sabi stared at it for a full minute, then shook his head. "Nobody I've ever seen. Is that why you came? To locate this man?"

"Indirectly. What I've learned is that Francesca's story involved joint action between China and Iran. Somebody killed her before she could reveal it. I'm trying to find out about the story. That'll lead me to her killers. Do you know anything about this?"

Sabi glanced around nervously. He signaled Craig to move with him behind the tree.

"Something big is going down. Iran has entered into a significant and far-reaching agreement with China, covering oil and military matters. Security has been exceedingly tight, so I don't know all the details. What I've heard is that Iran will be selling all of its oil to China. Meanwhile, the Chinese military will aid Iran in some kind of a military attack on large Arab oil producers."

"I'm wondering how high this goes in the two governments. Have you heard who's involved?"

"For us, the President and Supreme Leader. For them, I know General Zhou, the head of the Chinese military, has been meeting with people from our defense ministry. A written agreement exists between the two countries. I haven't seen a copy, and I don't know where one is."

"Is General Zhou related to Zhou Yun, the head of the Chinese Oil Company?"

"They are brothers."

For Craig, that added to the seriousness of the threat. Chinese military and oil interests were joined.

"Are nuclear weapons involved?" Craig asked.

"I don't know, but I've heard that after this goes down, Iran will be the dominant force in the Middle East. That's all I know now. I'll try to get more details and call you. We'll use the old soccer field for our next meeting."

"Good, but don't take any undue risks," Craig said.

Sabi laughed. "Every day I go into my office, I'm taking an undue risk. In this insane asylum we call a country, anybody could turn on me at any time."

"Thanks for everything. You leave first. I'll wait a while."

Sabi reached into his jacket pocket, took out a pistol and pressed it into Craig's hand. "You might need this. Be careful, my friend."

Craig waited until Sabi entered the lift cabin and it began its descent. Then he whipped out his cell phone and dialed. The numbers were indelibly committed to his memory.

"Yes." He recognized Yossi's Farsi with a barely discernable Israeli accent.

Using their old code, Craig responded in Arabic. "It's your friend,

Abdullah from Amman. I'm in Tehran and would like to meet with you as soon as possible."

"I'm in the south today. How about eight tomorrow morning for breakfast? The same place as the last time. Remember?"

"Of course," Craig could never forget the restaurant north of town, run by a blind man and his wife, which had been their usual meeting place. The proprietors were Muslims who detested the regime. Somehow, he and Elizabeth would have to make it through the night.

32

WASHINGTON

Kirby entered Franklin Square from Fourteenth and cut diagonally across the one-square-block park. On a warm sunny day, a scattering of people, lawyers and secretaries, the heartbeat of Washington, were eating sandwiches on benches. Two men in their twenties were tossing a Frisbee on the grass. He spotted Ali reading a newspaper on a bench. Kirby sat down next to him.

"Helluva steel wall you erected around Canada," Kirby said.

"What do you mean?" Ali sounded alarmed.

"Maybe you should pay me the one point seven five million dollars."

"You found them?"

"Craig's in Iran."

Ali was smiling. "That's great."

"What do you mean?"

"As I once told you, half of the SAVAK people came to the

U.S. The other half went over to the mullahs' side. So now we have Craig right where I can snuff him out. All I have to do is make a call or two."

Kirby had to hand it to Ali. The guy was undaunted.

"Shouldn't you go there yourself?"

"You're not serious?"

"Why not?"

"I have lots of friends in the country. But I also have plenty of enemies from the old days. Some of them were subjects of my interrogations under the Shah. Now they're in positions of authority. What do you think they'd do if they got hold of me?"

"Can you handle it from here?"

"Don't worry. My boys will find Craig and kill him. Elizabeth, too. I presume she's still with him."

"As far as I know."

"Good. It'll be a piece of cake."

Kirby replayed in his mind his conversation with Jurgenson. The Dutchman had become a liability.

"There's something else I need you to do."

"Sure. Anything."

"A Dutchman by the name of Hans Jurgenson runs the Rotterdam Carpet Company in Tehran." Kirby scribbled the address on a piece of paper and handed it to Ali. "He's in his office, waiting for a call from me. I want him eliminated ASAP. Got that?"

"He'll be a freebie."

"He damn well better be. And one other thing."

"Talk to me, Kirby."

Ali sounded eager.

"Based upon your track record, I don't have a lot of confidence that you'll have Craig killed in Iran."

"That stung. Even Michael Jordan didn't win every game."

"He did a helluva lot better than you."

"So what do you want?"

"If Craig manages to slip out of another of your steel walls, he may come home to McLean. I want his McLean house covered twenty four and seven."

"You've got it. I'll assign my best people."

"Stop bullshitting me and get the job done."

33

TEHRAN

After leaving that letch Reza, Elizabeth decided to walk back to the hotel.

A hot, dry, brown smog-laden layer of air had descended over the city. The beautiful snow-capped mountains outside of Tehran that Elizabeth had read about were barely visible.

On the residential streets, she passed people. No one nodded or said anything to her. Everyone walked with their heads down.

Approaching Lali Park, almost at the hotel, Elizabeth heard the sounds of shouting and amplified voices. The park was jammed with people holding up signs.

Like a magnet she was drawn to it. The investigative reporter in her wanted to know what was happening. As she got closer, the noise and shouting became louder.

At the edge of the square, she looked through a black wrought-iron fence. She saw a young man, wearing only pants, tied to a tree with his face flush against the trunk. From a loud speaker, she heard an announcement in Farsi, then in English: "This man is guilty of adultery." With that, a bearded man raised a leather whip and cracked it against the young man's bloody back. The young man screamed out in pain. His cries were futile. The whip came flying through the air again and again.

After the eighth lash, the protesters in the square, an angry, screaming mob being held back by the police, most of them wearing shirts that said Tehran University, rushed toward the man performing the public lashing, intent on stopping him. Their signs read: "THIS HAS TO END. RETURN IRAN TO THE TWENTY-FIRST CENTURY," and "DEATH TO THE TYRANTS."

Some of the students knocked the man with the whip to the ground. Others untied the young man from the tree. He quickly dashed into the crowd.

Without any warning, dozens of police in riot gear stormed into the square, spraying tear gas. Brandishing clubs, they beat the students on their heads. In an effort to escape, students raced in all directions. For a few seconds, Elizabeth was paralyzed. Finally, when students rushed by her, she ran to escape the oncoming riot police.

She kept running, willing herself to go as fast as possible back down the boulevard, in the direction she had come, to get away from the police. Coming from that direction were four motor scooters with bearded men, morality police, racing toward the park.

One of them saw Elizabeth running with her head uncovered. He stopped his scooter, jumped off with a wooden baton in his hand. "Whore," he yelled. "Whore."

He slammed the baton against Elizabeth's face, neck, and back. The blows were hard, the pain excruciating. She fell to the ground on her knees, trying to cover her head with her hands.

She struggled to get up. More blows rained on her. She collapsed to a prone position. Finally, the blows stopped. She made it to her feet and stumbled away. The guard didn't give chase, but continued to the square.

Elizabeth was limping. Every part of her body ached. Both of her knees were bloodied; her arms too. She had cuts and bruises on her face.

Gasping for breath, she entered the hotel and rode up in the elevator.

When she staggered in to the room, she found Craig watching Tehran television, "late breaking news," reporting the protest she'd witnessed. She heard the words on the television, "These were hooligans who tried to disrupt the lawful execution of justice in the Islamic Republic. Fortunately, most of the troublemakers were arrested."

"Holy shit," Craig said. "What happened to you?"

She pointed to the television screen. "I got caught up in that. I was observing the protest when I was blindsided by a couple of religious nuts."

"We have to clean you up."

He took her into the bathroom, filled the tub, and helped her off with her clothes. Then he washed her wounds while she soaked in the tub.

He kicked the door shut. "We can talk now."

"How much longer do we stay in this hell hole?" she asked.

"We can leave in the morning if you want."

"Not if we have more to do. I met with Reza, the head of PR from the Oil Ministry, who gave me no information, but came on to me. He gave me his cell number and claims if I let him take me to an underground club, he'll give me the real stuff I want about Iran and China. I figure it was a sorry excuse to get into my pants. Then I decided to check out a protest in the park, and the religious police beat up on me. So how was your day?"

Before Craig could answer, they heard sirens on the street.

Craig jumped up and raced over to the bathroom window.

Elizabeth climbed out of the tub, draped a towel around her body, and stood next to him, peeking out with him through the center of the drawn drapes. On the street, four floors below, she saw a police van pulling up in front of the hotel. Half a dozen baton wielding, black uniformed police scrambled out.

"Oh my God! They're coming for us," she cried out.

"Get dressed. A friend gave me a gun. If they knock on the door, we're shooting our way out."

She dressed, then stood next to Craig behind the door, holding her breath, waiting for a knock. It didn't come.

Instead, moments later, they heard a commotion on the street below. She ran over to the window. Police were dragging out a man and a woman in handcuffs, westerners, kicking and screaming. Police grabbed each of them by the shoulders and legs, then tossed them into the back of the van like sacks of garbage.

She and Craig went back in to the bathroom to talk.

"What else do you have to do here?" she asked.

"I have a meeting at eight tomorrow morning. I want you to stay in our hotel room. I'll be back by eleven."

"You don't have to worry. I'm not going anywhere myself."

"If I get the information I need, we're out of here."

"And if you don't?"

"I'll want you to call Reza, your lecherous PR friend. Set a meeting with him. We'll use your pussy as bait to lure the creep up here. If I have a few minutes with him, I'll find out what he really knows. Either that or he'll drown."

"Jesus, I'm glad you're on my side."

"With these people, you don't play Queensbury rules."

34

WASHINGTON

Kirby looked around the White House Situation Room at the top officials in the government. They had all dropped what they were doing, suspended meetings in the middle, canceled personal or other commitments. Kirby had passed the word: President Brewster said this meeting is top priority.

Seated at the heavily polished conference-room table, besides President Brewster, Kirby saw the Secretaries of State and Defense, General Braddock, the Chairman of the Joint Chiefs, and Jim Gorman, the President's Chief of Staff.

Brewster looked at Kirby, "I want you to kick this off. Give them the same Power Point you gave me this morning."

With a laser pointer, Kirby explained, "Here's the East China Sea. We have observed the Chinese Navy moving destroyers in the direction of Taiwan." He shifted the laser to Mainland China. "Here you will note the Chinese military moving troops over land toward the Straits of Taiwan." At the end, he said, "Our judgment is that this is the start of an offensive. They're finally making their move to take over Taiwan."

When Kirby sat down, President Brewster turned to the others. "Anyone else want to weigh in on whether this is the real thing or another exercise of the type the Chinese government periodically undertakes?"

The Secretary of State, Jennifer Nelson, responded, "You could call the Chinese President direct, tell him what we've observed and try to get some reaction from him."

"Too much of a sign of weakness," the ruddy faced Secretary of Defense, George Frasier, responded. "I recommend we make a show of force ourselves, moving our ships toward the area. They'll respect that more than a phone call."

"We have the forces ready to move," the Chairman of the Joint Chiefs said, "if that's what you want, Mr. President."

"So the issue," Brewster said, "is whether we respond with military movements of our own."

All of the heads in the room nodded.

Brewster looked at Kirby. "What's my brilliant director of intelligence have to say on the issue?"

"All I can do, Mr. President, is present our excellent intel to you. Beyond that, it's your call."

"Helpful as always," Brewster muttered. "Okay, you're right. The buck stops here." He pointed to the Chairman of the Joint Chiefs. "Begin moving American ships, aircraft carriers, whatever you have nearby in the direction of Taiwan. Do it visibly so the Chinese notice we're on the way."

Then he pointed to the Secretary of State. "Call the Japanese foreign minister. Tell him what we observed on our satellite reconnaissance and what action we're taking in response. Tell him we'll keep Tokyo informed, but they should go on full alert. If we do end up with a military confrontation with China, we'll be looking for support from the Japanese military as well."

Jennifer Nelson interjected, "Have you decided, Mr. President, that it is in the interest of the United States to go to war with China over the Island of Taiwan?"

"You always ask the tough questions, Jennifer."

"That's what you told me to do when you gave me the job."

Brewster smiled. "Well I didn't mean it." That prompted laughter... cutting through the tension.

Brewster said, "We have treaty obligations that require us to defend Taiwan. I don't know what decision I'll make if the Chinese attack, but I sure as hell want to deter them. Hopefully, our show of force will do it."

"With all due respect," the Secretary of State responded, "you're playing a dangerous game, Mr. President."

"I agree with you there." Brewster turned to the Chairman of the Joint Chiefs. "I might reconsider if General Braddock tells me our military is no match for the Chinese."

"I wouldn't tell you that, Mr. President," General Braddock said. "I believe we are up to the task. Our military is still more powerful. Frankly, it's as well for us if the battle comes now. In ten years, given the rate at which the Chinese military has been expanding, I might be required to give you a different answer."

The President rose, signaling the meeting was over.

Leaving the White House and walking to his car, Kirby was very pleased. Another piece had fallen into place.

His cell phone rang. It was Ali. "We have to talk."

"Where are you?"

"Downtown."

"Meet me back on the bench in Franklin Square in fifteen minutes."

When Kirby arrived, Ali was already there, with a smug expression on his face.

"I hope you're planning to tell me that your men found and killed Craig and Elizabeth."

Ali raised his hand. "Let me do this my way."

"Go ahead."

"For starters, Jurgenson's dead."

"What happened?"

"A fire at the carpet company. The whole building burnt to the ground. Nobody will ever know he was killed with a bullet before the fire started."

"Good. You finally did something right. Now, what about Craig and Elizabeth?"

"We don't yet know what aliases they're using or where they're staying in Tehran, but my friends have circulated their pictures to all of the police and intelligence agents. Also to security people at the airport. All hotels will be checked. They will be captured within a couple of hours at most, then promptly executed."

"Given your track record for apprehending Craig, I hope to hell you have people staking out his house in McLean, in case he slips through another one of your steel walls."

"He won't this time. Don't worry."

"Of course I'm worried. Do you or do you not have the house staked out?"

"Yes, with two of my best people. Twenty four and seven."

"If Craig and Elizabeth show, I want them both killed."

35

TEHRAN

It was 5:20 in the morning. Craig hadn't slept a wink. His instinct for danger had kicked in. Something was wrong. He knew it. He kept tossing and turning in bed.

Beside him, Elizabeth was snoring softly. He'd given her two extra-strength Tylenol for pain; they knocked her out.

The cell phone on the night table rang. He grabbed it immediately. Sabi was calling. Craig took the phone into the bathroom.

Sabi said, "I'm calling from the furnace repair company. We can do your work immediately."

"I'm sorry. You must have the wrong number." Sabi clicked off.

As he deciphered the message in his mind, Craig grabbed his clothes and dressed.

Sabi must be in the furnace room of the hotel.

He left the sleeping Elizabeth and took the elevator to the basement. At this hour it was deserted. He saw a sign on a door:

"UTILITY ROOM. PRIVATE." He twisted the doorknob and slowly opened the door. The room was dark. Then a flashlight lit up his face. He blinked his eyes.

"You have to get out of the country. Immediately," Sabi said.

"What happened?"

"The people you're up against know you're in Tehran. They killed Jurgenson."

"How?"

"A fire at the carpet company. They might have shot him first. They're planning on distributing your picture to all police and intelligence agents. Also to hotels and security personnel at the airport. Because it's the middle of the night and they don't move fast, you may have a narrow window."

"I can't thank you enough."

"Don't talk anymore. Just move."

Craig left Sabi, returned to their room, and woke Elizabeth. He led her into the bathroom. "I don't have time to explain. Dress and pack now. We're going to the airport."

Five minutes later, Craig and Elizabeth were wheeling their suitcases out of the hotel, walking toward a line of cabs.

He approached the first cab, expecting the driver to help them load their suitcases in the back of the old, battered, black Renault. The driver didn't move from his seat behind the wheel. Impatiently, Craig tapped on the front door, leaned in the window and said, "Take us to the airport."

"I won't do it," the driver said.

"What do you mean, 'You won't do it?'"

"You're an American. I could get into trouble, be forced to answer questions."

"Forget it then," Craig said. He moved on to the second cab. Again the driver didn't move. "We want to go to the airport."

"Get another taxi. We don't like to take Americans. Especially at this hour."

Craig reached into his pocket, pulled out a hundred dollar bill, and held it out in his hand while he leaned inside the cab through the window in the front on the passenger side. "Perhaps this will make a difference."

The driver was now hesitating.

Craig said, "And there will be another hundred when we reach the airport."

That changed the driver's mind. He climbed out of the cab, quickly opened up the trunk and piled their luggage inside. All the while he was looking around nervously.

Once they began moving, Craig watched the route the driver took. They were on the way to the airport. Music was blasting on the radio. That suited Craig. The driver couldn't hear him, he was convinced, when he called Swiss International and booked two tickets to Zurich. Repeatedly, he kept looking at the road behind them. He was confident they weren't being followed.

Thirty minutes later, they were about a mile from the terminal. Very few cars were on the road. Up ahead, Craig saw several red and blue flashing lights. Must be a roadblock. Searching for us. Before they reached the roadblock, there was one more exit from the airport access road. They were approaching it now.

"Turn off here," Craig barked to the driver. "We're changing our plans."

The driver hesitated. He slowed his speed without committing. They were almost at the exit. "I'll give you five hundred more U.S. to change our destination," Craig said.

The driver cut his wheel sharply to the right and onto the exit ramp. Midway down the ramp, he turned onto the side of the road, braked to a sudden stop, and cut off the engine.

"Give me the money now."

Craig reached into his pocket, took out three hundred dollar bills and tossed them onto the seat. "Three hundred now. The other two hundred when we reach my new destination."

"No. All five now."

Craig tossed two more bills onto the front seat.

"And five more when we get there."

"Okay," Craig said.

"Where do you want to go now?" the driver asked, while he pocketed the cash.

Craig described an intersection that was a short walk from the restaurant run by the blind man and his wife—his meeting point with Yossi at eight this morning.

The driver turned on the engine. Craig didn't trust him. He removed Sabi's gun from his pocket and leaned forward in the back seat, watching the driver carefully and the road.

The driver didn't continue down the exit ramp. Instead, he turned the wheel sharply to the left and looked at traffic coming from behind. He was preparing to make a U-turn and proceed to the airport where he would turn Craig and Elizabeth over to the police.

Before the driver had a chance to execute that turn, Craig pressed the barrel of the gun against the back of the driver's neck.

"You take me where I told you," Craig said, "or I'll pull the trigger, toss your dead body out of the cab, and drive there myself."

"No, no, I'll do it." He sounded terrified. "Take the gun away."

Craig withdrew the gun from the driver's skin but held it out so the man knew it was still there.

The driver continued down the exit ramp.

Craig handed Elizabeth the gun and told her in Farsi, for the driver's benefit, then English, "Keep the gun on him. If I signal you that he's not taking us to the right place, shoot him."

Craig took out his cell phone and dialed Yossi.

"Yes."

"It's Abdullah. Any chance we can have an earlier breakfast?"

"I'll be there in thirty minutes."

"Can you bring that truck you told me about?"

"I'll drive there in it."

36

TEHRAN

Craig hung up the phone and felt relief.

The Mossad agent had been a valuable source for Craig during his year in Iran. When the Shah ruled, the Israelis had a close relationship with the Iranian government. Though the country was Muslim, Iran, like Israel, confronted hostile Arab neighbors. The old adage, "the enemy of my enemy is my friend," applied well.

The Israeli military trained the Shah's army and sold arms to Iran. Other commerce flowed freely between the two countries. The Mossad played a pivotal role in increasing the effectiveness of SAVAK, the Shah's secret police, as well as the Iranian intelligence agencies. All of that was open and above board, with Israelis visible in Tehran when the Shah ruled. That relationship came crashing to a halt with the fall of the Shah and the Islamic revolution. From that point forward, Israel was viewed as Iran's second most despised enemy, with the United States first, although among some Iranian leaders, it was a close call.

Forced to go underground, the Israelis did in Iran what they had been doing successfully in Middle Eastern countries since the founding of their state in 1948. They recruited from the Israeli citizenry people who had either lived in the other Middle Eastern countries or were descended from those who had lived there and had the language skills as well as appearance to blend in. Yossi fit this bill.

The battered cab, bumping along with no meaningful shock absorbers, was approaching the intersection Craig had given the driver. The cab stopped. Craig took the gun from Elizabeth.

"We're here," the driver said.

"Continue a hundred yards further and pull into the parking lot for the restaurant on the right."

Craig turned to Elizabeth and said to her in Farsi, loud enough for the driver to hear, "My friend's picking us up here. He'll drive us across the border into Turkey."

The driver followed Craig's instructions. In the deserted parking lot, he got out and removed their bags from the trunk, then placed them next to the door of the restaurant. "Give me the rest of the money," the driver said to Craig.

"Back at the cab," Craig replied.

He motioned to Elizabeth. "Go inside. I'll pay him."

Craig turned and walked toward the cab. The driver was seated behind the steering wheel with his window open. Craig approached him and reached into his pants pocket as if he were pulling out cash. Instead, he withdrew his empty hand, rolled it into a fist and punched it hard against the side of the driver's head, knocking the man out. He pushed him across the seat. Then Craig climbed in and drove into the woods across the road. Once the car was buried in trees, Craig got out. He opened the trunk and took out some rope that he had seen when they were stowing the bags. Craig used it to tie the man's hands and feet. Then he tied the driver's torso to the seat. When he regained consciousness, he wouldn't be able to move.

Craig got out of the car, took the keys and tossed them into the woods. He searched the driver's pockets, found a cell phone, removed the battery and tossed it into the woods as well.

When Craig returned to the restaurant, Elizabeth was standing inside the door, the two suitcases next to her.

The owner's wife greeted him with a nervous look on her face. She gave him a nod and a wave of her hand. "Your friend's in there," she said, pointing toward a private room.

Craig led Elizabeth, with the suitcases, in that direction.

Yossi, who was pacing, came forward and hugged Craig. "After you called, I talked to one of my contacts in Iranian intelligence. It's good you didn't go to the airport. They'd have picked you up. Your picture has been posted all over the terminal. Security agents are running around showing copies to hotel personnel."

"This is Elizabeth," Craig said, "She's working with me."

"Pleased to meet you," Yossi said.

Craig, with anxiety in his voice, said, "I have an idea of how we can get out, a boat on the Caspian."

"I'm one step ahead of you. I've already lined up a boat to meet us in Lahijan. The captain's a Kurd. He hates the mullahs. He'll take you across the Caspian onto the western shore to Azerbaijan. He can leave you off near Baku and arrange transportation to the airport from there. A plane leaves once a day on British Airways from Baku to London. You might be able to make today's flight."

"Perfect. But I must talk to you about something. The reason I came to Tehran."

"It'll have to wait. We have to move now. They'll be putting up roadblocks in a ring around Tehran. Follow me now to the truck."

As the three of them cut across the parking lot toward a truck with a sign on the side, "TEHRAN PRODUCE." Yossi said to Elizabeth, "This truck was Craig's idea. We built it to take dissidents out of the country, including a Jewish nuclear scientist and his wife. I'm in the agriculture business so it's a great cover."

Yossi opened the back of the truck, filled with fruits and vegetables. He pushed them to the sides with a plastic shovel. Underneath were two wooden containers which he opened. Resembling large coffins, they were lined with foam.

Craig saw Elizabeth eyeing the containers apprehensively.

Yossi said to her, "You won't have any light, but a silent ventilation system will continually bring in fresh air. If I'm stopped, I'll tell them I have a shipment of produce for delivery to a boat. The destination is Baku."

Yossi lifted in her suitcase, then helped Elizabeth in. She was stretched out on her back. "Feels like I'm being buried alive."

"Sorry," Craig said. "There is no other way."

Yossi closed the lid and helped Craig into the other container. "I have a gun," Craig said. "If anyone but you opens the lid, I'll come out firing."

37

BEIJING

Captain Cheng walked into General Zhou's office, a somber expression on his face. His eyes were blinking. He'd begun doing that lately, General Zhou had observed. *Working with me is obviously taking a toll. So what? It's doing him good, giving him valuable experience, allowing him to participate in restoring the greatness of China.*

"Well?" General Zhou demanded.

"Mission accomplished, Sir. Admiral Xu is dead. She injected him exactly as you suggested."

"And the mistress?"

"I gave her the money and told her it would be wise to take a train to visit her parents in the country for a few months until this blows over. She agreed. I gave her a train ticket. Someone will pull her off at a midway point and eliminate her."

"Good. What else?"

The captain's eyes were blinking again.

"After she left, I checked her apartment. The Admiral didn't leave any papers. Then I searched his office. I've seized and shredded all documents relating to Operation Dragon Oil. I've also destroyed his computer hard drive."

"Now tell me about our arrangements for Paris."

Captain Cheng hesitated. The eyes were blinking.

"What is it?"

"Well I..."

"C'mon, spit it out. I won't consider you insubordinate."

"Yes sir. I didn't search Admiral Xu's house for materials relating to Dragon Oil."

"I didn't ask you to."

"I understand, but..."

There was a long pause.

"You think I should have? That I was wrong."

"I wouldn't express it that way. I only thought..."

General Zhou leaned back in his chair and weighed the issue again in his mind.

He doubted whether Admiral Xu took out of the office any materials relating to Operation Dragon Oil in violation of orders. Still having Cheng check the whore's apartment was a useful precaution. But having him search Admiral Xu's house, given the likelihood that nothing is there, was too risky.

General Zhou thought about Mei Ling, the Admiral's widow. A clever woman. She can't be underestimated. She's a member of the Central Committee, and she's close with President Li. Right now she has no basis to believe that her husband's death wasn't a heart attack, that fat blob having anxiety about whether his stalk would stand up. And if the whore managed to get it up, then straining while pounding away at her young cunt. But if military officials show up and search the house, Mei Ling will become suspicious. She'll talk to President Li. That might jeopardize Operation Dragon Oil.

"You were correct to raise the issue. But if you were to investigate the Admiral's house, there might be a complication which you can't appreciate."

The Captain looked relieved.

"Now tell me about Paris."

"The plane is fueled and ready to leave. The false flight plan has been filed. The Bristol suite reserved. The same woman you had the last time. Dinner for two of us in the hotel dining room. A box of Davidoffs waiting in the suite."

General Zhou was pleased. Captain Cheng did good work. He stood up and said, "On to Paris. I'll deal with those scheming, raghead rug merchants."

38

LAHIJAN, IRAN

Craig checked his watch, which glowed in the dark. He had been in the container a little over two hours. One leg felt stiff, but otherwise he was comfortable.

The truck had been driving fast, Craig realized. They only stopped once, about twenty minutes after leaving the restaurant, for about fifteen minutes. Craig's guess was that Yossi had encountered a roadblock.

During those fifteen minutes, Craig had gripped his gun so tightly his palm was moist with perspiration. Nothing happened. No one opened the box. Yossi must have talked his way out of it.

Now they were stopping again. Craig clutched his pistol once more, his eyes riveted on the top of the box. It opened slowly. He bolted to a sitting position, ready to begin firing. It was only Yossi.

"You can get out now." He held out his hand to Craig.

Craig climbed out, jumped down from the truck, and took a

deep breath, relieved to be breathing fresh air. Elizabeth was already out, doing knee bends. She looked at Craig. "Traveling with you is like nothing else."

Yossi handed them each a bottle of water. "Drink," he ordered. They gulped some down.

"We're in Lahijan," Yossi said. "Ten minutes walk from the port. I just spoke to the captain. He's on the water. He'll be here in about thirty minutes. Until he calls, we hold our position."

"A problem?" Craig asked.

"No. I beat the meeting time."

"I'm not surprised," Craig said. "You always drove like a maniac."

"I'm Israeli. What do you expect?"

Yossi pointed to a battered wooden building across the road. "We can wait in that deserted warehouse."

That suited Craig. He wanted to talk to Yossi. "What about security people?"

"So far I haven't seen anything out of the ordinary, but that could change."

Craig and Elizabeth followed Yossi into the warehouse. Elizabeth was walking in circles, stretching her arms.

Yossi shoved his hands into his pockets. "It was good hearing from you, but this isn't much of a visit."

"This country's as fucked up as ever."

"I gather it hasn't been a particularly good time for you personally."

Craig couldn't imagine Yossi knew about Francesca.

"What do you mean?"

"When I was in Tel Aviv, I heard that Kirby sacked you in a so-called reorganization."

Craig nodded.

"Now you're in the security business in Milan."

Craig was taken aback. "How do you know that?"

"You were the best American agent operating in our part of the world. We keep track of people like you. You might be interested to know there was a proposal floating around the Mossad to try and recruit you, as a covert agent. It went all the way up to Bennie, the director, who nixed the idea. He was afraid the benefits from having you on our payroll wouldn't outweigh the grief he'd take from Washington if the Americans found out."

"But we're supposed to be allies," Craig said facetiously.

Yossi laughed. "Yeah, everything works smoothly as long as we do it Washington's way. Now tell me what brought you to Tehran?"

"My daughter, Francesca, was a reporter for the *New York Tribune*. While working on a story involving China and Iran, she was murdered."

All of the color drained from Yossi's face.

"I'm so sorry."

"Well I wasn't about to sit in Washington and grieve. I want to find out who killed her and get revenge. The only way I can do that is by learning what the hell's going on between Iran and China. I've been able to piece together bits of information, but the picture's still murky. I was hoping you could connect some of the dots."

Yossi gave a deep sigh. "There is a written agreement between Iran and China. I've heard that from two different sources in Iranian intelligence. One of our Mossad agents in Paris reported there was a meeting at the Bristol Hotel a week ago between Iranian officials and General Zhou, the head of the Chinese armed forces."

"Also the brother of Zhou Yun, the CEO of the Chinese National Oil Company."

"You did you homework. None of my sources has seen a copy of the agreement, but they all believe it involves joint military action to seize Middle Eastern oil and secure it for China. The zero date is April 1."

"I've heard that date as well. Only eight days from now."

"In the meantime, Beijing's been arming the Iranians with huge quantities of sophisticated military hardware—offensive and defensive."

"Have you reported this to your leadership in Tel Aviv?"

"I had a meeting with Bennie last week. He told me to do everything I can to obtain a copy of the agreement. But so far I haven't been able to do that."

Craig finished the bottle of water.

"Do you know whether Bennie or anybody in your government has reported this information to Washington?"

"I know Bennie called Kirby. That happened while I was in his office after I gave him my report. He passed along to Kirby everything I've just told you."

"What'd Kirby say?"

"He didn't. He listened in silence. He thanked Bennie for the information and said that he would pass it along to other people in the American government. He promised to call Bennie back and let him know what happened."

"Did Kirby ever call back?"

"The next day I was still in Tel Aviv. Bennie told me that when he hadn't heard from Washington, he called Kirby again. The CIA chief said that Washington had to do some independent checking. But Bennie shouldn't worry. Kirby claimed that he had it under control. We don't believe him."

"That's for sure. You can never trust that man."

"Again, Kirby said he would get back to Bennie. I stayed in Tel Aviv three more days. Bennie never heard from Kirby."

"Why do you suppose Washington never responded?"

"Bennie's view was that Washington rejected our information because they believe we want the United States to launch an attack on Iran's nuclear facilities. To achieve that, they think we've invented the information. But that's not it at all. We were passing along reliable, hard information that should be enormously valuable to Washington. Let's face it. For us, Iran is a huge threat to our survival, but China's not critical. For Washington, Iran's important, but China's the nation the United States is most worried about. Anything Beijing does has to be of enormous concern to the Americans."

"Isn't there another possibility?"

"What's that?"

"Kirby's such an ego maniac and control freak with an inflated view of himself. It's possible that asshole took Bennie's information and didn't tell President Brewster or anyone in Washington. He's running with it himself, pretending he dug it up through Jurgenson. Under that scenario, he wouldn't get back to Bennie."

Yossi shrugged. "That's possible. I just don't know. Meantime, I'm hoping to get more detailed information from sources in the Iranian military about what they're doing with the Chinese. Security is incredibly tight, but I did get one bit of additional information."

"What's that?"

"One of the Chinese officials had too much to drink. He was running on at the mouth and said that China intended to attack Taiwan and retake the island by force on April 1."

Craig was stunned. "That is a bombshell."

Yossi nodded. "I learned that from an Iranian source yesterday and passed it on to Tel Aviv."

"Did they let Washington know?"

Yossi shrugged. "I assume so. We're not directly involved in the Taiwan issue. My job is to find out is what those Chinese military people are doing here that impacts our neighborhood."

"The two might be related."

"Agreed. Unfortunately, we don't have reliable sources in Beijing. The strength of our relationship with Washington has precluded that. Still, from what we know already, something big is going down in the Middle East, apart from the attack on Taiwan."

"Let me ask you something else." Craig removed the cell phone from his pocket and pulled up the picture of the man with the mustache from Calgary. "You've seen lots of people in Iranian intelligence over the years. Do you recognize this man?"

Craig handed Yossi the phone.

"Nope. Never saw him before. What's he have to do with this?"

"Somehow, he's involved with the people who killed Francesca. If I get my hands on him, I'll make him tell me who's the mastermind of this conspiracy."

Yossi smiled. "I wouldn't like to be that guy. I can imagine what you'd do to him."

Yossi's cell phone rang. Craig heard him say, "Yes… Yes… Yes."

He put away the phone. "That was the captain. He just docked. He says you better get on board fast. Security agents are moving into the area."

They walked rapidly along an old wooden, battered pier, Yossi leading the way, Craig and Elizabeth following, each wheeling a suitcase. At the end of it sat a fishing vessel, the Rasht, which looked like it had been working these waters for a hundred years. Yossi pointed to it.

"That's the one you're going on," he told Craig. Yossi continued talking while the three of them walked swiftly to the end of the pier. "It's a legitimate fishing vessel. I paid the captain plenty for this trip to Baku for the two of you, so you don't have to give him a thing. His crew, are all Kurds. You don't have to worry about them selling you out."

"That boat looks like it's ready for the junk heap"

Yossi laughed. "Don't be deceived. Last year, he equipped it with new, powerful motors that can outrun the Iranian Navy. Once you're on the open seas, nobody can touch you until you reach Baku."

"Could have fooled me."

"That's the idea. Camouflage the boat's power."

At the end of the pier, Yossi said, "This is as far as I go."

Craig turned to Yossi. "How can I ever thank you for everything you've done for us."

"Always a pleasure, my friend." The Israeli came over and hugged Craig. "Keep that gun handy. You're a long way from Baku."

39

THE CASPIAN SEA

The captain, with creased leathery skin, missing two front teeth, was waiting on the deck, smoking a pungent cigarette, as Craig and Elizabeth climbed aboard. "You two go down and hide in my cabin," he said. "Keep out of sight until we're clear of the port. Then you can come back up on deck."

"How soon do we leave?" Craig asked.

"I need a green light from the Harbor Master. I don't want to do anything unusual if I don't have to. Once I saw you coming, I put in the request. My guess is he'll give us a green light in thirty minutes."

Craig would have preferred to depart now, but he knew the captain was right. An unauthorized departure was likely to bring Iranian military in boats to block them while they were still in the harbor. The Rasht might be able to outrun military craft on the open sea, but they'd be sitting ducks in port. Craig took Elizabeth by the arm and led her below.

The captain's cabin, badly in need of a coat of paint, was paneled in dark wood with a myriad of scratches. Besides the bunk, Craig saw a battered wooden table, an old chest, and two chairs alongside of it. Off to one side was the head behind a wooden door, partially ajar. Elizabeth sat down on the bunk, Craig on a chair.

"Your friend Yossi is amazing," Elizabeth said. "I hate to think where we'd be without him."

"We don't even want to imagine it."

Twenty minutes later, Craig heard a knock on the door of the cabin. Gun in hand, he rose and moved toward the door, placing his body between the door and Elizabeth. "Yes," he said.

Without responding, the captain opened the door. "I have a departure time in twelve minutes."

"Good," Craig replied.

The Captain was frowning. "Not good is that I received a call from one of the regular soldiers who guards this area. A friend. He told me there are now intelligence agents swarming around the town and heading toward the dock. They're looking for a man and a woman. Must be you two. Best if you turn off the lights and wait in here."

"They might come down to search this cabin," Craig said.

"I'll do my best to stop them, but there's always a risk that I'll fail. When it's my departure time, I go unless somebody is on board to stop me."

Once the captain left, Craig led Elizabeth to the head. "We only have one gun. It's better if you wait in here."

"I agree."

"I'll let you know when it's clear."

"Where will you be?"

"Behind that chest," he said, pointing.

He closed the door to the head and turned out the lights in the cabin. From his position, he wouldn't be visible to someone who opened the cabin door, but by looking out, he'd have a clear view of the entire cabin.

Craig checked his watch with the illuminated dial. Only seven minutes until their departure time.

Two minutes later, Craig heard a knock on the door. He gripped the gun tightly. Glancing out from behind the chest, he was watching the door and holding his breath. Slowly, it creaked open. In the light from the corridor, Craig saw an Iranian soldier, pistol in hand. Tall, burley, unshaven, with an oil-stained uniform, he was standing in the doorway looking around while pointing his gun inside the cabin.

The soldier removed a flashlight from his pocket and shined it around the cabin. Craig concealed himself behind the chest. Once the light moved away from him, Craig looked out again. The soldier was walking around the cabin with the gun in one hand and the flashlight in the other. When he came to the head, he looked at the door suspiciously. He reached down with his hand holding the flashlight and grabbed the door knob. Craig couldn't let him go any further. Before the soldier opened the door, Craig stepped out from behind the chest with his gun raised. "Drop your weapon," Craig shouted in Farsi.

Stunned, the soldier pivoted and looked at Craig.

"Drop it, I said!"

Instead of complying, the soldier aimed at Craig and pulled the trigger. Craig leapt to the side, trying to get out of the line of fire. A bullet struck Craig in the side of his right leg, on the upper thigh. The gun fell from Craig's hand. He hurled himself through the air and slammed into the soldier, knocking him off his feet and onto the floor. Bleeding profusely from his leg, Craig was on top pounding the soldier's face with his fists. He felt bones break, but the Iranian was fighting back, kicking and scratching. Craig felt himself weakening. The man slipped out of Craig's grasp, sprang to his feet, and grabbed his pistol. He was aiming at Craig, preparing to fire. Before he pulled the trigger, Craig heard a shot from behind. The soldier went down, an expanding spot of blood in the center of his chest. Craig wheeled around to see Elizabeth holding his gun.

Ignoring the blood oozing from his leg, Craig dropped and checked the soldier. He was dead. Then he searched the man's pockets. All he found was an Iranian intelligence agent's I.D. and a folded piece of white paper. Craig opened it. Staring at him was his own picture with the name Jonathan Wilson on top and the words in Farsi: "FIND THIS MAN."

The captain walked through the open door into the cabin. He took a look at Craig and the soldier on the floor and shook his head. Craig hoped he wouldn't get cold feet about taking them. If need be, Craig could have Elizabeth hold the captain at gunpoint and take out the boat himself, but he didn't want to do that. He looked at the captain expectantly.

"Time to leave the port now," the captain said. "What do you want me to do?"

"Go to Baku."

"What about him?"

"He'll be gone by the time we reach Baku."

The captain nodded. He pointed to Craig's leg. "The medical kit's in the cabinet in the head. If you need help, I can get one of my men."

"I've had training," Elizabeth said.

As soon as the captain was gone, Elizabeth went into the head, grabbed a towel, wrapped it around Craig's leg and tied it as tightly as she could to stop the bleeding.

"You have to get off that leg," she said. She led him over to the captain's bunk, put another towel under him and helped him stretch out.

Craig heard a boat whistle. They were moving. Thank God for that.

Craig's leg was throbbing. Elizabeth was coming out of the head holding the medical kit.

"Don't worry," she said. "I once saw someone deal with a gunshot wound on Gray's Anatomy. Should be a piece of cake."

"Very funny. Where'd you have training?"

"With the U.S. military, before I went into Iraq as an embedded reporter in the second Gulf war. They taught us how to clean and suture a wound. It's not rocket science."

Before she had a chance to start on his leg, Craig heard the cell phone ringing in the dead soldier's pocket. "Grab his phone," Craig said to Elizabeth.

She pulled it out, still ringing and handed it to Craig. He heard in Farsi, "Where are you?"

Craig answered, "All clear on the Rasht. I've left the boat. On the way back."

"Well get a move on."

"Yes sir."

Elizabeth untied the towel and inspected his leg. "Looks as if the bullet grazed you and came out."

"That's what I figure."

Elizabeth unscrewed the top on a bottle of antiseptic. "This will sting."

"Do whatever it takes."

She poured the antiseptic on the wound, cleaning it. It hurt like hell. Craig bit down hard on his lip. He watched her remove sutures from the first aid kit.

"I'll have to stitch this up," she said. "Otherwise, it's never going to stop bleeding."

He admired the confidence with which she worked though she was a novice. Craig gripped the edge of the bed hard in response to the pain. Then she applied gauze and adhesive.

"My work won't win any prizes," she said. "Hopefully, it will hold until we get you to a doctor in Baku."

"Let's see how it goes."

"You don't want to run the risk of infection."

"We'll see what shape I'm in when we hit Baku or London."

Thirty minutes later, they were on the open seas.

"Anybody in sight?" Craig asked her.

She looked out of the porthole and shook her head.

They lifted the dead soldier and shoved his body through the porthole and into the sea. "Good riddance," Elizabeth said.

She led Craig back to the bunk, then asked, "Where are we going from London?"

"To Washington. I have to see President Brewster. Did you hear what Yossi told me?"

"Every word."

"Then you know we only have eight days to avoid disaster for the United States."

She nodded.

They docked in Baku without any further incident. Craig thanked the captain. They both left the boat. The captain had telephoned ahead. A taxi was waiting to take them to the airport. "We should get you to a doctor immediately," Elizabeth said.

"Not here. The flight to London leaves in less than two hours. We have to be on that plane. If not, we're stuck here for a full day."

At the airport, they bought tickets for the London flight and then a connecting BA flight to Washington.

At Heathrow, she pleaded with him to see a doctor, but he refused.

"Did anyone ever tell you that you're stubborn?"

"Never. Fact is you did such a good job fixing the wound. I'm fine."

"And you're such a liar."

As they walked around Heathrow, Craig's leg throbbed. He was feeling feverish. Without alarming Elizabeth, he looked down. The wound wasn't bleeding into his pants. The sutures seemed to be holding. There was a hospital in Uxbridge about half an hour ride from the terminal. He knew he should go there before flying, but he didn't want to waste the time. He had to get to Washington. The United Sates was on the brink of catastrophe.

PART THREE

THE OVAL OFFICE

40

MCLEAN, VIRGINIA

Elizabeth was worried and frightened. For the last two hours of the flight to Washington, Craig seemed increasingly listless. He was sweating. Once when he got up to go to the toilet, he fell back down again into his seat. He looked as if he might pass out. From loss of blood? Or infection?

Repeatedly, she glanced at his right leg. She noticed blood on his pants. She couldn't determine whether it was a reopening of the wound or old dried blood. When he dozed, she touched his forehead. He was hot. At least a hundred and two, she guessed. Infection must be setting in.

Approaching the rental car, she took charge. "Get in on the passenger side. I'm driving."

He didn't argue.

As soon as they were out of the lot, she activated the GPS system and entered "Fairfax Hospital."

"What are you doing?" he asked.

"Getting you to the hospital."

"You can't do that."

"This insanity has to end."

"As soon as they know it's a gunshot wound, the paperwork will be endless. They'll never release me without police authorization. We know somebody in Washington is mixed up in this. Once police reports start flying around on e-mail, I'll be good as dead."

"But if you don't get treated right now, you could lose your leg… or die."

"Call Dr. Rollins. Ed Rollins. He's a good friend of many years. He lives in McLean. About three miles from my house."

She pulled over to the side of the road and yanked out her cell phone. Before she had a chance to dial information, Craig said, "703-555-8944. You can tell him everything."

A man answered. "Hello."

"I want to speak to Dr. Rollins."

"This is Dr. Rollins. Who's calling?"

"My name is Elizabeth Crowder. I'm with Craig Page. He has a medical emergency."

"What's wrong?"

"Craig was shot in the leg in Iran. I sutured it in a boat on the way to Baku. Not very well, I'm afraid. We've flown back from there. Just arrived at Dulles. He needs medical help desperately. He refuses to go to the hospital."

"That sounds like Craig. Do you have transportation?"

"I'm in a rental car with him."

"Is he coherent enough to direct you to my house?"

"I think so."

"Good. Come immediately. My doctor's office is downstairs. I'm a cardiologist, but I'll get in touch with a surgeon friend of mine. We can treat it here."

A wave of relief passed over Elizabeth. "Oh thank you so much."

"If he passes out on you, call me back. I'll give you directions."

Elizabeth put down the phone and turned to Craig. "Dr. Rollins wants you to come to his place. He'll have somebody there to treat you."

"Good. After that, we can go to my house to spend the night."

Craig gave her directions. Traffic was insane. She'd forgotten how bad it was in the Washington area. The rush hour went on and on. And the drivers were fierce. Nobody yielded an inch. On top of all that, it started to drizzle. What should have been a fifteen minute drive became forty-five.

Near the end of the ride, Craig was moaning and mumbling to himself, fading in and out. He's going into shock. He's never going to make it, she feared. Her hands were shaking on the wheel.

Fortunately, he'd given her the address and directions. Dr. Rollins lived in a high-end subdivision. She pulled onto his street and frantically searched for numbers on mailboxes. There it was. She pulled into the driveway marked "MEDICAL ENTRANCE" of a sprawling red brick split level.

Outside lights immediately came on. A white haired, fit-looking man, in his early sixties, Elizabeth guessed, wearing a shirt and slacks charged out to the car pushing a wheel chair. He looked familiar. Then it hit her. He'd been at the cemetery for Francesca and at Craig's house afterwards. She'd never spoken to him, but she remembered his face.

Dr. Rollins opened the car door on the passenger side. He helped Craig out and into the chair. "What did you do to yourself this time?"

Dr. Rollins pushed Craig into the house, along a corridor to a treatment room, and helped him up onto an examining table. God, he looks so pale, Elizabeth thought.

"I called Harry Webster, the surgeon," Dr. Rollins said. "He's on his way over with a nurse and equipment."

"No," Craig protested, barely coherent. "Gun shot. Records."

"Don't worry. Harry owes me big time because I dropped

everything about a year ago when he had a heart attack and saved his life. He was happy to do a favor back. Everything will be off the books. He'll be here in about fifteen minutes. All I'll do is watch your vital signs until he arrives."

Elizabeth breathed a sigh of relief. Dr. Rollins was checking his blood pressure. She paced until she heard the doorbell ring. When Dr. Rollins opened the door, Elizabeth was startled to see Dr. Webster was about her age. How's a guy this young have a near fatal heart attack, she wondered. The nurse, following, could have been his mother.

Dr. Rollins approached Elizabeth. "Unless you have a burning desire to be a doctor, my suggestion is that you go out to the waiting room." He pointed down the corridor. "Read a magazine or watch TV. I'd love to have you meet my wife, Allison, but tonight's her bridge night."

"Thanks. I'll get out of the way."

She entered the waiting room and was surprised. This doesn't look like any doctor's office she'd ever seen. Dr. Rollins was not only a football fan, he was a Washington Redskins nut. The walls were plastered with memorabilia from the Redskins' glory days. Uniforms of famous players. Framed sports pages from the first Joe Gibbs era. Souvenir footballs. Everything she could have imagined. No *Time, Newsweek,* or *National Geographic* in the pile. Only *Sports Illustrated* with Redskins players or coaches on the cover and programs from games.

Elizabeth resumed pacing.

Please God, let Craig be okay. I don't want to lose him.

41

CULPEPER, VIRGINIA

As Kirby drove to the Johnnie Reb Saloon to meet Ali, in his mind flashed what he had learned earlier this evening from reading Craig's personnel file with the CIA, in the hope he'd find something useful.

Though he hated that bastard Craig, he had to concede, albeit reluctantly, that Craig had repeatedly shown great creativity and tenacity in completing assignments. He was also an incredible risk taker. But most of all, he had been damn lucky that he hadn't been killed on numerous occasions. Yeah, Kirby never knew anybody so lucky.

Once, three Hezbollah gunmen had him cornered in a waterfront café in the port area in Beirut. He jumped onto a fishing boat heading out to sea, then took cover, while their bullets whistled over his head. That boat being there was pure luck.

Another time he'd been pursuing Al Qaeda operatives in a motor boat off the coast of Oman. They turned their boat and opened fire with grenade launchers, which blew his boat apart. The terrorists were convinced he was dead and never went back to check. Miraculously, as he floated holding onto debris, a U.S. Navy vessel picked him up an hour later. Talk about luck.

Kirby had been in his office and had just finished reading about the Oman incident when Ali called to say, "I have information. We have to meet. I'll buy you a barbecue."

Kirby was excited. What had Ali learned? Perhaps Craig's luck had finally run out.

Kirby pulled into the parking lot, took off his shirt and tie.

At nine o'clock, the Johnnie Reb Saloon was crowded with a loud, raucous gang of men. A jukebox was blasting a Reba McEntire song, "Take It Back." A dozen men were milling around a pool table. Bells were ringing on pinball machines. Despite Virginia law, cigarette smoke wafted through the dimly lit air.

Walking across the sawdust-covered floor, Kirby spotted Ali at his usual table in the corner. As he sat down, Kirby said, "Hey, can we meet somewhere else in the future? Why do you like this place?"

"Because none of your rich and famous shiny ass Washington movers and shakers would ever set foot in this place. So we never have to worry about anybody who counts seeing us or overhearing what we say. That good enough for you?"

The skinny waitress, Kirby remembered from the last time, Jesus they must disregard child labor laws too, came over to the table.

"Something to drink?" she asked him.

Kirby saw Ali had a beer.

"Yes, a Bud." Having worked through dinner in the office, reading Craig's file, he was hungry. "And a plate of ribs."

"Make that two," Ali added.

When she was gone, Kirby said, "What's the news from Iran? Did your guys finally kill that bastard, Craig?"

Kirby held his breath.

"We're getting close."

Kirby's spirits sagged. That meant no.

"How close?"

"We've learned they were traveling under the names of Jonathan Wilson and Ann Wilson. Also staying at the Laleh International hotel."

"From which they no doubt fled by the time your guys got there."

"That's true, but…"

The skinny teenybopper returned with his beer and ribs. They looked good, Kirby had to admit. Ali paused to eat. Kirby, too. The ribs were tasty. He sipped some beer.

"Alright. You were saying?"

"We also found a cab driver whom Craig tied up and left by the side of the road in northern Tehran."

Kirby perked up. "Where was the cab taking him?"

"Originally to the airport. When Craig saw the roadblocks, he put a gun to the cabby's head and forced him to drive them to an intersection in the northern part of the city. The cabby overheard Craig telling Elizabeth a friend would pick them up there and drive them across the border into Turkey. We have every border crossing covered." Ali was smirking. "What do you think of that?"

"I think you're full of shit. Same as you were in Canada."

Ali was taken aback. "What do you mean?"

"You still don't know how he got out of Canada. Do you?"

Ali chewed on a rib. "That's true."

"Well, I'll tell you. He took a boat from Vancouver."

"How do you know that?"

"Because I read Craig's CIA file. He likes boats. I'll bet anything you're wasting your time at the Turkish border. He and Elizabeth are long gone from Iran. They took a boat to Baku."

The smirk was gone from Ali's face. Kirby continued, "I can prove this one."

"Yeah."

Convinced he was on to something, Kirby was excited.

"Tell me how you'd get out of Baku?"

"By plane. Either to Moscow on Aeroflot or BA to London."

Kirby took out his cell phone and called the airline tracking office at CIA headquarters. He could immediately tell that Cindy, the woman on duty, was pleased to be talking to the Director himself. "Yes, Mr. Kirby. What can I do for you?"

"Access the manifests for any BA plane from Baku to London in the last twenty-four hours."

"Sure. Give me a minute."

Seconds later she said, "There was only one. BA 694."

"Were Jonathan and Ann Wilson on that plane?"

"Let me check."

There was a pause. "Yes, Mr. Kirby. Both of them."

Kirby signaled Ali with a thumbs up. "I want to know where they went from London."

"That's harder. We don't know the airline. And I guess they could have stayed in London."

"Let's start with BA. Look at possible connecting flights with BA694 to New York? L.A.? Or Washington?"

"You want me to call you back?"

Kirby was too impatient for that. Besides, he had to keep the pressure on Cindy. "I don't mind holding."

Another pause. Then she said, "They connected to BA 126 and arrived at Dulles at 7:05 this evening, about two hours ago."

Kirby was elated. For Ali's benefit, he recited her words.

He thanked Cindy and hung up. Now it was Kirby's turn to smirk. "I'm damn smart. Aren't I?"

Ali took out his own cell phone. "We have to assume they'll spend the night at Craig's house. Right?"

Kirby nodded.

"I'll call my guys parked in front of Craig's house. See whether they've shown up."

Ali made the call, then put the phone down and said to Kirby, "No sign of them yet."

"They probably went out to dinner. They'll be coming home soon. Tell your men to move their car to a position three houses away to avoid suspicion. Wait until they're in the house. Then immediately break in and shoot them. I assume they have silencers on their guns."

"Of course."

"Make it look like a robbery."

"We'll do it. Craig and Elizabeth are good as dead." Ali stood up. "Pay the bill. I'm going over there myself."

42

McLEAN, VIRGINIA

Dr. Rollins walked into the waiting room. He wasn't smiling. That scared Elizabeth.

"How is he?" she asked anxiously.

"Dr. Webster is wrapping up. He's convinced the bullet's not in there. The wound, while serious, is superficial, no damage to the bone or nerves. He's cleaned and re-sutured it. By the way, he said you didn't do a bad job."

"Thanks."

"It was infected. He's given Craig some powerful pills for the infection, others for pain, because it will hurt like hell. Although knowing Craig, I doubt he'll use the pain killers. The wound's deep enough that it will take a while to heal. Here's where you can help."

"Sure. I'll do anything."

"Dr. Webster told him to stay off the leg whenever possible and not run. There's a possibility he could reopen the wound. I have no idea what you two are doing that got him shot, and I don't want to know. Just get him to take it easy on the leg. I realize that's easier said than done."

"I'll do my best. We were planning to spend the night at his house. Can I drive him over there?"

"Sure. You can borrow my wheelchair if you want. Hopefully, the medicine will work and his fever will be down in the morning."

She thanked Dr. Webster and his nurse, who left. Craig was sitting up on the treatment table, dressed in boxer shorts, a large bandage on his right thigh.

"You were great to take care of me," he said. "Thanks."

Dr. Rollins came in the room, carrying a pair of baggy white workout pants. "These should fit over the bandage."

"Ed, I can't thank you enough."

"I hope this is the last time for you."

Craig laughed. "I doubt it. Can she drive me home?"

"Sure."

Dr. Rollins and Elizabeth helped Craig into the wheelchair. The doctor was pushing; she was holding the front door open. Suddenly, a terrible thought hit her.

No! No! We'll be walking into a trap.

She closed the door, then said, "The people who tried to kill Craig and me may be staking out Craig's house. I have to check before taking him home."

"But if you drive by," Craig said, "they may stop you. They know what you look like."

"Who said I'm driving by? Listen, Dr. Rollins."

"Call me Ed."

"Okay. Ed. Do you have a good pair of binoculars?"

"Many. I take them to Redskins games."

"Good. Give me the ones with the highest magnification."

He left the room and returned a couple of minutes later with what looked like the Rolls Royce of binoculars.

"I was using these when they smashed Joe Theisman's leg. I could see the bone. And they have night vision as well. I'll show you."

"Also, do you have a street map of the area?"

He pulled a book with Fairfax County street maps from a closet.

"Craig, you can tell me what to use for my observation point?"

He gave her a detailed route to follow for the three miles to his subdivision. He told her to park two blocks from the house on a bluff next to a school that would give her a view down to his street. "Then crouch behind a mailbox and look down at the street in front of my house. They'll never see you that way."

With the map and binoculars on the seat next to her, Elizabeth drove off in the rental car.

She followed his instructions, binoculars in hand, moving in a crouch from the car to a position behind the mailbox. She held the binoculars up to her eyes. Below, she saw one car, a gray BMW, parked in front of a house three doors to the left of Craig's. That's where I'd park, she told herself, to avoid suspicion.

She increased the magnification, amazed at how good the binoculars were. She looked into the gray BMW. Two men were in the front. One appeared to be napping; the driver was sipping from a Starbuck's cup. She focused on the car seat. Between them was a rack to hold coffee cups. In it was a gun with a long silencer.

Elizabeth stood up, preparing to return to her car when she saw another car, a silver Jaguar convertible, XK8, pull up behind the gray BMW and park. She dropped down and raised the binoculars again. A man climbed out on the driver's side. Rapidly, he walked toward the BMW. She recognized him. The guy with the mustache who had followed her in Calgary. The driver of the BMW rolled his window down. The two of them talked for a few seconds, then the man with the mustache reached into his pocket, removed something and handed it to the driver, who looked at it. The object was a ski mask. The driver tossed it on the back seat, and the man with the mustache returned to the Jaguar.

He drove slowly down the street, made a U-turn, and parked three houses away from Craig's, on the right. They now had the house covered on both sides.

She'd seen enough. Keeping close to the ground, she beat it back to her car and returned to Rollins's house. Talking quickly, she told Craig and Ed what she'd seen.

As soon as she was done, Craig limped toward his suitcase.

Alarmed, she asked, "What are you doing?"

"Getting the gun I brought from Iran. I'm going over there. I'll find out who sent these goons."

"That's insane."

She raced ahead of him, rummaged through his suitcase, and grabbed the pistol. "No way I'm letting you do that."

He reached out his hand. "Gimme the gun."

She held it behind her back. "You'll have to physically take it from me. Even if I go with you, we're outnumbered by three to two, one of whom is a cripple. We'll have one gun, and they'll have lots more firepower."

"Gimme the gun, I said."

He was glaring at her. "I mean it." He was raising his voice, sounding angry. "Right now."

She held her ground.

I won't let you take the gun. Never.

Craig limped across the room toward her. Ed cut him off.

"Okay children," Ed said with the voice of authority. "That's enough. Craig, with your leg, you're not in shape to do anything like that tonight. Harry Webster and I didn't spend our evening fixing you up so you'd make a good impression if someone opened the lid of your coffin. Elizabeth's right. It's an insane idea. Both of you sleep here tonight and forget about them."

Craig said, "But…"

Elizabeth interrupted him. "Besides, you have to get to the White House tomorrow and talk to President Brewster. Stopping the April 1 attack is most important."

He sighed deeply. "I guess you're right."

"Don't worry. We'll get another chance to deal with these thugs."

"Okay," he looked at Rollins. "Can I at least have a glass of Armagnac?"

Rollins shook his head. "Alcohol's not good with the medicine."

"I'm being double teamed. To hell with both of you. I'm going to sleep."

"That's the smartest thing you've said in a while," Elizabeth told him.

43

McLEAN, VIRGINIA

Craig was surprised at how much better he felt in the morning. His leg had stopped throbbing. The pain, so great last night that he almost took one of those Percocets Ed gave him, was easing. He was definitely on the mend.

Wearing Ed's warmup pants, he limped in to the kitchen where Ed, Elizabeth, and Allison, Ed's wife, were having breakfast. Allison got up and gave him a hug. "Sorry I missed you last evening."

"Thanks. You didn't miss much."

Ed asked, "How are you feeling?"

"Much better."

Craig poured a cup of coffee.

"How about an omelet?" Allison said.

Craig looked at Elizabeth. "Morning," he said. "Sorry. I got a little carried away last evening."

She smiled at him. "I guess that's an apology."

He smiled back. "The only one you'll get."

He ate the omelet with toast and went into the den with the cell phone in one hand and a coffee cup in the other.

For openers, he talked his way past the White House switchboard to Kathy, the President's secretary. Then he took a deep breath and plunged right in.

"Kathy, this is Craig Page. About a year ago, I…"

"Oh, I remember you and your daughter, Francesca."

Hearing her name strengthened his resolve to find her killers and avenge her death.

"When I received the Medal of Freedom, President Brewster said if I ever needed to see him, I should call and tell you, and you would arrange it. I would very much like to see him today about a matter of national security. Also, I would appreciate it if he didn't mention my call to anyone else."

He held his breath, expecting her to say, "The President's awfully busy" or "submit your request in writing." Instead, he heard, "Just a minute. I'll go in and ask President Brewster about his availability."

A moment later, she returned to the phone, "The President can see you at eleven this morning."

"I'll be there."

He returned to the kitchen and told the others he had a date with President Brewster.

"You're in no condition to drive," Elizabeth said. "I'll drive you down there, hang out somewhere in the area. You can call me on my cell when you're done. I'll pick you up."

"I don't like that idea. I want you to come with me to the meeting. We've been together from the beginning. I wouldn't be here if it weren't for you. In fact, I wouldn't be alive."

She shook her head emphatically. "A reporter in the Oval Office will spook Brewster and chill your discussion. Also, McDermott's been blasting him in Trib editorials. When he hears I was with the Trib, you won't get what you want."

"I don't think Brewster's like that."

"Trust me. Now you're in my territory. I know a little bit about politicians and the press."

"Fair enough."

"Hey, you have a problem," Allison said to Craig.

"What's that?"

"I can see that big bandage bulging through Ed's warm up pants. You can't wear those to the White House, and I doubt if you'll be able to get on your own pants."

Allison loved nice clothes. Craig couldn't resist. "Oh my god, I'm going to the White House. What'll I wear?"

They all laughed.

Allison had an answer. "There's a men's store in the strip mall down the road, run by this Chinese couple."

Hearing the word Chinese, Craig looked at Elizabeth and smiled. She smiled back. "I'll call him," Allison said. "Ed buys a lot of stuff there. I'm sure he'll custom fit a suit for you while you wait."

"Great. Elizabeth and I will get our stuff together. Then we're out of here."

As he packed, Craig thought: Things are looking up. He was in a better mood. His leg was healing. He had his meeting with President Brewster.

Suddenly, he heard Allison scream, "Come quick."

He and Elizabeth raced into the den. The television was on the channel seven news. He saw a picture of his house on the screen. And the announcer saying, "Again repeating the hour's top story. In this quiet residential McLean neighborhood, at about 2:30 am, a woman saw a man in a ski mask break into her neighbor's house and another man parked in front. She called the police who responded immediately. There was a shootout. Two police officers were killed. Both men escaped in a gray BMW. Police believe it was a burglary. The house was unoccupied at the time."

Craig was stunned.

"Why'd they break in?" Elizabeth asked.

"Looking for information to help find me. Or to plant a bomb they could detonate by remote control if I come home. We're in an all-out war. And they're becoming desperate. God only knows what they'll try next."

44

PARIS

General Zhou preferred sex before dinner, not after. He found that, with age, alcohol dulled his senses and his libido. Also, there was the relaxation factor. Feeling satisfied, he could more thoroughly enjoy the meal.

On the last trip to Paris, as the General had directed, Captain Cheng asked the Military Attaché at the Chinese Embassy to find a woman who worked at the high end. "And I want her blonde, tall, and busty." She arrived wearing a fashionable, conservative, black raincoat, nothing to make her stand out on the sophisticated Rue St. Honore. Under it, she was dressed simply, but elegantly, in a pale pink silk blouse, black skirt, and five inch black stiletto heels. No heavy makeup. No tart look.

"Get her back again," General Zhou told his aide.

Bridgette—she called herself—liked champagne, he remembered. He had a bottle of Dom Perignon chilling in an ice bucket.

Adroitly, she opened the champagne and poured two glasses. General Zhou, dressed in a dark suit and tie, playing the role of a Chinese businessman, sipped a little and put it down.

"I'm glad your assistant called me again," she said. "I enjoyed being with you the last time."

He doubted her sincerity, but he had to admit she was good at what she did.

"I've never been with any other Chinese man."

"Was I different than you expected?"

"More considerate. Not so rough."

He smiled. "You thought we're all savages?"

She blushed. "No. Not that... I don't know what I thought."

Westerners' views of Chinese never ceased to amaze him.

And what was she? They had always spoken English. He had enough of an ear to know she wasn't from France. Eastern European? Perhaps Czech?

"Where are you from?" he asked.

She looked at him anxiously.

"I won't tell anyone."

"Russia. Moscow. My real name is Androshka."

He frowned and pursed his lips together. He hated the fucking Russians.

"You don't like Russians, do you?" she said.

"How could you tell?"

"Your face is an open book. Besides, as a wealthy Chinese businessman, I'm sure you must have clashed with our crooked oligarchs."

He nodded.

"That's why I left Moscow. I couldn't take the crime and corruption. Not to mention the contempt for women those people have."

"Were you the girlfriend of one of those billionaire Russian businessmen who behave like thugs?"

"Let's just say I had a relationship with one."

"Then you were lucky to escape Russia with your life."

"Believe me. I know that."

His cell phone on the desk rang. He walked over and picked it up. General Yang in Beijing.

"One moment," he told Yang.

Androshka said, "I can leave if you have to talk."

"No need to do that." He'd mostly listen. He doubted if she knew Chinese, but he'd make sure not to give anything away. Just in case.

"What happened?" he asked Yang.

"The Americans are responding to our preparations to retake the renegade province of Taiwan. They're moving warships and aircraft carriers toward Taiwan. Spies in Tokyo have informed us the Americans put the Japanese on alert."

Perfect. The brilliant Americans have fallen for the decoy.

"Keep me posted," he said.

He glanced across the room. Androshka left her chair and was sashaying toward the bathroom. Minutes later, she emerged, wearing only a white terry cloth robe and those stiletto heels, her clothes on a hanger.

He dialed his brother's cell. Smiling, she sat down on the sofa facing him.

"Our friends across the water are doing what we hoped."

"That's good news," Zhou Yun said.

"How about the other front?"

"Craig Page?"

"Precisely."

His eyes moved to Androshka. The robe was open. Her breasts, gorgeous, round and perfectly proportioned. Her legs were spread. Her bush, blond and welcoming, at the fusion of her long beautiful legs. She raised a finger to her lips, wet it, then touched herself between her legs. Becoming aroused, he wanted to end the call as soon as possible.

The General's brother said, "No news, I'm afraid. I called Kirby's father. He says his son's working on it."

"Tell him to work harder."

"I did."

General Zhou hung up, put down the phone, and stood up, his pants bulging in front. She slipped out of the robe, letting it drop to the floor, then walked over to him. She was the most beautiful woman he'd ever seen. In those heels they were the same height. He put his arms around her and kissed her. Her hands were busy. Undoing his tie; unbuttoning his shirt and pulling it off; unzipping his pants. She grabbed his erect penis. "You're rock hard," she said. "Just from looking at me. I love that. It means you want me."

"Oh, do I."

She dropped to her knees and took him into her mouth, playing with his balls as she sucked, her blond hair flopping over her eyes. He thought he'd explode in her mouth.

She stood and led him over to the bed where she ripped off the covers. "On your back," she ordered him. Then she climbed on top and lowered her breasts into his mouth. First one and then the other, her nipples pink and taut.

"Oh yes," she moaned. "Yes."

She sat up and guided him into her. With her hands behind her as an anchor and her legs alongside his body, digging those heels into the bed, she moved rapidly, breathing heavily, her forehead dotted with perspiration. He felt an incredible pleasure, on and on and on, like nothing else.

"I'm coming," she cried. "Now. You too."

He exploded inside of her.

As she rolled off, he said, "It's never been like that for me before."

"Nor me," she said.

He knew she was lying. He didn't care.

Minutes later, she got up and walked across the room. She

returned with two glasses of champagne and one of his Davidoffs from the box on the desk.

"You're a wonderful lover," she said.

They paused to sip champagne. Now he enjoyed the wine.

"Take me back to China with you."

He was flabbergasted. "What?"

She picked up a pack of matches from the night table, bit off the end of the cigar, placed it in her mouth, lit it, and handed it to him. No woman had ever done that before.

"I'm serious. I came to France with hopes. But they haven't been realized. It's a tough life in this country. Especially for a foreigner."

"China isn't easy. Even more difficult."

"But China's the future. That's where the growth is. And I'll have you, an important man. I'll be good for you, like this evening. We'll take care of each other. Nobody will have to know."

The idea of a gorgeous Russian mistress seemed fitting for the most powerful man in China, and his cow of a wife wouldn't dare question him.

"Before you leave," he said, "make sure my aide has all your contact information. He'll call you in a month and arrange your plane to Beijing. Meantime, start taking Chinese classes."

I'm on a roll, General Zhou thought. No stopping me now.

45

WASHINGTON

When Craig limped in to the Oval Office, President Brewster came out from behind his green, leather-topped desk, cut across the pale blue carpet with the Presidential seal in the center, and shook his hand. The bandage on Craig's leg produced a bulge on his thigh, even in the custom-fitted pants.

"Thanks for agreeing to see me, Mr. President."

"I told you my door would always be open to you, and I mean what I say. What happened to your leg?"

"That's why I'm here, Sir. I was shot in Iran."

Brewster's head snapped back. "What were you doing there? A CIA assignment?"

"It's a long story, Mr. President."

"I've got plenty of time." Brewster pointed to the sofa and chairs in a corner of the office. "Make yourself comfortable and drop the Mr. President."

"Yes, Sir."

"That too."

Before Craig sat down, the door opened and a tall, thin, bookish-looking man in a three piece suit, gold chain across the vest, entered. Brewster said, "You remember Jim Gorman, my chief of staff."

"Sure, from the awards ceremony."

They nodded to each other, then Gorman, pad and pencil in hand, moved to a chair in the corner. He won't participate. He'll only listen, Craig recalled.

Craig sat in a straight-backed chair, Brewster across from him.

He took a deep breath and began. "About six months ago, Kirby eliminated my job in a reorganization, so I left the CIA."

"Kirby let you go?" Brewster sounded incredulous and outraged. "A few months ago, I asked him about you. He said you decided to retire from the agency and open a consulting firm in Milan. 'A midlife crisis,' he called it."

"That's absolutely false. He fired me and dressed it up to look like a reorganization."

"Not somebody as good as you. What was he thinking?"

Craig didn't want to tell Brewster it was payback time because of Madison Square Garden. That would only divert from his objective today. So he simply said, "These things happen in all organizations."

"You should have come to me. I would have reversed that decision. Maybe even replaced Kirby, which I'm planning to do before long."

Craig was now sorry he hadn't called Brewster. "I appreciate your saying that. Anyhow, I started a consulting firm, based in Milan, assisting governments dealing with international terrorism. Also private companies. A couple weeks ago, I was in Rome, and I learned that my daughter Francesca had been killed in what seemed to be an auto accident."

"How awful. I remember Francesca. She was a reporter with the *New York Tribune*. Very smart young woman. I hope you're not going to tell me she was killed when she was in Iran working on a story."

Damn, Brewster was smart, Craig thought. "Not exactly, but you're close. She was murdered in Calgary, Canada. She had been in Tehran a few days earlier. The story she was researching involved an agreement between Iran and China. I went to Calgary, then to Iran to find out what the story was, figuring that way I'd identify her killers and bring them to justice."

"Have you?"

"Not yet. But I have uncovered a very serious threat to the United States."

Brewster leaned forward, concentrating on Craig's words. "You said an agreement between Iran and China?"

"That's right."

"What's it provide?"

"I don't know all the details yet. But here's what I've learned so far. On April 1, one week from today, China and Iran will implement a far-reaching agreement involving oil and joint military action. The Chinese are trying to control all of the oil in the Middle East. The Iranians will assist them by launching attacks on Arab oil producers with Chinese military equipment. I know there's a written document confirming this agreement, but I haven't seen it. Francesca was close to discovering this. So I'm convinced that Chinese or Iranian agents killed her. Or someone working with them."

Brewster looked stunned and horrified. "You've described a nightmare scenario. An agreement like that would do incredible damage to the U.S. Shutting off our Middle East oil supply would cripple this country economically. I don't even want to imagine the consequences."

"I agree. That's why I came to you."

"How confident are you of this?"

"I'm positive."

Craig had a firm policy of never disclosing his sources, but for the President he'd make an exception. "In Iran, I had confirmation from three separate sources: a CIA covert agent by the name of Jurgenson, who was murdered after he spoke to me, an Iranian intelligence official, and an Israeli covert agent."

Brewster gave a deep sigh. "That sounds like pretty good substantiation. You did all this yourself."

"I was accompanied the whole way by Elizabeth Crowder, formerly Francesca's editor at the *New York Tribune*. Elizabeth shared my view that Francesca was murdered. When she wanted to come with me to pursue Francesca's story, her boss, McDermott, refused to permit it. So she quit."

"I've heard of Elizabeth. She did a great series on the Taliban in Afghanistan a couple of years ago. She sounded like a gutsy woman."

"She saved my life by killing the Iranian soldier who shot me in the leg."

"Where is she now?"

"Waiting for me on the street near the White House."

"You should have brought her with you."

"I wanted to, but she thought…"

Brewster waved his hand dismissing Craig's thought before he completed it. "I wouldn't judge her by that asshole McDermott. I've had run-ins with him when he published distortions of what I said. Can you get her to join us?"

"Sure."

Craig took out his cell phone and called Elizabeth. "I'll be there in ten minutes," she said, sounding excited.

Craig told that to the President, who was now pacing.

"Why didn't Kirby know about this agreement? Is our intel so piss-poor?"

"Actually, he was informed about it by a CIA covert agent in Iran, the one I spoke with, and by the Director of the Mossad."

"Then why didn't he tell me?"

Craig shrugged. "Perhaps he's seeking additional substantiation before he comes to you."

"Damn that Kirby. I've told him I want to know about trouble early, even if it's not fully substantiated. He just came to me with information about a possible Chinese invasion of Taiwan. Also scheduled for April 1."

"I've heard about that, too. I was going to tell you about it."

"We're moving ships and planes to the area. I don't know whether the threat's real, or they're posturing. We may be on the verge of a war in the Pacific. Now you tell me the Middle East is about to explode."

"That pretty well describes it."

"One of my options, I suppose, is to call Chinese President Li direct, tell him what you learned, and tell him they had better call off their attack on Taiwan, as well as their agreement with Iran."

Craig swallowed hard. He didn't know Brewster that well. Contradicting the President of the United States could be risky, but he had to do it. "I have to disagree with that approach, Mr. President. I'm afraid if you went to the Chinese President now, when we don't have a copy of the agreement with Iran or more concrete information about the attack on Taiwan, you won't have much chance of getting him to call off the Chinese action. If you don't have hard evidence, he'll simply deny everything and forge ahead."

"Then what do you think I should do?"

"If we learned all the details of the Chinese-Iranian agreement, and more important, if we obtained a copy of the written document before April 1, you might be able to intimidate the Chinese into backing down. And if they won't, with that kind of evidence, you might be able to mount joint action by many affected parties. Meantime, you'd be able to prepare the Saudis and other oil producers for an attack. Or even launch a preemptive attack on Iran."

"All of that's fine, but..."

The intercom buzzed. Brewster walked across the room to the phone. "Yes."

Kathy replied, "Elizabeth Crowder is here."

"Send her in."

Brewster walked over and shook her hand. "I hear you saved this young man's life." He pointed to Craig.

She blushed. "That may be an exaggeration."

"I appreciate everything you've done for the country. Come sit down," he said warmly.

She sat on the sofa, facing Craig.

"The big question," Brewster said, "is how can we obtain a copy of the written agreement between China and Iran?"

Craig took a deep breath. Well here goes. "Authorize me and Elizabeth to go to Beijing as your representatives to obtain it."

"Do you have a chance?"

"We'll give it our best shot."

"You've never been stationed in China."

"That's an advantage. They won't know me."

"Is there enough time? If you're right, we're operating on an April 1 deadline."

"If we take a day to prepare and fly there the next day, that'll leave us five days."

"I can provide you with help in China."

"Who?" Craig asked, holding his breath, hoping the President didn't want to involve Kirby.

"Our Ambassador in Beijing, Bill March, is an old friend. He was a New York investment banker, partner in Hansell Gray. Bill and I go way back. I appointed him right after I took office, so he's been in Beijing two years. He's very bright and a hell of a good man. When Bill visited Washington about a month ago, we spent time together. I was impressed with how much he's been able to accomplish in Beijing in terms of developing lines of communication with key Chinese officials. Bill will help you."

"That's an excellent idea." Craig was delighted to have assistance from someone like March.

Brewster gave Craig March's private telephone number. "I'll let Bill know you're coming. I'll also tell him you may be using a different name. I presume you will be using some kind of alias."

"That's correct, Mr. President."

"With March, use the code Madison Square Garden so he'll know who you are."

"Will do, Mr. President."

"Meantime, I'll get Kirby down here and explain to him what you'll be doing in Beijing. I'll also tell him to give you any assistance you need, either from Washington or with agents he has stationed in Beijing."

"I don't need help from Kirby or the CIA, Mr. President. I say this with all humility. Also I'm afraid that once e-mails start flying from Washington to Beijing, talking about my mission, somehow the Chinese will pick up the information. I'll be stopped before I ever get started. So I respectfully ask you not to tell Kirby about my mission to China."

"You want to do this on your own? You and Elizabeth?"

"With the help of Ambassador March, of course."

Brewster stood up and paced around the office. "I don't know," he said softly.

"At least give us a shot this way."

"Okay. Do it," Brewster finally said.

"I appreciate your confidence, Mr. President."

"Keep me informed about what you learn concerning both the Chinese agreement with Iran and the attack on Taiwan. March has a secure phone at the Embassy. Any time you need it, he'll make it available."

"Will do, Mr. President."

Craig stood to leave. Elizabeth too.

Brewster said, "There's a great deal riding on your mission in Beijing. Preventing the outbreak of a war in the Pacific and avoiding serious adverse economic consequences from an agreement between Iran and China."

"I'll do my best, Mr. President."

Elizabeth added. "We promise you that."

"Get that agreement. The security of the United States depends on it."

46

WASHINGTON

"What do we do now?" Elizabeth asked Craig as they walked through the White House gate onto Pennsylvania Avenue.

"We eat. I'm starving. Can't remember the last meal I've had."

"Good. You're feeling better."

"There's a terrific Italian place nearby, Tosca."

"Let's go."

Craig asked the maître d' to seat them in an alcove in the back. They wouldn't be visible from most of the restaurant. If they kept their voices down, they could talk freely.

After they ordered, grilled octopus for her, pasta with seafood for him, Elizabeth said, "I feel as if we've won the lottery. Five days in China."

"Let's hope it's not a one way ticket."

She looked grim. "Do you have to put it that way?"

"Sorry. We have to assume the names Craig Page and Elizabeth

Crowder will ring all the bells at Beijing Airport."

"So you have a plan for getting us in the country."

He nodded. "This evening we fly to San Francisco. Tomorrow we get the documents we'll need in the names of Alexandra and Richard Collier. Passports and visas at a black market place above a produce shop on Grant Street in Chinatown. Then we fly out the next morning."

"Sounds good. For our covers, let's pretend you're a businessman and I'm along for the ride as a tourist. Then I can break off and do some digging myself."

"You have relationships in Beijing?"

"I hired Carl Zerner, the Trib's bureau chief. He could be a source of useful information, and we don't have to worry about him blowing our cover. He hates McDermott almost as much as I do."

Craig was pleased. "I have one other thing to do today."

He visualized Betty sitting at her desk at CIA headquarters, her eyes close to her computer screen, in her hand a cigarette that couldn't be lit because she was inside the building, but would be as soon as she went outside. He was afraid to call her at the office, even though she had a secure phone. "I know Kirby bugs my office," she had told Craig on more than one occasion.

When he dropped out of normal CIA communications to follow Achmed from Dubai to New York and thwart the Madison Square Garden attack, Betty had helped him. They established a secret code.

He took out his cell phone and sent her a text message: "Verona Wine Merchants will be at Calvert Woodley at seven this evening. Hope you can come."

He was asking her to meet him at the M&H Grill in Herndon at three this afternoon. Four hours sooner than the time in his message.

Thirty seconds later, he saw her reply. "I'll be there."

The waiter brought their food. Craig stood up and surveyed the restaurant, which had filled up. The Washington power lunch was going full blast. From pictures in the press and on television, he recognized two presidential assistants, two senators, a congressman, and a couple of powerful lobbyists. But nobody he knew personally, he thought with relief. They'd be able to stay and eat. Instead of dropping cash on the table and running.

At ten minutes to three, Elizabeth pulled into the parking lot for the M&H Grill. Craig told her to park on the side of the restaurant, giving them a view of the entrance to the parking lot. They remained in the car.

When he saw Betty's red Dodge truck, he waved. She drove over and parked next to them. Betty climbed out and got in the back of their car.

Before Craig had a chance to open his mouth, Betty said, "Did you hear what happened at your house last evening?"

"Only what was on TV. Do you know any more than that?"

"Kirby has been leaning hard on the police not to release your identity and background as the owner of the house that was burglarized. He's told them this could be related to your former CIA work. He doesn't want to invite copycat actions against other former or current CIA employees. The intruders killed two cops with high-powered assault rifles. Obviously this was no burglary."

"Very thoughtful of him."

"Apparently, none of the neighbors know what you do. Tell me what's going on?"

"Meet Elizabeth Crowder," Craig said. "She's working with me."

"We spoke briefly at Craig's house after the funeral," Betty said. Elizabeth nodded to her.

"Working with you on what?"

"Francesca didn't die in an accident."

He gave Betty a summary of everything they'd done, including the meeting with Brewster.

"That's a mouthful," she said. "You have to find out who killed Francesca and make them pay for it."

"You can be sure I'll do that."

"Good. Now let's turn to the Chinese-Iranian agreement. If they implement something like that on April 1, we're in deep trouble. What can I do to help?"

"For starters, tell me who's the Agency's station chief in Beijing?"

"Guy by the name of Peter Emery. I don't know anything about him. What are you looking for?"

"Ideally, I'd love it if he were a bit of a maverick like me."

Betty laughed. "A bit?"

"As I was saying, if he's an independent spirit, willing to operate under the radar, without reporting to Kirby or anyone else at headquarters, I might be able to use him in addition to March. We don't have much time. Any chance you can get some info for me?"

"Sure. I'll wait until the office is quiet tonight, then tap into personnel records. I'll call you from home on your cell first thing in the morning."

"Good. We'll be in San Fran. I'll sleep with the phone next to the bed."

She smiled. "Don't you always?"

"Speaking of cell phones," Elizabeth said to Betty, "When we were in Calgary, I took a picture of a man following me. Maybe you could identify him."

Elizabeth pulled up the picture on her cell and showed it to Betty.

"I don't recognize him. Forward the picture to me. I have a number of ID sources."

"Will do."

Betty wrinkled up her nose and continued staring at the picture. "I'm sure I'll ID him. I just need a little time. I have a nagging feeling I've seen him before."

47

PARIS

General Zhou was standing in the living room of his suite in the Bristol as Captain Cheng led in the two Iranians. One, dressed in a western business suit, white shirt, and tie, to conduct the business. The other, bearded with a turban, representing the mullahs, to check on the businessman and make sure he doesn't get out of line.

Zhou didn't bother with formalities. "You asked for this meeting," he said curtly, while pointing to three plush bergiere chairs around a marble top coffee table.

Once they were seated, General Zhou said, "I don't know what you want, but I'm willing to meet with you." He made no effort to conceal the irritation in his voice. He was a busy man, particularly right now. The last thing he needed was a quick trip to Paris. "It's already the twenty-sixth of March. Our agreement is scheduled to be implemented on April 1. At our end, everything is in place. We're ready to proceed."

The Iranian in the business suit stared hard at General Zhou. "It would be premature to proceed. We don't yet have an agreement. Certain important terms haven't been resolved."

General Zhou kept his anger in check. He reached into his pocket and pulled out a copy of the signed document. "You signed it yourself."

The Iranian refused to be intimidated. "Yes, I signed that piece of paper, but it only sets forth a preliminary and partial understanding."

A bunch of fucking rug merchants and liars.

"I don't understand. Everything is spelled out in this document. The commitments that each of us undertakes. Both sides are to implement beginning April 1." General Zhou held the document out in his hand, then waved it around.

The Iranian remained calm. "Of course I know what that document says. As you pointed out, I signed it myself. It specifies that China agrees to provide certain military equipment to my country."

"That's right. And it spells out precisely what that equipment is."

"Yes, but our understanding at the time we signed the document was that it was only a partial list. To be supplemented by further agreement prior to April 1."

"What else do you want?"

"We must have twenty additional batteries of surface to surface missiles, as well as twenty long-range missiles. Also, we must have more sophisticated electronic detection devices that will permit us to detect not only airplanes approaching our territory at a distance of five hundred miles, but also any ships approaching our coast at a distance of five hundred miles as well. The ones you supplied can be jammed by American technology. We want the next generation."

"You have no need for those."

"That's easy for you to say. We'll be the ones facing the entire United States military. If we implement the agreement, you can be certain they will attack us and not your country. This is equipment we need in order to thwart that response by the Americans. It's absolutely essential for us."

"You're worrying needlessly," General Zhou said. "I've reassured you before that you don't have to be concerned about an American response."

"Your nation won't be in the line of fire. Besides, you already have a full range of defensive missiles to safeguard China."

"I've explained to you we have a very high American official working with us on this matter. We have received assurances from him that there will not be an American military response. That should be sufficient for you."

"Who is this American official?"

"I'm sorry. I can't disclose his identity."

"Then I'm equally sorry that our government cannot implement the agreement as it is written. We need the additional protection provided by the supplemental arms which I outlined."

General Zhou felt his face reddening. "Perhaps, we should simply call off the agreement."

Before the Iranian in the business suit had a chance to respond, the bearded man stood up, said something in Farsi to his colleague, and started toward the door.

His colleague in the business suit gathered together his papers and was rising to his feet.

If this is a bluff, it's a good one.

General Zhou said, "I'll tell you what. We could agree to supply ten long range surface-to-surface batteries and the missiles that go with them."

"Ten is not enough. It will have to be fifteen. And fifteen surface to air missiles as well."

"Fifteen it will be." General Zhou said.

"Also additional cash. Another ten million euros."

More graft and corruption finding its way into the mullah's pocket.

"Okay," he said reluctantly. "But that's it, and I want it in writing. The agreement is final."

The Iranians both nodded.

General Zhou pointed to Captain Cheng, who had been standing in front of the window, overlooking a center courtyard. He took two pieces of Bristol Hotel stationery from the desk, removed a pen from his pocket and prepared two copies of a document. He showed it to General Zhou. It specified the additional equipment to be supplied, as well as the cash, and stated, "This is now a final agreement."

General Zhou signed both copies and handed them to the Iranian businessman, who carefully studied the document.

"I assume this is acceptable," General Zhou said.

"Correct."

"Good, then we're finished. Implementation proceeds on April 1."

"Absolutely," the man in the business suit said as he handed a signed copy to General Zhou. He reached out his hand. With a pained look, General Zhou shook it. The bearded man was nodding.

With the meeting over, General Zhou took Captain Cheng aside. "Walk the Iranians downstairs to the lobby and outside to their waiting car. Make certain they're gone from the Bristol and won't be making further demands."

Once Captain Cheng returned, General Zhou gave him a series of orders relating to the movement of Chinese forces, Army, Navy, and Air Force. "I want you to call military headquarters in Beijing," General Zhou told Captain Cheng, "and relay these orders. Tell them to proceed immediately for our April 1 implementation of Operation Dragon Oil."

48

SAN FRANCISCO

The cell phone ringing on the night table woke Craig out of a sound sleep in the two bedroom suite at the four Seasons. It was 4:45 a.m. in San Francisco and Betty was calling. "What did you learn about Peter Emery?" he asked.

"You won't like it."

"Break it to me gently."

"Emery is three years younger than you. He joined the agency a year after you did. He came to the CIA right out college. BA at Yale. Magna. Skull and Bones. Majored in Chinese studies. They have an excellent Chinese department. He was immediately assigned to Asian operations, and he's been there ever since."

"That explains why I never met him."

"But he'll know what you look like. He attended a seminar at headquarters two years ago when you made a presentation about how Al Qaeda cells communicate."

Betty had done good work to dig that out. The audience was about a hundred. He didn't recall Emery. "Do you have a picture?"

"In color. I'll forward it to you."

Seconds later, Craig had it. Emery was heavyset, chunky. What stood out was his carrot-red hair. Unlike Carolyn's, which had been red bordering on brown. He remembered seeing that red hair when he had given his presentation. He was certain he never spent time with Emery alone or in a small group.

"What was he doing at the conference?"

"He was stationed in China at the time. The Chinese were lending support to the Muslim government in the Sudan, which had been waging a cruel and relentless war on Christians in the country. It had become a breeding ground for terrorists."

"What jobs has he had with the agency?"

"He's obviously a bright guy. They put him on a fast track. His first posting was to Japan, where all his reviews were absolutely tops. Then Deputy Station Chief in Thailand. All along he was pushing for China, telling people at headquarters about his Chinese education and language skills. Three years ago, he was sent to Beijing as third in command. Six months ago, Kirby jumped him over the Deputy to make him station chief in record time. He operates out of our Embassy under the cover of cultural attaché."

"What did you get from reading between the lines?"

"As I said, all his reviews have been very good. Strong performance. No weaknesses shown. What comes through to me is that he's no Craig Page. He's a real company man. Also a suck up to Kirby, particularly after Kirby promoted him out of turn to be station chief. He'll follow orders to the letter. Does everything by the book. Whatever he's instructed to do. He won't make any waves. He'll do it well, but he's the kind of agent who will follow the script prepared in Washington and the instructions coming from headquarters. He's ambitious. His main concern is his next promotion."

"Great. So I won't get help from Emery."

"That's an understatement. I'd say do your best to avoid him. He'll notify Kirby if he finds out you're operating under cover for the President."

"What about the man Elizabeth photographed on her cell phone?"

"I haven't been able to ID him, but I'll keep looking. What's bugging me is I think he's one of ours."

"CIA?"

"No. I ran though all our personnel files. Those defense agencies have so many off-the-book operations. He could be with one of them. I'll keep looking."

Her words reinforced Craig's conclusion when they left Calgary. This was a three-headed monster. One Chinese. One Iranian. And one American.

"What else do you have for me?"

"Just some advice. After what happened in McLean, watch your six o'clock. These guys play rough."

"Thanks. I already figured that out."

Craig tried to fall back asleep, but it was hopeless.

Only five days to obtain the document.

49

WASHINGTON

Kirby was puzzled by Kathy's call summoning him to the White House.

As he waited in the reception area, Senator Rogers, the chairman of the Senate Finance Committee, walked out of the Oval Office, saw Kirby and said, "Good luck. He's in one pissy mood today."

Kirby's whole body began shaking when he recalled his meeting with Ali at three yesterday morning, along the tidal basin near the Jefferson Memorial, and Ali telling him about the two dead cops in front of Craig's house. Kirby realized he was now on the hook for conspiracy murder. But Ali glibly said, "Shit happens." Ali wanted to continue watching Craig's house from a remote location, but Kirby told him, "Don't do another Goddamn thing. Kirby was finished dealing with that psychopath and his incompetent lackeys.

Sitting in the Oval Office reception area, Kirby couldn't stop thinking about those two McLean cops. He felt a tugging on his arm. It was Kathy. "I've been telling you, Mr. Kirby, that President Brewster is ready for you, but you haven't heard me. Are you alright?"

"Yeah. I'm great. Sorry. I'm preoccupied, engrossed in thinking about CIA business."

"I can understand that," she said politely.

Feeling crummy, Kirby shuffled into the Oval Office. He saw Brewster, his mouth drawn tight, standing behind his desk, in front of the thick, bulletproof-glass windows. Kirby slouched into a chair in front of the desk.

Still standing, Brewster blurted out, "I'm not feeling very good about of the state of our intelligence."

Kirby stiffened in his chair. "What's the problem?"

"What do you know about an agreement recently entered into between Iran and China?"

Kirby moved forward, onto the edge of his chair. "Why are you asking me that?"

"I'll tell you in a minute. First I want to hear what you know about this agreement."

The President's voice had a sharp edge. Kirby decided he better answer the President's question. "We had an agent in Tehran by the name of Kurt Jurgenson. A Dutchman. His cover was running a Dutch carpet company. About ten days ago, I flew to Holland and met Jurgenson, who told me that he had heard some kind of agreement had been entered into between Iran and China, involving perhaps oil and military supply. Jurgenson didn't know any of the details of the agreement. I told Jurgenson to go back to Tehran and obtain some additional information. I never heard any more from him. That's all I know."

As Kirby was talking, the President's face was growing red with rage. The instant Kirby finished, Brewster pounced.

"Why wasn't I told about this agreement?" He was raising his voice.

"With all due respect, Mr. President, I didn't have any support for the information Jurgenson passed along, or confidence it was reliable."

"Didn't the Director of the Israeli Mossad come to you with information about the agreement between China and Iran?"

Where the hell did he get his information?

"Yes, but it seemed to me, absent some confirmation, that we were dealing with misinformation supplied by the Israelis, because they want us to launch an attack against Iranian nuclear facilities."

"But you know how important I think the whole Iranian subject is."

"I'm well aware of that," Kirby said, remaining calm. "On the other hand, I didn't want to bring you information that we weren't satisfied was reliable."

"Shouldn't I be the one to make the decision of what is and isn't reliable? What can and can't be acted on?"

"With all due respect, Mr. President, that's precisely the problem that President Bush got into in connection with the weapons of mass destruction in Iraq. He was given information that was unreliable, that hadn't been checked, that hadn't been verified, and the President proceeded to act on the basis of that information. It created a problem for the President and the country for some time thereafter."

"Even if your summary of what happened with Bush was accurate, and I could take issue with that, it misses the point. I should have been given the information and told it was of questionable reliability. Whether or not I choose to act on the basis of the information is my decision. You have no right to be an intelligence gatekeeper and decide what I get to see and what I don't see."

"With all due respect again, Mr. President, it is my job to be a gatekeeper. Hundreds of thousands of pages of intel are generated by our intelligence agencies day in and day out. We can't inundate the White House with all of that material. It is *my function* and the function of my office to sift through and decide what's worth passing on to you."

The President shook his head. "You have a general point with some validity, but we're dealing with something as important as an agreement between China and Iran that could blow up the Middle East. You were absolutely wrong not to have brought it to my attention."

"I understand you feel that way, Mr. President. I disagree with you, but you're of course the President of the United States. I'll act accordingly in the future. And by the way, when I had confirmed information about the Chinese plans for an attack on Taiwan, I immediately came to see you. So you have no right criticizing me."

The President pounded on his desk. "Don't you tell me what I have a right to do, you insubordinate little pipsqueak."

Kirby realized he had gone too far. He couldn't risk being fired before Operation Dragon Oil was over. "I'm sorry, Mr. President. I misspoke. Please forgive me. I was simply doing what I believed was best to serve you."

"Humph."

"Can I ask you, sir, how you learned about this agreement between China and Tehran?"

"Craig Page. A man you had no business terminating."

For Kirby, the words hung in the room like a cloud of poison gas. Craig had been talking to Brewster. He felt perspiration breaking out under his arms.

"I am firmly convinced," Kirby said, "that it is all Israeli disinformation. That it isn't reliable. That Craig Page is off chasing rabbits running down rabbit holes. There's nothing here. Absolutely nothing at all. No agreement. I'm thoroughly convinced of that."

"Even after Jurgenson was murdered?"

How the hell did Craig know that?

"I will redouble my efforts," Kirby said, "to find out what if anything is going on between China and Iran. I have a very good station chief in Beijing, Peter Emery, he…"

"Wrong. You're not to do anything more about this agreement."

"But…"

"Whether you like it or not, I've sent Craig Page and Elizabeth Crowder to Beijing as my personal representatives to find out the details of this Chinese-Iranian agreement, and most important, to obtain a copy. I don't want you interfering with Craig's mission in any way. Ambassador March will give him the help he needs. You people bungle things."

Kirby was so upset he couldn't speak, which was just as well because the words out of his mouth would have been: "Is Craig Page Superman?" That sarcasm would have further infuriated Brewster.

Brewster continued, "Craig asked me not to tell you about his mission to China, but the more I thought about your intelligence failure, the angrier I became. I had to tell you. Also, I became concerned that one of your people may spot him in China, and I don't want anyone employed by the CIA interfering with Craig's assignment. Do you understand me?"

"Yes, sir."

"What Craig's doing is dangerous. If anything happens to him, I'll hold you personally responsible."

50

WASHINGTON

Shaken and trembling, Kirby stumbled out of the Oval Office.

He needed time to think, to develop a strategy for dealing with what he'd just heard. He directed his driver to take him back to his office in Langley.

Kirby stood behind his desk and tossed darts at the board across the room. Most missed the bullseye by a wide margin, but he decided what to do: let the Chinese deal with Craig. To implement that, he had to call his father at the old man's house in Aspen, where Kirby had installed a secure line.

He spit out the information that Craig and Elizabeth were going to Beijing, then said, "It's time to unleash the dogs of war in China. I think you should call Zhou Yun and tell him to eliminate Craig and Elizabeth once they're on Chinese soil."

There was a long pause.

"Well?" Kirby said.

"I think that would be a mistake," his father finally replied. "I'm afraid that Zhou Yun and his brother, the General, will conclude that by letting Craig slip away from us and go to China, we're not holding up our end of the bargain. They'll cancel the deal. You have to take care of Craig yourself in Beijing. You understand what I'm saying?"

His father had a point. "I'll get on it right away."

"Good. Meantime, I'm flying back to Washington. I'll be at my Watergate apartment until this is over."

"Well, at least we have to call…"

His father cut him off in mid sentence. "I'm well aware of that. You think I'm looking forward to telling him what happened and having him chew me out?"

Kirby heard the phone slam down. He dialed Peter Emery at home, waking him in the middle of the night.

"Get to the Embassy ASAP," Kirby said. "Call me on the secure phone."

Forty minutes later, Emery was on the line.

"Yes, sir, Mr. Kirby. What do you need?" He sounded excited to be talking to the Director.

"Did you ever meet Craig Page when he worked with the CIA?"

"Once at a CIA conference on terrorism."

"Would you recognize him?"

"Yes, sir."

"I fired Craig for insubordination. A review Board approved my action. As you might imagine, he's embittered about it."

"I would expect so."

"Anyhow, Craig is on his way to China, traveling with a female reporter, using aliases, claiming he came to China to tour and find clients for his security consulting firm based in Milan. But we have received evidence that he's gone over to the other side, determined to get even with us. He's engaged in a plot with officials of the Chinese military to attack American military bases."

"Are you serious?"

"I wish I weren't."

"That son of a bitch."

Good, he's buying it.

"What can I do to stop him?"

"For now, I want you to track him—who he's meeting with and where's he's going. Keep me informed, but don't take any action."

"I'll do that."

"Also, Craig has some type of personal relationship with March. So don't be surprised if he meets with March. But don't tip March off about my call or involve him in any way. This has to remain between us. You understand?"

"I do, Mr. Kirby."

He fired a dart. Scored a bullseye.

Then he called Ali, who seemed surprised to hear from him. "Meet me in Great Falls in an hour," Kirby said. "Near the footbridge on the Virginia side."

When Kirby arrived, he saw the area was deserted, except for Ali standing on the edge of the Potomac River bank, hands in his pockets, looking into the river. Ali's back was to Kirby. He was sorely tempted to sneak up and push Ali into the swollen Potomac, rushing past, in flood with spring runoff. But he wanted to get rid of Craig far more than Ali.

Kirby coughed to clear his throat. Ali walked over.

"Listen," Ali said, looking and sounding chagrined. "I know you're angry about those two cops, but we've been through a lot together."

"Don't worry, I've gotten over it."

"Glad to hear that. I could set up remote surveillance of his house."

"No point in that. Craig's gone to China with Elizabeth at the President's request."

"I have good contacts in China."

Kirby shook his head. "Forget China. I can handle that myself. Eventually, Craig will come back to the United States. He'll land at Dulles Airport. I want you to wipe him out, the girl, too, once they arrive. If they're in a car, hit them on the Dulles access road. If they're in a chopper, shoot it down."

"When are they coming back?"

"I don't know yet. Probably before April 1. Keep your men on standby."

"I'll do it myself," Ali said. "With one of my people."

"Good. I'll let you know the flight number and time."

51

SAN FRANCISCO

Elizabeth was staring at the Four Seasons dinner menu, but not reading it. She was thinking about all the incredible things she'd done since she met Craig. Even today, when they weren't getting chased or shot at, she had her picture taken for phony documents above a produce shop in Chinatown. What a wild ride.

Meantime, she had gone shopping to buy suitcases, clothes, books, cameras, and film. She had to look like a tourist accompanying her husband on a business trip to China when they flew to Beijing early tomorrow morning.

She glanced out of the window at Market Street below. A trolley car was passing by, pedestrians scrambling to get out of the way.

Craig signaled for a waiter who rushed over. She told the young man, "I'll have the mixed salad and crab." Craig ordered a salad and another of those steaks he loved. Then he said to the waiter, "We'll have bottle of the Brunello by Antinori."

She looked at him with alarm. "Do you think you should drink? Dr. Rollins said that with the medication, which you're still taking…"

"You worry too much. I'll just sip a little."

During dinner, he said softly, "How ironic that China and Iran are uniting to try and dominate the world." He explained to her what those two countries were doing in the sixth century, B.C. Cyrus had expanded the Persian Empire to include over fifty million people. At about the same time, Confucius was the seminal thinker of the period.

"There are so many astounding developments in Chinese history. The Ming Navy was crossing the Indian Ocean and traveling to Africa almost a hundred years before Columbus and the European explorers. A great creative age for technology and culture came two centuries before the renaissance in Europe."

As he spoke, pausing from time to time to eat and drink wine, she was astounded at the depth of his knowledge. She was listening enough to ask questions from time to time, but they weren't really engaged in a discussion. He seemed so serious. It was as if he were giving a seminar. This was a side of him she'd never seen before.

Her mind wandered, thinking about him.

Suddenly, she wanted him to make love to her. He'll probably be a good lover. Strong, but sensitive. Concerned with her pleasure, too.

Thinking about it, she was becoming wet, her face flushed.

"What's wrong?" he asked.

"Nothing. Why?"

"You look red."

"Maybe it's the wine."

He smiled at her, then reached over and placed his hand on hers. The waiter refilled their glasses.

When the waiter took their dessert order, he said, "We have a Grand Mariner soufflé."

"I love that," she said with enthusiasm.

"One for the two of us," Craig said.

Waiting for the soufflé, they talked about San Francisco and their visits over the years. Beneath the surface of their conversation was the tension of what awaited them in China.

Suddenly, she remembered. Today was March 26. She stood up, "Be right back. I have to go to the ladies room."

En route, she passed the waiter. "Will you please put a candle in the soufflé?"

Moments later, it arrived with a lit candle.

"Happy birthday," she said.

"How'd you know?"

"Francesca told me she wanted a few days off. Your birthday was on the twenty-sixth. She planned to fly to Milan."

"Thanks. I still can't believe she's gone. We'll catch the bastards."

For several minutes, they ate in silence. He looked peculiar, bleary eyed. She was watching him as he stood up, looking woozy. She took his arm and led him out of the restaurant.

A waiter rushed over. "Should I get a doctor?"

She knew it wasn't necessary. Ed Rollins had warned him about alcohol with the medication, but Craig Page thought advice like that was for mere mortals. He was invincible.

She led him up to their suite and tucked him into bed.

Too wired to sleep, she sat in front of the floor-to-ceiling window, stared out at Market Street below, and thought about where they were going.

Though she'd never been to China before, she had edited several of Carl Zerner's articles about Chinese dissidents and persecution. She knew how tightly the Chinese military and intelligence ran the country. She and Craig only had a narrow window until Chinese intelligence was pursuing them. And those people were brutal.

PART FOUR

THE CHINESE CHALLENGE

52

BEIJING

As the plane descended over Beijing, Craig looked out of the window. Never having been in China, he was struck by how massive the city looked, in breadth like Los Angeles and in height, with its myriad of skyscrapers, like New York. How in the world will they be able to obtain what they need in such a vast place in five days?

He was also struck by the thick brown layer of pollution hanging over the city and the power plants spewing out fumes. Economic progress had a price.

Craig was relieved the long flight was ending. Though he had stood up and walked around every half hour, his bandaged right leg was stiff.

He'd passed the time reading books about the current political and economic situation in China. When he needed a break, he turned to maps of Beijing. He memorized the layout of the streets in and around central Beijing, particularly near the American Embassy in the international compound across from the St. Regis Hotel. Meantime, Elizabeth studied guidebooks, then slept. He envied her. He'd never been able to sleep on airplanes.

He kept thinking about their mission in China.

Having Ambassador March for assistance will be a real asset. He just hoped Brewster complied with his request and didn't tell Kirby.

"We're on our final descent," the pilot announced. "Please make sure your seatbelts are tightened."

Craig reset his watch to Beijing time. Fifteen minutes past noon.

Elizabeth was awake. She squeezed his hand. "Show time," she whispered, leaning toward him.

When they reached the head of the line at immigration, Craig slid the U.S. passports of Alexandra and Richard Collier into the opening under the thick glass, along with their forged visas, then held his breath.

The agent glanced at their faces, after that, at their documents. In a routine way, he asked, "Purpose of visit?"

"Business for me," Craig said.

Elizabeth spoke up, "And, I'll be touring. Visiting the sites. Climbing the Great Wall."

Looking bored, the agent stamped their documents and waved them through.

Okay, we're in, Craig thought. So far, so good. Now the fun begins.

For transportation into the city, Craig selected the route any well-healed American businessman would follow. In San Francisco, he had called the St. Regis Hotel in Beijing and told the concierge when they would be arriving. In the baggage claim area, a petite woman in a dark blue business suit and starched white blouse was waiting with a sign: ALEXANDRA AND RICHARD COLLIER.

Once they had their luggage, she led them out to the curb, on a windy, blustery day, then called for a car—a large, four-door,

Chinese-manufactured, black sedan. The driver in a blue blazer that said "St. Regis Hotel" raced out to open the door for Craig and Elizabeth and assist with their baggage. They settled into the back seat, as the driver pulled away.

"Is this your first visit to Beijing?" the driver asked in halting English.

"Yes," Craig said.

"You will like it. Much to see in Beijing."

"We've been looking forward to it."

From the time that they left the airport access road and pulled onto the main highway, they were in the midst of a ferocious traffic jam, often involving gridlock. Bicycles were a thing of the past.

The drive was painfully slow, lots of stop and go. Even worse than driving from Dulles Airport to downtown Washington in the middle of the afternoon.

Here, the roads were wider, but there were cars and more cars. Thousands and thousands of cars, as he looked around. Some manufactured by American and Japanese companies, more manufactured by Chinese companies.

Close to the heart of Beijing, Craig saw a huge number of high-rise office buildings and apartments, virtually filling the landscape. Not merely a dozen or a score, but hundreds, even thousands of high-rise buildings in every direction. Modern, spanking new office towers, apartments, glass, steel, all the newest modes of construction. Next to the buildings were cranes. Dozens and dozens of cranes for additional buildings under construction.

In the back of the car, Elizabeth said to Craig, "I had no idea the city was this large, with so many buildings."

Craig smiled. She was playing the role of the tourist well. They both knew that, while this might be a free economy, the government was still a totalitarian regime. Their driver might be working for the government, as well as the hotel, and filing reports with an intelligence agency on the passengers he drove.

"Tired from the long plane ride, hon?" Craig asked Elizabeth.

She yawned. "A little. I might take a short nap when we get to the hotel. I want to be ready for dinner. I've heard the food is very good in Beijing."

"A nap sounds like a good idea," Craig said, "although I may walk a little to stretch my legs."

As their car approached the St. Regis, Craig looked across the road at the foreign embassy compound—a cluster of buildings inside a walled complex, with barbed wire on top. Armed Chinese guards patrolled the entrance to the compound. Anyone who wished to get in or out had to cross through that Chinese border point, effectively blocking Chinese political dissidents from seeking asylum in an embassy.

Walking into the front of the hotel, Craig was surprised by how modern and luxurious the wood-paneled and marble-floored lobby was, with a wide staircase rising up two floors. The back area of the lobby was lined with shops displaying French and Italian high-end imports. He saw Chanel, Yves St. Laurent, Armani, and Louis Vuitton.

After they checked in and went to their suite, a tuxedo-clad butler showed up with their bags, offering to help them unpack. Craig sent him away.

Once they were alone, Craig lifted his hand and raised one finger to his lips, reminding Elizabeth of what he had told her in San Francisco. "I don't know whether our rooms will have listening devices or not. We have to assume they do."

She nodded, indicating she understood. Elizabeth began wandering around the suite. "Oh my," she exclaimed. "You've got to see the bathroom. It is beyond belief."

He followed her into the bathroom which was lined in marble. It had a huge shower with built-in steps. A marble double sink. Jacuzzi tub. "Beats anything I've ever seen," Elizabeth said. "I'm going to use it and take a long bath. What about you?"

"My legs are sore from all the sitting on the plane and in the car. I think I'll walk a little outside. I shouldn't be too long. I'll have the concierge make us a dinner reservation."

Craig exited the hotel, turned right and walked three blocks to a main boulevard with shops, office buildings, and apartments. More bumper-to-bumper traffic.

He walked for about half a mile, stepping in and out of shops, looking around, behaving like a tourist. He crossed the street and returned in the direction of the hotel on the other side. All the while, he was looking around, glancing at his reflection in shop windows. He used his three turn rule. No one was following.

While he walked, he took out his cell and called Ambassador March. A secretary answered in an official sounding voice, "This is the office of Ambassador March."

Craig replied, "Richard Collier calling from Madison Square Garden Associates. I'd like to speak with the Ambassador."

"I'll put you right through."

March had an enthusiastic, cheerful voice. "Delighted to hear from you, Richard. I gather that you've arrived in Beijing."

"I just did. We've checked into the St. Regis. I was thinking of stopping by to say hello."

"That's great. I'd be delighted to see you again," March sounded like an old friend. "How soon do you want to come?"

"I could be there in fifteen or twenty minutes."

"Perfect. You know where the Embassy is?"

"In the compound across from the St. Regis."

"I'll be waiting for you."

53

BEIJING

General Zhou had scheduled his meeting with Admiral Xu's widow, Mei Ling, in a remote corner of the Army headquarters. He wanted to avoid anyone other than Captain Cheng knowing about it.

To say that he had been compelled to have this meeting was an understatement. When she had called General Zhou's office and Cheng answered, the General had refused to talk with her. He relented when Cheng returned with a message: "Tell him I have certain issues to discuss with President Li, but I want to give him a chance to deal with them first." Now, the scheming shrew was ten minutes late.

He paced in the sparsely furnished room, with only two old, wooden chairs and a battered table.

Captain Cheng finally led her into the room.

She was tough-looking, with coal black eyes, a predator's eyes, that could bore in on someone like lasers. Her hair was freshly coiffed, and she was dressed in a fancy European two-piece gray suit. He had no doubt she was a rich widow. It wasn't much of a secret that the Admiral skimmed from Navy contracts. That was how he set up and supported his mistress. And General Zhou had heard that Mei Ling demanded two RMB for every one her husband gave the peasant girl.

General Zhou waited until Cheng left to say, "My condolences to the grieving widow."

She shook her head and sneered at him in contempt. "You're such a hypocrite. I know you had him killed."

I can't underestimate her.

He appeared indignant. "A ridiculous allegation. The official autopsy was a heart attack from over exertion." He gave a short, dirty laugh. "We all know what he was doing at the time."

"A heart attack can be induced by drugs."

"Really? I never knew that."

"Traces of the chemicals may have been left behind."

"The body's gone. The autopsy finished."

He felt relief, even boldness. This must be all she had, mere suspicions. "You can talk about this with President Li all you want. You have no proof."

She gave him a hard cold smile. "I have something else to talk to him about."

"What's that?"

He was holding his breath.

"My husband brought home a copy of your agreement with Iran for Operation Dragon Oil. Even though he kept his mistress, we had a close relationship, and he cared about the country. Unlike you. He discussed the agreement with me. He was concerned that you were plunging China into war, that you and your brother would destroy the country for your own personal gain. He didn't know whether President Li approved Operation Dragon Oil or not, so he was considering talking to Li. Then you ordered his murder. That convinced me. President Li doesn't know. You're operating on your own."

General Zhou was shaken to his core.

"That document wasn't final," he said weakly.

"Then you won't mind if I show it to President Li?"

"You wouldn't dare."

"Don't try me. It would give me pleasure to destroy you."

"What do you want?"

"My son's an officer in the Navy. I want him to have my husband's job, in charge of all Naval operations."

He had to buy time to get past April 1. "Your son is a fine officer, but I'm afraid he doesn't have the experience for the position."

"You need young blood at the top. It'll be good for the Navy."

He frowned. "Do you have any idea how many higher ranking officers there are? How could I justify promoting him over them?"

She locked eyes with him. "Don't give me that stuff. You run the armed forces like your own fiefdom. You can do anything you want."

"But there are limits. I can't risk a mutiny. Suppose I promise he'll have the job in five years."

She spit on the ground. "That's what I think of any promise of yours."

"Two years. Will that satisfy you?"

"You take me for a fool. I know very well if my son's promotion isn't announced by April 1, and you launch your attack, I lose my leverage."

He had no response.

"You leave me no choice, General Zhou. I'll give President Li your regards."

"Bitch," he hissed. He wanted to strangle her with his own hands.

As if reading his mind, she said, "Don't even dream of killing me as you did my husband. And don't dream of trying to steal the document. I've hidden the agreement. Only two people know where it is. If I'm arrested or anything happens to me, they will immediately take it to President Li."

"You think of everything."

"My father dealt with Mao for many years before Mao had him purged. He taught me: When you're dealing with a snake, you have to get down on the ground and slither around with him."

"I should be flattered that you compare me with our honorable Chairman Mao."

"I didn't intend that compliment. You're venal, but you're still not close to him."

He decided to make one more stab at the two-year deception. "I would be willing to give you a written statement confirming he will be promoted to head of Naval operations in two years." He removed a pen from his pocket.

She shook her head. "I knew I was wasting my time meeting with you."

She rose to leave.

"Sit down," he commanded angrily.

She remained standing. "You have something to tell me?"

"I'll do what you want." He made it sound as if his surrender was painful, so she'd believe her son would be promoted. "You drive a hard bargain."

"When will it be announced?"

"I'll begin processing his promotion today, but these things take a couple of days. I'll have to follow protocol."

"Just make sure it's announced before April 1, or I go to President Li."

"It will be. You can count on it."

She seemed satisfied and left.

General Zhou summoned Captain Cheng. "Call Jiang, President Li's Appointment Secretary. Tell him to alert you immediately if

Mei Ling arranges a meeting with President Li. Then when she's en route to the meeting, have her snatched and killed. Her son, who's at sea, will fall overboard and drown. Do you understand?"

"Yes sir."

When Cheng had gone and General Zhou was alone, he said softly, "Goodbye Mei Ling. And goodbye to your son."

54

BEIJING

By showing the Richard Collier passport, Craig was waved without difficulty through the Chinese checkpoint into the embassy complex. He identified himself to the two Marines on duty in front of the American Embassy. Inside, the receptionist led him up the stairs to the Ambassador's second-floor office.

"Would you like coffee or tea, Mr. Collier?" March's secretary asked as he entered the Ambassador's suite.

Before Craig had an opportunity to respond, he heard a powerful voice. "He'll have tea, Phyllis. Our visitor has to get used to the way people do things in China."

Coming toward Craig was a tall, professorial-looking man in his mid-fifties, with thinning black hair and wire-framed glasses. Bill March exuded self confidence as he held out his hand.

"Welcome to Beijing," March said. They were alone in the large corner office.

"Delighted to be here."

"Let's take a look at the view, while we wait for Phyllis to bring the tea."

Craig followed March over to the window. As the Ambassador identified the other embassies in the complex, Craig looked at March through the corner of his eye. Craig remembered reading a profile of March in a newspaper when Brewster named him U.S. Ambassador to China. March had no prior State Department involvement. He had spent his career on Wall Street, rising to become a partner in Hansell Gray, one of the large Wall Street investment-banking firms. He had jumped onto the Brewster campaign bandwagon early and become chairman of the committee that organized fundraising from the wealthiest individual donors.

Following Brewster's election, March wanted to be Secretary of the Treasury, but the position went to a California banker, responsible for delivering that state to Brewster, which had been the decisive edge in the election. March's second choice was Ambassador to China. According to the article, March was fluent in Chinese, and he had, in his investment banking business, represented Chinese companies. He believed that the future of the world economy depended upon China and the United States, and how they handled their economic interaction. In the article, March was quoted: "As Ambassador to China, I hope to build bridges of cooperation between our two great nations and avoid the confrontation that some believe is inevitable."

Once Craig and March each had a cup of tea and had settled in chairs across a circular table, the Ambassador turned to his visitor. "We can talk freely here. Peter Emery, the CIA station chief, has our Embassy scanned twice a day for bugs."

Craig sipped some tea.

"Your reputation precedes you, Craig. I've never heard President Brewster so effusive about anyone."

Not used to compliments, Craig shifted uncomfortably. "How

much did the President tell you about my mission in China?"

"Nothing. He thought it best if I hear it direct from you. What he did tell me was that I should roll out the red carpet for you. Anything you want. You're 'working on the single most important issue facing the United States,' Brewster told me in a grim voice. You can imagine with that as a backdrop, I'm entirely at your disposal."

"I appreciate that, because I need your help."

"Okay. Start talking."

Craig summarized for March everything that occurred since he had been informed of Francesca's death.

"Bottom line," he said at the end, "is that China and Iran have entered into an agreement involving oil and military action. April 1 is their zero date."

A frown settled over March's face. "China and Iran working closely together." March sounded skeptical. "Are you confident your sources are accurate?"

"Absolutely."

March grimaced. "That would be a dreadful development for the Unites States, if it were to happen."

"Remember this is in addition to our intelligence assessment that China is planning to launch an attack on Taiwan to retake the island on April 1, as well. I assume you've heard of that."

"Brewster called me himself. He told me he's moving U.S. military forces into a defensive posture. I told Brewster these are only exercises. Not the prelude to an attack."

"What was his reaction?"

"He told me, 'Satellite photos don't lie. I have to act accordingly.'"

Craig's facial muscles tightened. "We have to stop this fast-moving train."

"But how?"

"My objective is to get a copy of the agreement between China and Iran, then forward it to President Brewster before April 1. If he confronts the Chinese with the document, they may back down."

March shook his head in trepidation. "That's a helluva mission in five days."

"We don't have a choice. If the President approached the Chinese leaders without hard evidence, they'd dismiss him."

"Agreed. Now tell me what I can do to help?"

"For starters, tell me whether you've heard anything here in Beijing that, when you reconsider it in light of what I've told you, might be related to the Chinese-Iranian agreement."

For a minute, March didn't respond. Finally, he said, "Not a word, I'm afraid."

The Ambassador took off his glasses and fiddled with them. "One thing I don't understand. Assuming all of your information is correct, what do these two Chinese operations have to do with each other? Why the attack on Taiwan at the same time they are implementing an agreement with Iran? There has to be some connection between the two. But I sure don't see it."

"I don't know that either."

March pulled his lanky frame up from the chair and paced around the office. "Since I've been here, I've spent time with the top Chinese civilian leadership, their President, the Premier, the Deputy Premier, and others at the top of their government. I can't say I know these people well, and they're certainly not telling me everything on their minds. On the other hand, I find it very surprising that the ones I've met would be engaged in these aggressive actions. Right now, they're trying to address some internal domestic problems. Until they've done that, I can't see them launching a serious foreign adventure, much less the two you outlined."

Craig hoped that by listening to March talk about China's current political situation, he'd get an idea about how to proceed. "Tell me a little about their internal domestic problems."

"The Chinese government never fully recovered from the Tiananmen Square protest and massacre. The hardliners, the old communists, the party people, still have control of the governing apparatus. A grip on running the country politically. They control speech. Access to Western movies and books. They limit and stifle dissent. There has been relatively little in the way of political liberalization. Political dissidents are usually arrested or somehow quieted down. Those who protest publicly against the regime are often thrown in jail without anything like due process."

"It strikes me as odd that China has been able to expand so much economically without political liberalization."

March smiled. "Many Americans have told me that. They don't appreciate Chinese history. Autocratic rule has always been the norm, and the population by and large submits. The magnitude of the changes this government is managing is breathtaking. I don't approve of their methods, but I have to respect the results."

"You mean economically?"

"Precisely. In the last ten years, China has undergone the largest economic expansion in the history of the world. More Chinese people have moved from the countryside to the cities to take jobs than twice the entire U.S. workforce. It's been the largest single migration in the history of the world. Their economy continues to grow at an incredible pace. Current estimates say that in another twenty years, China will surpass the United States in the size of its economy. If things keep moving the way they are, we'll find ourselves like England a century or so ago, surpassed by a larger, more aggressive economy with more resources, more people, and more of a will to push ahead."

"You really think they'll be able to continue their economic expansion and surpass us in that short a period of time?"

"It's a virtual certainty, unless their political situation leads to unrest. There could be missteps in governing. The whole structure could unravel. For example, they're now having considerable problems with poverty for those who remain behind in the countryside. Peasants and farmers are growing poorer at the same time those in the cities are growing richer. That dichotomy in a society this large could lead to major problems. That's one of the internal issues the Chinese government is trying to address."

"Is it possible that the regime in Beijing wants to launch these military ventures to divert attention from their internal domestic problems?"

March thought about Craig's question for a minute. Then he responded in a thoughtful voice, "I don't think so. The great economic snowball keeps rolling. That's what the leadership cares most about."

"Let's assume you're right about the civilian Chinese leadership. That they do not want a confrontation with the United States, at least not right now. That they're fully consumed with internal domestic issues. On the other hand, are there some in the Chinese military who want to pursue a more aggressive approach?"

March stopped pacing, wheeled around and faced his visitor. "In that respect, China isn't any different than the United States. I've had a number of Pentagon briefings about China's developing military. The threat that they pose to the United States, Japan, and others in Asia. We have some hawks in the Pentagon, who want to launch a preemptive strike against China. We also have many others in the Department of Defense who come at it from a view similar to mine. The objective for both countries is keeping the hawks under control."

As March sat down, Craig continued, "Let me add one more fact to the mix. When I was in Iran, I learned that the Iranians had a meeting in Paris to discuss their agreement with China. On the Chinese side, General Zhou was there. Does his presence affect your analysis?"

March raised his eyebrows. "I know quite a bit about General Zhou. He's the Commander of the People's Liberation Army, which makes him the highest-ranking military official in the country. He's in charge of all the Chinese armed forces. Sort of like our Chairman of the Joint Chiefs, but with more power. In prior governments, that post was often held by a civilian, a leader of the Communist Party or the President of the country. However, through skillful political maneuvering, Zhou was able to get that prestigious and important post. The concept was that, even though General Zhou would have this position, the Chinese President and Premier would still have ultimate decision-making on military issues. In reality, ever since his appointment, General Zhou has been consolidating his authority over the military and asserting his independence from civilian leadership."

"I gather that General Zhou takes a hard line on military issues toward Taiwan and presumably toward the United States."

"Correct."

"Are there some in the military leadership who don't agree with this hard line?"

"Over the last couple of years, General Zhou has had them purged. Some were forced to retire. Others have been arrested and charged with treason."

"Do you know any military leaders who were outspoken foes of General Zhou and have been retired?"

"What do you have in mind?"

"I'm looking for someone who might be willing to talk to us."

March shook his head. "It won't happen. Nobody who had been at a high level would be willing to do that on matters this sensitive. Not with the risks that would entail."

Craig thought March was being too negative. "Over the years, I've repeatedly been surprised at how much information I've obtained from former government and military officials. People who, for one reason or another, believe their country is on the wrong course or who have personal motivations. It's our only possibility of obtaining the information we need in the available time."

When March didn't respond, Craig pressed him. "All I need from you is a name and contact information. I'll take it from there."

"I don't have one."

Craig was feeling frustrated. He always believed in finding ways to get things done; he hated it when others took a pessimistic approach.

"President Brewster said you could help me." Craig was raising his voice. "I'll have to call and tell him he was wrong."

March sighed. He crossed over to his desk, opened up the center drawer and pulled out a pile of cards which he examined. After several minutes he retained one and returned the others to the drawer. He handed it to Craig. It was printed on one side in Chinese characters. Craig flipped the card over. On the other, he read: "General Ming Liu. Fellow at the Institute for International Affairs. Beijing China."

Craig turned back to March. "What's the Institute for International Affairs?"

"A high-level think tank."

"How well do you know General Ming?"

"I first met him at a diplomatic reception a couple months ago. He retired from the military about six months prior to that. He may have had a falling out with General Zhou. The organization he's with is a Beijing equivalent to the Brookings Institute in Washington. A top-dog organization. Lots of prestige. The reception was at the French Embassy, in honor of the new French Ambassador. Ming went out of his way that evening to talk to me. He suggested we schedule a lunch. If I was interested, I should give him a call. I took him up on his invitation, and he asked me to come to his Institute. They set us up in a private room. We had lunch and we talked for a couple of hours."

"Was he critical of General Zhou?"

"We didn't discuss General Zhou. The thrust of what Ming told me was that he was aware of my position, that there need not be enmity between our two governments, that, by cooperation, we would both gain, and the entire world would benefit. He wanted me to know that he agreed. He offered to come to the United States and make speeches about United States-Chinese relations. He asked me if I knew any groups who might invite and pay him. That's all I know about the man."

"Do you think he was reaching out to you on his own, or operating as an agent for the Chinese government?"

March shrugged. "Good question. I don't know. I've never operated in your world, where you have to tell agents from double agents."

"Besides General Ming, do you have any other people we could talk with?"

March shook his head.

"That settles it. I'll have to take the chance that General Ming will help without reporting to General Zhou."

"Let's be clear about one thing," March said, in a grave voice. "Any further meeting which I have, or any meeting you have with General Ming, would be dangerous. Even if he disagrees with the hard-line views of General Zhou and wants to help us, if Zhou found out, particularly about a meeting with someone who had been in the CIA, it would be death for Ming, as well as you. As for me, I would probably just be expelled from the country. It's your call."

Without hesitating, Craig said, "How do I get a meeting with General Ming tomorrow?"

"He gave me a phone number at his home. He asked me to use it if I had to reach him on short notice. He said there's less chance of someone listening in on that line. I'll call him this evening. Tell him I have a friend whom I think he might like to meet. I'll see what he suggests as far as a time and place. How can I get in touch with you this evening?"

"Call me on my cell," Craig wrote out the number and handed it to March. "Just give me a time. I'll come to the Embassy. We can then talk here, where we're assured of privacy. From here, I can proceed to any meeting with or without you, however you arrange it."

March took a deep breath and exhaled. "Sounds like a plan. Now what else can I do for you?"

"Tell me about General Zhou."

March glanced his watch. "I'm due at the Chinese Finance

Ministry in thirty minutes to discuss currency issues. How about if we do it tomorrow?"

"That should work."

"Before I leave, do you want to talk with Peter Emery, our CIA station chief, who was in the building earlier today. I don't know whether he's still here."

"Glad you mentioned Emery. That was my next topic. President Brewster asked me to undertake this assignment working directly for him. No CIA involvement. Not Kirby. Not Emery. He doesn't even want them to know that I'm in China or what I'm doing here."

March shook his head in disbelief. "Seems to me like a hell of a way to run a railroad. But then again, there's very little that surprises me about Washington these days. Sometimes, since I took this job, which is my first one with the government, I feel like Alice in Wonderland."

Craig cracked a smile. "It's possible Emery will see me in the building and recognize me. I intend to stick with my cover. Tell him I'm in private business as an international security consultant, and I'm visiting China as a tourist and to develop new clients. You're an old friend of my family. I stopped by to say hello."

"Anything else?" March asked, standing up.

"That's about it."

"Phyllis will see you out. I'll get in touch with you this evening, after I've spoken with General Ming."

55

BEIJING

From Ambassador March's office, Phyllis led Craig down a long corridor toward the staircase in the center of the building. Coming from the other direction was a chubby, red-headed man with a cherubic face, dimples on his cheeks and a big broad smile: Peter Emery.

"Well, well. Craig Page. What a surprise."

Phyllis looked bewildered. And why not? She thought she'd been walking Richard Collier to the stairs.

"Since you two obviously know each other, I don't have to make any introductions."

"That's right," Emery said. "We're old friends and colleagues from way back. Why don't you leave our visitor with me? He and I have a little catching up to do."

Phyllis retreated.

Kirby must have tipped off Emery.

"Let's go back to my cubby hole and chat," Emery said.

Craig didn't want to talk with Emery, but there wasn't anything he could do about it without creating problems for his mission. So he dutifully followed Emery.

Once they reached Emery's office, the CIA station chief kicked the door shut and pointed to two chairs.

"It's a pleasure to meet the great Craig Page. You made a helluva presentation at a CIA conference a couple years ago. Since then, I've heard a lot about you."

"Not much good, I presume."

"The way I heard it, you're a bit of a legend in the agency. You accomplished some phenomenal things."

"And I was terminated all the same."

Emery laughed. "After I found out they sacked you, I did some checking around. Just curiosity. It seemed bizarre that somebody could be a top agency man one day and ushered out of the door the next. From what I learned, it was all a personal vendetta by Kirby. You basically made him look like an ass in connection with the Madison Square Garden business. It was his way of gaining retribution."

Craig waved his hand. "All ancient history. I've moved on."

"I hear you set up a security consulting firm in Milan."

"How in the world did you hear that?"

"Oh, you'd be surprised. News travels fast. There's always plenty of gossip in the agency. You've been the subject of quite a bit. You have respect among the professionals. Many of us are sorry you ended up in the middle of Kirby's buzz saw."

Craig laughed. "Is that the way it's being characterized these days by soldiers in the trenches?"

"Yeah. Something like that. So what are you doing in Beijing? Do you have a client with security problems, or are you over here trolling for business like most other foreign companies that see China as the place to cash in?"

Craig smiled. "Actually, I am trying to drum up some business from Chinese-based international companies. Also, this trip has a pleasure component. I'm here with a friend. The two of us want to see China, as well as do a little business and travel around."

"How do you know the Ambassador?"

"An old friend of the family. I called and told him I'd stop by and say hello when I arrived in Beijing." Craig was looking at Emery. His face showed no reaction.

"How about having dinner with me tonight? You and your friend. I'm not married. I'm here by myself. I could fill you in on things to do in China. Help you out with guides and touring. Get your trip off to a good start."

Craig decided to accept the invitation. Maybe he'd be able to flush out Emery. "Sure. We'd love to."

"Where are you staying?"

"The St. Regis."

"I'll swing by and pick you up at eight. Driving a blue Toyota sedan."

"We'll be in front. By the way, if you have to leave a message, we're registered as Richard and Alexandra Collier. I didn't want to take the risk of Chinese intelligence running the hotel guests' names through their computer and getting a hit for Craig Page."

"Smart. Never underestimate those Chinese intelligence people.

Elizabeth finished soaking in the tub and picked up her cell phone from the desk. She had to select each word with care, assuming Chinese intelligence would be listening, if not on her phone, on Carl's, at the Trib office, for sure. But Carl was smart, and in the last several years they'd had a number of oblique calls. It was an advantage that he'd recognize her voice.

He answered on the first ring. "Carl Zerner here."

"Hi, Carl. It's your friend Alexandra Collier, the pitcher on your old team in New York."

Short pause. Surprise on his part, she guessed. McDermott had no doubt told Carl he'd fired her.

"Where are you?"

"Beijing. Richard and I just arrived. We're staying at the St. Regis. He's on business. I'm doing the tourist thing. I was hoping we could get together tomorrow afternoon."

"Love to. Let me check my schedule."

He was back in five seconds.

"How about if we meet at two at the East Gate of the Summer Palace? You can easily get there by cab. It's one of the sites you don't want to miss. We can catch up while I show you around."

"See you then."

She was pleased that she had her meeting. Anyone who heard their conversation couldn't possibly be suspicious.

56

WASHINGTON

The secure phone rang on Kirby's desk. He glanced at the caller ID. Peter Emery in Beijing.

"Yes Peter."

"Craig arrived. I'm having dinner with him and his friend tonight. They're staying at the St. Regis. I wanted you to know I'm on top of it. Tracking him, just like you asked."

"Good."

"I already have some critical information for you."

What has the suck up learned so soon?

"What's that?"

"Well, because you told me Craig would be meeting with Ambassador March, I planted a bug in March's office, and I…"

"You did what?" Kirby was panicked, raising his voice. "I told you March shouldn't be involved in any way. Didn't I?"

"Yes sir, but…"

"Don't you know how to follow orders?"

"I didn't think planting the bug involved March."

"Oh, for Christ's sake."

"Okay. Okay. I'm sorry. As soon as March leaves the office, I'll pull the bug. But at least you should hear what they talked about."

"Did you type this up?"

"No. It's only on an audio tape. I heard it once quickly and decided I better call you."

"Alright. Now listen carefully. I want you to give me an oral summary now. Then destroy the tape. And no written reports. You got that?"

"Yes sir."

By the time Emery finished his summary, Kirby's shirt was soaked with perspiration. What if Ming helped Craig. That would ruin everything. It was time for more extreme measures. And he had to move fast.

He pulled up airline schedules on his computer.

"Listen, Peter, have dinner with Craig this evening. Then tomorrow morning there's a 5:15 plane on ANA to Tokyo. Take it and meet me in the ANA business lounge at Narita."

Kirby picked up a dart from his desk and fired it across the room. He missed the entire dart board.

57

BEIJING

Elizabeth didn't like Emery from the first time he opened his mouth. He said to Craig, who had introduced her as my friend Elizabeth, "I can't believe a guy like you found someone so attractive to travel with."

Once they were in the car, Emery said, "I hope you two don't mind eating native tonight." Craig was in the front, Elizabeth in the back. Emery eased the car onto the road.

"Whatever you suggest," Craig said. "You know the territory."

"Great. The place I have in mind has the best duck in town. You probably call it 'Peking Duck,'" he said turning to look at Elizabeth. "But at any rate, it's fabulous. Also, you'll notice that we'll probably be the only non-Chinese people in the place. I not only like the food, but I like the fact that Westerners don't go there. It has another advantage. Typically Chinese Intelligence stations a couple of their agents in restaurants which are frequented by large groups of foreigners. They want to keep track of everything that's happening, overhear conversations and the like. It's unlikely they'll have anybody in this place. But still, out of an abundance of caution, it's best that we don't talk politics."

He looked over his shoulder at Elizabeth again, making certain she understood the message.

"I wouldn't think of doing otherwise," she said. "From what I've read, I understand there's still a fair amount of repression in China and very little dissent tolerated. At least in public, talking politics can be dangerous."

"That's true," Emery said. "On the other hand, there's lots of dissent in the country. People are just careful about how they express it."

The proprietor of the restaurant, who greeted Emery at the door, led them to a table in a corner, separated from the others. The restaurant was crowded. Emery was right about one thing, Elizabeth saw. They were the only Westerners. As they walked to their table, some heads turned to follow their movement. The waiter came over and said something in Chinese to Emery.

"None of the help speaks any English," Emery said. "He asked what we want to drink. My recommendation is go with the beer. They have good Chinese beer. The wines in this country aren't worth drinking."

Emery look at Elizabeth. "Beer," she said.

Craig nodded. "Same for me."

Three beers arrived along with glasses and menus. Emery ordered for them.

"How did you get so facile at Chinese?" Craig asked Emery, after the waiter had departed.

"It started when I was a freshman at Yale. I went to college, figuring I would study American government, or political science, or something like that then go to law school. My dad is a partner in a large law firm in New York. I knew enough to understand that the world didn't need one more lawyer, but at that point, I didn't have any better idea of what I wanted to do. Then during freshman orientation, I met this good-looking blond woman and asked what she would be taking. She said one of her courses would be Chinese. I thought that sounded pretty nifty. I had read that China was the way of the future, but I was really interested in this woman more than the course. So I enrolled." He laughed.

"What's so funny?" Craig said.

"Well, it didn't work out with the woman. We went out two or three times. We liked each other, but there was no chemistry. More important, when I made my commitment to change my courses to include Chinese, she hadn't told me that she was in love with a Chinese-American who was getting an MBA at Harvard and planning to go back to Shanghai after he got his degree and become a banker there. So I was wiped out with this girl before I got started."

Elizabeth couldn't resist laughing.

"It's not funny."

The waiter brought platters of food, which he put in the center of the table. He then divided up the dishes on three plates.

"What are we eating?" Craig asked Emery.

"One is the duck dish I described. Another is scallops and shrimp with snow peas. The third is braised beef and bok choy flavored with ginger, water chestnuts, cilantro stems, and Szechwan peppercorns."

After taking a little food on his chopsticks, Emery turned to Elizabeth. "Enough talking about me. As for your friend here, I know a little about his history. He's kind of boring. Tell me about yourself. I have to say you are so good looking. You could be a model. Have you ever done that?"

Oh please. What a pathetic line.

"I work for an advertising agency in New York. Craig and I have been friends for a while. I've never been to China before. So I decided to tag along. I'm looking forward to doing some serious site seeing here and later when we go to Xian."

"You'll love touring in Beijing. I can help you arrange a good guide. That's critical."

"I spoke to the concierge at the hotel this afternoon," Elizabeth said. "He scheduled a guide for us for each of the next three days."

Emery was frowning. "The trouble is some of those guides are very good and others aren't."

"Well, I asked the concierge for an English-speaking guide. I figured if the hotel recommends somebody, they'll be good."

"Not necessarily. Some of them are terrific and their English is fluent. Others, even recommended by a hotel like the St. Regis, can say, 'good morning Mrs. Collier' in perfect English, but that's about the only decent English you'll hear from them all day. Some don't even know the history and the sites. When we get back to the hotel, I'll go in and speak to the concierge. I know a couple of guides who work out of the St. Regis and are absolutely first rate."

Emery turned to Craig. "I assume you're going along with her on these site seeing jaunts?"

"That's the plan," Craig replied deadpan. "I'm anxious to see the city. When we get to Shanghai, I'll have some business meetings."

Emery insisted on paying for dinner. As they were leaving the restaurant, he turned to Elizabeth. "If he's ever tied up and you have time by yourself, give me a call." He removed a card from his pocket and handed it to her. "I'd be happy to show you some things myself."

She was astounded Emery was making such a blatant play for her with Craig right there.

Back at the hotel, Emery left his car with the doorman. He walked in with Craig and Elizabeth and led them to the concierge desk. There, he had a heated discussion in Chinese with the man on duty, forcing him on the defensive. When it was over, Emery turned to Craig and Elizabeth. "You're all set. I've now lined you up with Dan, one of the best guides. He'll be here at eight in the morning."

As soon as Emery departed, Elizabeth said to Craig, "Let's go downstairs and look at the workout facility."

Once they walked into the deserted room, with its dozens of machines, Elizabeth moved close to Craig and whispered, "What do you think of Emery?"

"He was tipped off by Langley. He's watching us for them."

"What a jerk. He's condescending, superior, obnoxious, and fancies himself a great lover. I knew men like that at Harvard from wealthy families, and I hated them."

"Don't hold back."

"You know I'm right."

Craig's cell rang. He listened, then hung up.

"March wants to meet me at his office at one."

"He must have gotten the meeting with Ming."

"That's what I figure. We can tour together in the morning, then split. You meet Zerner. I'll go to March. We only have four days left. The clock's ticking."

58

BEIJING

"We have a meeting at three this afternoon with General Ming," Ambassador March said to Craig when the two were alone in March's office.

"Excellent. I appreciate your setting it up on short notice."

March raised his hand. "Before you start thanking me, let's see whether it accomplishes what you want."

"Fair enough. Yesterday, you said that you know quite a bit about General Zhou. I want to pick your brain."

"Phyllis is bringing lunch into my office. We'll eat while we talk."

"Good. There is one other thing I'd like."

"What's that?"

"I assume the Embassy communications department retains copies of messages to and from Washington as well as a phone log."

March nodded. "We keep them for up to a year. Then they're forwarded to Washington for safekeeping. What do you have in mind?"

"I want to see any messages to or from Peter Emery in the last three days from Washington."

March raised his eyebrows. "What are you looking for?"

Craig didn't like the idea of sharing his suspicions with the Ambassador, but he had no choice. "Emery twisted my arm to have dinner last night, so we did. He and I and my friend, Elizabeth, who's traveling with me. I had the distinct feeling he's trying to keep tabs on me in Beijing. I'm afraid he may have been tipped off about my coming by Langley. That of course would be inconsistent with what President Brewster wanted. I have to know what I'm up against. I don't want Kirby or the bureaucrats in Langley fucking up my mission."

"I'll get copies of all messages Emery received as well as calls to or from his line. You realize, of course, that he has one or more secure lines that I have no control over. The origin of calls he received on those phones or the numbers he called will be outside my reach."

Having worked at embassies and wanted to conceal his actions from the Ambassador, Craig knew very well what March was saying. "I appreciate that. On the other hand, normal modes of communication may have been used, either by Langley or by Emery. Sometimes, people are in a hurry; they don't take all the safeguards."

March walked across the room, picked up his phone and gave the instructions to Phyllis. Then he turned to Craig. "We'll have the materials up here shortly."

After lunch arrived and they ate a little, Craig said to the Ambassador, "Now tell me about General Zhou."

March put down his chopsticks. "He's from a remarkable family. For two hundred years, until the Second World War, they were one of the leading industrial families in China. At the beginning of the twentieth century, General Zhou's grandfather moved to San Francisco with his Chinese wife, to establish a trading company as a subsidiary of the family business, based in Shanghai. General Zhou's father was born in San Francisco. He attended Stanford, received an engineering degree, then went to work in the family business."

"What areas were they in?"

"Initially banking, but General Zhou's father understood the importance of oil. He made a number of very successful investments in U.S. oil exploration and refining companies, operating in the huge east Texas oil field. He bought a lot of real estate in that part of the country, including some of what later became downtown Houston."

Craig paused to eat, thinking about what March had said. "Do they still have operations in the U.S.?"

March shook his head. "The Japanese killed off the family in China during the war. In 1949, when the Communist government took over under Mao, General Zhou's father liquidated his operations in the United States, placed the money in American and Swiss banks, and moved to China. He wanted to be a part of building the new China. He had a dream that one day China could be restored to its former greatness from the Imperial period, but that would require developing a modern economy. The man was a visionary. He could see China emerging from the ashes and the rubble to become a major economic competitor of the United States. I doubt if anyone else had that notion at the time."

Craig's injured leg felt stiff from sitting. He stood up and limped around the room. March asked, "Can I get you something? I have some pain killers. Percocet."

"No, I hate those things. I'll be fine. Continue your story."

"General Zhou's father married a woman in Shanghai. They had two sons. Zhou Yun, born in 1952; and General Zhou, born in 1954."

"How'd the capitalistic man, General Zhou's father, fare under Mao's version of communism?" Craig said cynically.

"Most people don't realize," said March, smiling at Craig. "That Mao was willing to sacrifice communist principles for economic expansion. In 1950, Mao put General Zhou's father in charge of the Chinese national oil company, CNOC, which at the time was owned by the State. During those years, China was the largest oil exporter in East Asia."

"What happened to him during the cultural revolution?"

"Good question. It's hard to believe how arbitrary and whimsical Mao could be, frequently turning on his most loyal supporters without warning." March pointed with his chopsticks for emphasis. "Mao sent General Zhou's father and mother to the countryside to live with peasants. To be indoctrinated with the proper Communist philosophy. The boys remained in Beijing. The mother starved to death; the father somehow survived. But when the campaign ended, Mao permitted General Zhou's father to resume his position in charge of CNOC. Talk about irrational."

His leg was feeling better. Craig sat back down. "What role has General Zhou's father played in China's economic expansion?"

"He made billions as the largest stockholder in the privatized CNOC and from a construction company he started, now one of the largest in China. The old man died five years ago. General Zhou's brother took over the business, including CNOC, while General Zhou pursued his military career."

"How do you know all this?"

"Before I become Ambassador, I was an investment banker with Hansell Gray in New York. General Zhou's father was a client of the firm. I worked with him. Also with Zhou Yun, General Zhou's brother, after he took over the company."

"You mean your capitalist New York firm was doing deals for a company based in Communist China?"

March laughed. "Americans don't understand how pragmatic and shrewd Chinese business people can be."

Craig closed his eyes and leaned back in his chair, processing the information March had given him.

"What I should add, and I can't emphasis enough," March said in a stern voice, "is that General Zhou and his brother—like their father—are extremely determined. We're talking about talented individuals, ruthless but savvy, who must not be underestimated."

"You sound as if you admire them."

"I simply want you to know what you're up against."

There was a buzzing on the intercom. "Mr. Barker is here. He has the communications that you wanted."

"Tell him to leave the documents with you," March told Phyllis.

A few minutes later, March walked to the outer office and returned with a pile of documents about half an inch high. He placed them on the conference table next to the remains of the now cool and congealing Chinese food.

It took Craig only fifteen minutes to go through the documents because there was very little of substance. It was obvious that Emery didn't communicate with Washington on sensitive matters through these routine communication channels. No mention of Craig Page. No mention of an agreement with Iran. No mention of a Chinese attack on the Island of Taiwan.

"Nothing here," Craig said. "Is Emery in today?"

"Let me look." March went over to his desk, punched a few keys on his computer, and said to Craig, "I like to keep track of the people in the Embassy so I require them to submit their daily schedules. Emery is out at a meeting from eleven to three p.m."

"Do you know with whom?"

"I can't obtain that information for Emery. He made it clear to me, and he had the backing of Kirby, that his comings and goings were not to be reported to me."

"How soon do we have to leave for our meeting with General Ming?"

March consulted his Frank Mueller wristwatch. "I would say in about fifteen minutes."

"Good. I think I'll walk up and down the hall to keep my leg loose."

59

NARITA AIRPORT, JAPAN

Leaving the plane at Narita after the long flight from Washington, Kirby shifted his briefcase into his left hand. He wanted to easily grab the passport with his right hand when he reached immigration. He slowed down, trying to blend into the surge of passengers. He didn't want to be recognized by Japanese intelligence agents. Always plenty of them at Narita.

Recognition would mean questions.

By the time he reached the front of the line, the officer asked, "Occupation, sir?"

"U.S. government employee."

"Agency?"

"Defense."

"Purpose of visit?"

"Business."

"Length of stay?"

"Depends on how my meetings go."

He hoped the officer didn't access Kirby's flight itinerary. A return flight in three hours would have raised red flags.

The man yawned. He had no desire to probe any further. He stamped Kirby's passport.

Moving into the terminal, Kirby thought about immigration examinations at U.S. airports. How thorough were they? How easily terrorists could slip into the country.

Making his way to the ANA business lounge, Kirby walked slowly to minimize attention. He checked in and was told by the smiling receptionist, "Mr. Emery is in private room 46." The door was ajar.

Kirby entered and slammed it shut. Even that didn't wake Emery who was in a chair in the corner, sound asleep.

Kirby walked over and shook him. "Peter, wake up."

Emery sprang to his feet, his face red with embarrassment. "Sorry sir. Late night with Craig and his girlfriend. Early plane."

Kirby was exhausted from the flight as well, but glad he had made it. He had to give Emery instructions in person. With so much on the line, Kirby had to observe his expression, his body language.

"What happened last night at dinner?"

"Uneventful. Craig stuck with his cover. He's in China to check out business opportunities with companies in Shanghai for his Milan security business. He's touring in Beijing."

"Did you press him?"

"As much as I could without making him suspicious. Craig's a good liar."

"What would you expect? We trained him well at the Farm. What about the woman?"

"She's in the advertising business in New York."

"She told you that?"

"Yeah."

Kirby reached in to his briefcase and pulled out a Tribune article.

"Foreign Editor Replaced." It contained pictures of Elizabeth and Sy Harrison, her successor. He passed it to Emery, who shook his head while he read.

"So she was lying to me."

"You got it. They both were."

Emery puckered up his lips.

Kirby asked, "What names are they using?"

"Richard and Alexandra Collier."

"I made this long trip to talk to you in person, Peter, because our latest information is that Craig and Elizabeth pose even a more immediate and severe threat than we thought. You have to find a way to get them out of China immediately. Otherwise, they'll have time to solidify plans for an attack against United States bases."

Emery ran a hand through his red hair. "I'll tell Craig that I learned Chinese Intelligence is looking for them. They better get on the first plane out. Otherwise they'll be arrested and thrown into jail. That should scare the hell out of them."

Kirby frowned. "Call that Plan A. I doubt if it will work, because Craig's a gun-slinging cowboy—and he thinks he's invincible. But it can't hurt to try. After that?"

"I don't know. I have to think about it."

"You think Craig cares about Elizabeth?"

"Absolutely. Usually, I can get women like that. I made a soft move on her, but it was hopeless."

"Suppose you arranged to have someone abduct Elizabeth? You must know Chinese who would do that for money. Then have them threaten to kill her unless Craig leaves China. Once he's out, they'll release her and put her on the next plane. Make that Plan B."

Emery gave a long low whistle. "That's a bit excessive. Isn't it?"

"Not in view of the threat they pose. You've been through training courses and case studies. We did lots of stuff like that during the cold war, and against Muslim terror suspects after 9/11."

"But they're American citizens."

I need Emery's buy in.

"Right now they're enemies of the United States. I'm telling you to do this for the good of the country."

Emery was nodding.

"Besides, nobody will get hurt."

"I understand, Mr. Kirby. I'll do it."

"Good. That'll be Plan B. Keep me informed."

"Yes sir. I'll do that."

"After this is over, I'll give you a promotion. You'll come back to Washington as Deputy Director for Eastern Asia."

Emery's face lit up. "That's a plum of a job."

"You'll deserve it. You can get the job done."

They separated at the door of the business class lounge. Emery had to hustle to make the next flight to Beijing. Kirby had an hour before his plane to Washington.

He stopped in a bar and ordered a double scotch.

Then Kirby called Cindy in the CIA Transportation Tracking Office. "I want you to start examining the manifests of all planes out of Beijing or Shanghai for Richard and Alexandra Collier. If their names appear, please call my office and let me know immediately. If I don't answer, leave it on my voice mail."

"I'll do that Mr. Kirby."

The scotch arrived. He toasted. "Success." Ali would make sure Craig and Elizabeth had a proper welcome when they returned to the United States.

60

BEIJING

Elizabeth had read about the Summer Palace, but when the cab dropped her off twenty minutes before her meeting with Zerner and she wandered around, she was astounded. This place is huge. Hundreds of acres of Qing style pavilions, bridges, walkways, and gardens spread along the shores of Kunming Lake. She understood why the Empress Dowager Cixi made it her full time residence.

She checked her watch. Two. No sign of Zerner. He did say the East Gate.

At two fifteen, she became worried. This wasn't like Carl. Had Chinese intelligence picked him up because he was meeting her? Don't become paranoid, she told herself. But after Calgary and Tehran, who could blame her?

She looked over the crowds. With relief, she saw Carl coming toward her, moving rapidly, dodging around tourists. At thirty two, he was prematurely gray. The thick mop of hair on top of his six-foot-two thin frame fluttered in the breeze.

"Sorry I'm late. Traffic accident on the road in, and I couldn't get around it."

"I'm just glad you're here."

"Let's walk along the lake. It'll be easier to talk."

He set a fast pace; she followed alongside. Once no one could overhear them, he said, "What's going on with you, Liz?"

She disliked being called Liz. She'd corrected Carl lots of times, but he still did it. Today, she decided not to push the issue.

"What do you mean?"

"Sy Harrison e-mailed to say he replaced you as foreign editor. I meant to call you, but I never got around to doing it. Now suddenly you show up in Beijing. What's going on?"

"It's a long story."

"I told Janet I'd be home for dinner at eight. We've got plenty of time."

"Did you ever meet Francesca Page?"

"Yeah, at our retreat at that terrible place McDermott picked in the Catskills last November. I liked her. Smart. Good sense of humor."

"Well, she was murdered in Canada while covering a story."

"Jesus. Start at the beginning."

The sun came out, reflecting from the water, pushing the temperature into the sixties. They stopped walking and sat on a bench, facing the lake.

"I'll give you the whole story, Carl, but you can't write it up. At least not yet. I'll let you know if that changes."

"I understand."

For the next thirty minutes, she summarized everything she and Craig had done, while he peppered her with questions.

At the end, she asked, "Have you heard anything about a Chinese agreement with Iran, or an attack on Taiwan?"

"Negative. But you have to remember being a reporter here is different than most other places. With very few exceptions, government officials, even private parties, won't talk to foreign reporters, especially Americans. They're too frightened. Since Tiananmen, the repression has tightened, even in the internet age, which is pretty astounding. So, for the most part, we're relegated to official handouts. That suits most of my colleagues, who are lazy or too petrified to dig up and publish information that could be considered a state secret… which is most everything here."

"But you're not like that?"

"Of course not, Liz. You and I are cut from the same cloth. We live for a story like this. Francesca may have just been a kid, but I'll bet she knew in her first year she had the story of a lifetime. I have to say, though, McDermott firing you makes no sense. What's his game?"

"He's cheap. And he's a control freak. Jerks like that shouldn't own newspapers."

Zerner shook his head. "I can't buy that. Has to be something else."

"You sound like Craig Page."

"I'd like to meet him."

"You may before this is over. Craig thinks McDermott's working with an American who's part of this conspiracy."

"Sounds like it to me."

"What do you know about General Zhou?"

"He's a mean, tough SOB. Very much of a hawk. I'm not at all surprised he's planning to launch these operations. I wonder whether President Li has given approval, or whether General Zhou's running rogue operations."

He paused for a minute, then continued thoughtfully, "I should add that I've never met General Zhou. What I just told you came from people who aren't exactly fond of him."

"Who are they?"

"Admiral Xu and his wife Mei Ling. The Admiral had been head of Naval Operations until his death a few days ago. Rumors have been swirling that General Zhou had the Admiral killed, but no one's dared to suggest that in the media."

"How do you know Admiral Xu? And Mei Ling?"

"I was reaching out for Chinese officials to talk with, acting like a burglar who tries door after door, hoping to find one unlocked. The Admiral invited me and Janet to dinner a couple of times with his wife Mei Ling. He always used care in what he told me, but he wasn't able to conceal his dislike for General Zhou. I, of course, never printed that."

"What about Mei Ling?"

"She hates General Zhou even more. Her father had been a close confidant of Mao's until he was purged near the end of the tyrant's life, when he became a nut case, imagining conspiracies against him among his most loyal supporters. So that makes her Chinese aristocracy—so to speak."

Elizabeth watched a rowboat pass by. Strong and self confident, a young man in his twenties rowed while a beautiful, dark-haired woman looked at him in awe.

Mei Ling could be the break Craig and I need.

"You think Mei Ling would talk to me?"

"I can try to set it up. When?"

"Anytime. Call me on my cell and let me know. Nothing's more important than this. We're desperate to get a copy of the agreement between China and Iran. Maybe she can help with that."

61

BEIJING

"General Ming set our meeting at a furniture store," March said to Craig. The two of them were riding in the back of the Ambassador's bulletproof-paneled black Lincoln.

"How did he sound?"

"We had a strained conversation. My guess is he's fearful someone is recording his calls. I told him I enjoyed our last discussion and suggested another meeting to expand my knowledge of Beijing and China. Once I asked if he could meet today, he understood the urgency. He said I would learn a great deal from a visit to this furniture store because it has numerous antiques from the Qing Dynasty, some of the best anywhere in China."

"Did you mention me, or tell him you would be bringing someone?"

March shook his head. "Too risky. He may be surprised by your presence, but once he hears what you have to say, he'll be savvy enough to deal with it."

"How do you plan to introduce me?"

"As a representative of President Brewster."

"He may abort."

March folded his hands and put them in his lap. "That's a possibility. Unfortunately, he's the only choice you have in the available time."

They continued along the main road for half an hour into a business area with spanking new shopping malls and office buildings. Wedged in between them were blocks of older shops. It wouldn't be long, Craig guessed, before the wrecker's ball demolished them and made room for other high rises with indoor malls.

In the middle of a block of older, wooden buildings, the driver slowed while March looked out of the window, searching for the furniture store. "It's right here, John," March said to the driver. "Make a right turn at the corner and find a place to wait. I'll call you on my cell when we're coming out."

"Yes, sir, Mr. Ambassador. I'll do that."

Craig followed March into the shop filled with furniture and art. He quickly checked the people: three Japanese male customers and four young female clerks, each of whom had a white badge on a navy blue jacket.

March cut across the room and examined wooden chairs. Craig tagged along, pretending to be looking at the same objects. They were waiting for General Ming to appear. Craig hoped his presence wouldn't drive Ming away.

After a couple of minutes, one of the young women approached March. "I see you're interested in looking at some of our objects."

"You have some very beautiful things."

"We also have some items in the back in a special collection. Perhaps you would like to look at those."

"Yes, please."

With Craig two steps behind, the clerk led March toward the rear wall. After glancing around to make sure no one was observing her, she pushed a button on the wall, opening a concealed door to a crowded storeroom. In one corner, a Chinese man was sitting on a wooden crate. As soon as he saw them, he sprang to his feet. He was tall and distinguished-looking, with a full head of black hair, graying at the temples. He wore black-framed glasses and was dressed in a dark blue suit, white shirt, and tie. Without saying a word, the young woman retreated through the door and back into the shop. The door closed behind her.

"General Ming," March said. "I'd like you to meet a friend of mine from the United States, Craig Page."

Ming held out his hand and shook Craig's firmly. "Good to meet you, Mr. Page."

"Please call me Craig."

"I apologize for having us meet in this manner, but after our lunch at the Institute, I was forced to answer many questions. A colonel from military intelligence came to conduct an aggressive interrogation. I don't want to go through that again."

"I would not have called if it weren't an urgent matter."

"I understood that. Last time we met, you spoke with frankness and candor about your objective of having our two great nations work together. And not be adversaries. As you know, I share that objective. What is this about?"

"Craig is here as a representative of President Brewster. I have advised him to come right to the point with you, if you don't mind our being so forthright."

"No. Quite the opposite. I don't believe these walls have ears, but I don't know if someone followed me to the store and might be waiting outside. So it would be best if we kept our discussion as brief as possible."

March nodded to Craig.

"General Ming, I was recently in Iran. There, I learned about two critical developments, both of which involve China."

Ming was watching Craig.

"First," Craig said, selecting his words carefully, "it appears from satellite photos and other information that China is planning an attack on Taiwan to capture that island, and the attack is scheduled for April 1."

"What do you want from me?" General Ming asked, his eyes moving from Craig to March and back to Craig again.

"I'd like confirmation that this attack is scheduled for April 1. That the troop movements weren't merely saber rattling or a practice exercise."

"And if it is, are you seeking this information to permit your country to better prepare for the defense of Taiwan? You're asking me to betray my own country and to assist your nation in inflicting enormous casualties upon China?"

"No. That's not it at all. If an actual attack is planned, I will report that to President Brewster, who will initiate discussions with President Li in an effort to resolve the issue by peaceful means. Ambassador March told me that you share his view of wanting to avoid a confrontation between our two great nations. As a result, I'm hopeful you could be of help in this situation."

"You ask a great deal, Mr. Page. You realize that."

He won't help me. I'm finished.

"You told me there were two developments," General Ming said. "What is the second?"

"When I was recently in Tehran, I learned that an agreement had been entered into between China and Iran. My understanding is that it involves oil and a joint military operation. I don't know all the details. I was told that a written agreement exists. I haven't seen it or been able to obtain a copy. As you might imagine, President

Brewster is anxious to find out what is involved in this arrangement. An agreement of this type would run counter to the interests of all people wanting to have peace and prosperity."

"I understand that very well. As soon as you mentioned China and Iran entering into an agreement, I had some concern that it was aimed at the United States. I agree that it would be important to ascertain what this agreement provides and perhaps to foil it. Do you know when this agreement will be implemented?"

"My understanding is that the date is also April 1. Somehow, these two actions are linked, but I haven't been able to learn in what way."

General Ming glanced at his watch. "April 1 is only four days from now."

"Unfortunately, that's correct." Craig decided to press ahead. "Prior to today's meeting, have you heard anything about either of these two Chinese operations?"

General Ming hesitated for a second, then responded, "A few days ago, I heard some talk about a possible attack on Taiwan. Specifically, that there were Chinese troop movements both on land and in the water in the direction of Taiwan. I had assumed, until I met with you, that those were one of our routine and periodic military exercises. With respect to an agreement between China and Iran, I have not heard a single word."

Doubt crept into Craig's mind. Could the information he obtained from Yossi and Sabi about the agreement be wrong? Did he deceive President Brewster?

Sensing Craig's body language, General Ming added, "That doesn't mean an agreement like this doesn't exist. Since I was retired, I haven't been informed about military developments. On the civilian side, I have some contacts in the premier's office, but those aren't as good as I would like. If this is a recent agreement or something that's moving quickly, then I might not know about it."

Craig swallowed hard. "Is there any way you could find out whether an agreement between China and Iran has been concluded and what it provides?"

General Ming took off his glasses and cleaned them slowly with a handkerchief.

"What I could do," Ming finally said, "is make inquiries, on a confidential basis, without leading a trail back to either of you, about what is happening between China and Iran. I want to be clear, however, that I'm doing this because I've spent my life in the military. I'm aware of the horrors of war. By helping you, I might be able to avoid one."

"I understand that," Craig said. "I'd be grateful for any help."

"I'll need a bit of time."

"Time is something we don't have. You heard the schedule."

"Believe me, I'm well aware of the deadline. What I would like to have is until two o'clock tomorrow afternoon. I will do my best in the next twenty four hours to find out whether a Chinese attack on Taiwan is imminent. Also whether our nation has reached an agreement with Iran, and if so, what it provides."

Craig was relieved. "That would be perfect, General Ming."

"We should meet again tomorrow," Ming said, "at two o'clock in this store."

General Ming turned to Ambassador March. "Will you be coming tomorrow also?"

"No. I don't think I will. I wanted to make this introduction. It's a matter for Craig to handle himself."

"The two of you leave first," General Ming said. He walked over to the door and gently pushed it open, while concealing himself along a side wall.

Leaving the furniture store, Craig was worried. All his eggs were in one very fragile basket.

62

BEIJING

For Craig, dinner with Elizabeth had been a two-hour respite from the tension they faced in Beijing. He liked the restaurant Zerner had recommended, a twenty minute walk from the St. Regis. Afraid to discuss what they were doing in Beijing, they talked about Italy, France, and other places they'd both been.

But once they walked back in the cool air, the weight of their mission hung over him.

Craig told Elizabeth, "General Ming is our best hope, but I don't have confidence in him. The odds on Mei Ling are even longer."

Approaching the St. Regis, Craig saw a blue Toyota sedan parked along the street, in front of the hotel. The driver's door opened. In the bright lights illuminating the area, Craig immediately recognized Peter Emery. He was walking in their direction, looking worried.

Once he was three feet away, Emery said softly, "Craig, you and I have to talk. Let Elizabeth go upstairs. C'mon in the car with me."

Elizabeth was visibly alarmed.

"It's okay," Craig said to her. "I'll meet you in the room."

Craig followed Emery to his car and climbed in the front on the passenger side. Emery started the engine.

"Where are we going?"

"For a ride around the block. We have to talk."

"What happened?"

Emery eased the car onto the road.

"I received a call from a source in Chinese Intelligence. He wanted to meet with me on an urgent matter. I saw him about an hour ago."

"And?" Craig said impatiently.

"He told me they've cut through your cover. They know you're not Richard Collier. You're Craig Page."

"How did they figure that out?"

"He didn't say. I stuck with what you told me yesterday. That you're Richard Collier. Your wife is Alexandra. You're a family friend of Ambassador March's. In Beijing you're touring with your wife. When you reach Shanghai, you intend to meet some business contacts, but I don't know what business you're in. That went over like a lead balloon. They're convinced you're in China as a spy, working for the CIA. They intend to arrest you and Elizabeth for espionage."

Craig tried to appear calm. His insides were churning. How the hell did they find out so soon? he wondered. He couldn't confide in Emery. Instead, he said, "Well they're wrong."

Emery parked at the side of the street. He turned toward Craig. "If you are here to spy on China and you don't want to tell me, that's your business. But you better listen to what else the Chinese intelligence agent told me."

"Go ahead."

"He said you and your girlfriend are in such extreme danger you must leave China immediately. 'If I were Craig Page, I'd be on the next plane out.' Those were my contact's exact words."

"How did you respond?"

"I said I would pass along his warning to you."

Craig remained mute, digesting Emery's words.

Emery continued, "I know our government does strange things. Keeping the CIA station chief out of the action on a critical issue involving China wouldn't surprise me. If there's something like that going on, it's between you and Kirby. I can tell you, however, that my contact is right. Now that they're on to you, the two of you have to leave China immediately."

Emery had made a slow circle around the hotel. When he pulled up to the curb in front, he said to Craig, "I'll do anything to help you get out of the country. Make airplane reservations. Drive you to the airport." He paused for a minute. "I'll wait here while you and Elizabeth pack. Once you come down, we're good to go. The most important thing I have to do right now is help you and Elizabeth get out of China as quickly as possible."

Craig had no intention of leaving until he obtained the agreement. "Thanks for the warning, Peter, but I'm not going anywhere."

Emery ran his hand through his hair. "You've got to be kidding. Are you crazy? They'll haul you in for interrogation. They'll torture you and Elizabeth. Then they'll execute both of you. Nobody will even know what happened to you. The Ambassador will file a protest, and it'll be ignored. They'll say they have no idea where you are. Believe me, I've seen it happen. Remember that Harvard professor last year? The protests haven't done squat."

"I hear you."

"Man, you better reconsider. You can't be that insane. You've been in countries that operate the same way, I'm sure, in the Middle East."

Craig was getting annoyed at Emery. Peter had done his job. Craig knew the risks. The decision was his.

"Your concern is duly noted. I'm not going."

"What do you hope to accomplish? What do you think you can possibly do now that Chinese Intelligence is on to you?"

"Thanks for your advice."

Craig reached for the door handle.

"Even if you're too much of a fool to save your own ass, think of Elizabeth. You can't subject her to what they'll do."

Craig opened the door.

"Tell Elizabeth what I told you. She'll have the sense to make you rethink the issue. Tell her. I know she'll want to leave. I'll wait here for another hour. When she persuades you to change your mind, I'll drive you to the airport."

"Forget it," Craig said, with the ring of finality. "I'm not leaving China. You can go home now. Your waiting is pointless."

When Craig entered their room, Elizabeth was still dressed. He put a finger to his lips and signaled with his hand toward the door. Out in the corridor, they took the elevator to the lobby. Guessing Emery would still be in front of the hotel, Craig led her through the rear entrance, to a garden with a pond in the center. The area was deserted. Fat orange fish were swimming in the water.

"What'd that jerk want?" she asked.

"He said he learned from a source in Chinese intelligence that they know I'm Craig Page. According to Emery, they think I'm here spying for the CIA. So the two of us better get out before we're arrested."

"You sound as if you don't believe him."

"I just don't know. Something about it didn't ring true. If they knew about me, why haven't they picked me up? We were walking to and from the hotel to dinner."

"Could Kirby want us out?"

"I thought of that, but it doesn't compute. Kirby has to think I'll fail in China. So why not leave me here?"

Craig was trying to come up with another explanation. He couldn't.

"What'd you tell Emery?"

"I'm staying. He said I should at least give you the chance to leave. And it may not be a bad idea."

She looked at him sharply. "Forget it. I'm staying until we're done."

"But Emery may be passing along accurate information. That Chinese intelligence is…"

"I have a chance to meet with Mei Ling. Remember, Carl said she hates General Zhou. He may have killed her husband. She could be very valuable to us. I won't leave at least until I talk to her, or find out she won't meet with me."

"Chinese prisons aren't pleasant places."

"Tell me about it. I edited a piece by Carl on the subject in January."

"God, you're as stubborn as I am."

"The supreme compliment."

"Okay, somehow we have to get through the next couple of days."

"We should take one precaution." She gave him Carl Zerner's cell number. "We can use Carl as our intermediary if we can't reach each other."

"Why don't you go back to the room," he told Elizabeth. "I'll meet you there."

"What are you doing?"

"Stopping in the hotel kitchen."

At this late hour, he saw only two women mopping the kitchen floor. He waited until they were looking the other way, then he snatched two sharp knives from a rack—a butcher knife and a skinning knife for fish or poultry. He concealed them in his jacket.

They were sharing a king sized bed. He put one knife on the night table on each side. Guns would have been better, but he had no idea where he could get one at night on the streets of Beijing.

He put the deadbolt on the door, then turned the television to max volume so they could talk. "If they come for us, it'll probably be at night," he said. "We'll sleep in our clothes. Once we hear them at the door, we go for the knives. I'll try to grab one of their guns. If we make it out of the room, we use the inside staircase to the lobby. From the entrance, it's a short dash to the embassy compound. We'll have to take out the guards in the booth to get in. The good news is I've only seen two of them each time I've passed through."

"Can you run with that leg?"

"It's almost back to normal. I will if I have to."

Three hours later, he was still awake, staring at the ceiling, his ears trained on the door. He couldn't hear a sound. He checked his watch. 3:10 am. He recalled other sleepless nights over the years, in many different places.

Elizabeth whispered, "Are you asleep?"

"No."

"I'm scared. Hold me."

He met her in the middle of the bed and wrapped his arms around her, pressing the front of his body tight against hers.

Without thinking, he reached down and kissed her. It seemed like the most natural thing to do. She was clutching him tightly.

He ran his hand down her body along her leg, then under her skirt and inside of her silk panties. She was so wet; she moaned with pleasure as he stroked her moist folds of flesh, which aroused him. He found her clit with his finger and thumb. In seconds he felt her body shake as she came in his hand.

Then she reached down and unzipped his pants, grabbing his hard cock and stroking it. She helped him off with his pants. Then took his cock in her mouth.

Abruptly, she pulled away. "I want you inside of me. I'll come on top. It'll be easier for your leg."

She climbed up and mounted him, her hands at her sides, not touching his leg. She felt so damn good moving her body up and down.

He was waiting for her. "Now," she cried out.

They came together.

"That was wonderful," she said sliding off and lying next to him.

After several minutes, they put their clothes back on. Holding each other, they fell asleep.

63

BEIJING

As soon as the waiter left the breakfast table and departed, Craig turned on the television and increased the volume to the max. With the CNN announcer droning on, he moved close to Elizabeth and whispered, "What if Peter Emery is right?"

"But nothing happened last night."

"They could be making their move today. I think you should cancel your touring and stay in the hotel. If Carl calls, you can go out."

"That's ridiculous," she whispered back. "There may be doubt about us in Chinese intelligence. We have to maintain our cover. Let them think we really are tourists. If they've made up their mind, it won't matter. Besides, they can snatch me as easily out of this hotel room as they can off the street."

"I think you're being foolish."

"C'mon, Craig. We talked about it last evening."

"You need a weapon. Take the skinning knife. It'll fit in your purse."

"Good idea. What do you have?"

"I brought a pocket knife in my luggage. The butcher knife's too large."

"Alright. It's settled. We tour together this morning. You break off about noon. I'll leave if and when Carl calls."

Dan, the guide Emery had selected, was waiting in the lobby. He was a short, squat Chinese man in his mid-fifties, who spoke perfect English and was smoking a foul smelling Chinese cigarette. From the time he'd met Dan yesterday, Craig was struck by the perpetual frown, the sour, sullen look, on his crease lined face. And his dark, sad eyes.

On the other hand, as Peter Emery had promised, he was a phenomenal guide. "We'll begin our tour in the Forbidden City," Dan had told Craig and Elizabeth yesterday once they were in the car and the driver pulled away from the St. Regis. "In order to appreciate our current situation in China, it's absolutely critical to understand our history. In Beijing, that lesson must begin in the Forbidden City."

Dan had moved slowly and deliberately in the well preserved cluster of ancient buildings, which had been home to two dynasties of emperors who lived almost exclusively in the palace complex. From within these palace walls, the entirety of China was governed for centuries until the 1911 revolution marking the end of the Qing Dynasty. He reeled off for Elizabeth and Craig in a careful, methodical way details about each of the buildings and the code of rules and protocols that governed life in the royal court. When they asked questions, Dan was always patient with them, providing full and complete answers. His English was flawless. Still, Craig wished that the man would have smiled.

This morning, with Dan leading them, Craig and Elizabeth visited sites in old Beijing. First, Prince Gong's mansion, the home of the last emperor's great uncle. At eleven o'clock, they reached the Drum Tower. Dan went first, climbing the sixty nine high and uneven stone stairs to the top platform to reach a tenth-century Yuan dynasty drum used to send warnings to people in the surrounding area. Elizabeth followed behind the guide. Craig took up the rear.

Once they reached the top, Dan moved close to the edge, next to the narrow metal railing and told them about the drum.

Craig was listening only slightly. He was more concerned with watching the guide. Ever since they had met Dan in the lobby this morning, Craig had been struck by how nervous he seemed. He was chain smoking cigarettes, already on his second pack. His eyes were twitching today. They hadn't yesterday.

On the other side of the railing, exposed in front of them, was much of Beijing. Instinctively, Craig remained several feet back from the precipice and kept Elizabeth close to him. No sign of Chinese intelligence.

When it was time to descend the stairs, Craig let Dan go first again. He held Elizabeth back. Once the guide reached the next landing and couldn't hear them, Craig whispered to her, "I have to leave once we reach the bottom. I think you should go back to the hotel now."

"I thought we settled that this morning."

"There's one difference. I don't like the guide. Something about him bothers me."

"You're being silly. He's a bit of a nervous fellow, but he's okay. Besides if I stop touring, that'll raise suspicions about our cover."

"My gut tells me that you don't want to stick with Dan any longer."

"Aw, c'mon Craig. You're worrying too much."

He decided to back off, let her continue touring while he went off for his meeting with General Ming.

Once they reached the ground, Craig said to Dan, "I have some other things to do on my own around Beijing. So I'll leave you two now."

"Can our driver drop you somewhere?" Dan asked.

"The nearest subway stop."

After Dan gave the driver instructions in Chinese, the car pulled into heavy noonday traffic. Craig noticed that Dan was glancing at his watch again as he had repeatedly in the morning, acting like someone on a tight schedule.

64

BEIJING

Thin briefcase in hand, General Zhou exited the elevator on the top floor, the fiftieth, of the Zhou Enterprises Building. Distraught, he ignored the receptionist, making a beeline for his brother's huge, richly paneled, corner office with a commanding view of the city.

He couldn't believe what he'd just learned.

"We have a problem," General Zhou said, as he kicked the door shut behind him.

Zhou Yun looked up from his computer screen. "What happened?"

General Zhou reached into his briefcase, pulled out a man's picture and tossed it on the desk.

"This man has entered the embassy compound twice in the last two days to go the American Embassy. We took his picture as part of routine surveillance. We forwarded it to our agents around the world. Two of them in the Middle East recognized the man. He's…"

"Craig Page," Zhou Yun completed the sentence and shook his head in disgust. "Do we know what name he's using?"

"We checked with passport control at the airport. He's traveling with a woman. They're using the names Richard and Alexandra Collier. We have her picture too."

He handed that one to his brother. "Elizabeth Crowder, Francesca Page's editor."

"You made a serious error," Zhou Yun said. "You should have given these pictures to passport control as soon as we knew his daughter Francesca was the reporter in Calgary. We could have stopped Craig Page at the airport."

General Zhou bristled. He had no intention of accepting the blame.

"You never suggested that then. Besides, we were depending on Kirby. That fucking Kirby. He can't do anything. And as long as we're assigning blame, don't forget it was your idea to involve him in the first place, convincing me that…"

Zhou Yun raised his hand. "Okay, okay, brother. Enough finger pointing. The situation's not dire. Chances are Craig won't find out anything in a few short days. But we don't even have to take that risk. We deal with it by eliminating Craig Page—and the woman, too."

"I agree. Their entry documents show they're staying at the St. Regis, but we can't send troops into the hotel. President Li has given edicts in the past against snatching foreigners from their hotels. I don't want to do anything to involve him. Not now. We'll have to grab and kill Craig outside of the hotel."

"Can you station troops outside of the hotel to watch people going in and out?"

"Absolutely. I'll move on it right now. We'll seize him on the street."

"Good. Meantime, I have some civilian strongmen I use for business enforcement. I'll get them on it immediately. Let them do the killing rather than your soldiers. We wouldn't want to alarm our dear President."

65

BEIJING

After leaving Elizabeth and Dan, Craig took the subway to a stop close to the St. Regis. Exiting the station and walking along the street, he was constantly looking around, eyes darting in every direction. He was satisfied that nobody was tailing him. Perhaps Emery's information was wrong. Or Chinese intelligence intended to pick him up when he was with General Ming.

He returned to his hotel room to check for messages before leaving for his meeting with General Ming. No one had called, but he was alarmed. He had been careful to leave his guidebooks and his papers, though innocuous, in specific places on the desk. He had also placed inside the safe, along with cash and passports, some pieces of paper which had incomprehensible doodling. He had taken careful note of how he had lined them up. Now he found the papers and books on the desk had been moved. That could have been the maid. But the ones inside the safe had been disturbed as well. Nothing was missing, but he was certain someone had been in his room and searched it. Craig opened the top drawer that held his clothes. The butcher knife from the kitchen was still there.

He left the room and rode down in the elevator. In front of the St. Regis, he climbed into a taxi and asked the driver to take him to the Palace Hotel. From the Palace, he began walking the ten blocks to the furniture store.

Covering the first two blocks, Craig didn't see anyone suspicious on the crowded sidewalk. In the third block, a large construction site was on his right. When he was opposite the site, he noticed two heavyset Chinese men in Western business suits moving up behind him. One was on his right, the other on his left. He picked up his pace to get away from these two. As he did, the man on his left, without any warning, swung his right arm and smashed his elbow into Craig's kidney. It was a powerful blow, perfectly aimed. The pain was excruciating. Craig dropped to his knees. His vision was blurred.

The man who assaulted Craig grabbed him around the waist and pulled him into the construction site. None of the pedestrians was paying attention.

Once they were through the gate of the construction site, they dragged Craig to a shed that held building supplies. They opened the door and pulled Craig inside, shutting the door behind them. It was only Craig and the two men in the shed.

At first, Craig's eyes refused to focus. Then his sight came back and his mind cleared. He saw one of the men pick up a piece of wood, a two by four, three feet long. Meantime, the other man yanked Craig, who had been on the ground, to an upright position. He was strong. Standing behind Craig, he had his hands wrapped around Craig's waist, while his colleague held the piece of wood as if he were preparing to swing a baseball bat.

Craig tried to appear more groggy than he was to gain the element of surprise. He mumbled in an almost incoherent voice, "What happened?... Where am I?..."

"Hey, you American," the man with the piece of wood said. "You play baseball. Yes… hey?…"

"What did you say?…" Craig muttered. His act was having the desired effect. He felt the man holding him loosen his grip.

The man with the piece of wood said, "I use your head for baseball. We beat you to death. You understand that?"

"Don't understand… Don't understand…"

"I tell you one more time. I use your head for baseball. Beat you to death."

The man wound up to swing.

Now I have to make my move. Before he brings the wood forward.

With a sudden burst of motion, Craig pulled himself away from the man who was holding him. He threw himself at the assailant with the wood. As he did, in a single roundhouse motion, Craig brought up his right hand, tightened it into a fist, and swung it with all of his might toward the side of the man's head.

He hit the man so hard, knocking him unconscious, that he could feel bones crunch in the side of the man's head. Meantime, Craig's hand hurt from the blow. He hoped to hell he hadn't broken it.

Craig then wheeled around to face the second man who tore into Craig knocking him down and falling on top. Craig rolled away. The two of them were on the dirt ground. The Chinese man was on top again. He raised his hand and tried to punch Craig in the face. Craig deflected the powerful blow with his forearm. He clawed Craig's face, tearing the flesh, then lunged for Craig's eye. Craig was too fast for him. He twisted away and flipped the Chinese man on his back. Craig, blood dripping from his face, was straddling his assailant, both of his hands around the man's neck.

"Who sent you?" Craig shouted as he tightened his grip. When the man didn't answer, Craig continued tightening. "Who sent you? You tell me now or I'll kill you."

The man still didn't respond. Craig knew he was close to cutting off air from the man's windpipe. Still, he wouldn't talk. He'll die before he tells me anything, Craig decided. No point killing him. Whoever sent him must have plenty of others.

Craig let go, reached out and lunged for another piece of wood on the ground. He rose to his knees, then smacked the man in his head, not hard enough to kill him, but hard enough to knock him out. "I use your head for baseball," Craig said.

He pulled himself to his feet and straightened his clothes. His pants were torn at the knees. He checked the bandage on his leg. The wound wasn't bleeding. He squeezed his right hand open and shut. Not broken.

Leaving the two unconscious Chinese men on the ground, Craig exited the shed. Bloody and dazed, he resumed walking toward the furniture store. As soon as he entered the shop, he saw, standing next to the cash register in front, the young woman who had taken him and March to the back of the back store yesterday. The minute she saw Craig, she moved away from the register, walked up to him and said, "Please come with me."

She had to be startled by his appearance, but she didn't make any comment. Craig followed her into the storeroom, as he had with March yesterday. He remembered seeing an employee's bathroom there and he asked to use it for a minute. He washed his scratched face and combed his hair, hoping not to alarm Ming, who would already be nervous, any more than necessary.

Once Craig came out of the bathroom, he asked the woman, "Where is General Ming?"

"He's not coming."

Craig's spirits fell. All this for nothing.

"He sent a car to take you to him."

She led him to a rear entrance which opened into an alleyway. A dark-blue sedan with tinted windows was parked there, it's engine idling. She opened the door to the backseat, and he quickly climbed in. A Chinese man was behind the wheel, but no one else in the car. She slammed the door and quickly returned to the shop.

The driver slammed his foot on the accelerator and roared down the alley. For ten minutes, he drove on secondary roads, in an area of high rise buildings, apartments rather than office buildings. The streets were deserted for the most part, because it was mid afternoon in a residential area.

The driver pulled up to the curb and stopped the car. He got out and opened the door for Craig. Then he pointed to an identical-looking dark blue sedan with tinted windows parked five yards away. He motioned to Craig to get into that car.

Craig found Ming in the back seat. A driver in front. No one else in the car. General Ming reached into the pocket of his jacket, extracted a pair of glasses with black lenses and handed them to Craig. "I have to ask you to wear these. They'll completely block your vision."

"Is that necessary?"

"Personally, I don't think so, but the individual you'll be talking with insisted on it as a condition of meeting with us. He doesn't want you to know where you're going."

"I'll do it then."

A glass partition separated the front of the car from the back. General Ming slid open the glass and said to the driver, "You may proceed." He then closed the partition. Craig put on the glasses. The car began moving.

"Who will we be meeting with?"

"I can't give you his name. He's prepared to tell you about the agreement between China and Iran."

"What about the Chinese attack on Taiwan? Will he have information about that as well?"

"You're very impatient. I planned to tell you about that next."

"Forgive me. I sometimes do that."

"It's not just you. It's a cultural difference I've noticed. When I talk with Americans, they frequently interrupt other speakers without letting them finish. We don't operate that way here. My suggestion is that you be very careful in our meeting. We don't want him to be offended by this cultural discrepancy."

"I understand. I'll try to bear it in mind." Craig wanted to ask General Ming again, "What about the Chinese attack on Taiwan?" but he took General Ming's cautionary note seriously. He waited.

Ten seconds later, Ming said, "We don't have to talk to the man about the Chinese attack on Taiwan. I've been able to obtain information about that myself."

Craig held his breath and waited for Ming to continue.

"What I learned is that there won't be a Chinese attack to retake Taiwan."

"But I thought our information on that point was reliable."

"A considerable amount of disinformation has been spread by the Chinese military to suggest they are planning to launch such an attack. It included movement of troops, naval destroyers and other ships as well. General Zhou is doing this to divert attention from the agreement he reached with Iran. He believes what he is doing with Iran is so critical to China and has such serious adverse consequences for the United States that it was essential that the Americans not find out about it before April 1. These military movements were undertaken to suggest that China would be launching an attack on Taiwan. They were all elaborate diversions."

"Can you tell me anything about the man we'll be meeting with?" Craig asked.

"He emphasized to me how critical it was that you not know his identity. All I'm permitted to tell you is that he's a high ranking official in CNOC. As you may be aware, General Zhou's brother, Zhou Yun, is the Director, or what you Americans call the CEO, of CNOC. This man knows he's risking his life by talking to you. However, he believes what's being planned is not in the best interests of China."

Craig thought about Peter Emery's warning. Was he being led into a trap?

Kirby's office had an adjacent suite containing a bedroom and bath. The DCI used it for crises when he remained at CIA headquarters around the clock. He was now in a crisis mode.

At midnight, he stripped to his underwear and lay down in bed. He kept open the connecting door to his office. He didn't want to miss Emery's call on the secure red phone.

Sleep was impossible even after a double Johnny Walker blue label.

The phone rang at one fifteen in the morning. Kirby jumped up, raced into his office, and grabbed it. "Yes," he said in an anxiety filled voice.

"Peter Emery here. I want to give you a progress report, Mr. Kirby."

"Go ahead."

"Plan A didn't work."

"Big surprise. And?" he asked impatiently.

There was a long pause.

He doesn't want to do it. Well, that's too fucking bad.

"And?"

"Everything is in place for plan B. The gentleman should be on a United plane out of Beijing for Washington at midnight Beijing time."

"Excellent."

"I'll call you when he's in the air."

66

BEIJING

During lunch at a small restaurant with Dan, after Craig left them, Elizabeth learned why he was such an unhappy man.

"You speak very good English," Elizabeth said as she struggled to pick up her food with chopsticks. "Did you travel in the United States or England?"

Dan paused to sip some water before responding. "The rates for guides are set by the government at a ridiculously low amount. We're not permitted to charge any more. With what I earn from this job, I can't even travel to Shanghai, much less to Europe or the United States."

Sorry she had asked the question, she tried to change the subject. "I know we've been looking at the history of your country, and it is truly magnificent. What I have found breathtaking as well is all of the modern construction around the city. I've never seen so many cranes or large buildings that are new or under construction. The rapid growth of the Chinese economy is truly phenomenal."

"You must not be deceived. It is true there has been phenomenal economic expansion. It is also true there has been an enormous increase in wealth. However, you must recognize that the wealth is not being shared among the entire population. Quite the contrary. The beneficiaries of this great economic boom are a small minority. The vast majority, not merely peasants on farms, but poor struggling working people within the cities are not sharing in this economic miracle. For those of us at the bottom of the economic chain," he said with bitterness, "there has been no economic miracle. We toil and struggle long hours simply to have enough to eat. We have no prospect of doing better."

"You're so knowledgeable about the city," Elizabeth said, changing the subject again, "How long have you been a guide?"

"More than fifteen years. Before that, I was a professor of history at Beijing University."

She raised her eyebrows. "Do you still teach when you're not taking people around to see the city?"

"I was fired from my job after the Tiananmen protests. I'm not permitted to teach any longer."

"Your English is good. Have you ever considered teaching Chinese history in the United States?

"I would like that, but I would need a loan to pay for the airplane and expenses while I found a job there."

Elizabeth expected him to ask her for money, but he didn't. He checked his watch, then said, "Time to visit the hutongs."

She and Dan climbed in the back of a pedicab, a contraption Elizabeth had never seen before, and sat on a faded and torn leather seat. Up front the driver, an elderly man with powerful legs, peddled. She removed her cell phone from her jacket pocket and checked whether she'd missed a call from Carl. No missed calls. No messages.

"The term hutong literally means alleyways," Dan said, between drags on his vile-smelling Chinese cigarette.

In a few minutes, they left behind the glamour and glitz of modern Beijing with its steel and glass high-rise office buildings, its new automobiles and shopping malls. They entered a world of the past with tiny, narrow streets. Some of them not even paved. Covered with dry dirt and dust that kicked up as they rode. On both sides of the narrow road were one-story ramshackle dwellings that Elizabeth had read about as being historic courtyard houses.

"This used to be what all of Beijing was like," Dan said. "Rows and rows of homes like these. This is how people lived in the city. Large courtyard houses for wealthy families. The entire family could live there. Smaller ones for poor people. Gradually, as the city grew and expanded, coming into the modern world, these clusters of hutongs, as the houses are called, are being destroyed, one by one, to make way for the new modern Beijing."

"Sad, isn't it?" Elizabeth said. "After all, it's more than a house. A way of life. Part of the history and culture of the city. What a shame to see it lost."

The guide shook his head in disgust. "It's a lot worse than that. Once I had some American clients whom I took on a tour. The man was a lawyer. He explained to me that in the United States before the government can take someone's house or property, they have to pay that individual for the value of his house. Here we don't have anything like that. The government simply says, 'you have one week to get out.' After that, the bulldozers destroy the house. That's it. No payment or compensation. The government has been destroying approximately ten thousand of these dwellings a year. They keep bulldozing them to make way for the new modern Beijing. Then the wealthy developers and builders come in. They make a fortune selling the new apartments, and as usual, the poor people get nothing."

Elizabeth didn't respond. She wasn't interested in prolonging the discussion with Dan about Chinese politics and his animosity toward the regime and its economic policies. The guide tossed his smoldering cigarette out of the pedicab, onto the dirt road, and lit another. "I think it would be worthwhile for you to go inside and visit one of these hutong houses."

She glanced at her cell phone, willing it to ring. C'mon Carl. Nothing.

"I would like that."

"Good. There's one up ahead. I know the people. They have a son, a teenager who speaks very good English. He'll explain how the hutong houses were built and how people like his parents live."

The driver pedaled through a few more blocks and made a left turn. They were now proceeding down a narrow, dirt-covered alleyway. The guide tapped the driver on the shoulder. They stopped alongside a building of faded and peeling pale yellow wood. As Dan helped her out of the pedicab, Elizabeth looked around. The dusty road was deserted except for a small tea house about fifty yards away. In front of it, two elderly men sat at a table playing chess. To the left was the entrance of an old courtyard house. The gates were stone. She saw several large trees.

Dan pointed to the two ornate stone statues in the shape of dragons on either side of the entrance. "These are intended to keep out evil spirits. This courtyard house was constructed approximately two hundred years ago. Right now it's not much different from when it was built."

Following the guide, Elizabeth walked down the tree-lined lane. Based upon the odor, they passed the outhouse.

"Originally this was all a single house," Dan said, "but as you can tell, it's been divided into many separate units."

"How do they heat the houses?"

"With a wood-burning stove or perhaps coal in one of the rooms."

They walked twenty more yards, then turned right into an old creaky wooden doorway. What caught Elizabeth's eye as soon as she stepped inside the cramped living room, jammed with furniture, was a young man, maybe sixteen, seated at a desk. His eyes were focused on a computer screen.

"I see you're surprised by the computer," Dan said. "Don't be. Even in a complex like this, computer usage is widespread, particularly among young people."

The young man stood up and stuck out his hand. "Pleased to meet you, Miss."

Dan said, "Would you mind showing her around the house, and explaining how people live. I'm going down the street to pick up a package of cigarettes." He looked at Elizabeth. "I hope that's okay with you."

"Of course. I'm sure he'll be able to explain it to me."

The young man seemed tense and awkward. Elizabeth guessed he wasn't accustomed to speaking with foreign visitors. He stuttered for a moment, then began in halting English. "This was once a house that belonged to a wealthy nobleman. After the revolution, the house was taken over by the government. In China, all property is owned by the government. It was broken up into a number of smaller units. My grandparents were assigned this unit by the government. I was born here, in this room."

Through the corner of her eye, Elizabeth watched Dan leave the house. "How many rooms do you have?" she asked.

"This one and another in the back where some of us sleep. Others sleep in this room." He walked over to the wall and placed his hand on what looked like an old makeshift stove. "This is where we get heat." He showed her the kitchen area in a corner off the living room. "Let me show you the bedroom."

"I don't want to disturb anyone."

"No one else is here. You can walk into the other room. I'll follow you."

She obeyed the young man's instruction, moving toward the bedroom. As she crossed the narrow threshold, a heavy set, muscular Chinese man, dressed in a white T-shirt cut off at the shoulders, who had been lurking around the corner, stepped out to block her path. "Hey," she cried out.

Before she had a chance to say any more, he yanked the purse out of her hand and threw it onto a table. With one powerful arm, he grabbed her around the waist. With the other, he picked up a burlap sack from the floor. In a single sweeping motion, he tossed the sack over her head and pulled it down the length of her body. Then he picked her up and threw her over his shoulder. She was kicking and screaming, waving her arms, trying to get free, but the man was too strong. He tossed her onto a bed.

Then he used two pieces of rope, she guessed, to wrap around the burlap, one locking her arms against her sides; the other tying her ankles together.

She saw a knife blade sticking through the burlap near her face, and she was terrified and helpless. She had no way of getting at the knife in her purse. She closed her eyes to protect them. He was only cutting two holes.

"You breath now," he said.

She could breathe, but she couldn't move.

"What do you want?" she shouted frantically, trying to make herself heard through the burlap. "What do you want?"

The man didn't respond.

"Money? I'll give you money."

Still no response. "When the guide comes back, you'll be in trouble. You'll be arrested. You'll go to jail. I'm a tourist. You can't treat me this way."

The man laughed caustically. "Save energy lady. You better to remain quiet."

"What do you want? Tell me. I'll give it to you. Money. Anything. Tell me what you want."

The man laughed again.

She realized further protest was hopeless. Dan wasn't coming back. He'd arranged her abduction. She had been so stupid, dismissing Craig's concerns about the guide.

How will he ever find me?

67

BEIJING

Though Craig couldn't see, he knew the car was approaching an oil refinery. In the Middle East, Craig constantly lived with the distinctive odor from the processing of crude. The car slowed to a stop.

"We've arrived," General Ming said. "Please keep the dark glasses on until we're inside the building."

The car door opened. General Ming took Craig's arm and led him along a cement path.

"We're entering a warehouse," General Ming said, "and walking down stairs. Hold onto the banister on the right. I'll take your left arm."

Craig followed Ming's instructions. Without being able to see, he had to use his other senses to gain as much information as he could of his physical surroundings. The steps were wooden and rough. He counted them. Twenty altogether. At the bottom, his feet encountered a dirt floor.

Maintaining his grip on Craig's arm, General Ming led him along the dirt surface. Craig heard a door slamming behind them at the top of the stairs and a lock click into place, isolating them. When Ming stopped moving, Craig reached out his arm. He struck a wooden object with his hand. "That's a chair," Ming said to Craig. "You can sit down."

Craig felt his way into the chair.

General Ming took off the dark glasses and placed them on an oil-stained wooden table.

It took Craig almost a minute before his eyes became accustomed to the surroundings. The room was dimly lit. He saw three chairs around a table. He was seated on one side. General Ming across from him. The chair at the head of the table was empty. In front of it was a computer. On the far wall, a screen for a Power Point presentation or a video. Craig rubbed his eyes; the room came into focus.

A door at the far end opened. A man entered, wearing on his face a mask that revealed only his eyes and his nose. He had a black baseball cap on his head with CNOC in white letters across the front. As the man in the mask moved toward the chair at the head of the table, he said, "Accept my apologies for insisting we conduct our meeting this way. As General Ming told you, I believe it is imperative."

"I very much appreciate your talking to me under these or any circumstances."

"Before I begin, there's something else you must understand."

"What's that?"

"I am an official of CNOC, and I believe in what is best for China. Some have launched a course of action that would do great damage to my country. It would be better if they were not permitted to carry out the acts they have planned. That is the only reason I have agreed to speak with you. I want no money or anything else. I simply want you to listen to what I have to say. If you have a way of blocking what is planned, that would be sufficient reward for me."

The CNOC official was speaking good English, which revealed traces of a Boston accent. Craig's guess was he had attended an American university in the Boston area.

"Let me first share with you background information necessary to understand the agreement between China and Iran," the man said.

He turned on the computer and flashed a chart on the screen. "Let's start with the supply side.

"These are the proved oil reserves for the ten countries with the largest reserves. You'll see that Saudi Arabia is first and Iran is second. Most of these countries including, Saudi Arabia, are close to or at their maximum production. You're no doubt familiar with Hubbert's Peak."

Craig nodded.

"Soon total maximum oil output will begin declining in the world."

Craig had seen information like this many times over the years.

"Now let's turn to consumption." The next slide went up on the screen.

"The world consumes 84 million barrels of oil a day. The United States, with about five percent of the world's population, consumes almost 21 million barrels a day, or twenty-five percent of the world's total, making it the largest consumer of oil. The United States imports approximately sixty percent of its oil or 12.6 million barrels per day. In 1970, U.S. oil production peaked. Even with the addition of Alaskan and off-shore wells, your domestic production has been in a steady and sharp decline. The oil the U.S. is consuming is not available in the U.S. at any price. Hence, your dependence on imported oil must increase over time, even if your total consumption remains the same. Which it won't, of course. It is increasing. If the average price for oil this year is $80 a barrel, the United States will spend more than a billion dollars a day on imported oil, or $367 billion a year. Every dollar added to the price of oil per barrel costs

Americans $7.7 billion a year, and $4.62 billion of that goes for imports."

"China is catching up with the United States in all these categories," Craig interjected.

"Precisely where I was going next." The man hit a button on the computer. Figures for imports and consumption by the largest countries appeared on the screen.

"As you can see, China is now second, both as an importer and consumer of oil. We recently passed Japan, which is third. For many years, China was not an importer of oil. In fact, our nation was a net exporter. It's only since our economic breakthrough in the last decade that we have become a huge importer of oil, which drives our industrial machine and fuels our huge and ever-increasing number of cars on the road. As you know from being here, the days of Chinese bicycles are over. We now rival only the United States in terms of imports." With pride he said, "passing Japan was an enormous accomplishment for our country."

Craig shrugged. "All you've shown me so far is that both the United States and China are heavily dependent upon imported oil. That imported oil is what drives both of our economies. I knew all of that very well."

"I'm getting there. This is all critical background information."

Ming was looking at Craig and shaking his head in disapproval. I'll have to be more patient, Craig admonished himself.

"There is a critical difference between our two nations on the oil supply side," the man continued. He pressed computer buttons and another image flashed on the screen. "Here is the breakdown of countries supplying China's oil. We have a broad and diverse group of suppliers. We receive about forty-five percent of our oil from the Middle East. Roughly, twenty-eight percent from Africa, particularly Angola and the Sudan. Another fourteen percent from Europe and the western hemisphere, and finally, twelve percent from Asia and Pacific. Over the last several years we've broadened our suppliers enormously, including many nations which have difficulties politically with the United States, such as Venezuela, Burma, the Sudan, Russia and some of the former states of the U.S.S.R. We've promised them arms and other concessions to lock up long-term, oil-supply contracts. At the same time, we also import from Canada, Australia, and Mexico."

The masked man flashed another set of images on the screen. "Now look at the number of nations supplying oil to the United States and the relative quantities. You'll note a far smaller list of suppliers for the United States than for China. You'll also note that the United States is very heavily dependent upon Middle Eastern oil. That's in part because, unlike China, your country has not moved to lock in supplies of foreign oil from specific countries. You live by the free market... and you'll die by the free market."

Craig couldn't argue. He had the same thought many times over the years.

"Now I recognize, of course," the man said, "that our government has succeeded in exploiting political problems and in offering benefits to induce countries with whom the United States would not deal to supply oil, but all of that is beside the point. What is critical is that the United States is heavily dependent on Middle Eastern oil and on that oil being available on the free market. If the United States were to suddenly lose its supply of Middle Eastern oil, then..."

Craig completed the sentence. "There would be short term chaos for the American economy. Gasoline prices at the pump would exceed ten dollars a gallon for those stations that managed to have a supply. People wouldn't be able to heat their homes. We'd have runaway inflation and double-digit interest rates. Huge unemployment. The dollar would tumble. Longer term, there would be a devastating impact on every aspect of American life."

The man turned off his computer, "You've expressed that better than I ever could."

"What do you know about the agreement China entered into with Iran?" Craig bluntly asked.

Ming frowned. A heavy silence settled over the room.

"Are you familiar with General Zhou?" The man's voice was cracking.

"The commander of the People's Liberation Army," Craig replied.

"Precisely. The highest-ranking military officer in our country. General Zhou has concluded that China has an opportunity to leapfrog over the United States and to become the world's greatest economic and military power. He believes the United States is like a patient in a hospital hooked up to life support, which happens to be Middle Eastern oil. All we have to do is cut that line."

This must be what Francesca discovered.

"And how does he intend to do that?"

"General Zhou, with his brother, has conceived Operation Dragon Oil. The key part is an agreement with Iran, which will permit China to corner Middle Eastern oil. Under that agreement, Iran will sell all their output to China, and China will help develop new oil fields. On April 1, Iran, with Chinese military assistance, will attack Saudi Arabia and other Arab Gulf oil producers with long range missiles. The Shiites in those countries will rise up and take control of the oil."

"Wait a minute," Craig said. "What makes you think we'll have a Shiite uprising?"

"The Iranians have been secretly arming the Shiites in those countries and solidifying their relations with the Shiite leaders. The same as they did with the Shiites in Lebanon under the Hezbollah banner. In Saudi Arabia, the Shiites have their own area, which happens to be in the eastern part of the country, where the richest oil fields are. The Saudi government has no idea what's going on in the Shiite community."

Craig nodded. "I can understand that."

"The plan is for those Shiites to sell their oil to Iran, who will sell it to China. The Shiite government in Iraq will also join with Iran to cut off the United States' oil supply, while giving China unlimited oil. The agreement will wreak economic destruction on the United States. Your economy will collapse. The economies in Western Europe will be in a nose dive as well. China will leap ahead of the U.S."

"You said that implementation is scheduled for April 1. That's only three days from now."

"Exactly. That's zero date. All that is needed is a green light from General Zhou on that date."

"Through this whole discussion, you've spoken about General Zhou. You haven't talked about the Chinese civilian leadership. Are the Chinese President or Premier behind this agreement with Iran, or is this a rogue operation by General Zhou?"

After a pause, the masked man said, "I don't know. It's been explained to me as being General Zhou's agreement."

General Ming interjected, "I haven't been able to learn that either."

"Have you ever seen the written document memorializing this agreement?" Craig asked.

"I'm quite certain it exists," the masked man said. "I've heard discussion about a written document, but I have never seen it and I don't know where it is."

"You said that the agreement with Iran is a key part of Operation Dragon Oil. What else is involved?"

"My boss, Zhou Yun, has entered into agreements to take over oil production of Venezuela, Nigeria, and Sudan. Also the five largest Canadian oil producers, cutting the United States off from that oil."

"Did you go to Calgary with Zhou Yun, a few weeks ago, when those agreements were made?"

"Yes. I was part of our delegation."

"Do you know anything about an American reporter who interviewed Zhou Yun?"

"A young woman from New York interviewed him. She had gotten information about Operation Dragon Oil in Iran. Zhou Yun arranged to have her killed following his interview."

The words struck Craig hard. The masked man sounded as if he were describing a nameless, faceless woman. But she wasn't.

She was my daughter.

Craig paused in the questioning. He leaned back and closed his eyes. Images of Francesca popped into his mind. Teaching her to play baseball. Attending her graduation from Northwestern. The two of them walking into the White House to meet President Brewster.

"Are you alright?" General Ming asked.

Craig had been driven into this because of Francesca's murder. Now he was close to understanding what had happened. He forced himself to continue. Ignoring General Ming's question, Craig asked the masked man, "How did Zhou Yun arrange the reporter's death?"

The masked man shook his head. "I don't know."

"Did he have an American helping him?"

"I overheard a conversation Zhou Yun had with an American about the reporter, but I don't know who it was. Why are you so interested in this reporter?"

"She was my daughter." Craig's voice was quavering.

The masked man pulled back with a start. "I'm sorry for your loss. I had no idea."

"Nor did I," General Ming added.

"She was a brilliant and beautiful young woman, cut down in the prime of life."

The masked man closed down his computer. "I've told you everything you wanted to know. Now I would like to terminate our discussion. It's important that you and General Ming leave first." He now sounded more nervous.

"Thank you for meeting with me," Craig said.

"Never forget, I did so for the good of my country. I'm afraid General Zhou and Zhou Yun are ignoring the terrible consequences for China if they launch Operation Dragon Oil. The United States will respond militarily, and we will suffer tremendous casualties in a devastating war. I don't want that to happen. I hope you can stop it."

Elizabeth felt disoriented. She couldn't see her watch. She had no idea how long she'd been held. Her arms and legs ached. She couldn't move. Escape was impossible.

She heard the cell phone in her jacket pocket ring, but she was helpless to answer. It had to be Craig looking for her. Or maybe Carl setting up a meeting with Mei Ling. She tried desperately to move her hands, but she couldn't. The phone stopped ringing.

She strained her ears to hear what her captors said, but she couldn't hear a word. Only silence.

No one will ever find me.

68

BEIJING

General Ming's driver eased the car to a stop near the entrance to Longtan Park. "Will you walk with me for a few minutes?" Craig asked.

General Ming got out with him. They walked along a path, cutting through trees toward a pond.

"I have a serious problem," Craig said. "It is essential that I obtain a copy of the agreement between China and Iran."

"But you know all of its terms."

"I realize that. However, for my government to take action, I must have a copy of the document. Otherwise, everything can be denied. We'll have no chance of blocking it."

Ming lowered his head, not responding. Coming from the other direction was a woman pushing a baby stroller. Once she passed, Ming said, "Are you certain you can't move without a copy of the document?"

Craig reached his hands up in the air as if pointing to the sky. "I won't have a chance of success without the document. Somehow, I have to get a copy. It's critical. Is there any way you can help me?" Craig was pleading.

"You're asking an enormous amount."

"I realize that. But let's face it. President Brewster is known to be quick on the trigger. If the President feels that the United States is boxed in between China and Iran, he's likely to respond aggressively. It could mean war. We have to find a way to shut this down before April 1. Our only hope is if I can supply him with a copy of the document. He'll be able to use that to launch a powerful diplomatic effort, which could succeed in derailing the agreement. If I can't, then events take on a life of their own. War between our countries and chaos will be the result, China being the target of a devastating attack by the United States and then responding in kind."

Craig turned to Ming for a sign of acquiescence, but Ming was looking away.

"You know I'm right, don't you?"

Ming sighed deeply. "Unfortunately, you are."

"Then how can we get a copy of the agreement?"

"There may be a way. It's a long shot, but I'm willing to try."

"What is it?"

"Captain Cheng, General Zhou's chief aide, was once my aide. He could get a copy. I don't know whether he would."

"But talking to someone so close to General Zhou would be risky for you. I don't want to expose…"

"I'm afraid I'm already highly exposed."

Craig was impressed by General Ming's courage.

General Ming pointed to a nearby bench. "Meet me here at ten this evening. I'll be sitting on that bench. If I've gotten a copy of the agreement, I'll give it to you. If not, I'll tell you then. I don't think we should talk by phone."

Ming turned and walked back to the car.

Craig had to hook up with Elizabeth. He called her cell phone. No answer. It kicked into voicemail.

He checked his watch. Five minutes past five. Surely, she was done touring.

He called the St. Regis and rang their room. Again, voice mail.

He told the operator, "Try paging her in the gym." She might be down there working out.

He waited patiently for a full two minutes until the operator came back on the line. "I'm sorry, sir, we tried paging her there and in all the restaurants in the hotel. We haven't had any answer to the page. I even tried your room a second time."

He tried her cell again. More voice mail.

Something happened to her. He was frantic with worry.

He remembered her telling him they could use Carl as an intermediary. He tried Carl's number. He heard: "Carl Zerner here."

"This is Richard Collier. I'm trying to reach my wife. Is she touring with you?"

"Afraid not. I've tried her a couple of times on her cell, but got voice mail. Too bad, I've lined up some interesting sights for her."

Craig was alarmed. Zerner must have arranged a meeting for her with Mei Ling, which she didn't make. That meant she was in trouble. He decided to go back to the St. Regis, hoping she left him a coded, cryptic message in the room.

His heart racing, he tore down the path toward the St. Regis—two miles away.

69

BEIJING

"The situation with Craig Page has gotten more serious," Zhou Yun said to General Zhou. They were in Zhou Yun's office. His brother's words made General Zhou cringe.

"What happened?"

"I've heard from one of my CNOC people that your old friend, General Ming, whom you drove out of the army, has been assisting Craig Page."

General Zhou stiffened. "You're not exaggerating. The situation has become lethal."

Zhou Yun asked, "How much does General Ming know about Operation Dragon Oil?"

"It was developed after he was dismissed from the military. He shouldn't know anything about the agreement or our plans, but we have to assume he knows people who do have knowledge."

"And one of them might be willing to talk to General Ming."

General Zhou sighed deeply. "Do you have any idea how much progress Craig Page has made, working with General Ming?"

"All I know is that Page had one meeting with General Ming yesterday. He was on his way to a second this afternoon. I arranged for two people to intercept him before he got there. They were ordered to kill him and make it look like a robbery and murder perpetrated by a street gang against a wealthy, foreign visitor."

"And?"

"Unfortunately, though the two men I sent were experienced and tough, Page overcame both of them. He killed one and left the other unconscious in the storage shed of a construction site. Then he went off to his meeting with General Ming. I don't know what he did after that. He obviously mustn't be underestimated."

"You should have called me earlier," General Zhou said. "I would have sent troops. They would have known how to deal with Page much more effectively than your men."

"I thought about that, but since he's an American, I decided it best to avoid the appearance of involvement by the Chinese military, in case there was an eye witness."

"But at this point, we have to run that risk."

Zhou Yun stood up and walked over to the window.

"Do we know where Page is now?" the General asked.

Zhou Yun shook his head.

General Zhou said, "I have troops from my personal bodyguard brigade, whom I can trust, in front of the St. Regis. They have pictures of Page."

Zhou Yun nodded.

General Zhou continued, "When these soldiers see Page exiting the hotel by himself or with a woman, they'll seize them and put them into a military van. We'll keep them in isolation until after April 1. We'll interrogate them to find out what they know about our agreement with Iran and how much Page has conveyed to President Brewster."

"Good."

General Zhou clenched his hands into fists. "Meanwhile, I'll kill that traitor General Ming."

"Before you do that, I suggest you arrest him and make him tell us where we can find Page? And how much he knows?"

General Zhou's eyes were blazing. "It'll be my pleasure. I'll have one of my elite units grab him. We'll torture him worse than he ever imagined, until he talks. One way or another, I'll make sure Page doesn't block our agreement with Iran."

70

BEIJING

At a distance of a hundred yards from the St. Regis, Craig, frantic with worry, spotted three armed soldiers standing in front of a military van.

He made a wide loop around the hotel. In the back, he saw a six-foot-high wall. After looking around to make sure he wasn't being watched, he scaled the wall. The sun had set. In the dusk he slipped into the hotel through the rear service entrance.

From the elevator, he charged down the corridor to his room. No sign of Elizabeth. He searched the hotel gym and restaurants. She wasn't there. Called her cell. Again, voice mail.

Seconds later, his cell phone rang. The caller ID was blocked.

"Is this Craig Page?" a man said in English with a heavy Chinese accent.

"I'm sorry. You must have the wrong number. My name is Richard Collier."

"Don't play games with me," the man said tersely. "We have Elizabeth. We will kill her unless you are on the midnight United plane to Washington. Once the plane takes off, she will be released."

"Who is this?" Craig demanded.

No response. The phone line went dead.

Craig took the elevator to the lobby and cut across the white marble floor to the concierge desk. A young man was on duty, tall and thin, with a narrow face, in his late twenties. He was wearing wire-rimmed glasses.

"I'm Richard Collier, from room 710," Craig said. "My wife went out with a guide this morning. She hasn't come back. I'm trying to reach her."

"How can I help you?" the concierge asked.

"I want the home telephone number and address of the guide, so I can contact him to find my wife. Since the hotel arranged for the guide, you must have that information."

The concierge frowned. "I'll be happy to call the guide for you. It'll be much easier that way."

"I'll make the call myself. Just give me his address and telephone number."

"I can't do that."

Craig glared. "Why not?"

"As I told you, I'll make the call. I'm not able to give out the telephone number and home address of a guide."

"And why can't you give me that information?"

"Those are our rules. We're not allowed to give out personal information about any of the guides. If any contact is to be made, it has to come through me or one of my colleagues."

The concierge had a self righteous air. "Those may be your rules," Craig said, now raising his voice, "but you're sure as hell going to give me the information." Craig was shouting. People in the lobby were staring at him.

Unintimidated, but now flustered, the concierge held his ground, "I won't do it."

Craig leaned over the desk and grabbed the man by the lapels of his black jacket. He pulled him so hard that he lifted the startled man off his feet. His body was stretched out horizontal across the concierge desk. His face close to Craig's.

"You damn well are going to look up the information right now and you're going to give it to me."

In response to the shouting, a man in a security uniform rushed across the lobby. As he approached Craig, he was reaching for the gun at his waist.

"What's the problem?" the security man asked.

Craig let go of the concierge, who fell to the ground, landing on his feet. "There's a helluva problem," Craig said. "My wife went out this morning with a guide the hotel arranged and never came back. This idiot refuses to give me the guide's name, home address, and phone number, so I can locate him and find out what happened to my wife."

"I offered to call the guide," the concierge said defensively. "He wouldn't let me do that."

"That's right. I want to talk to him myself."

The security man put his gun away and turned to Craig. "Listen. My name is Hu Wuen. I'm the director of security at the St. Regis. Let's move over to the side of the lobby where we can talk."

Craig followed Hu to a deserted desk.

"Okay, now tell me what this all about."

"I'm Richard Collier, in room 710. I'm here with my wife, Alexandra. We're visiting Beijing for the first time. We went out together this morning and did some touring with a guide, the concierge arranged. I left her around noon, because I wanted to see some things on my own. The guide was planning to take her to the hutongs, and I didn't want to do that. So we split. I left her alone with the guide. We said we'd meet back at the hotel around four o'clock. She never came back."

"Maybe your wife decided to go shopping. We have wonderful boutiques and malls in Beijing."

"Exactly what I thought. But then a little while ago, I received a call from a man speaking English with a Chinese accent. He told me my wife has been kidnapped."

Hu's head snapped back. "Kidnapped?"

"That's right."

"What else did he say?"

"That they seized her because we're wealthy foreigners. They want to get a large ransom from us. He said he would call again with details. How much money I would have to pay to get her back and where I should meet him with the money. If I go to the police, he said they would kill her. I was astounded that something like this could happen in Beijing. It's the sort of thing we expect when we travel to places like Mexico or Brazil. We certainly didn't expect it in China."

Hu looked mortified. "You're right. This kind of thing never happens in Beijing...Well, almost never. It's the first case of this type we've ever had involving a guest at the St. Regis. I'll do anything to help. Believe me I will. We can't have something like this happening to one of our guests."

"I'm happy to hear you'll help, unlike that idiot concierge. I figure we should start by talking to the guide, because he'll know where he left my wife. Perhaps the guide was with her when she was kidnapped and the guide was threatened. Perhaps he was bribed. Maybe he's even a part of this scheme." Craig was holding out his hands. "I didn't want the concierge calling him. If the guide's involved, that would tip him off. Then he'd disappear." Craig paused. "Do you understand what I'm saying?"

Hu nodded.

"I was afraid to go to the police after what the caller said. My idea was to get the address of the guide from the concierge and go directly to the guide's house. Surprise him there, and hopefully find out what he knows about my wife." Hu closed his eyes without saying a word.

Finally, Hu opened them and said, "I like your approach. Let me talk to the concierge. I'll get the guide's name and address. Then I'll go with you to the guide's house."

"I'm very grateful for your assistance."

"I'll also tell the concierge that under no circumstances is he to call the guide, alerting him."

"Good."

"You wait here. Let me handle the concierge. Then we'll go."

Three minutes later, Hu returned. "I have what we need. My car is in the hotel employees' garage. Ride down in the elevator with me."

I hope we're not too late. That Elizabeth is still alive.

71

BEIJING

Craig admired the way Hu drove. They were going fast, racing around cars on the streets of Beijing, cutting in and out of lanes. Cars were honking at them. Hu didn't seem to mind.

"How long have you been with the hotel?" Craig asked.

"About four years. Before that, I was with Chinese Intelligence."

Oh oh, Craig thought. Better be careful. Hu might still be involved with those people. Craig had to risk it. Hu was his only hope of rescuing Elizabeth.

"Where do you live in the United States, Mr. Collier?"

Craig would have preferred that Hu concentrate on driving and not talk, but he wasn't calling the shots. "Pittsburgh, Pennsylvania," Craig said, sticking with a city he knew well, while wondering if Hu would try to cut through his phony story.

"Once I went to the United States. I liked Philadelphia, Washington, and New York."

Hu stopped for a red light. When the car began moving again, he resumed talking. "I was astounded at how much crime you have in the United States. I hope what happened to your wife doesn't signal the beginning of a situation like that in China."

"I hope not either."

At that point, Hu happily went silent.

Twenty-five minutes later, they arrived at the guide's residence, an apartment on the twelfth floor of a high-rise building. As they rode up in the elevator, Hu had his hand close to his gun, holstered at his waist. In the twelfth floor corridor, Craig hung back three steps behind Hu. When they reached the guide's door, Hu took his fist and pounded on the wood. Seconds later, a cry came from inside, "Who is it? Who's there?" Craig recognized Dan's voice.

"It's Hu Wuen from the St. Regis hotel security. Open up right now. And I mean right now."

"Just one minute please."

"No. Not one minute," Hu said in a loud commanding voice. "You open this door now, or I'll break it down."

The door immediately opened. Craig followed Hu inside and looked around. The apartment consisted of one tiny room which had a bed, table and chairs, and a cooking stove off to one side. Standing in the middle of the room was the guide. Dan was dressed in an undershirt and a pair of boxer shorts. "Why do you barge in like this?" the guide said.

Hu pointed to Craig. "We want to know about his wife."

The guide's eyes were twitching. "We toured this afternoon. I took her to a hutong area. After that, we went back to the hotel. I left her there."

"You're lying," Hu said. "At the hotel, they told us she never came back."

"Oh, I must have made a mistake."

The guide was speaking English, obviously for Craig's benefit. "I remember now. She wanted to go shopping… Yes, that's it. She said something about shopping. So I left her off at a large mall about five blocks from the hotel... That's right... That's where I left her off." The guide was looking down at the floor.

"And if I talk to your driver, he'll tell me the same story?" Hu said.

"Yes. For sure."

Hu took the cell phone out of his pocket. He also removed a piece of paper. "I have the driver's phone number." Hu dialed the number and conducted a conversation in Chinese. Once the call was over, Hu slammed shut his cell phone, put it back into his pocket, and took out his gun. He gripped it by the barrel. Without any warning, he smashed the handle against the side of the guide's face. "You lying piece of dogshit," Hu shouted at the guide.

Craig wasn't surprised by Hu's actions. He knew very well how security people conducted their interrogations in autocratic regimes. The rules NYPD followed didn't apply in most of the world.

The guide collapsed to the floor onto his back. His face was red and swollen. His nose broken and bleeding.

Hu didn't stop. He walked over and raised his right foot, kicking the guide sharply in his side. Blood was running from the guide's nose. A couple of teeth were broken in the front of his mouth. He was coughing and gagging blood.

Hu grabbed him by the arm and yanked him to his feet. Then he slammed him down in the only chair in the tiny apartment. Hu picked up his gun and aimed the barrel at the guide's genitalia. "Now you tell me the truth, or I shoot and destroy your manhood. No more lies. Tell me the truth. Everything that happened to his wife, or I fire this gun."

The guide was shaking.

Craig hoped to hell Dan talked before Hu killed him.

"I had nothing to do with kidnapping his wife," the guide stammered. "Believe me."

"So you know she was kidnapped?"

The guide nodded.

"Who did it?"

"I don't know the man."

"What do you know about him?"

The guide hesitated for a minute. Craig watched Hu tighten his grip on the gun and glare at the guide.

Dan began talking. "Late last night, someone came to see me here in my apartment. An American. He offered me ten thousand dollars in U.S. cash and a visa to live permanently in the United States with a grant of political asylum, as well as a plane ticket to New York."

Once he heard the words, "An American," Craig wanted to jump in and take over the questioning. But realizing Hu would be more effective, he held back.

"What did he ask you to do?" Hu said.

"He wanted me to deliver his wife…" the guide was pointing to Craig, "to a house in the hutong district at three this afternoon. He said I should leave her there and go. I wouldn't have to worry about her anymore. He said he was a friend of hers. He would make sure she returned to the hotel safely."

"But you knew the man was lying, didn't you?"

"I didn't know. I swear I didn't know."

Hu snarled. "Don't lie to me again."

"I suspected there was more to it than that." Dan said softly.

"Did the man deliver the money to you, the visa and the plane ticket?"

"Yes. A couple of hours ago. All of that."

"Where is the stuff now?"

The guide pointed toward his bed. "Under the mattress."

"Go get it."

The guide hobbled across the room. He paused to wipe blood from his nose with his arm. Then he reached under the mattress and removed an envelope. He walked back to the chair, handed it to Hu, and sat down. Hu poured the contents of the envelope onto the small table the guide used for eating.

Craig walked over and examined it. Everything the guide had described. The money consisted of two wrappers, each containing fifty one-hundred-dollar bills.

"So, for ten thousand dollars," Hu said, "a visa and a plane ticket, you were willing to let this man harm an innocent woman."

"I had no idea he would harm her. Believe me, if I had any idea that…"

"Don't you lie to me again." The guide didn't respond. "What's the address of the hutong where you left the woman?" Hu asked.

"I don't remember."

Hu raised his pistol by the barrel and slammed it against the other side of the guide's face. "You'll remember now."

"Yes. Yes." The guide mumbled the address of the hutong.

Craig couldn't hold back any longer. "What's the name of the American?" Craig asked.

"He never told me his name."

"What did he look like?"

"He was short and heavy. He had bright red hair. Like a carrot. He had spots on his cheeks. That's all I remember."

Peter Emery. That shit Peter Emery!

Hu turned to Craig. "We should go to the hutong house. Hopefully your wife's still there. If not, whoever's in the house may be able to help us locate her."

"I agree. What do we do about him?" Craig pointed to the guide.

"Leave him here. What do we want with him?"

"I'm worried he might try to call or contact the people in the hutong house. Give them a warning."

"Good point. Wrap towels around your face," Hu shouted at the guide. "I don't want blood in my car. You're coming with us."

Before they left the apartment, Hu placed the money, visa and plane ticket back in the envelope. "We're taking these with us," he said. "We're not letting him keep this blood money."

"I want the visa," Craig said. "That could be useful."

Hu handed it to Craig.

Once the three of them were in the car with the guide stretched out in the back seat and Craig sitting next to Hu in the front, Hu told Craig, "At this point, I could call the police, and I'll do that if you insist. I'd prefer to do this ourselves, at least for now. Not only because they told you not to call the police, but for me it's a matter of pride. I want to make sure we take care of guests and do everything possible to ensure their safety. But as I said, if you would feel better bringing in the police, I'm willing to do that. It will become much more of an incident, however."

"No. No police."

Searching for information, Craig turned on the map light in the front of the car and looked at the visa. It had been issued by Helen Franklin in the American Embassy in Beijing at nine thirty this morning.

Elizabeth watched scissors cutting away the burlap sack, and she was terrified.

The first thing she saw was the Chinese man who had grabbed her and threw her into the bag. He was cutting the ropes binding her arms and legs.

She looked around. Standing in the doorway was Peter Emery.

"Oh Peter, thank you for rescuing me."

Horrified, she watched him pull a nine millimeter Beretta from a shoulder holster and aim it at her.

Emery? What the hell?

Emery signaled to the Chinese man, who exited the Hutong, leaving her alone with Emery.

"Why are you doing this?" she cried out.

"Shut up!" he said roughly. He walked over and pressed the gun against her forehead. With his other hand, he removed a cell phone from his pocket and handed it to her.

"Call Craig and tell him to take the United midnight flight to

Washington. Once he boards that plane and it takes off, you'll be released. And that's all you better tell him."

"Okay," she said. "Give me the phone."

He handed it to her. Craig answered on the first ring. "Craig, it's Elizabeth."

"Are you okay?" he asked frantically.

"Peter Emery has…"

He grabbed the phone and cut off the power. Then smacked her across the side of her face with his forearm. "You're a stupid woman. You'll pay for this with your life."

She spat in his eye. "Go fuck yourself."

72

BEIJING

Staring at the dead phone, Craig thought: I just hope Emery didn't move her from the hutong house.

In the back of the car, the guide was moaning in pain. Hu ignored him and drove with determination, his eyes riveted on the road. Craig was thinking about that bastard Peter Emery. He had to free Elizabeth, and he had to know who was pulling Emery's strings.

They entered the hutong district. The streets were dimly lit. They struck a crater-sized hole in the road. The car bounced. The guide shrieked. "Shut up," Hu called out.

Hu braked to a stop in front of the black gate to one of the hutong houses. "Is this the place?" Hu shouted over his shoulder.

The guide pulled himself up to a sitting position and looked out. "Yes."

"Which unit?"

"Go down the main center walkway. It's the third door on the right."

"You better not be lying."

"I'm telling the truth. I promise."

"Alright. Let's go," Hu said to Craig, as he grabbed the gun out of the holster.

"What do we do with the guide?" Craig said.

"Leave him here for now. If he runs, he knows I'll come and kill him. He's not going anywhere… Are you? Lying piece of dogshit."

Craig suggested to Hu, "We should check the building first. Look in through the windows."

"No. We go straight in," Hu said with an air of finality. "Surprise them. That's how I work."

"Okay, we'll do it your way," Craig said reluctantly.

He followed Hu along the dimly lit path. The courtyard was quiet and deserted. Craig heard voices coming from a couple of the houses. Also a television set. Nothing suspicious.

Once they reached the third door on the right, Hu didn't knock. He slammed his shoulder against the old wooden door smashing it open. Hu had his gun raised. Right behind him, Craig's eyes scanned the living room of the hutong house. He didn't see anyone.

Silently, Craig pointed his finger toward the doorway leading to another room in the back. Hu nodded and moved stealthily in that direction. Before Hu had a chance to enter the room, Peter Emery walked through the doorway. He was holding Elizabeth with his left arm around her waist and forcing her to move forward, using her as a human shield. In his right hand, he held a Beretta raised close to the side of her head. Emery stopped moving once he was in the doorway connecting the two rooms. Elizabeth had a terrified look on her face.

"Let her go," Craig shouted at Emery. "We can work this out. Tell me what you want. I'll make sure you get it."

"Maybe I should speak Chinese," Emery said. "You obviously

don't understand English. If you want her released, then you better get out to the airport and on the midnight plane to Washington. Once that plane takes off, I'll let her go."

"I have another proposal," Craig said. "What you want is to get me out of the country. So let's do it this way. You drive me and Elizabeth to the airport. You can keep your gun aimed on us if you'd like until I board the plane. As long as she's with me, I'll leave the country."

"You know damn well that won't work. I'll never be able to keep a gun on you at the airport. I'm no fool."

Emery pulled the gun away from Elizabeth's head and aimed it at Hu. "First of all, Craig, you better get your Chinese buddy to drop his weapon. Maybe then we can find a way of working this out so I get what I want and you get the girl back."

Craig watched Emery's arm loosen around Elizabeth's waist.

Make a break for it now! Go Elizabeth! Go!

And she did. In a sudden, swift move, she raised her right leg and kicked it behind her as hard as she could, aiming for Emery's groin. Her heel smashed into his balls. Then she ducked down hitting the floor. That was all Hu needed. He fired off a shot aiming for Emery's right arm, holding the gun. It nicked Emery's shoulder. The gun fell out of his hand before he could get off a shot.

"Oooh, oooh, oooh," Emery cried out in pain.

While Hu still had his gun aimed at Emery, Craig picked up Emery's Beretta and pointed it at the CIA station chief. "Now you're going to answer some questions. Who ordered you to kidnap Elizabeth?"

"You should know that," Emery said.

"Is it somebody in China? Or Washington?"

When Emery didn't respond, Craig aimed the gun. "I swear you're going to tell me. Hu already hit your shoulder. I'll go for your other body parts. One at a time. And you know damn well I'll do it, because you had the same training I did. You'll tell me exactly what I want to know."

Emery removed a handkerchief from his pocket and held it against his right shoulder to stop the blood flow. "You don't have to do any of that," Emery said. "I'll tell you."

"Who was it?"

Elizabeth was on the floor crawling away from Emery. As Emery opened his mouth to speak, the window on the side of the house opened. A Chinese man stood there brandishing a gun. He aimed at Emery. Craig pivoted to his left and shot the man in the chest. He fell backward. Craig heard a loud clomping noise on the roof.

Hu raised his gun toward to the ceiling. "I'll go outside and get that one."

Before Hu could leave the house, the door flew open. Another Chinese gunman was staring inside the room. He raised his weapon, aimed at Emery and fired off a shot, hitting Emery in the center of his face, blasting apart his head. Hu immediately raised his own gun and took down the man who had killed Emery.

Craig put his arms around Elizabeth and held her tight. "It's over now. You're safe. I'll make sure nothing else happens to you."

"I'm okay now… The Chinese man didn't even try to shoot us."

"He was here to kill Emery. So Emery couldn't talk."

"Why?"

"I don't know. We have to catch the person on the roof and make him talk. Meantime, let's get out of this house. We'll meet Hu back at the car."

"Who is that guy, Hu, you came with?"

"Director of Security at the St. Regis."

When they reached the car and were waiting on the street for Hu, Elizabeth said, "My cell phone. Messages."

She took out the phone and listened. Then she turned to Craig. "Besides you, I had a message from Carl. He said, 'I've arranged for you to see the site you wanted. Meet me at midnight at the same place we met yesterday.' So he must have arranged a meeting for me with Mei Ling at the East Gate of the Summer Palace. I'll call and tell him I'll be there."

Hu came running up breathless. "Sorry, he got away. He was one more gunman, also, Chinese. I chased him, but he was too fast. Let me drive you two back to the hotel."

Hu opened the back door. The guide was lying on the seat, bleeding and whining.

"Oh my God," Elizabeth said. "Dan. What happened to you?"

"Don't feel sorry for him," Craig replied. "He set you up for Emery in return for ten thousand dollars, a visa and an airplane ticket to New York."

Hu reached into the car and pulled the guide off the back seat. Roughly he threw him on the ground. "You can find your own way home, you piece of dogshit." Then Hu opened the trunk of the car and took out some towels, "Sit on these," he told Elizabeth.

As Hu turned the key in the ignition, Craig said, "What about the three bodies back in the house?"

"We'll give the Beijing police an anonymous tip. They'll have someone come over and pick them up. Once they learn one of them is an American attached to the Embassy, they'll let your Ambassador know. What you tell him is up to you."

While he was driving, Hu placed the call to the police. When he hung up, he turned to Craig. "You're not a tourist. I realized that from the way you spoke to Emery."

Craig tightened his grip on Emery's gun. Hu kept driving. "You're obviously an intelligence professional, CIA or one of the other agencies."

"Yeah. Is that a problem?"

"You can relax," Hu said. "You don't have to worry. As I told you before, I was with Chinese intelligence myself. What I didn't say is that I left the organization under less than favorable circumstances. I don't want to get involved with those people again. But you have another problem."

"What's that?"

"A couple hours ago, I saw three soldiers standing in front of the St. Regis, next to a van. I went out and asked them what they were doing. They told me in the strongest possible terms to mind my own business. It was none of my affair. My guess is they're waiting to see you on the street. At that point, they'll pick you up. They probably don't want to go into the hotel. They're patient. These people. They figure sooner or later you have to leave or enter the St. Regis. So you can't go back to the hotel. Tell me where to take you."

Craig checked his watch. In an hour, he had to meet General Ming in Longtan Park. Then get to the Summer Palace. Cabs would be a huge risk. Hu was a valuable ally.

"You want to stick with me a while longer?"

"Sure. I haven't had this much fun in a long time."

General Zhou's palms were moist as he dialed his brother's cell phone.

"I just received a strange call from the Beijing police chief," the General said. "About a shootout in a hutong. A member of the U.S. Embassy staff is dead. Peter Emery, their CIA station chief. Craig Page had to be involved in this."

"Do you know where Craig is?"

"He hasn't come back to the hotel. If he does, we'll pick him up. Also, I've given his picture to the guards at the entrance to the embassy compound. We're checking every occupant of cars going to the U.S. Embassy. If he tries to get in, we'll grab him."

"What about General Ming?"

"We've been at his house. No one's there. We have soldiers outside. But more important, Ming called Captain Cheng, asking whether Cheng had ever seen a copy of our agreement with Iran. Cheng wisely said no and kept Ming on the phone long enough to trace the location of the call. Ming's in a car, heading toward Longtan Park. We're following it, while assembling troops to move in and arrest him."

Approaching the north entrance to the park, Hu slowed the car.

"Here's the plan," Craig said. "I'm going out alone to meet Ming. Elizabeth will wait with you."

"I don't like that," she said. "You need back up."

"We must do it that way. You have a second meeting at midnight. If I get killed or captured, you have to still keep that. You know I'm right."

"Okay," she said reluctantly.

"Once I'm out of the car," Craig said to Hu, "drive around to the south entrance to the park. If I have to run, I'll go that way."

Craig stuffed Emery's pistol into his pocket. He checked his watch. Ten minutes to ten.

The path was dimly lit by the almost full moon in a cloudless sky and street lamps about fifty yards away. Walking rapidly, Craig reached Ming on the bench exactly at ten. Ming had a cell phone plastered to his ear.

Craig sat down next to him. "We don't have much time," Ming said, spitting out the words staccato.

"First, I spoke to Captain Cheng. He can't or won't help. So I failed you."

"I'm sorry to hear that."

"Second, General Zhou and his men are pursuing me. Right now, they're very close and preparing to arrest me. You better run."

Craig heard noises, men shouting at the north entrance to the park. Dogs barking. A bright light was shining from that direction.

"Run now," Ming ordered.

"Come with me," Craig pleaded. "I'll give you sanctuary in our Embassy."

Ming shook his head emphatically. "My situation is hopeless. You go."

"You're a brave man."

Ming took a pistol from his pocket. "Atoning for what I didn't do at the time of Tiananmen Square. Now run."

Craig put his head down and raced toward the south entrance of the park. From behind, he heard a single pistol shot.

Ming killing himself.

His leg was aching. The shouting louder. The area behind him lit like noon. The dogs barking louder. He didn't stop running until he reached Hu's car. Winded, he threw himself into the back seat next to Elizabeth, out of sight.

"Go," he said to Hu. "As fast as you can. We have to get out of the area."

73

THE SUMMER PALACE, BEIJING

At fifteen minutes before midnight, they pulled into the parking lot. Elizabeth spotted Carl through the open window of his car. "Park next to him," she told Hu. Theirs were the only cars in the lot. The entire area was deserted.

Quickly, she climbed out of Hu's car and into Carl's. "Mei Ling told me she'd come at midnight," he said. "In disguise. Completely covered in black. Her only ground rule is that she talk to you one on one. You should follow her into the Palace. I have to remain in the car."

Elizabeth was concerned. "I don't speak Chinese."

"She spent a year at Stanford, Liz. Here, take this." He handed her a flashlight.

Elizabeth returned to Hu's car and explained the set up. Craig said, "I have Emery's gun. After you walk into the palace with her, I'll follow behind. Just in case."

"We don't want to spook her."

"I'll hang far enough back. She'll never know."

"Okay."

Craig said to Hu, "I want to thank you for everything. I'm sure Carl can drive us…"

"Not yet. I'm not leaving until I know the two of you are safely out of the Palace. I'll stay in the car unless trouble comes."

Elizabeth watched another car park across the lot. A woman, whose face was covered by a long black cape, got out of the back. Shining a flashlight at her feet she walked swiftly, never hesitating for an instant, toward the gate. Elizabeth followed her at a distance of ten feet.

She watched Mei Ling insert a key in the lock on the gate. It snapped open. She followed Mei Ling inside, then watched with trepidation as Mei Ling, without saying a word, locked the gate behind them.

"Sorry, Craig," she muttered under her breath.

She followed Mei Ling across the courtyard to Renshou Dian, the Hall of Benevolence and Longevity, the Palace's main hall, where Empress Cixi received members of the court. Once inside that building, Mei Ling, closed the door, let the cape fall to the floor, and shined her light on Elizabeth.

"You're a very courageous woman," Mei Ling said.

"My courage is nothing compared to yours."

"I have the document you want." Mei Ling reached in to her pocket, extracted an envelope and clutched it tightly.

"I want you to know why I'm doing this," Mei Ling said, holding the envelope at her side.

"Please tell me."

"I have both personal and patriotic motives. General Zhou," she said his name with contempt, "promised me my son would receive a promotion, but a nephew in the Navy told me that General Zhou selected someone else for the job after he made his promise to me.

I have no doubt he will kill me and my children after April 1, if he launches his attack. Only if you and your President succeed in stopping the attack will we be able to live. Do you understand?"

"Yes."

"I told General Zhou that I would take a copy of this document to President Li if he refused to promote my son. And I was planning to do that when a friend in the President's office alerted me that General Zhou arranged to have the President's Appointment Secretary call and tell him if I scheduled a meeting with the President. I'm certain he would have me killed on the way to the meeting. I should have guessed that devil would do that. But he never figured I had another way of blocking him—giving it to you."

Elizabeth reached out her hand. But Mei Ling had more to say.

"I have patriotic motives, too. I re-read the document and thought about the issue some more. Regardless of whether that lying sneak, General Zhou, promoted my son, his agreement with Iran is detrimental to our country. I'm not the traitor. He is. He'll wreck China if he's not stopped. I'm the true patriot. Not that power hungry demagogue."

She paused to take a deep breath. "I want you to know all this because you are a woman. You will understand."

Elizabeth nodded.

"Also, Carl Zerner has told me you are a newspaper reporter."

"I am."

"I want you to promise to keep my involvement confidential. There could be repercussions for my family. Promise me that."

"I promise."

Mei Ling shined her light on Elizabeth's face. "Tell me again that you promise to keep it confidential."

"I promise."

"You have an honest face. I believe you."

Mei Ling handed Elizabeth the document.

74

BEIJING

Gun in hand, Craig crouched behind a tree on the edge of the parking lot and watched Mei Ling's car pull away. Then he raced over to Elizabeth who was sitting next to Carl on the front seat.

"Did she give it to you?" he asked anxiously, as he climbed into the back.

Elizabeth handed him a sealed envelope and the flash light. With trembling fingers, he opened it carefully. Inside was a copy of a three page document entitled "Agreement between China and Iran for Operation Dragon Oil. In Chinese, Farsi, and English."

He began reading and nodding. It was precisely what he wanted. Astounding. The agreement was consistent with what the CNOC official told him. It spelled out Iran's commitment to shut off the flow of Middle Eastern oil to the United States, including their missile attacks on Saudi Arabian oil fields and other producers across the Gulf. The weapons China has and will send to Iran. The help China will give Iran in developing nuclear weapons. The terms of sale of Iranian oil to China and development of new oil fields in Iran. It was all there. If Operation Dragon Oil was implemented on April 1, the United States would be subjected to a massive squeeze play between China and Iran.

My God, Francesca had it right. And died for this.

Craig's eyes dropped to the bottom of the document. There were two signatures: General Zhou for the People's Republic of China, and the President of Iran.

Craig returned the document to the envelope and slipped it into his jacket pocket.

He told Carl, "Elizabeth and I must get to the American Embassy as soon as possible. I have to call President Brewster. But I don't want to expose you to any more risk. It would be better if Hu drove us to the gate of the embassy compound."

Carl shook his head. "When you were both out of the car, I received a call from my office. Chinese troops have initiated intensive surveillance of Americans at the gate of the embassy compound. All Americans are being checked. Cars are being searched. They're even opening trunks of U.S. Embassy cars or cars being driven by Americans."

"Could we scale the wall surrounding the embassy compound?" Craig asked.

"Definitely not an option," Carl replied. "The compound is too high. Barbed wire on top."

"Then what the hell are we going to do? General Zhou must have the airport covered."

Dammit think.

Elizabeth turned to Carl. "Other embassies are in that compound. Do you have a friend in one of them who'd be willing to sneak us in the trunk of his car?"

Carl brought his hand up to his mouth, thinking. "Jean Pierre, a French diplomat, owes me a very big favor. I gave him an alibi when his wife suspected him of sleeping with Mary Ellen, a secretary in our office, which he was. I can try him."

"What do you think?" Elizabeth asked Craig.

"We'd be vulnerable in the trunk of a car, but it might work. I don't have another way to get in." Craig looked at Carl. "Call Jean Pierre. Let's give it a shot."

Carl took out his cell phone and dialed. Craig's French was good enough to follow Carl's end of the call. Carl wasn't having an easy time. Using their friendship, he began with coaxing. Then cajoling, finally conveying a subtle threat. "Mary Ellen wants to talk to your wife. I've told her if she does that, she'll lose her job and be sent home. As long as I stick with that, I'm sure she'll keep her mouth shut."

A few seconds later, Craig heard Carl say, "If you do this for me, you don't have to worry... Good I'm glad we have an understanding... No, I won't ask you for anything else... Yes, they'll be there."

Carl powered off the phone. "You're all set. We arranged the handoff for a residential street near his house. He'll drive you to the French Embassy inside the compound. From there it's a short walk to the American Embassy."

Craig turned to Hu. "I appreciate everything you've done for us. I can't thank you enough."

"Yeah. Well, a security job at the St. Regis is pretty boring compared with what I used to do in the intelligence service. The most exciting thing I've had in the last several months was to arrest a prostitute who robbed one of our guests in his hotel room after their encounter."

Hu took Craig around to the back of his car and opened the trunk. "You have one gun," he said. He put a second gun in a leather bag. Also four hand grenades. And a bag of bullets.

"You better be armed," he said. "General Zhou isn't finished with you yet."

75

U.S. EMBASSY, BEIJING

As they crossed the courtyard leading from the Marine checkpoint, Craig was astonished to see March waiting for them in front of the Embassy.

"I didn't know Ambassadors work all night," Craig said.

"They do when the police call to say their CIA station chief was killed in a shootout."

March led the way inside. Craig introduced Elizabeth. "I have a cot upstairs, Elizabeth, if you you'd like to rest," the Ambassador said.

"We stick together," Craig replied. "She was with me in the Oval Office. She'll be with me here. Besides, she was the one who got a copy of the document."

Craig took Mei Ling's envelope out of his pocket and held it up.

March looked surprised. "How did she do that?"

Craig intended to respect Elizabeth's commitment of confidentiality to Mei Ling—even with March. "I'm not at liberty to tell you."

"It wasn't General Ming?"

Craig shook his head. "He tried to get it. And paid with his life."

"I'm sorry to hear that."

The three of them went into March's office. Craig waited until he closed the door to say, "Peter Emery was a traitor."

March pulled his head back. "What did he do?"

"He arranged to have Elizabeth kidnapped to force me to leave China before I got the document."

"Why in the world did he do that?"

Craig shrugged. "I don't yet know. Probably for money. General Zhou and his brother are spreading a lot of it around."

"Humpth. Did you kill Emery?"

"No. I was trying to interrogate him to find out whom he was working with, when some Chinese broke in and shot him. There were three of them all together. Two are dead. One escaped."

"What did you learn before his death?"

"I didn't have time to get any information."

"Been a hell of a night for you."

"It's far from over. I have to call the President. Can you set me up on a secure phone?"

"Sure. The communications room is in the basement. I asked the Embassy's Director of Communications to come in tonight. I thought you might need her."

"I appreciate that. Speaking about your Embassy staff people, who is Helen Franklin?"

"What did she do?"

"She issued a visa this morning to a man involved in the kidnapping. Who would have told her to do that?"

"Any one of a number of people. I can call her at home and ask, or I can tell her to come in right now."

"Do that. The phone's too risky."

March picked up the phone and woke Helen. He said he needed

her in the office without telling her why. He put the phone down and said, "She'll be here in thirty minutes."

"Alright. Now let's go down to the communications room," Craig said.

"I should be on the call with the President," said March.

"I agree. You know the local players."

The Director of Communications was an attractive African American woman, whose name was Sara. As soon as Craig entered her domain, he smelled strong coffee. "How much do I have to pay for a cup?"

She smiled. "Free for you, but I'll warn you I'm from New Orleans. This is the real stuff. It'll keep you awake for days if you're not used to it."

"Just what I need." He picked up a mug and poured some coffee. Elizabeth did the same.

Sara opened the door to a room resembling a large closet with thick metal walls. She pointed to the table inside which held a red phone and a black phone. "If you pick up the red one, you'll have direct access to the Oval Office. If you pick up the black one, you'll have direct access to the State Department, to the Secretary of State's office. Both are hooked up to secure lines. If you don't mind, I'll stay inside this room only until I see that you're able to reach the party you're trying to speak with."

Craig picked up the red phone. Elizabeth and March pulled chairs up to the table. In a couple of seconds, Kathy was on the line.

"This is Craig Page. I want to speak with President Brewster."

"I'll check on his availability."

Through the corner of his eye, Craig watched Sara drift out and close the thick metal door behind her. A moment later, Kathy was back. "He's in a meeting with the Secretary of the Treasury, which he will conclude in the next couple of minutes. He wants you to hold on this line."

"I'll be here."

In a little over a minute, Craig heard Brewster's booming voice. "Yes, Craig. Where are you?"

"The American Embassy in Beijing on a secure phone. Elizabeth and Ambassador March are with me. I'm putting the phone on speaker."

"Go ahead."

"I'm calling to tell you that I have in my hand a copy of the agreement between China and Iran for Operation Dragon Oil."

"Good work. How did you obtain it?"

"I have a friend, who had a friend, who knew someone." He hoped Brewster didn't press him.

The President laughed.

"Spies never like to divulge their sources. Do they?"

"I guess not. It's an old habit. I want you to know that Elizabeth was instrumental in getting it. Without her, I wouldn't have it."

"Thank you, Elizabeth," Brewster said.

"You're welcome Mr. President."

"How about the Chinese attack on Taiwan? What did you find out?"

"There won't be one. It was all a ruse to divert attention from their agreement with Iran."

"So I can call off our preparations to defend Taiwan?"

"That's correct."

"Good. Will you transmit a copy of the document electronically? You have a way of encrypting documents and transmitting them, don't you, Bill?"

"Absolutely, Mr. President."

Craig said, "I'll do it right now." He opened the thick metal door. Sara was sitting at her desk in the outer office. Once he told her what the President wanted, she took the document and slid it inside a device resembling an ordinary copying machine.

"It instantaneously encrypts and transmits documents direct

to the White House, to a machine outside of the Oval Office." Thirty seconds later, Sara handed the document back to Craig. "The President should have it by now."

He left Sara and returned to the room with the red telephone. "Has it arrived?" Craig asked.

Brewster said, "I'm reading it as we speak. Damn those people. If they implement this agreement, the price of gasoline will skyrocket. It would be catastrophic for the American economy. We have to find a way to block this agreement from going into effect."

"You'll notice that, for China, the document is signed only by General Zhou. He's the head of the Chinese Armed Forces."

"Let me look at it... That's right."

"What we don't know, and what my Chinese sources were unable to determine, is whether the President of China and the civilian government leadership has accepted, authorized, or agreed to the terms of this arrangement with Iran... or whether it's a rogue operation by General Zhou."

"Bill has told me that in the past there have been conflicts between the military and civilian rulers in China, so you may be on to something. Even if that's the case, the issue will be moot in three days, when General Zhou and the Iranians implement this agreement."

"Agreed. Whatever we do, we'll have to move quickly."

"What time is it over there?"

"Two forty-five in the morning."

"I want to get together several key people in my administration ASAP to discuss a course of action. In exactly three hours, call me back on this phone. Can you do that?"

"Yes, Mr. President."

"Good. I'll set up a meeting here, with the Secretaries of State and Defense. Also General Braddock, the Chairman of the Joint Chiefs, to consider military options. I'll include Kirby in that discussion."

At the mention of Kirby's name, Craig sat up straight in his chair.

"There's something else I haven't had a chance to tell you," Craig said.

"What's that?"

"A couple hours ago, I learned that the CIA station chief in Beijing, Peter Emery, hired some Chinese thugs to interfere with my mission. They kidnapped Elizabeth. She's okay, but Emery was killed when I rescued her—before I had a chance to find out whether anyone else in the American government is working with the Chinese."

March interjected. "We don't know what was motivating Emery. As Craig just told me a few minutes ago, it may be money. General Zhou has lots of it at his disposal."

"Do you think Kirby's involved?" Brewster asked.

"I have no basis to believe that," Craig said.

"Okay," Brewster replied, sounding sorely troubled. "I'll call you in three hours."

They went back to March's office where Helen Franklin was waiting for them. She was a petite woman with long black hair, which she constantly pushed back from her face in nervous movements as March introduced her to Craig and Elizabeth. "They have some questions for you."

Craig handed her the visa issued to the guide. "Do you remember preparing this visa yesterday morning?" Craig asked.

"Yes. Peter Emery came into my office and told me to do it immediately. He gave me no other information, only the individual's name. He was in a rush and rude. I did what he wanted."

"Was anyone with him?"

"No. He was by himself."

"Did anyone else talk to you about this visa?"

She pushed back her hair. "Nobody."

"Was it consistent with normal agency protocol for you to issue a visa solely on the basis of a request like this from Emery?"

"Yes. Emery has need for visas from time to time. Under my

operating instructions, I'm supposed to prepare them for him."

"Do you ever seek approval from the Ambassador or any other Embassy official for visas requested by Emery?"

Craig was listening for nuances. Helen didn't sound defensive. "Those aren't my instructions. Can I ask what this is about?"

"I'm afraid I can't tell you."

"I understand."

"Thank you for your help," March said. "Would you mind staying in the building?"

"I'll be here, Ambassador."

When Helen was gone, Craig asked March, "How long has she worked at the Embassy?"

"About ten years."

Elizabeth interjected. "Any reason to believe she can't be fully trusted?"

"None at all. All her reports show the highest degree of loyalty, as well as conscientiousness in her work. Everything she told you is consistent with my understanding of protocol."

Craig said, "Let's search Emery's office."

"What are you looking for?" March asked.

"Anything that will show whether other Americans were involved. Also evidence of any payments he received."

The three of them conducted the search and turned up nothing.

They were preparing to leave when the red phone on Emery's desk rang. Craig knew that was the CIA station chief's direct, secure line to Langley.

Craig picked up the phone and remained silent. "Peter, are you there?" He recognized Kirby's voice.

"It's Craig Page."

"Where's Peter Emery? I want to talk to him about Chinese preparations for the attack on Taiwan."

"There won't be an attack on Taiwan."

"How do you know?"

"I did the job the President asked me to do, and I reported that to him."

"Well, let me talk to Emery."

"You can't. He's dead."

"Dead? How?"

"He tried to blackmail me and Elizabeth from carrying out our mission. He was killed when I freed her. My guess is he was on the take from the Chinese. I'm trying to determine whether anyone else was involved."

"You've made a serious charge. I'll launch an immediate investigation."

Stunned, Kirby let go of the phone. It dropped onto his desk with a thud. He put his head into his hands.

That damn Craig Page!

In a fog, his heart pounding, he heard the phone ringing. He ignored it until his secretary buzzed. "It's Kathy at the White House. The President wants you there immediately for a meeting about China."

76

WASHINGTON

When Kirby entered the Situation Room, he looked around and saw four grim, long faces: George Frasier, the Secretary of Defense; Jennifer Nelson, the Secretary of State; General Braddock, the Chairman of the Joint Chiefs; and Jim Gorman, the President's Chief of Staff. He sat down next to Jennifer.

Moments later, Brewster walked in. Another grim, long face.

"The Chinese will not be attacking Taiwan," he said.

Jennifer said, "That's good news."

"Don't get too excited. The bad news is the Taiwan troop movements were all a decoy to deter us from finding out what they are really up to." Brewster paused.

Under the table, Kirby dug his fingers into his pants legs. The room was deathly still. Everyone waiting to hear what came next.

"Unfortunately, they are planning something far worse than an attack on Taiwan. The Chinese have entered into an agreement with Iran for Operation Dragon Oil, to be implemented on April 1, which would have a devastating impact on the United States."

Brewster distributed copies of the agreement.

Kirby stared at it and feigned disbelief along with the others.

"The question," Brewster said, "is what should be our response?"

George Frasier offered the first proposal. "We have to take the hardest possible position. Make it clear to the Chinese that we're ready to go to war if they implement this agreement. Let's get aircraft carriers and ships moving toward the coast of China today. Then, first thing tomorrow morning, deliver a message: Unless they cancel the agreement, we bomb some of their military bases. Also bases in Iran."

Kirby, in a frenzy, could barely follow the discussion.

"Whoa." The Secretary of State said, raising her hand. "We can't possibly move that quickly. We have to give them some time to save face and back down now that we have a copy of the agreement. We should give them an ultimatum. Maybe seventy-two hours to reconsider the agreement. Tell them that if they don't, we'll move forward without specifying what we'll do."

The President looked at General Braddock. "What do you think about the idea of a military response? How strong are we now relative to the Chinese military? Could we do what George here," the President said, pointing to his Secretary of Defense, "wants to do?"

Braddock gave a nervous cough clearing his throat. "For the last several years, in the Pentagon we have watched with alarm the continuous Chinese military buildup. They've grown at an unprecedented rate, constantly exceeding our intelligence estimates. I have no doubt they intend to supplant U.S. power in the region."

"But you haven't answered my question," Brewster said irritably.

Another nervous cough by Braddock. "I believe we still have naval and air superiority."

"There's something I've been wondering," President Brewster said. "Take a look at the agreement again. All of you. It's only signed on the Chinese side by General Zhou. We don't know whether the Chinese President has authorized this action."

"We have to assume he has," Frasier said.

"Not necessarily," the Secretary of State spoke up.

"There is one other issue I want to raise," said General Braddock.

All eyes in the room turned toward the Chairman of the Joint Chiefs. "When we discuss a military response, we keep talking about targets in China. There's something else we could do militarily that would have an enormous impact on China. It would be a response in kind to what the Chinese are doing. I'm not suggesting it be the final step, but it could be an initial step."

General Braddock had President Brewster's attention. "Go on."

"Most Chinese oil goes though the Straits of Malacca. We control those seas in Southeast Asia. Our Navy there is considerably stronger than the Chinese. If we were to move immediately to close those Straits, we would be blocking ships with oil from getting to China. They haven't been able to build pipelines yet. So they're heavily dependent on oil being brought by sea. Shutting off those sea lanes would strangle their economy. That would give us a response in kind to what they're doing. I'm not advocating one over the other. That of course is your decision, Mr. President. I'm just suggesting that you have a military alternative to bombing as an initial action."

Brewster's eyes lit up. "It's an excellent idea. Let me throw something out. You all can shoot at it."

No one said a word.

"Suppose we take the following three steps," the President said. "Number one, have Craig Page go with Ambassador March to Chinese President Li, first thing in the morning, which is about two hours from now, and tell the Chinese President that we know about this agreement. Craig can hand a copy of the document to the Chinese President and tell him that, if China implements this agreement with Iran, the United States will regard it as an act of war, to which we will respond militarily.

"Second. Craig and March should also tell the Chinese President that the United States will immediately close down the Straits of Malacca to oil shipments to China as well as cut off other sea lanes that bring oil to China. This will be our initial response. Unless they cancel the agreement, we will take further actions, including bombing military targets in China and Iran, and General Braddock, I want your people to prepare a list of strategic military sites to be hit.

"Third, I want you, Jennifer, to notify the governments of Saudi Arabia and the other key Middle Eastern countries to go on high alert for possible attacks against their oil facilities. Don't mention China. Don't mention Iran. Simply tell them we have information that there could be an attack against their oil facilities. All actions should be taken to secure those facilities. Meantime, we place our antimissile defense systems in the Gulf area on full alert."

Brewster paused. "For openers, this combination should do the job. What do you think?"

The Secretary of State said. "I think it's an excellent approach. Definitely the way to go."

Frasier spoke up. "Do you think that's strong enough? They could attack first."

"That's as far as I'm prepared to go at this point. As long as there is a chance the Chinese President is not behind this agreement, we have to give him an opportunity to get General Zhou under control."

"I'm not sure that he'll be able to do that," Frasier retorted. "General Zhou has gotten powerful. He may implement the agreement, regardless of whether the Chinese President is on board."

"That may be," President Brewster said, "but before we go to war with China, we have to exhaust every other possibility. You've been awfully quiet, Kirby. What do you think?"

"I'm in agreement," Kirby mumbled.

Kirby didn't even know to what he was agreeing. His mind was fully occupied by one overriding thought: Craig Page was destroying his entire life.

77

BEIJING

Craig placed the call from Brewster to the Embassy communications room on speaker, with Elizabeth and March seated across from him.

"Here's what I decided," Brewster said in a solemn voice. "Bill, as soon as people are in their offices over there, I want you to call the Chinese President. Arrange a meeting with him, or the highest ranking Chinese civilian official who's available to meet with you, Craig, and Elizabeth. I want Craig to take a copy of the agreement between Iran and China to that meeting."

"I understand," March said.

"At the meeting I want you to give a copy of the agreement to the Chinese President, or whomever you're meeting with. Tell them in the strongest terms that, unless they cancel this agreement with Iran, we will regard it as an act of war, and the United States will respond accordingly. Immediately, we intend to close the Straits of Malacca, blocking all oil shipments coming to China from Iran as well as everywhere else in that part of the world. You can tell them we believe that we still have naval superiority over China. We intend to use that to block oil shipments, not only coming through the Straits of Malacca, but from any other direction to China. We will impose an oil blockade on China, responding in kind to the action they're taking against the United States. That will only be our initial action. If they persist and implement the agreement, we will take further military action, more directly against China, including bombing military targets. We'll back off only if we receive from China a clear signal they do not intend to implement this agreement. Am I making myself clear?"

"Absolutely, Mr. President," March said.

"You on board with this, Craig?" Brewster asked.

"Yes sir. I believe it's the right course of action."

"Good. Then the three of you have your work cut out for you. Convince them to back off. When you return to the Embassy, I want you to call and give me a report."

"Will do, Mr. President," Craig said.

As soon as they entered March's office, the Ambassador picked up the phone and called the office of the Chinese President. All Craig could do was watch, because March conducted the discussion in Chinese.

When March hung up, Craig looked at him anxiously. "Did we get the meeting with the Chinese President?"

"Not with him," March said.

Craig looked dejected.

"It's not so bad. We're scheduled to meet with Wang Shi, the Deputy Premier. I impressed upon him the urgency and told him that I was asked specifically by the President of the United States to arrange this meeting. He's waiting for us now."

"This isn't a good development," Craig said glumly. "If the

Chinese President won't even meet with us, I'll bet he knows what we want and he's trying to shield himself."

March shook his head. "I disagree. Wang spent a year in the United States, attending the Kennedy School at Harvard. He's their expert on the American government. The man speaks perfect English." March paused and looked at Craig thoughtfully. "On the other hand, regardless of whether the Chinese President knows or doesn't know about the agreement, if we have to talk to a subordinate first, it still buys him some wiggle room."

March held out his hand. "Why don't you give me the agreement. I'll have my secretary make two copies. One we'll take to the meeting with Wang. The second I'll put in my office safe. The third you can keep with you."

After the copies were made, March told Craig and Elizabeth, "We better get going. I'll call John Donovan, my driver. Have him meet us in the car out front."

Elizabeth said, "We have a problem: Getting through the checkpoint at the embassy compound guard station. Should Craig and I ride in the trunk?"

"That won't be necessary. I told Wang we were concerned about passing through security when we exited the embassy compound, that there were problems with people on my staff getting in and out last evening. Wang assured me he would give an order to the personnel in charge of that security point, letting them know that when the car containing the U.S. Ambassador leaves the compound, neither the car nor its occupants are to be examined in any way. His instructions will supersede any directive of General Zhou."

"And they'll recognize your car?"

March smiled. "It has a very distinctive license plate."

Craig recalled what Hu told him when they were separating last night: "General Zhou isn't finished with you yet."

He said to March, "We'll get our stuff together."

Craig took Elizabeth aside. He handed her one of Hu's guns and two hand grenades. "Put these in your bag just in case. I don't want to alarm March."

"I understand," she said somberly.

"I assume you know how to use hand grenades."

"Part of my Iraq training. Just watch me."

"I hope I don't have to."

78

BEIJING

Approaching the Ambassador's black Lincoln, Craig glanced at the license plate. Besides, the Chinese identification, it contained in English: Diplomat-US-1. Anybody who wanted to attack them would recognize the car.

Craig tapped on the thick bullet proof side panels and windows. It cost a fortune to assemble this car, but it wasn't a tank. It would never repel powerful new weapons.

Craig told March to sit in the center of the back. He and Elizabeth were on March's right and left. Donovan was alone up front, Elizabeth behind him.

Donovan started the engine and eased the Lincoln along the path toward the guard house. Craig pulled the gun from his pocket and gripped it tightly. Elizabeth removed hers from her bag. March, looking alarmed, removed his ID from his wallet and clutched it in his hand.

He didn't need it. Before Donovan stopped, the gate went up. Craig exhaled with relief.

They were driving on a narrow two-lane road, which, in a hundred yards, intersected with a wide boulevard. As they approached the first intersection, still on the narrow road, Craig, looking over the front seat out of the front window, saw a road crew making repairs. One of the workmen held up a red international stop sign, while a dump truck, loaded with hot asphalt, moved into the center of the road, blocking both lanes. Donovan brought the car to a halt.

"Can we back up?" Craig asked Donovan, who was looking in the rearview mirror.

"I'm afraid a car's right behind us."

"I want to check this out," Craig said, gripping his gun.

He grabbed the door handle. Before he had a chance to open it a missile blasted through the right front side window, flew across the front seat, ripping into Donovan and blasting his body out of the left front side of the car.

Craig grabbed March by the neck and shoved him down on the floor. "Stay there," he barked.

The missile had come from the right. Craig didn't see anything on the left. "Get out," he told Elizabeth. "Take cover behind the car."

As she did, he scrambled over the back seat and landed on the ground next to her.

Quickly, he surveyed the area to find their assailants. In front, the road construction workers were scattering. He couldn't see anyone in the civilian car behind them.

Along the right side of the road at two o'clock, he saw a small booth, where a woman had been selling DVDs yesterday.

Craig's eyes zeroed in on the booth. A man was reloading a grenade launcher. He raised it onto his shoulder.

Before he fired, Craig aimed and shot, striking him in the chest. He dropped to the ground, the weapon falling on top of him.

Craig noticed two more men jumping up in the booth, automatic weapons in hand, and firing. The bullets bounced off the car.

Elizabeth had the pistol in her right hand, a grenade in the left. "Use that pitching arm on the booth," he told her.

She yanked the pin from the grenade, jumped up for an instant and let go. The grenade scored a direct hit, blasting the booth to fragments.

Pedestrians and motorists were screaming and taking cover.

Craig noticed two men racing down the street toward the front of the car, automatic weapons in hand. "That way," he shouted to Elizabeth while pointing.

"I see them."

"You take the one on the right."

They sprang up and fired, each of them taking out a gunman with a single shot.

Still standing, Craig scanned the area. "All clear." Then he said to Elizabeth, "Get in the back with March. I'll drive."

The front door on the driver side had been blown out along with Donovan. Craig got behind the wheel. "Let's hope this sucker starts," he said, as he turned the key in the ignition. It did.

Craig floored it, driving as fast as he could. Up on the sidewalk. Around road construction. Narrowly missing pedestrians.

He smashed through a construction barricade. Pedestrians scattered.

At the boulevard, he turned right. He didn't stop for red lights. He drove as if he had an emergency vehicle with a siren and flashing lights on the roof.

"We'll have the local police on our tail," March cried out as Craig dodged two cars to cross a busy intersection on a red light.

"That's what I'm hoping," Craig shouted back.

"We'll all land in jail." March sounded terrified.

"I don't think so. I'll bet the gunmen were sent by General Zhou.

The local Beijing police weren't clued in."

Seconds later, Craig heard sirens. Three police motorcycles converged on the moving Lincoln.

"What will you do now?" March wailed. "Try to outrace these people?"

"Nope. You'll see."

Craig stopped the car. One of the policeman approached on foot and reached for his gun. Clutching it in the holster, he said something in Chinese to Craig, who turned to March. "Tell him, you're the American Ambassador, and we're on our way to an emergency meeting with Deputy Premier Wang. It's critical we get there as quickly as possible. Give him the number for Wang's office."

March leaned forward and spoke in Chinese to the policeman, who immediately made a call on his cell phone while the two other policeman came over, gawking at the car.

This better work.

The policeman returned his cell phone to his pocket and said something to March.

"You can continue driving," the Ambassador said to Craig. "They'll give the Deputy Premier's honorable guests an escort. You're one helluva a good gambler."

79

BEIJING

Wang Shi, the Deputy Premier, was a slight figure, with ridges in his forehead, black framed glasses, and an intense, serious expression.

March said to Wang, "For the benefit of my colleagues, I would like to conduct this meeting in English."

"Of course."

"I want to introduce you to Craig Page and Elizabeth Crowder. Mister Page is a special emissary of President Brewster. I can assure you he speaks as a representative of the United States. He will be telling you what President Brewster asked him to communicate. This is an official message on a matter of great urgency and gravity."

"Before you convey your message, Mr. Page, I am sorely troubled by a call from the Beijing police a little while ago. Something terrible happened to you on the way to this meeting. I want to know about that."

"When we were in the Ambassador's car," Craig said, "gunmen opened fire and tried to kill us. Fortunately, we were able to kill the attackers."

As Wang listened to Craig's words, a worried expression appeared on his face. "I find that hard to believe."

"Unfortunately, it occurred," March said.

"Beijing is not like one of your crime ridden American cities. We don't have people running around with guns in the manner of your wild west."

"That may be true," Craig said, "however, Ambassador March's driver was killed by a missile fired into our car before we shot back. This occurred about one block from the embassy compound. If you check with the local police, you'll obtain verification."

"I'm not doubting you. I'm simply indicating my surprise, and I want to offer my sincere apologies on behalf of the government. At some future point, I will discuss with Ambassador March the matter of compensation. Now, we can move to the subject of this meeting."

He pointed to a round table with four chairs.

When they were seated, Wang knotted his hands together in front of his starched white shirt and tie, narrowed his eyes, and stared directly at Craig. "I have great respect for your President Brewster. I would be pleased to receive officially on behalf of my government any message he wishes to convey."

While they were walking into the building, March had told Craig it would be up to Craig to make the presentation, and he should play it however he thought best. The one bit of advice March offered was, "Wang Shi is a no-nonsense individual. Unlike some Chinese officials, perhaps because of his year in the United States, he doesn't like people, particularly Americans, talking to him in riddles or obliquely. Lay it out straight, whatever you have to say."

Following this advice, Craig handed him the document without saying a word.

He watched the Deputy Premier's face as Wang read it once, then a second time. The man would've been a great poker player. His face disclosed nothing.

After his second reading, Wang put the document down.

"Where did you get this?"

"I'm not at liberty to disclose that." Feeling remorse for what happened to General Ming, Craig had no intention of putting Mei Ling's life at risk. Craig continued, speaking slowly to avoid any misunderstanding, "Unless you tell us that this agreement is cancelled before April 1, President Brewster will regard it as an act of war and respond accordingly, with military action." Craig described the actions Brewster said he would take. While he spoke, Wang was staring at the last page of the document, his face still not showing any emotion.

"If you won't tell me where you obtained it," Wang said, "that presents me with a dilemma."

"Which is?"

"How do I know the document's authentic? That you didn't fabricate it? It could easily have been prepared in the United States."

"I can tell you categorically that we did not do that. Moreover, as I think about your question, it occurs to me there's absolutely no reason we would want to make up this type of document."

"Perhaps you are engaged in a vendetta against General Zhou, who is well known as a hardliner against the United States. Perhaps you wish to have him disgraced and removed from office."

"We may not be fond of General Zhou, but that is not something my government would do. That type of action could rebound against us, to our detriment."

Wang picked up the document and stared at it.

"You could," Craig said, "verify that General Zhou's signature is authentic by checking it against other documents he's signed."

"I've thought of that. However, we both know it is not difficult to forge a signature."

"In addition to the document," Craig said, "we have other information about collusion between China and Iran."

Wang was staring at Craig, waiting to hear what came next.

"We've learned that General Zhou had at least one meeting in Paris with Iranian leaders in the last month. He stayed at the Hotel Bristol. That's where he negotiated the agreement."

"If that's the case, then Paris hotel records will confirm what you're telling me."

"Also, if you examine military supply records, I'm sure you'll find confirmation that the equipment promised to Iran was in fact shipped."

"I'll do that, Mr. Page."

"In your investigation, you will also find that Zhou Yun, the General's brother has been an active participant in this venture."

March said, "I have to ask you, Deputy Premier Wang, whether it's possible, even if you knew nothing about the document, that the Chinese President did?"

"Anything is possible, Ambassador March. However with what's involved here, given my relationship with President Li, I do not believe that could have occurred. What I intend to do, after you have gone, is take this document and meet privately with President Li. Following that meeting, one of us will get back to you, Ambassador March, with an appropriate response."

March followed up. "When can I expect to hear from you?"

"As soon as possible."

Craig pressed the point. "Since April 1 is two days from now, I would like to suggest that we schedule a call now between President Li and President Brewster. This is not a matter for emissaries. The issues are of sufficient importance that they should be discussed by our respective heads of state."

"I will certainly pass along that suggestion to my President," Wang said, without making any commitment.

Craig felt like a quarterback in one of his football games. His team had been on the field a long time and had nothing to show for it.

"Is there anything else we should discuss?" Wang asked, sounding as if he wanted to terminate the meeting.

"One other matter," Craig said. He noticed March fidgeting in his chair. He must be wondering where I'm going next. "Our safety. In view of what happened on the way to this meeting, steps should be taken to protect us from another attack."

"I completely agree. I will place at your disposal, Mr. Page, and if you would like as well, Ambassador March, armed Chinese guards for your protection for as long as you would like."

"That won't be necessary for me," March said. "We have our own Embassy security staff."

Wang looked at Craig with a grim expression on his face. "Mr. Page, the moment you and Miss Crowder walk out of this office, until you board a plane to leave China, I will make certain you are under constant surveillance by state security guards, directly under the control of the President's office and fully independent of General Zhou and the military."

Craig nodded. "Thank you. I appreciate that."

"Under the circumstances, I could do no less. We're an advanced, civilized country. We confer hospitality and welcome our guests. Those who have official business with our government need not worry about encountering personal difficulties. You may be assured of that. Whatever happened in the past, I can't explain. I don't know who was responsible. Every society has hooligans. If that's what it was, then I sincerely apologize. If it was something more ominous, well…" his voice trailed off. He never completed the sentence.

80

BEIJING

Back at the Embassy, the three of them returned to the communications room. With March and Elizabeth standing next to him, Craig placed the call to President Brewster. "We had our meeting."

"What did the Chinese President say?" Brewster asked anxiously.

"We never got to meet him. We had to settle for Deputy Premier, Wang Shi."

"The nerve of those people. You should have been able to see President Li."

March interjected. "Based upon the structure of their government, we can't read anything into that. Also Wang Shi is the point person on American issues."

"That may be, Bill, but I still don't like it. Okay, take me through the meeting in detail."

Craig provided a close to verbatim report.

"At the end of the day," Craig said, "the three of us came away with the same conclusion: We don't know whether the agreement with Iran goes beyond General Zhou to the top of the Chinese government."

"But leaving that aside, Craig, do you think they'll cancel the agreement before April 1?"

"I presented your ultimatum in the clearest terms. Either they cancel the agreement before April 1, or you'll launch military action. All we received from Wang was a commitment to talk to President Li and respond to us as soon as possible."

"So you have no idea is the answer to my question." Brewster sounded frustrated.

"Unfortunately, that's correct," Craig said.

"Bill, do you have anything to add on this critical point?"

"Unfortunately not."

"Elizabeth?"

"Craig expressed it very well."

"I can't run the risk of having them launch their attack with Iran first. I must preempt them to avoid catastrophic losses. Today's March 30. Wang gave you no reason to believe they wouldn't go forward. Am I right?"

"Yes sir," Craig said.

"So I could make a strong case for pushing the button and launching our own offensive, attacking both China and Iran today."

Brewster's words sent a chill up Craig's spine.

The United States and China were on the brink of war.

"May I suggest an alternative course?" Craig said.

"Go ahead."

"Have Ambassador March call Wang and give him a deadline, noon, Washington time, on the thirty first. If you don't hear by then that they've cancelled Operation Dragon Oil, you'll take military action."

"The risk is that they'll move up their zero hour, and we'll lose the first strike. You really think I should do that?"

Craig remained mute. The others, too.

Brewster pursued it. "You were in the meeting, Craig. I'm asking you for your best judgment."

Craig swallowed hard. "Don't act now. Have Bill call Wang and give them the deadline of March 31, noon, Washington time."

March spoke up. "I second that."

There was a long pause. Finally Brewster said, "Alright, Bill, make the call."

Craig said, "I'm prepared to stay in Beijing as long as you'd like."

"I don't see the point. You've done your job. I can't thank you and Elizabeth enough. Bill's there if they want to talk to him. Besides, God only knows when you'll get back if we're at war with China."

"I understand, sir. Elizabeth and I will get to Washington as quickly as possible."

"As soon as your flight lands at Dulles, come right to the White House."

PART FIVE

EVENING THE SCORE

81

NORTHERN VIRGINIA

Craig thought Elizabeth was sleeping in the seat next to him in the first class cabin. But she tugged on his arm and whispered, "Will we still be in danger? Even in the United States?"

"I don't know. Whoever was controlling Emery might be coming after us."

Craig checked his watch. They'd be landing at Dulles in an hour, at five past seven in the morning.

Craig and Elizabeth were the first ones off the plane. They walked along a sealed corridor toward a transport vehicle taking passengers to Customs and Immigration. Twenty yards along the corridor, a door opened and a heavyset man in a blue suit walked in. "Craig Page," he said, "please come with me. And your friend too."

"Who the hell are you?"

The man reached into his pocket and extracted an ID identifying him as Roger Bardilino, U.S. Secret Service.

To avoid blocking other passengers, Craig, with Elizabeth in tow, followed Bardilino through a door leading to a gate boarding area.

"What do you want with us?" Craig asked apprehensively.

"We were sent by President Brewster," Bardilino said softly. "We're supposed to take you straight to the White House."

"Nobody told me that."

Bardilino whipped out a cell phone. "Call the White House for confirmation."

Craig reached for his own phone. When he heard Kathy's voice, he said, "This is Craig Page. We've just arrived at Dulles. Did the President send someone to meet us?"

"There should be two men, Secret Service agents, a Mr. Johnson and Bardilino. They're supposed to transport you to the White House."

Craig hung up. "Another man with you?"

"In the car, Bill Johnson."

"Okay, let's go."

Bardilino led them through a door, then down stairs running to the airfield. The waiting car was a black Cadillac with a thick, metallic bulletproof shield. The windows were also bulletproof. Standing next to the car on the driver's side was a burly African American built like a linebacker. "Bill Johnson," Bardilino told Craig.

"Good. Let's go," Craig said.

Once they exited the airport, they pulled onto the Dulles access road, a two lane limited-access highway that ran to downtown Washington. On the right was a grassy strip with a swale in the center, about twenty yards wide. To the right of that, a second two lane highway—a state road used by drivers who were weren't going to or from the airport.

Johnson reached to the floor, removed a flashing light, and put it on the roof. "We can make better time with this. I was told to get you to the White House ASAP."

Craig leaned forward in his seat, alternating his gaze between the front and rear windows, looking for anything suspicious.

Ten miles from the airport, the Cadillac was in the right lane when a large tractor trailer, an eighteen wheeler, approached from behind at a high speed. Sitting in back of Johnson, Craig watched the fast-moving truck. The driver cut into the left lane to pass the Cadillac. When the truck was alongside, Craig looked through his side window up at the truck's cab. The window was rolled down on the passenger side. Leaning out, holding a gun, was the swarthy man with the thin mustache who had followed Elizabeth in Calgary and had been at his house in McLean. The man raised his hand and aimed at the rear window of the Cadillac, next to Craig, who instinctively ducked. Craig heard the "ping... ping" of the two shots. Both ricocheted off the bulletproof glass.

"They'll try to ram us," Johnson shouted. "Tighten your belts and hold on."

The wheels of the truck moved closer to the Cadillac. Before the truck crashed into them, Johnson cut the steering wheel hard to the right. At the same time he smashed his foot on the brake. The Cadillac spun off the road onto the grassy swale. It ground to a halt a few yards short of the parallel state highway.

The heavier, bulky truck aped the movements of the Cadillac. It ended up jackknifed in the swale. The two vehicles were parked about twenty yards apart.

"I want the two men in the truck alive," Craig said to Johnson and Bardilino. "Do you have a gun for me?"

Bardilino reached down to an ankle holster, pulled out a pistol, and tossed it to Craig. Craig jumped out of the car and ran toward the truck. Bardilino and Johnson were two steps behind. As Craig watched, the driver got out of the truck, shaken from the crash landing. He was a big man, with thick, curly black hair. The shooter was out as well. Both of them took cover behind the trailer. They opened fire from two directions.

Being exposed was too dangerous. Craig, Bardilino and Johnson retreated and dove for cover behind the Cadillac.

As bullets flew back and forth, Craig saw the man with the thin mustache, running across the swale toward the state highway, while the other man kept firing.

I can't let him escape. Moving into the open is risky, but a chance I have to take.

Craig made a circle around the truck, trying to keep the truck between him and the man with the moustache.

Craig was running with the gun in his hand. The driver spotted Craig. He leaned out from the truck to get a better shot. As he raised his gun, exposing himself, a shot from Bardilino took him down. The firing stopped.

The man Craig was chasing reached the state highway. He waved his gun in the air to flag down a vehicle. A dark blue Toyota SUV. The driver rolled down the window. Craig saw a terrified young woman behind the wheel, two small children in infant seats in the back. Craig held his position, twenty yards away. He watched the man grab the woman by the neck with one hand and pull her head close to his.

Craig had his gun raised, but was afraid to fire.

"Drop your gun," the man shouted to Craig, "and throw it across the road. Or I kill this woman and her children."

When Craig didn't move, the man shouted again. "Do it now or I kill all three of them."

Through the corner of his eye, Craig saw Johnson and Bardilino aiming at the man. Neither could get off a shot without the risk of hitting the woman. Reluctantly, Craig tossed his gun across the road.

"I'm getting into the SUV and driving away with these people. I'll be looking in the rearview mirror. If you or your buddies make any effort to come after me, I'll kill the woman and her kids. You can be sure of that. So you better stay right where you are and don't move until I'm out of sight."

Craig did what he was told. In frustration, he watched the man open the door and take the wheel, while the frightened mother scrambled to the passenger side in the front. All the while, the man had the gun in one hand. He started the engine. The car began moving slowly. Then he opened his door, leaned out and took a shot at Craig, who hit the ground. The bullets flew over Craig's head. The car roared away. Craig saw the license plate of the SUV: REX 220. Virginia plates.

He wanted to kill me. But his first priority was saving his own ass.

Once the car rounded a bend, Craig whipped out his cell phone. He called the Virginia State Police, but was met with bureaucratic resistance. "Are you with a law enforcement agency?"

"I want to report a kidnapping. I have a license plate. You have to get State police moving on it immediately."

"I repeat. Are you with a State law enforcement agency?"

After a minute of useless back and forth, Craig abandoned his effort. He ran back to Bardilino and Johnson, who were standing with Elizabeth, next to the truck looking at driver, stretched out on the ground.

"Dead," Elizabeth said, reading his mind.

"Oh damn."

"Sorry," Bardilino said. "We tried to avoid that. Did you get a license plate on the SUV? We were too far away."

"Virginia plates. REX 220. A woman and two children in the car. I couldn't get anybody in Virginia State Police to help me. You guys will have to call them. Get them to locate the SUV, but be very careful. Tell them he's armed and he threatened to kill the woman and children."

"Will do," Johnson said. He took out his cell and placed the call. After twenty seconds, he turned back to Craig. "They're on it, a full court press."

Two State Police cars roared up to the scene. One on the Dulles access road, the other on the parallel state road. Both ground to a halt near the truck and the secret service car in the swale. As officers jumped out, they had their guns raised. Bardilino displayed his secret service ID.

Bardilino explained what had happened. "How about you guys taking over from here? We're supposed to be at the White House with our two passengers. We want to get moving."

"Is your car drivable?"

"Damn right. Not even a dent from the shots fired at us."

"Okay. We'll clean up your mess here."

Johnson maneuvered the car out of the swale. The rest of the ride to sixteen hundred Pennsylvania Avenue was uneventful.

Once they reached the reception area to the Oval Office, Bardilino said to Craig, "Mission completed. It's been swell."

"Let me know what happens with the kidnapper."

"I'll get right on it. I want to catch that guy, too."

82

WASHINGTON

Kathy said, "He's in with Jim Gorman, his Chief of Staff. They're on a call with the House Speaker. I'll let him know you're here."

She opened the door and slipped into the Oval Office. Craig's cell rang. He checked caller ID. Betty Richards, his long-time friend at CIA.

"Yes, Betty."

"We have to talk. Where are you?"

"The White House. Waiting to see Brewster. I have no idea how long I'll be."

"I'll head into town from Langley. Be waiting in Lafayette Park, in the center, near the fountain. Don't leave the area without talking to me."

Kathy said, "He'll see you now."

As Craig and Elizabeth filed in, Brewster came forward to greet them. Craig noticed Jim Gorman seated in his usual place in the corner. He rose and nodded to Craig.

Brewster signaled Craig and Elizabeth to sit in front of his desk.

"I spoke to Ambassador March after you left Beijing. He told me about the attack on the way to the meeting with Wang. That's why I sent a driver and security to pick you up. I'm glad I did. I heard what happened on the Dulles access road. Who do you think sent those people?"

"Unfortunately," Craig said, "we didn't capture either of them. One's dead; the other escaped. If we nab him, we can interrogate him and get the answer to your question. Without that…"

"What's your best guess?"

Craig took a deep breath. "We know Emery was a traitor."

Brewster nodded. "Go on."

"There are others in the United States who were working with Emery. They knew when we were coming back to Washington."

"You think they tried to kill you today to stop you from finding out who they are?"

"Precisely. Before, they wanted to prevent me from obtaining the Chinese-Iranian agreement. But now we have it."

"You think they're in the CIA or U.S. intelligence community?"

Craig paused to ponder the question. "At this point, I don't know, Mr. President. It could be anyone in the government, or outside, for that matter, who knew Emery was our station chief in Beijing. For money, they could have gotten Emery to assist them. Once you give me the word, I intend to find out who the other traitors are."

Brewster raised his hand and pointed a finger at Craig. "That's precisely what I want you to do as soon as we learn what's happening with China. If I don't need you in connection with the Chinese Iranian agreement, I want that to be your top priority."

"I understand, Mr. President. Have you heard any more from March or the top people in the Chinese government about whether they intend to implement their agreement with Iran?"

Brewster sighed deeply. "We have a little more than two hours until my deadline. So far, we've had a deafening silence from Beijing. I've ordered our military to move up ships and planes. To close off the Strait of Malacca and blockade ships going into China. We did it in a visible manner. I want the Chinese to understand we're serious. Our Air Force is on full alert. At noon, I'll give the order to bomb Chinese and Iranian military targets. I'm not bluffing."

The intercom rang. "Mr. President," Kathy said. "Ambassador March is calling from Beijing."

"Put him through." The President hit the speaker button.

"Bill," Brewster said. "Craig and Elizabeth are with me. What do you have?"

"I received a call from Deputy Premier Wang a couple of minutes ago. He and Chinese President Li would like to speak with you, thirty minutes from now. The discussion will be conducted in English. Wang will translate for the Chinese President. What should I tell him?"

"Did he give you any idea of their position on the agreement?"

"Not even a hint, though I pressed him."

"Call Wang and tell him that I'll be available to take the call. I'll have Craig and Elizabeth with me. I want you on the line."

"I'll take care of the logistics. We'll call you then."

Brewster hung up and turned to Craig. "What do you think?"

"My guess is an internal battle has been raging in Beijing between the hard liners and those who don't want to challenge the United States. Wang's call doesn't give us any idea who prevailed. Still, it's good they're willing to talk."

"Now that we have a few minutes, why don't the two of you tell me in detail what happened in Beijing, particularly with Peter Emery and everything you know about traitors in my administration."

Craig and Elizabeth used the thirty minutes to give Brewster the report he wanted, including March's help arranging the meeting with Ming, her kidnapping, and how she obtained the agreement from an unidentified "source of Carl Zerner." As they spoke, Brewster interrupted from time to time. Craig could see that the President was deeply troubled about Emery. They had reached the end of the discussion when the telephone rang. Kathy said, "We're ready for the call Mr. President."

Craig felt a tightness in his stomach.

March spoke first.

"This is Ambassador March in Beijing. I have on the line Chinese President Li and Wang Shi, the Deputy Premier of the People's Republic of China. Would you please identify who you have with you in Washington?"

Brewster said, "I have with me Craig Page and Elizabeth Crowder, who had a recent meeting with Wang Shi, and Jim Gorman, my chief of staff."

Wang Shi said, "My role will be as translator for our President. He will be speaking Chinese, and I will be translating for him if that is acceptable to you."

"Yes," Brewster said tersely.

"Good," Wang continued. "First our President wishes to convey his regrets for this unfortunate situation. He wants to assure you that what purports to be an agreement with Iran was not an official act of the Chinese government, authorized by our President or the lawful leadership of our country."

Brewster rolled his right hand into a fist and shook it in a sign of victory. He looked at Craig and mouthed the word, "Yes."

Craig breathed a huge sigh of relief.

Wang continued in a somber voice, "Our President wants you to know that all of the negotiations with Iran were conducted by General Zhou. Air Force General Yang was working with him. It was what you Americans refer to as a rogue operation. Our President appreciates your calling it to our attention while there was still time to prevent any action from being implemented. We have taken several steps to nullify this situation."

"Could you tell me what those steps are?" Brewster said.

"First our President has notified the President of Iran that the commitments made by General Zhou were not commitments of the People's Republic of China. That the agreement they believed they were entering into with our nation has no legal significance, and we have no intention of complying with any of its terms. Moreover, we would urge the government of Iran not to take any action against other oil producers in the Middle East. We would regard those as hostile acts as I'm sure your government would."

"What was the reaction of the Iranian President?"

"In light of our position, he assured us they will not take any of the actions called for under the agreement."

"What about Taiwan? We also had some reports that an attack would be launched by the Chinese military against Taiwan."

"I can assure you that no attack is contemplated against the renegade province of Taiwan. As you well know, our position with respect to Taiwan is in disagreement with the American position. Nevertheless, at this time no action will be taken. To the extent there were troop movements in the direction of Taiwan, those were part of military exercises. The exercises have been concluded."

"General Zhou and General Yang. What action has been taken against them?"

There was a pause while Wang translated Brewster's question. The Chinese President then responded in his own language, which Wang translated.

"General Zhou and General Yang have been relieved of their positions. They have both resigned from the Chinese military."

"Will they be punished further for these acts?"

Another pause while Wang translated. Then he responded. "Our President believes that their further punishment is an internal matter. This subject is not appropriate for further discussion."

Brewster opened his mouth to pursue the issue. Before he uttered a word, he halted. "Mr. Wang, please inform your President we appreciate his actions. We are pleased we will not have a military confrontation. On our side, in view of what you have told us, we will redeploy American ships which have moved into the Strait of Malacca and which are off the coast of China. Those will be returned to their normal positions."

"Excellent. We are sorry this difficult situation arose. Our two great nations both benefit from the trade between us. We wish to continue for many years our peaceful and mutually beneficial economic relationship."

The Chinese hung up first. Then Brewster thanked March for his participation and cut off the line in Washington.

Brewster turned to Craig and Elizabeth. "I can't thank the two of you enough. With your help, we were able to head off a dangerous military situation."

"Thank you, Mr. President," they both said in unison.

"As I was listening to Wang on the phone," Brewster continued, "what kept running through my mind was whether in fact it was a rogue operation by General Zhou, or whether the Chinese President, now that they've been caught with their hands in the cookie jar, and are faced with the threat of strong American action, has decided to call off their agreement with Iran."

Craig replied, "I had the same thought. It's a close question. I guess we'll never know. I wish to hell General Zhou was being imprisoned or executed."

Brewster stood up and paced with his hands behind his back. "I would have liked that, too. As they said, there were internal considerations involved. I understand from Bill March that General Zhou's brother is an important industrialist."

"Bottom line is we don't know whether General Zhou and his brother were operating on their own. Li and Wang managed to leave the situation sufficiently ambiguous."

"Deliberately so, no doubt. However, let's not lose sight of the most important fact. We managed to avoid a tremendously dangerous situation for this country."

"Agreed," Craig said.

The President turned to Elizabeth. "I know you're a journalist. I hope you won't publish any of this now. Perhaps later, with the passage of time, it may be alright."

"I wouldn't think of doing it, Mr. President. I realize it would be detrimental to our country's best interests."

The President pointed to Gorman who had been listening from his chair in the corner. When he did, Gorman stood up.

"Jim," Brewster said. "I want you to call the Secretary of Defense, the Secretary of State and the Chairman of the Joint Chiefs. Let them know we're to stand down militarily. The Chinese blinked. There will be no military confrontation."

"Kirby also?" Gorman asked.

"No, not Kirby," Brewster said tersely.

"I'm glad it's over," Gorman said.

"But it's not over," Brewster replied in a sharp voice. Then he turned to Craig. "I want you to find out who the other traitors are in my government. Besides Peter Emery. Commence your investigation right now. Call me if you need help. Any time. We have to catch all of them."

83

WASHINGTON

Craig left the Oval Office with Elizabeth. In the reception area, he heard Brewster shouting into the intercom in an angry voice, "Get Kirby over here, right away."

As they passed Kathy's desk, she handed him a note, "Call agent Bardilino. 202-555-6521."

Craig called immediately.

"Bad news," Bardilino said glumly. "Virginia State Police lost the guy who kidnapped the woman and her kids. They located the SUV parked in Roslyn next to the Metro station. The woman was in the car with her two children. Hysterical. When they finally got her to talk coherently, she said the carjacker had gone down the escalator into the Metro. He could be anywhere in the Washington area."

"Great," Craig said, sounding dejected.

He and Elizabeth left the White House through the front gate, then crossed Pennsylvania Avenue to Lafayette Park. Sitting on a bench near the fountain in the center, smoking a cigarette, was Betty. Craig and Elizabeth sat down on each side of her.

"You asked me to ID a man who's photo Elizabeth took," Betty said.

"He tried to kill us this morning on the ride in from Dulles," Craig replied.

"I found out who he is."

Craig couldn't wait to hear.

"His name is Ali Hariri. Born in Iran. He was a colonel in SAVAK. One of the most dreaded members of the Shah's intelligence agency. He had the nickname 'Ali the Assassin,' because he was responsible for torturing and killing scores of Iranians. No one knows precisely how many."

She paused to puff on her cigarette.

"After the fall of the Shah, he came to the United States. He volunteered to work for the CIA, but the agency passed him off to one of the intelligence agencies operating under DOD. He's been stationed in Tampa at SOCOM."

"If he's been working on Iranian issues, I should have met him before or during the year I was undercover in Iran."

"He hasn't been involved in Iranian issues."

"Why am I not surprised? I wouldn't expect our leaders to use expertise they have at their disposal."

"Cynical as always."

"Accurate. So what's he been doing?"

"Involved for years in Afghan issues and the hunt for Al Qaeda leaders. But he's been carefully concealed, with limited exposure. I think whoever hired him was worried if his former SAVAK connection was disclosed, with the kind of torturing and killing he did, they would take heat. So they decided to give him a low-visibility position without Iranian involvement. Also, he doesn't need the money. From his file, it's obvious he stole plenty during the Shah's regime. He lives well in the Tampa St. Pete area." Betty put out her cigarette and lit another.

"Is it possible," Craig asked, "that Ali came to the United States pretending to be loyal to the Shah, acting as if he was thrown out by the revolutionary regime, but in fact he had turned and was working for the mullahs? So for all these years, Ali was a mole planted by the mullahs right in the heart of the DOD. That would be great, wouldn't it?"

Betty shrugged. "You know a lot about what Ali's been doing that you haven't told me. All I can say is it's certainly possible."

"I have to get hold of Ali. Interrogating him is the way to blow this wide open. The last we heard is that he disappeared into the Metro at the Roslyn station. He could be anywhere in the Washington area."

Betty shook her head. "I don't think so. If I tried to kill you and missed, I'd get the hell out of town. From Roslyn Metro Station it's only a couple stops to National Airport. That means a plane to sunny Florida."

"Do you have an address for Ali in the Tampa St. Pete area?"

"I thought you'd never ask." She reached into her bag and took out a piece of paper. "Address in St. Petersburg, phone number, and personal e-mail address."

She took out her cell phone and dialed. "Who are you calling?" Craig asked.

"Cindy in the CIA's transportation tracking office. To see if Ali Hariri was on a flight to Tampa this morning."

Craig watched her anxiously.

"He's on U.S. Air 1855, which left Reagan National half an hour ago. Arrives in Tampa in two hours."

Craig whipped out his cell and dialed a charter air service operating out of Dulles.

"Haven't heard from you in a long time," Weldon Blake, the owner of the company, said.

"I've been off traveling the world."

"What do you need?"

"I have to fly to St. Petersburg, Florida ASAP. I'm in downtown Washington and can be at Dulles in twenty minutes. You'll have two passengers. What can you do for me?"

"That's a tough one. All my pilots are in the air."

Craig groaned. "C'mon Weldon, I've been a good client. You have to do something."

There was a pause. Finally Weldon said, "Tell you what. For double my regular fee, I'll fly you myself."

"You're a thief, but I love you."

"Where are you going from St. Pete?"

"Lord only knows. Stay loose. We might see more of America together."

As soon as Craig hung up, Betty reached into her bag. She pulled out a Beretta and handed it to him. "You might need this. Ali plays rough."

"So we've found."

He tucked it into his pocket, while she reached back into the bag again. "More goodies. A transponder and a burglar's tools to open a door. You never know."

84

WASHINGTON

When he entered the Oval Office, Kirby had no idea what to expect. Last night he had told Ali that Craig and Elizabeth were on ANA Flight 28, due into Dulles at 7:05 this morning. Ali had said, "Don't worry. I'll eliminate both of them." But so far he hadn't heard from Ali, and his repeated calls to Ali's cell ended up in voice mail.

Feeling apprehensive, he took a chair in front of Brewster's desk. Through the corner of his eye, he noticed Gorman sitting in the corner studying some papers.

"The crisis with China has been resolved," Brewster said.

Kirby was in agony. "Resolved how?"

"When confronted with a copy of the agreement between China and Iran, the Chinese President backed down."

"That's really good to hear."

"No thanks to you. Last year this country spent more than fifty billion dollars for intelligence, and you had no idea about this collusive action between China and Iran that would have wreaked havoc on the United States."

Kirby didn't respond.

"How do you explain such a massive U.S. intelligence failure?"

"I was waiting for confirmation from our agent in Tehran."

"Pointing the finger at a subordinate won't do the job for you, mister."

"In addition, I didn't want to burden you with unsubstantiated information."

"We've had this discussion many times. You just won't listen. I've told you again and again you should come to me with all the information you have. I'll decide what's reliable and what's not."

"I didn't think…"

"That's just it. You didn't think. The intelligence failure here is so huge, on a matter so significant to the United States, that you're fired."

Kirby sat up straight. "I have influential friends in Congress. They'll go to bat for me. You'll suffer mightily in your legislative program if you remove me from office."

His face beet red, Brewster shot to his feet. "Don't you threaten me! If I go to anybody on the Hill and tell them you missed a planned suicide bombing in Madison Square Garden and then an effort by China and Iran to cut off oil imports to the United States, do you really think any of your so-called friends will support you? You can't be such a fool to believe that you'd have a single supporter in the Congress."

Kirby's jaw dropped.

"And what's more," Brewster added, "I have no intention of making it look like you resigned, as these things are usually handled in Washington. The story I'll release is: "President Removes CIA Director.""

Kirby wanted to protest, but he realized it was futile. All that was left for him now was to find a way to kill Craig Page.

Kirby stood. "Where is the great Craig Page now?"

"Forget about Craig Page. What you should do is get your ass out to the CIA and clean out your office."

Kirby struggled to keep his composure. Like a punch-drunk fighter, he stumbled toward his car parked in the back of the White House. Before getting inside, he took out his cell and tried Ali again. More voice mail.

He told his driver to drop him at the West End Hotel, two blocks from the Watergate. Though it wasn't even noon, he ordered a double Johnny Walker on the rocks. A solitary and pathetic figure, he sipped his drink, trying to imagine what could have been if it weren't for Craig Page.

85

BEIJING

Barging into his brother's office, General Zhou was distraught. "I can't believe that Li and Wang didn't have the balls to stand up to the Americans."

"Well they didn't," Zhou Yun said somberly.

General Zhou was charging around the office like an angry bull in a ring. Words spewed from his mouth, "A military coup is our only option. I have my top generals standing by. All I have to do is give the order. They'll arrest both Li and Wang. We can seize control of the government."

"Then what?" Zhou Yun said thoughtfully. "A civil war? Millions of Chinese dead." He shook his head. "I don't like it, neither would our father."

"What do you propose? If we do nothing, they'll arrest both of us for treason. I won't sit still and take that."

"I didn't think you would. Neither does President Li."

"I don't understand."

"Could you stop pacing? You're driving me crazy."

General Zhou slumped into a chair. "Now explain."

"Wang called a few minutes ago."

"I hope you told him that he's the scum of the earth."

General Zhou realized he was ranting. He didn't care. He was so furious.

"He had a proposal from President Li."

"We don't want their proposal."

"Just hear it out."

"Alright."

"Neither of us will be arrested or executed. You'll quietly leave the country and live in any place of your choice outside of Asia."

General Zhou was dumbfounded. "And you?"

"I'll continue to run CNOC. I'll continue to buy up foreign oil assets except in Iran or elsewhere in the Middle East. I'll forward you all the money you want."

"They want to banish me. A life of exile. To Elba like Napoleon."

"You pick your place."

"I hope you told him 'Hell no!' to his offer. They want a civil war. That's what they'll get."

With a dirgeful expression, Zhou Yun walked over and put his hand on his brother's shoulder. He spoke softly. "This is extremely difficult. We're so close. We've been through so much together. Those six years, alone without our parents, we survived only because we took care of each other. Your leaving will be as if someone had ripped away one of my arms."

"You're telling me we should accept?"

"I tried to think what our father would do. He despised Mao for always putting himself ahead of the state—of the people."

"And you're accusing me of behaving like that devil, Mao?"

Zhou Yun gave a deep sigh. "I would never compare you to Mao." He walked over to the window and stared out for a minute. Then he pivoted. He looked sad. General Zhou thought his brother was going to cry.

"You think we should accept the offer?" the General said.

"We have no choice."

"You're the only person in the world who could tell me to take it."

"I realize that. And I know you will."

I can't deny my brother. And he's right about our father. He would have accepted it.

"I'll do it," he said reluctantly.

"Where will you go?"

"To Paris."

"But what will you do there?"

"Wait until Li and Wang are gone. Then I'll be back. And I'll be plotting to gain revenge against Craig Page."

86

WASHINGTON

Kirby walked into his father's Watergate apartment and blurted out the words he rehearsed while sipping scotch. "Operation Dragon Oil has turned to shit. Because of Craig Page. And President Brewster has fired me."

His father was flabbergasted. "That's certainly a mouthful. Take it from the top. Give it to me in detail."

For the next fifteen minutes Kirby walked his father through everything that had happened in the last few days. The old man got redder and redder. Kirby thought he might explode. At the end, he tapped his fingers on the green-leather-topped desk. Then he said, "All may not be lost."

Kirby felt the stirring of hope. "What do you mean?"

"Perhaps General Zhou and Zhou Yun will launch a coup, take control of the Chinese government, and proceed with Operation Dragon Oil."

"You think so?"

"Only one way to find out."

Kirby watched his father pick up the phone and call Zhou Yun. It was a one way conversation. Kirby's father only listened. When he hung up, he had a glum expression.

"What'd he say."

"They've acquiesced in President Li's decision. They're blaming you for everything. Zhou Yun said, 'Tell your son to watch his six o'clock. My brother's a vengeful man.'"

"There's something you and I have to do," his father said, "to avoid spending the rest of our lives in jail."

"What's that?"

"Clean up and damage control. That means destroying every piece of paper and computer memory relating in any way to Operation Dragon Oil and our involvement. I'll do it here in my Washington apartment. This evening I'll fly to San Francisco and sanitize the Silicon Valley office and my home there. You do the same at your Georgetown and Middleburg houses. Then get on a plane this evening and fly to Aspen. Sanitize my Aspen house. Particularly destroy the documents in the safe. That stuff would nail us for sure."

"I'll do it."

"Get started now," Kirby's father said. "At this point, we can't think about the money we lost. It's gone. All we can think of is not getting caught."

But Kirby had something else to think of: Killing Craig Page.

Out in the street, Kirby took out his cell and called Ali again. This time the Iranian answered. "Where have you been?" Kirby asked. "I've been trying to reach you all morning."

"In a plane on my way to Tampa. We just landed."

"But you can't do that. I need you to finish the job of killing Craig Page. He wrecked everything. I'll pay you millions more. Whatever you want if you bring me his head."

"Get somebody else. I'm finished working with you. I figure

they'll be coming after me. Just as soon as I get my boat ready, I'm heading down to Brazil. I'll be able to live well there. And not worry about extradition."

"But you have to kill Craig Page for me," he whined. "You promised."

"I'll give you some advice. You're crazy to keep going on this vendetta. Quit now before you destroy what's left of your life."

"I'm telling you to fly back here, and…"

"Don't you understand English? NFW. No fucking way."

"You'll think about the money and change your mind. Call me on my cell when you do. I'm flying to Aspen this evening to my father's house. Sometimes my cell doesn't work in the mountains. If you can't get through, call me on my father's house phone. He's Winston Kirby. I don't remember the number. You can get it from information and then…"

The phone went dead. He tried calling back. He got voicemail. "You'll change your mind," he muttered, and climbed into his car.

He called the CIA transportation office. "Del, this is Director Kirby. I need an airplane this evening."

There was silence, then Del said, "I'll transfer you to Deputy Director Norris."

"But…"

Del hung up. The call was being transferred. Kirby heard, "This is John Norris. I'm afraid you can't have the plane."

"You're joking. Right?"

"Afraid not. I received a call from President Brewster a little while ago. He told me that I'm now acting director. He also told me you're not to be permitted in your office except with an armed escort. And all perks, including the plane, are to cease immediately. You must have really pissed him off. I'll let you keep the car and driver for the rest of the day."

"That's big of you, considering I gave you your job."

"It's too bad, but Brewster's the President."

"And you're his lackey."

"I'm sorry you feel that way, but I…"

Kirby hung up and called United Airlines.

"I want to book a first class seat on your last plane from Washington to Denver, connecting to Aspen this evening."

"Denver and Aspen airports are both shut down because of snow. We're expecting them to reopen first thing in the morning. I have space on the 6 am out of Dulles to Denver. The connection will get you into Aspen at 11:02. Is that okay?"

"It'll have to be," Kirby grumbled.

87

ST. PETERSBURG, FLORIDA

They flew into Central Florida in a powerful rainstorm. The Learjet was vibrating so badly that Craig knew they were pushing the stress tolerance to the limit. With any more wind, the plane might break apart.

Craig looked at Elizabeth, sitting next to him. She was white as a ghost. She had thrown up what little breakfast she had in an airsickness bag over northern Florida.

On the plane's intercom, Weldon said, "storm's moving in faster then they thought."

"You think we'll be able to land?" Craig asked.

"It'll be close. I'm cleared for landing at St. Pete/Clearwater, subject to change. We're only fifty miles out. Just make sure those seat belts are tight and don't worry. I flew through typhoons in 'Nam."

Craig checked Elizabeth's seatbelt. "Grab onto the armrest. This will be a rough landing."

That proved to be an understatement. They bounced around as the plane descended, then finally hit the ground with a thud in swirling wind and heavy rain.

"We were the last plane in," Weldon said when he came out of the cabin. "They're shutting down until the storm blows through." Craig checked his watch. Ali had landed in Tampa two hours ago. Craig hoped he was still at the house. If not, they'd wait for him there.

"Were you able to book a rental car?"

"Hertz has one on hold. My plan is to hang here. You've got my cell number. Let me know where we're going next."

As Craig drove away from the airport, Elizabeth, next to him, was beginning to recover her color. "Sorry, Craig, I don't do well flying in rough weather."

"You okay now?"

"I will be when we get to Ali's house."

They headed toward the water. Ali's house was near Pinellas Point on Tampa Bay, a high-income, secluded area with large homes on the waterway. Most of them with private piers. They drove by Ali's, without stopping, to check it out. Built to resemble an antebellum mansion, it had four large, white columns in front. The house was huge.

The rain was coming down in sheets. The neighborhood deserted and deathly still. No other cars on the street.

They turned the corner. Craig stopped the car. "You drive," he told Elizabeth. He climbed over her as they changed positions. Then he took the gun out of his pocket.

"Turn around and drive slowly toward his house," Craig said.

Approaching the house, which was on their right, Craig noticed lights on inside. As they drove past, he saw a fifty-foot motorboat tied to a dock in the back. Ali was walking out of the house toward the boat, carrying two large suitcases.

They passed the house.

"Make a U-turn just ahead," he told Elizabeth. "Drive back and park immediately across from Ali's house." No one else was on the street.

As soon as Elizabeth stopped the car, Craig jumped out and raced across the street. Elizabeth was right behind. In a few seconds, they were both soaked. They got to the house without Ali spotting them. Once they were concealed, Craig asked Elizabeth, "Ever operated a motorboat?"

"You're not planning to take it out in this weather. Are you?"

"I might."

"You're crazy."

"You're right. Now tell me what you know about boats."

"My Dad had one on a lake in the Poconos where we had a summer place. When I was a girl, he showed me how to operate it. Told me one day it would be mine. That never happened. The bank repossessed it. It wasn't as big as Ali's, but a boat's a boat, I guess."

"That's good enough." Looking out from behind the house, Craig watched Ali on the boat. He was taking suitcases down below—one at a time. The water was rough and choppy. Craig waited until Ali walked down with the second suitcase. Then he said to Elizabeth, "Let's go for it now. You jump on board. I'll untie the boat. I'll worry about Ali. You pull away from the dock and get the boat out into the water. It'll be a helluva nasty ride, but it's our best shot."

They sprinted toward the boat, Elizabeth alongside of Craig. He grabbed for the rope knotted around the pier, while she climbed on board. By the time he had it unknotted, Elizabeth was on board. Ali was still below. Craig gave Elizabeth a thumbs up signal and jumped on the deck.

She started the engines. They were moving away from the pier. Gun in hand, Craig was standing at the top of the stairs.

Looking startled, Ali flung open the door, which had blown shut. "What the hell…" he cried out.

"Surprise," Craig said, pointing the gun at him. "We decided to take a boat ride with you."

"Are you out of your fucking mind? We're in the middle of a storm."

"But you and I need to have a little discussion. And we'll do that out on the water where nobody can hear us."

"You're insane. We'll all be killed."

"Funny to hear you say that. People have been trying to kill me for the last couple of weeks. I can handle danger. Let's see about you."

"What do you want?"

"Information."

The boat hit a surge of waves that lifted it into the air. Craig watched Elizabeth gripping the wheel hard, struggling, but keeping it under control. She had them on a steady course, moving into Tampa Bay on a line perpendicular to the shore. The wind kept gaining in intensity. The rain was pelting them, running down Craig's head and over his face.

"Just take us back to shore. And I'll tell you what you want to know."

"I'm in charge. We're doing it my way. The sooner you give me the answers I want, the sooner we take you back." Craig pointed to the single deck chair. "Why don't you sit down and make yourself comfortable."

Craig aimed the gun at Ali.

Ali obeyed. "What do you want to know?"

"Who hired you, and why were you attacking us in Calgary and on the Dulles access road? Also staking out my house in McLean?"

"I wasn't attacking you. You're mixing me up with somebody else."

Craig fired a shot into the air. "Now, I'll ask my questions again, and I'll keep asking them. Each time you don't answer, I'll shoot one of your body parts, starting with your right knee cap. I'll move to your left knee cap. After that, each of your shoulders. Your dick and your eyes. Then I might kill you and put you out of your misery, or I might not. I might just have Elizabeth take the boat back to shore, tie it up and leave you to bleed to death. Am I making myself clear?"

They hit a large wave and bounced.

"I don't know what you're talking about," Ali said. "You've made a mistake. I swear to God. I work for the United States government. I'm part of SOCOM. You're attacking a United States agent. This is a serious crime. You're going to go to jail for a long time."

Craig stared hard at Ali. "You had your chance to do this the easy way." He raised the gun and fired at Ali's right knee cap, splintering the bone and tissue. Ali screamed in pain. Elizabeth turned to see what was happening.

"Better keep your eyes on the water and the wheel," Craig cautioned her. She turned back around.

Grimacing in pain, Ali screamed, "You dirty bastard!"

"Now I'm ready to go for knee cap number two. You know, missing one knee, they can do wonders for you. There are all sorts of prosthetic devices. You could still be a useful citizen. If I shoot the second one, you're in deep trouble. What'll it be?"

Ali stammered, "I've been taking orders from Kirby, the CIA Director. He told me what to do each step of the way and paid me a huge amount of money."

Gripping a side rail for support, Craig said, "Why did Kirby do it?"

"Kirby's father..arghh..." Ali winced and moaned in pain, "Kirby's father is a big Silicon Valley investor. He's involved somehow with the Chinese. I don't understand what their game is. He promised the Chinese that President Brewster wouldn't find out about the Chinese-Iranian agreement until after April 1. That way the United States couldn't do anything to block it from being implemented. Then it would be too late. And he'd make a lot of money."

"Are you still working for Kirby?"

"No. He called me an hour ago and told me he wanted me to kill you because you wrecked everything. I told him no fuckin' way. I'm finished working for him."

"Where's Kirby now?"

"He called me from Washington, but he said this evening he was flying to Aspen. His father has a big house there. The man's name is Winston Kirby. He said if I couldn't reach him on his cell, I should call him at his father's house. Everything I told you is true. I swear to God. And I don't know any more than this."

Ali's chair was sliding across the deck. It reached the back panel and stopped moving. His leg was bleeding profusely. Craig saw Elizabeth struggling with the wheel.

"Now, you have to take me back to shore," Ali said, moaning in pain. "I have to get to a hospital. I've told you what you wanted."

"Not everything. Tell me about Calgary. About the reporter you killed."

Ali's eyes opened wide with terror. "Kirby was responsible for planning that. All I did was make a couple of calls for him. And I wasn't driving the truck."

"She was my daughter."

"I didn't know. I swear. I was just doing what Kirby told me."

Craig moved up close to Ali and smashed the handle of his gun across Ali's face, knocking him out. Then Craig lifted the unconscious Ali out of the chair and tossed him into the swirling, foaming water. He watched Ali go under. Then he walked over to Elizabeth. "Let me give you a hand with the wheel."

The windblown rain was pouring out of the skies, washing Ali's blood off the deck.

"Will we get back okay?" Elizabeth asked.

"You're damn right." With confidence, he took the wheel. "Hold on tight. We'll be tossed around, but we'll make it."

He brought them back to shore and tied up the boat. In the heavy, drenching rain, they ran from the pier, along the house, climbed into their rental car, and drove away.

When they reached the highway, Craig pulled into a mall. "What are you doing?" Elizabeth asked.

"We're going shopping. We have to get out of these clothes."

An hour later, they were in clean, dry clothes, sitting in a food court sipping coffee.

He asked Elizabeth, "Do you suppose Kirby's going to Aspen to lick his wounds?"

"Nope. He's going there to destroy incriminating documents." She said it with confidence.

"How do you know that?"

"While you were killing terrorists, I was an investigative reporter. I covered Wall Street before I got hooked on international. Once the bad guys think they're at risk, the first thing they always do is destroy the documents."

"Then we have to get to Daddy's house before Kirby."

He took out his cell and called Weldon. "Can you fuel up and prepare a flight plan for Aspen, Colorado? We'll be there in twenty minutes."

"I'll check with the tower here. See when they expect to reopen."

Ten minutes later, when they were on the road, Craig's cell rang. "Sorry, Craig," Weldon said. "Aspen's socked in because of snow. Denver too. From the forecasts, the best we can do is an early take off here in the morning, which is just as well. By then the storm will be out of here."

"We'll meet you at the airfield anyhow. Find a place nearby for the three of us to stay."

"Bummer," Elizabeth said. "But at least Kirby won't be able to get to Aspen until tomorrow morning."

"If Weldon can get out of here later today, we could fly back to Washington and surprise him there tonight."

"I know you're anxious to get your hands on Kirby, and I don't blame you. But the only way we can nail him and Daddy, too, is with incriminating documents. Otherwise, what's our evidence, Ali's testimony? Dead men don't talk."

"You're right. I just hate sitting around for twelve or so hours with nothing to do."

She yawned. "I don't know about you, but I'm planning to sleep. I can't remember the last time I slept in a bed."

"With me in Beijing. How could you forget that night?"

"Sorry, Craig. Things like that don't mean as much to a woman." She laughed and poked him playfully.

88

ST. PETERSBURG, FLORIDA

The hot shower in their suite at the Airport Hilton felt so damn good that Craig let it run over his head for several minutes. When he emerged from the bathroom, a towel around his waist, Elizabeth was sound asleep in the king sized bed, on her front, the covers pulled halfway up her back.

He slipped into bed next to her, reached under the covers, and stroked her back.

"Um, that feels good," she said.

He moved his hand lower, just above her rear, and rubbed her there. Slowly, he worked his hand down. First, over the backs of her thighs and then reaching between her legs, playing with her lips until she moaned with pleasure and flipped over.

He buried his head in her bush, fondling the clit with his tongue while she writhed under him, grabbing his head and forcing it tight against her, screaming out with pleasure.

He climbed on top and entered her. Together they moved, their two bodies fused into one. His cock was so hard. He was ready to come, but he held back, waiting for her.

"Now... Now," she cried out, and he came inside her.

He rolled off and took her in his arms. "That was so good," she said.

Hugging, they fell asleep.

The ringing of his cell phone woke him. He jumped up and grabbed it. "Hey, it's Weldon. You guys want to come up for food?"

Craig looked at his watch. Eight in the evening.

"Sure, we'll meet you in the dining room in fifteen minutes."

When the waitress stood, pad in hand, he let Elizabeth order first. She pointed to him and said, "The two of us are having house salads and grouper."

"Hey, I need red meat," he protested.

"You don't need any more red meat."

Weldon was roaring with laughter.

"Besides, we're in Florida. Here you eat fish."

By the time they finished the first bottle of a Riserva Chanti, the best the Hilton had, and were on the second, Elizabeth and Weldon learned they'd both been in Iraq in the second Gulf war. While she was an embedded journalist, he was flying cargo planes for a private firm on contract with the Air Force. Craig leaned back and listened to them trading war stories, like two of the guys.

But he quickly lost interest in their discussion. All he could think about was Kirby and what lay ahead in Aspen. Not merely evening the score for everything Kirby did, beginning with Madison Square Garden. Finally gaining some measure of revenge for Francesca's death.

To redirect his mind, he glanced at the television, playing above the bar, tuned to CNN. What the?... Kirby's picture was on the screen. Craig rushed over.

"This just in, the White House announced that President

Brewster has fired CIA Director Kirby. No reason was given. The action is effective immediately. Until a new Director is appointed, Kirby's Deputy, John Norris will be acting Director."

Craig glared at Kirby's picture on the screen.

I'm coming for you Kirby.

89

ASPEN, COLORADO

The tiny Aspen airport was jammed with private planes. The rich and famous enjoy early-spring skiing. And unlike Washington, once the snow stops, they have the roads cleared in record time.

When they were still in St. Pete, Craig had obtained Winston Kirby's address from information. On the plane, Weldon had printed from his computer a map of the Aspen area. Craig examined the gun Betty had given him. Fully loaded. Extra bullets in his pocket.

By the time he and Elizabeth climbed down the plane's stairs and headed for the Hertz desk, they were good to go.

On the plane, he had asked Weldon to check arrivals into Aspen from connecting Washington planes.

"We have about a twenty minute lead on Kirby," Craig told Elizabeth. "Not much. Better than nothing."

Kirby's father's house was on Red Mountain. With Elizabeth behind the wheel, they drove on the clogged road into the center of

Aspen, before veering to the left. Ploughed snow was piled along the sides of the road. Traffic moved slowly. He was becoming impatient.

"He'll have the same traffic," Elizabeth said.

"But he might know a shortcut."

"There are none. You looked at the map."

"There are always shortcuts."

Finally they were on Main Street in the center of town. Then a left turn onto Mill. They headed up the mountain. The temperature was dropping. Lots of patches of ice on the narrow, winding road. Elizabeth was taking it slow. "We don't want to roll off the mountain," she said.

Climbing, they passed one mansion after another. "These houses must go for ten million each," Elizabeth said.

Craig was checking the numbers. "Should be coming up around the next bend."

On the left, he saw the mail box with the numbers above it: 1020. Winston Kirby's house.

"That's it," he said. "Pass it slowly. Don't stop."

They were still climbing.

It was in keeping with those around it. Huge two-floor structure. Lots of land separating it from other homes. On the edge of a cliff with a great view down toward the town.

Inside, the house looked dark, but the driveway was shoveled.

No cars in the driveway. The garage door was down.

After Elizabeth was fifty yards past the house, Craig told her to turn around. Executing the U-turn on the narrow road was tricky, but she did it with aplomb.

"Drop me in front of the house. Then turn around, go back up to the point where you just made the U-turn, turn around and pull over. That'll be a good observation point. I'll be inside, looking for the evidence we need. Call me immediately on my cell if anybody approaches the house."

"Will do."

Craig got out into the biting cold. The wind was whipping down the mountain.

Parts of the shoveled driveway and walkway had iced over, making it treacherous to get to the front door.

With only a simple lock on the door, breaking in was easy. Using Betty's tool, it took Craig twenty seconds. Inside, he disabled the alarm in another twenty seconds. Then he went to the study off the entrance hall. The desk drawers weren't locked. Craig rifled through the papers inside. Lots of them dealt with start-up companies, which was consistent with Kirby's father as a Silicon Valley investor. Craig glanced at them one by one. Nothing to do with China or an agreement with China.

He looked at his watch. He had about ten more minutes—at most. "Must be a safe somewhere," he said aloud.

Craig looked at the walls covered with a chocolate cloth-like material. On one of them hung a Monet, or a good copy of one. Craig noticed it was a bit off center. He lifted the painting from the wall. Sure enough, behind it was a wall safe.

Craig went to work on the safe. Before he had a chance to open it, his cell phone rang. It was Elizabeth. "Kirby just parked in the driveway. He's leaving the car and walking toward the front door."

"Thanks. I'll be waiting for him."

"What do you want me to do?"

"Stay put until I call you. Kirby may have others coming."

Craig made no effort to return the Monet. He hid behind a wall separating the study from an adjoining bedroom and pulled out his gun.

As soon as he entered the house, Kirby charged into the den. Seeing the Monet off the wall, he stopped and stared at the safe.

Watching Kirby, Craig stepped into the den, moved forward, and raised his gun. "Stop right there," Craig said.

"What are you doing in my father's house?"

"Is that any way to greet an old friend?"

"You ruined my life, you bastard," Kirby sounded unstrung.

Craig calmly replied, "I didn't make the deal and sell out the country. You have nobody to blame but yourself."

"I'll call the police. They'll arrest you for breaking and entering." Kirby took two steps toward the phone.

Craig pointed his gun menacingly at Kirby. "You touch that phone and you'll lose your hand."

"What do you want?"

"I'm here to arrest you for treason."

"You're mad."

"I don't think so. Ali Hariri and I had a little chat in St. Petersburg. He's been taken into protective custody after he cut a deal with me. He told me you and your father, in return for a huge payoff, agreed to help the Chinese implement their agreement with Iran, which would have had a devastating effect on the United States. In my book, that's treason. And, I remember, a capital offense. You and your father will both be executed, or if you're lucky, spend the rest of your lives in jail."

"I don't know Ali Hariri."

"Sorry, it's too late for lies like that. We already have his signed confession. He's prepared to testify."

"Nobody will believe him."

"Wrong. He recorded his conversations with you."

All of the color drained from Kirby's face. Craig's bluff was working.

"You're finished. Now you're going to sit down in that chair," Craig said pointing. "Once you do that, you can give me the combination or watch me open the safe. I'll bet there are documents that will corroborate Ali's story."

"You're wasting your time looking in the safe," Kirby said. "What you want isn't in there. The information is in my head. I'm prepared to give it to you in return for your getting a commitment from President Brewster of total immunity for me and my father."

Craig looked hard at Kirby. "Immunity?" he said in disbelief. "Why would the President give the two of you immunity? What do you have to offer?"

"My father and I were only bit players in this business. Somebody much bigger and closer to the President was calling the shots. He engineered the deal. He would have received the majority of the benefits. I can give you that individual."

"Before I even consider calling the President," Craig said, "you'll have to give me more than that. I need some facts. Then I'll decide whether to make the call."

"Fair enough. Let me go in to the kitchen, get a bottle of scotch and a couple of glasses." He motioned to the bridge table on the side of the room, next to a glass door that opened to a patio, overlooking the mountain. "We'll sit down there and we'll talk. I'll give you some critical information, but not the name of the individual calling the shots. Then you can make your call to the President. After I get immunity, I'll give you his name."

"This better not be a trick."

"If it were, do you think I would have told you everything I have so far? Do you think I'd be willing to have you call the President to cut a deal for immunity if I didn't have something to offer?"

"Go get your scotch. You only need one glass. I'm not drinking with you."

As Kirby walked into the kitchen, Craig followed, keeping the gun pointed at him. Craig watched Kirby pull a bottle of twelve-year-old McCallums from a cabinet and retrieve a glass. He put in two cubes of ice, then took the glass and the bottle back into the den. When they were seated at the table, Kirby poured himself a drink and took a sip. Craig was sitting across from him, the gun still in his hand. "Okay. Start talking."

"About three months ago, I was approached by someone whom I'll call Mr. X. He promised me a financial windfall if I agreed to prevent President Brewster from obtaining any information about a Chinese-Iranian agreement until after that agreement was implemented on April 1."

Craig sneered at Kirby. "So you decided to sell out your country and commit treason because somebody agreed to pay you a little money. That's despicable."

"It was a great deal of money. I was told my father should establish a new corporation which was to be called Mountain Air, a Silicon Valley Company, which we did about three months ago."

"Go ahead. I'm listening."

"I was to have twenty percent of the stock in the company. My father was to have twenty percent. Mr. X was to have the remaining sixty percent. The Chinese agreed to give exclusive rights to Mountain Air for all the computer technology, hardware and software, developed at fifty of their leading universities. This agreement would go into effect once the Chinese-Iranian agreement was implemented."

"But the Chinese Iranian agreement was never implemented. So I presume there will be no transfer of rights to Mountain Air?"

"That's correct. Once the Chinese-Iranian agreement was canceled, thanks to you, the agreement between the China and Mountain Air was canceled as well, under its terms."

"I don't care how much money was involved. It doesn't justify the treason you committed. Even if you would have had access to all of these Chinese inventions, I don't see how you could have done it."

"Don't be so sanctimonious."

"Tell me who Mr. X is?"

Kirby picked up the glass and finished his drink in one large gulp. "Only when I have immunity from President Brewster. So you better take out your cell phone and call Washington. I'm sure you can get through to the President or his Chief of Staff. I'll give you a fax number here. Once they fax a written document giving me immunity, I'll give you the name of Mr. X."

"Okay, I'll call Brewster."

Craig placed his gun on the table and took his cell phone out of his pocket. He began punching in the numbers of the White House. Before Craig completed the call, Kirby, in a single, swift motion, lifted the table from underneath and flung it at Craig. Craig's gun fell to the ground. He landed on top of it.

Before Craig could recover, Kirby slid open the glass door to the patio. He grabbed the bottle of scotch and raced across the stone patio toward the black wrought iron railing on the outside perimeter. Craig, now on his feet with his gun, realized Kirby was trying to escape by going down the mountain on foot.

I have to take Kirby alive. To learn the identity of Mr. X.

Craig ran out of the house with his gun in one hand and his cell phone in the other. "Don't be a fool, Kirby," he shouted as he tried to move toward Kirby without slipping on the icy patio. Kirby had a huge advantage: Rugged snow boots, against sneakers from the Florida mall. "I can call Brewster for you. I can get you that immunity."

Close to the railing, Kirby pivoted. He smashed the bottle against the railing breaking off the bottom part. He raised his arm with the sharp jagged top. "Here's my answer, you bastard." He threw it at Craig's face.

Craig ducked, losing his footing. The cell phone and gun fell out of his hands and skidded away.

Struggling to his feet, Craig saw Kirby lunge for the black railing, planning to vault over it.

Craig grabbed Kirby from behind. The former CIA Director wheeled around, swinging wildly. One of Kirby's fists slammed into Craig's head. Craig was dazed for a second. Kirby then brought up his leg and smashed his heavy boot against Craig's testicles. Craig felt a jolt of searing pain. For an instant, he thought he'd pass out. But he refused to give up. He refused to go down.

He rolled his hand into a first. With all the force he could muster, he hit Kirby in the jaw. The powerful blow knocked Kirby off his feet and over the railing. Craig watched helplessly as Kirby rolled down the snowy mountain.

Craig shrugged off the pain and climbed over the railing. With difficulty, he made his way in the snow down the mountain, desperately trying to reach Kirby. But Kirby was rolling fast, far ahead of Craig. Unconscious from Craig's blow, Kirby rolled like a boulder down the mountain. He reached a precipice and flipped over it, his body and his head crashing against sharp rocks. He continued rolling until he hit a gulley.

In the snow and in pain, it was slow going for Craig, but he made his way down the mountain, holding onto small branches and trees to maintain his footing. By the time he reached Kirby, the man's body was entangled in a small shrub. One look at Kirby told Craig it was hopeless. Kirby's head was split open. Blood was spurting out, congealing and freezing. Kirby was dead, his face covered in blood.

Climbing back up was even more difficult for Craig. He was feeling numb from the cold and snow. Several times he thought he would lose his footing, but he finally made it back to the patio.

Bruised and weary, Craig staggered into the house, leaving the patio door open.

He rubbed his hands together to restore circulation. Took off his wet and icy sneakers.

He remembered Elizabeth outside, waiting in the car. He thought about bringing her in, now that Kirby was dead. But he couldn't risk it. Not until he opened the safe and found out whether there were documents that identified Mr. X. Kirby might have asked Mr. X to meet him here.

Craig squeezed his fingers together several times. Then he went back to work on the wall safe.

At ten minute intervals, Elizabeth turned on the engine and ran the heater for five minutes to warm the car without having the battery die.

She looked at the clock on the dash. It had been close to an hour since Kirby arrived, and neither he nor Craig had come of out of the house.

She thought long and hard about going in to find out what was happening. But what if someone else came?

In the hour, only one other car had passed. Now she watched a gray Hummer making its way up the road. She expected it to pass Winston Kirby's house too, but the Hummer pulled into the driveway and parked next to Kirby's car.

Frantically, she dialed Craig's cell and got voice mail.

A man got out of the Hummer, dressed in high boots, a fur hat, and a dark green military coat, collar up, concealing his face.

I have to warn him.

She tried Craig's cell again. It rang and rang. Then went into voicemail.

She watched the man try the front door. It was locked.

He trudged in the snow around to the side of the house.

She dialed Craig. "Answer," she cried out. "Dammit answer." He didn't.

90

ASPEN, COLORADO

At last, Craig heard a click and the safe snapped open. Inside he saw bundles of cash and a pile of documents. Craig pulled out the documents and examined them. The third one in the stack was entitled, "Articles of Incorporation of Mountain Air Corporation." Precisely what he wanted.

The first page was simply legalese for the start up of the company.

On the second page, Craig saw a list of shareholders. First, Kirby's father with two hundred shares of stock. Then, Kirby with another two hundred. Craig's eyes ran down to the next line. He couldn't believe what he saw. The owner of six hundred shares of stock.

"My God! It's William March," Craig blurted out.

From behind, Craig heard a voice, "Unfortunately that information won't do you any good."

Holding the Articles of Incorporation, Craig turned around. March, who had slipped in through the open patio door, was facing

Craig with a pistol in his hand and a frenzied look on his face. "You ruined everything," March cried out in a cold fury. "If it weren't for you, the Chinese agreement would have been implemented. But you'll pay for what you did. I'll kill you and take the document with me."

I have to stall him. To find a way out.

"But you introduced me to General Ming," Craig said. "Why did you do that, with what you had at stake?"

"I had to give you a name, or you would have gotten suspicious and gone to Brewster. I knew Ming would never be able to deliver the agreement, and I was right. I never dreamt Elizabeth would find another way."

"You had Emery killed. Didn't you?"

"Of course. I couldn't believe Kirby came up with such a stupid idea—convincing Emery you were a traitor and persuading Emery to kidnap Elizabeth. When Kirby described it to me, after he talked Emery into it, I knew he was panicking. That brown nose Emery had no chance of persuading you to leave China. So I had one of our geeks put a tracking device on Emery's cell phone. Once I located him, I arranged for Chinese hit men to take him out. I couldn't take the risk of Emery talking to you or being arrested. He would have given up Kirby, and Kirby would have give me up."

"Why didn't you have your goons kill me and Elizabeth?"

"I didn't think it was necessary. Ming wasn't going to give you what you wanted. Besides, you're Brewster's fair-haired boy. He'd have moved heaven and earth to find your killer. Now we're finished talking."

"Just one more thing. Why did you do it? I can't believe for the money. You must already have so much from your investment banking business."

"You can never have enough. There'll always be somebody with more. Although, I have to say, if this deal had gone through, I would have been right up at the top of the world's wealthiest people. Higher than Bill Gates. But you're right. Money wasn't the only motive."

"Then what?"

"The way I see history evolving in the next decade, the Chinese are on the way up, while the United States is on the decline. Besides energy, technology is our soft spot. We've lost our superiority. I want to be on the winning side."

Craig shook his head in disagreement. "You're selling the United States short. Don't count us out."

March sneered. "Always the patriot, Craig. Your entire life. The honorable spy." He said it with contempt. "Now you're going to die, still being the good and loyal American."

March raised his gun. He tightened his finger on the trigger. Before he could pull it, a cell phone flew through the air from the patio toward March. It struck the unsuspecting March on the side of his head, momentarily dazing him. That was all Craig needed. He took three steps toward March, flew off his feet and smashed into March, bringing him down to the floor in a flying tackle.

March tried to struggle, but Craig was too strong. In seconds, he overpowered March. Craig grabbed March's gun and pointed it at him. "Get up," he ordered March. Once March was on his feet, Craig pushed him down on a sofa. Craig then turned toward the patio.

Elizabeth was walking into the house.

"You're one helluva pitcher," he said. "I'm glad you're on my team."

He picked up her phone from the floor and dialed the White House. "Mr. President, I now know who the other traitors are."

91

PARIS, APRIL 14

General Zhou went out on the balcony of his fourth-floor apartment with the view of the Eiffel tower across the river. A myriad of lights sparkled in the evening Paris sky. He lit up a Cuban cigar and thought about his situation.

He should have been happy.

As soon as he arrived in Paris two weeks ago, he bought a large penthouse apartment off Place de l'Alma in a fashionable part of Paris. He rented the adjacent apartment for Captain Cheng.

Then he called Androshka.

"Oh, it's so good to hear from you," she had said.

He gave her the address and asked how soon she could come.

"I'm on my way," she sounded excited.

Though it was noon, he cracked a bottle of champagne and poured two glasses. After they sipped, he told her, "We have a change of plans. You and I aren't moving to China yet. But we will one day soon. And then I'll be President of China."

"All I want to do is be with you," she had said.

Obviously the right answer, he thought. The woman's no dummy. "Good. Would you like to move in here with me?"

"I only need an hour to pack up my things."

She walked over and kissed him, at the same time grabbing him in the crotch. "I'll be good for you."

As she started for the door, he said, "There's only one condition. You can't see any other men."

"You don't have to worry about that."

"And if you do, I'll kill you." He said it coldly.

"I wouldn't even consider it."

In the last two weeks, the sex with gorgeous, sensuous Androshka had been incredible. Meantime, his brother Zhou Yun had funneled a hundred million euros into accounts for General Zhou in Switzerland and Singapore.

Last week General Zhou took Androshka to San Tropez. They liked the South of France so much he bought a huge estate in the hills overlooking the Mediterranean in Cap d'Antibes, a favorite spot for movie stars and other celebrities.

All of this made for comfortable living, but General Zhou was still miserable. He loathed being exiled from China. He despised President Li occupying the presidency that should be his.

Most of all, he was consumed with hatred for Craig Page. The American had destroyed General Zhou's carefully laid plans. But Craig Page would pay for it, General Zhou vowed. One day General Zhou would gain his revenge, and that revenge would be sweet.

92

WASHINGTON, APRIL 15

Craig cut across Lafayette Square on an idyllic spring day.

How bizarre. Almost exactly one year ago, he had come with Francesca to the White House to receive the Medal of Freedom. Now, Brewster had summoned Elizabeth and him to receive the award this morning.

Trees were in full bloom, birds fluttering from branches. The square was mobbed with tourists—in town for the cherry blossoms, now winding down.

So much had happened in the last two weeks. After FBI agents took March away from Winston Kirby's house in handcuffs, in an unmarked car, Elizabeth and Craig split. He wanted her to fly with him to Washington to brief Brewster. But she demurred. "I need some time alone after the whirlwind to catch my breath. Leave me here. I'll be okay. We'll talk." Reluctantly, he agreed.

They spoke briefly several times, but she refused to tell him where she was or what she was doing. "I'll meet you at the White House," was all she told him.

In Washington, he spent seven grueling days briefing and working with the Attorney General, Wes Simmons, and Justice Department lawyers, helping Brewster decide whether March, being held without bail and without charges in a maximum security prison, should be charged with treason. Brewster was still pondering the issue.

Prosecuting Kirby's father quickly became moot. He fled to Beijing before he was arrested and suffered a fatal heart attack. Craig was convinced Zhou Yun had him killed.

Then Craig received a call from Giuseppe, the Director of the Italian Intelligence Agency, asking him to fly to Brussels for a meeting of the EU Defense Ministers. Following three hours of intensive questioning, they offered him the job of Director of a new counterterrorism agency, based in Paris. He had to give them a decision tomorrow.

Elizabeth was waiting for him in the reception area outside the Oval Office, wearing a stylish khaki suit, hair done, and face tanned from being in the sun, smiling warmly.

"You look great," Craig said.

Before she had a chance to respond, Kathy led them into the Oval Office.

"I don't have words to express my gratitude," the President said. "I'm only sorry I can't do this publicly." He laughed. "But you're used to that, Craig."

"Afraid so,"

"Seriously, I can't imagine where we'd be if it weren't for you. A war with China would have been devastating. No three people were ever more deserving of this award."

"Three?" Craig said.

Brewster directed them to his desk. On top were three Medals of Freedom. "The third one is for Francesca, posthumously."

Craig's eyes filled with tears. "Thank you, Mr. President. This means a great deal to me."

"If it hadn't been for her, we would never have known about any of this."

Brewster led them over to the sitting area. "I've been meeting with Congressional leaders about energy policy. We have to consider this a final warning to wean ourselves from imported oil. The first strike was the '73 Arab oil embargo. This is the second. Our economy may not survive the third."

"I couldn't agree more," Craig said. "What about March?"

"I've made a decision. And I don't think you're going to like it."

Brewster paused for a moment as if he hated saying what came next.

"He'll be resigning as Ambassador to China, but we won't charge him with a crime."

Craig shook his head.

How absurd.

Brewster continued, "Look, I don't like it either. He betrayed me personally as well as the country. I'd give anything to keep him locked up and throw away the key, but Wes has persuaded me a public trial would have a devastating effect on our relations with China."

"I'll finish your thought. And since the Chinese are the principal bankers for our huge national debt, we can't afford that."

"Precisely."

At least Kirby and his father are dead.

"Let's talk about you, Craig. I want to nominate you to be CIA director. I can't think of anyone more qualified."

"I'm extremely flattered, Mr. President. Truly I am. It's a great honor. I would like to think about it overnight and give you an answer in the morning."

"Anything I can do to persuade you?"

"No, sir. A couple days ago, I was asked to be Director of a new EU counterterrorism agency."

He glanced at Elizabeth. She didn't seem surprised. Judging from her face, he concluded that she already knew.

"I have to let the EU know tomorrow, and I need a little time to weigh these two wonderful opportunities."

"I'll understand if you decide to take the EU job. You'll be valuable to the United States in that position." Brewster added, "We have to coordinate so much with them on terrorism matters."

Moments later, as they left the White House grounds, Craig said to Elizabeth, "How about lunch?"

They walked east along Pennsylvania Avenue to Michel Richard's Central. At 12:15, only about half the tables were occupied. Nobody he recognized.

"I don't normally drink at lunch," she said, "but today's special. We both were awarded the Medal of Freedom, as well as Francesca. As for you, I doubt anyone ever received two of them."

She signaled the waiter, then ordered a bottle of Roderer champagne.

Waiting for it to arrive, he said, "I really missed you the last two weeks. Where'd you get the suntan?"

"On the beach at Laguna Niguel, south of L.A."

"What were you doing there?"

"Arranging a job offer at the *L.A. Times.*"

"Is that where you're going to live? L.A.?"

"It's not so bad. Lots of sun. I'll never need a winter coat."

He felt a knot in his stomach.

I don't want to be thousands of miles from her.

The champagne arrived. They raised their glasses. "We were pretty incredible," he said. "We make a great team."

"I'll drink to that."

They clicked glasses and sipped. "How'd you find out about my EU job offer?"

She smiled. "Spies and reporters don't disclose sources. Also, don't underestimate my investigative prowess."

"I'll never underestimate anything about you."

"You're leaning toward taking the EU job. Aren't you?"

"It's a hard decision. CIA Director is a fabulous position, but I'm sick of the politics and bureaucracy in Washington. I've had it for years. And lawyers always calling the shots. March skating is a travesty. The bastard should be in jail for the rest of his life."

"You think they don't have politics and bureaucrats in Europe? Also, don't forget national rivalries."

He nodded. "You're right, of course. But I'm hopeful I'll have more freedom there."

The waiter brought menus. They both ordered lobster burgers.

When the waiter left, she said, "So you'll go to Paris?"

He hesitated for a moment, "I'd like to, but it's important for me to know what you're doing. The distance between LA and Paris is too great. Washington and L.A. is manageable."

Her head snapped back in surprise. "You're factoring me into the equation?"

"You're damn right. We have something special. I want to be with you."

"In that case, I have to tell you I have another offer, too. From the International Herald, based in Paris. To be an investigative reporter with Europe as my beat."

"Quite a coincidence, both of us having Paris offers."

She smiled. "Life's full of coincidence. I have to decide between the two in the next couple of days."

She stopped talking and looked down at her hands.

Suddenly his difficult decision had become easy.

He leaned over and kissed her. "Let's go to Paris together," he said. "Sounds great."

ACKNOWLEDGEMENTS

My heartfelt appreciation to my agent, Pam Ahearn, who understood what was needed and helped shape *The China Gambit*. To Joe Pittman, whose enthusiastic support and brilliant editing, enhanced the novel. And to my wife, Barbara, who added valuable story and character suggestions to draft after draft, while always providing encouragement.

Turn the page for a special preview of
Allan Topol's next Craig Page Thriller,

THE SPANISH REVENGE

Coming Soon from Vantage Point Books

MARCH, AVILA, SPAIN

AT FIVE MINUTES to midnight the heater in the battered gray Renault van died. Omar, in the front passenger seat, was astounded that the vehicle had made it all the way from Clichy-sous-Bois, the suburb of Paris.

They were parked outside the gate of the Franciscan Monastery. Thirty minutes ago, the last light had gone out.

"Cut off the engine," Omar said to Habib, seated behind the wheel, puffing on a foul-smelling Turkish cigarette. "Time to move."

Omar got out of the van, stretched his legs, and checked the pockets of his black leather jacket. Gun and map Musa provided in one pocket, knife and flashlight in the other. He grabbed the two shovels from the back and tossed one to Habib.

The air was cold for this time of year. The moon full in a cloudless sky. The light would make their job easier, but increase the risk of someone spotting them. It would have to be one of the monks. The monastery was surrounded by woods.

With Habib at his side, Omar walked swiftly along the dirt road toward the monastery entrance. The black, wrought-iron gate was padlocked. He reached for his gun, then reconsidered. The monks inside the building might hear the noise. He pointed to the six-foot stone wall. Habib nodded.

Omar easily scaled it, then moved away while Habib tossed over the shovels, following behind. No need to consult Musa's map. He had committed it to memory. That bastard Tomas de Torquemada's grave should be fifty meters away at the end of the road leading from the entrance gate. He walked swiftly along a narrow path bisecting ancient weatherbeaten stones.

Approaching the spot, he recognized from pictures the large stone cross.

"We dig here?" Habib asked.

"One thing first."

Omar unzipped his pants, pulled out his prick and peed on the cross. "For all those Muslims you killed cruelly and without mercy," he said softly.

Then he grabbed a shovel.

Fortunately, it had rained yesterday, and the ground was soft. Still it was tough work. On one side, they created an incline to get out. Once they were down three feet, Omar's face and shirt were soaked with perspiration. Drops ran down his cheeks and into his eyes.

He drew strength from the importance of his mission. The cause he and Musa had labored so hard for over many months was now at a critical point. With the parchment, their success would be assured. Europe and the world would be irretrievably transformed.

"The dead man's spirits are talking to me." Habib was trembling. "Telling me it's wrong to disturb a grave."

Omar pulled out his Glock and aimed it at Habib. "You fool. No Christian spirits are talking to you. You dig or this will be your grave too."

Reluctantly, Habib resumed.

Forty minutes later, Omar's shovel struck a metal box about a meter from the coffin as Musa had said. He could barely contain his excitement.

The parchment will be in the box.

Suddenly, he heard the rustling of leaves. Footsteps near the building. Now getting closer. It might be an animal. Or…

"Stay in the hole and keep quiet," he whispered to Habib. Then he climbed out and slipped behind the cross. A black-clad monk was approaching, lit torch in hand, making a beeline for the open hole. He shined his light down and looked into the hole. As he did, Omar, shovel in hand, circled behind him. He watched the monk calling to Habib, cowering in a corner of the hole "Who are you?" Omar raised the shovel and swung it like a baseball bat, with all his force, striking the monk on the side of the head. He crumpled to the ground away from the hole, blood pouring down the side of his face. "Help me," he mumbled. "Help me." Omar ignored his pleas, lifted his shovel and smashed the metal against his face. The monk stopped moving.

Omar stepped over the body and climbed back into the hole. He had to work fast or others might come looking for the dead monk. He dug around the box, being careful not to damage the old metal. When he got closer, he handed his shovel to Habib. With his fingers he clawed furiously, grabbing the soil, pushing it aside until he freed the box.

Cradling it in his arms, he climbed out and placed it carefully on the ground. The box was sealed shut. Using his knife, he pried the top open. Habib was leaning over Omar. He felt Habib's hot garlic breath on the back of his neck.

He pulled the top off, then grabbed his flashlight and shined it inside. For an instant the light blinded him, the reflection from jewels and gold coins. He reached in and moved around the contents searching desperately for the parchment. He came up empty.

"No," he wailed. "No."

I have to get the parchment. I can't face Musa without it.

Musa didn't tolerate failure. He won't understand. There must be another way.

Eyes bulging, Habib was staring at the gold and jewels. "Let's take what's here and leave. Nobody will ever know."

"We can't do that, you imbecile. If we're caught by the police with that stuff, we'll be tortured. You'll lead them to Musa, and all will be lost."

"Then let's just go."

"No. Somebody inside must know where the parchment is. Musa said there are five monks altogether."

Omar looked at the stone building. Dark inside. He raced toward the nearest door. Habib was right behind him. The door was ajar. He opened it carefully and shined his light inside. The room was deserted, its stone walls muting the reflection. They must all be asleep. He spotted a bell and rang it.

Minutes later four monks stumbled out of the wing on the right in night clothes. Omar held up his gun and herded them toward four wooden chairs in the reception area. One was praying. "Shut up and listen." Omar called out.

"No comprendo," one monk said in Spanish.

"Any of you speak French?" Omar asked in that language.

A tall, thin, gray haired monk said, "I do."

"Good. I'll talk to you. A parchment was buried in a box next to Tomas de Torquemada's coffin. We dug up the box, but the parchment isn't there. I want to know where it is."

The tall, thin man was flabbergasted. "You disturbed his grave?"

"Someone already had. The parchment was gone. I want to know where it is."

"I have no idea."

"Then ask your colleagues in Spanish. One of them must know."

The tall, thin monk said something to the others. All shook their heads in denial.

Omar didn't believe them. He was becoming angry. "This monastery has been here since before his death in 1498. At some point one of your monks must have taken it and hidden it. This must be a secret passed down here through the ages."

"How can you be sure it was buried with him?"

Omar raised the Glock and aimed it at one of the other monks. He fired at his head, blasting it apart. Two others wailed.

"Don't you challenge me," Omar said. "Tell me where it is."

"You can kill us all," the tall, thin monk said, "but you won't get the information."

"Because you don't know—or because you won't tell me?"

"That's your riddle to solve," he replied in a taunting voice.

Omar used his knife to gouge out the eyes of one of the other monks. Despite the man's screams, nobody said a word.

Omar killed that one and the other, leaving only the tall, thin monk. "I'll make you suffer more than you can imagine," Omar said.

"I am a man of God. I have no fear of mere mortals."

Omar knew it was hopeless. He shot and killed the man. Then he and Habib searched the building. Even the basement, beneath a concealed trap door. No sign of the parchment.

To extend the time until they were discovered and pursuit began, Omar decided to move the dead bodies down the stairs. "While I do that," he told Habib, "Rebury the box. Toss the other dead monk in the hole and start to refill it. I'll be out in a couple of minutes to help you."

He searched one more time, then dragged the bodies across the floor, flung them down the wooden stairs, and closed the trap door.

After leaving the building, he crossed the grassy swale back to the graveyard. He couldn't believe his eyes. Habib was stuffing gold and jewels into his pockets. Omar stood behind a tree and watched. Once his pockets were full, Habib ran toward the wall. As he began scaling it, Omar raised his gun and fired dropping Habib with a single shot. Enraged, Omar raced over and pumped three more bullets into

Habib's dead body. Then he removed Habib's ID, dragged him back to the hole and kicked him in.

For the next two hours he worked until he was so exhausted he could barely lift his arms. But it was all done. Habib, the monk, and metal box all buried.

The work had been brutal, but he knew an even worse chore awaited him in Marbella: Explaining his failure to Musa.

I don't have the parchment.